TITLE WAVE

Berkley Prime Crime titles by Lorna Barrett

MURDER IS BINDING

BOOKMARKED FOR DEATH

BOOKPLATE SPECIAL

CHAPTER & HEARSE

SENTENCED TO DEATH

MURDER ON THE HALF SHELF

NOT THE KILLING TYPE

BOOK CLUBBED

A FATAL CHAPTER

TITLE WAVE

Anthologies

MURDER IN THREE VOLUMES

TITLE WAVE

Lorna Barrett

BERKLEY PRIME CRIME, NEW YORK

BERKLEY
PRIME
CRIME

An imprint of Penguin Random House LLC
375 Hudson Street, New York, New York 10014

This book is an original publication of the Penguin Random House LLC.

Copyright © 2016 by Penguin Random House LLC.
Penguin supports copyright. Copyright fuels creativity, encourages diverse voices,
promotes free speech, and creates a vibrant culture. Thank you for buying an authorized
edition of this book and for complying with copyright laws by not reproducing, scanning, or
distributing any part of it in any form without permission. You are supporting writers and
allowing Penguin to continue to publish books for every reader.

BERKLEY® PRIME CRIME and the PRIME CRIME design are trademarks of
Penguin Random House LLC.
For more information, visit penguin.com.

Library of Congress Cataloging-in-Publication Data

Names: Barrett, Lorna, author.
Title: Title wave / Lorna Barrett.
Description: First edition. I New York : Berkley Prime Crime, 2016. I Series:
A Booktown mystery
Identifiers: LCCN 2016003928 I ISBN 9780425282700 (hardback)
Subjects: LCSH: Miles, Tricia (Fictitious character)—Fiction. I Women
booksellers—Fiction. I BISAC: FICTION / Mystery & Detective / Women
Sleuths. I FICTION / Mystery & Detective / General. I
GSAFD: Mystery fiction.
Classification: LCC PS3602.A83955 T58 2016 I DDC 813/.6—dc23
LC record available at http://lccn.loc.gov/2016003928

FIRST EDITION: June 2016

PRINTED IN THE UNITED STATES OF AMERICA

10 9 8 7 6 5 4 3 2 1

Cover illustration by Teresa Fasolino.
Cover design by Diana Kolsky.
Interior text design by Laura K. Corless.

This is a work of fiction. Names, characters, places, and incidents either are the product of
the author's imagination or are used fictitiously, and any resemblance to actual persons,
living or dead, business establishments, events, or locales is entirely coincidental.

PUBLISHER'S NOTE: The recipes contained in this book are to be followed exactly
as written. The publisher is not responsible for your specific health or allergy needs
that may require medical supervision. The publisher is not responsible for any
adverse reactions to the recipes contained in this book.

Penguin
Random
House

To
Valerie Bartlett
Nothing on earth can replace a mother's love.

ACKNOWLEDGMENTS

There's nothing like a cruise for relaxation, seeing new sights, and having fun. I'd like to thank my cruising buddy Nancy Cooper for sharing her insights; my go-to girl for all things Irish, Edel Waugh; and my friend for all things Bermuda, Sylvia May, for tips and suggestions made while writing *Title Wave*. Members of the Lorraine Train—Maria Pullman and Claudia Wilson—jogged my memory to fill in some gaps and bring back several of my favorite characters, and Cyn Rielly came up with some cute names for the shipboard bars and casino.

Special thanks go to my editor, Tom Colgan, for having faith in me and letting my characters step out of their comfortable (maybe not-so-safe) village to explore a whole new world. Tom has always given me free rein to push the cozy boundaries. Thanks, big guy. You rock!

CAST OF CHARACTERS

Tricia Miles: owner of Haven't Got a Clue mystery bookstore

Angelica Miles: Tricia's sister, owner of the Cookery, Booked for Lunch café, and half owner of the Sheer Comfort Inn. Her alter ego is Nigela Ricita, the mysterious developer who has been pumping money and jobs into the village of Stoneham.

Ginny Wilson-Barbero: Tricia's former assistant; wife of Antonio Barbero

Antonio Barbero: the public face of Nigela Ricita Associates (NRA) and Angelica's stepson

Mr. Everett: Tricia's employee at Haven't Got a Clue

Grace Harris-Everett: Mr. Everett's wife

Ian McDonald: the *Celtic Lady*'s security officer

Millicent Ambrose: entertainment director on the *Celtic Lady* cruise ship

EM Barstow: *New York Times* bestselling author of thrillers

Dori Douglas: EM Barstow's fan club president and sometime assistant

Arnold Smith: superfan of various mystery authors

Cast of Characters

Cathy Copper: EM Barstow's editor

Mary Fairchild: owner of the By Hook or By Crook crafting bookstore

Muriel and Midge Dexter: elderly twin sisters who reside in Stoneham

Chauncey Porter: owner of the Armchair Tourist in Stoneham

Fiona Sample: cozy mystery author

Victoria Burke: cozy mystery author

Sidney Charles: cozy mystery author

Helen Evans: cozy mystery author

Norma Fielding: cozy mystery author

Carmen Hammond: cozy mystery author

Diana Lovell: cozy mystery author

Kevin Mitchell: nonfiction author

Steven Richardson: thriller author

Hannah Travis: cozy mystery author

Mindy Weaver: tour guide from Milford Travel

ONE

It was almost four in the afternoon, but already it had been a very long day. Too long a day, Tricia Miles decided as she shifted from one foot to the other.

The day had started many hours before daylight, when she'd awoken to the sounds of her cat, Miss Marple, having a hairball at the end of her bed. She'd managed to whisk the cat off the snowy white spread in time to save it, but that was the end of her rest. Tricia still had so many things to accomplish before she; her sister, Angelica; and many friends and colleagues from the Stoneham Chamber of Commerce boarded a bus and headed for the Big Apple.

No doubt about it, once the holidays were over, the shops along Stoneham's main drag might as well shut down until April, when the tourists came back in full force. What better time for everyone to take a much-needed vacation? At least, that was the pitch Angelica had given the Chamber members the previous fall when Milford Travel, a new member, had proposed the excursion. The Authors at Sea cruise would be filled with two dozen authors and thousands of their readers. Tricia had spent the previous six winters in Stoneham, with very little in the way of downtime. A vacation to the south that was dedicated to her favorite subject—reading—had sounded heavenly, but now she felt she needed a vacation from her vacation.

The weather had held, but the bus had encountered a gigantic traffic jam outside of Boston that had put them more than an hour behind schedule, and so they'd had to cancel their planned breakfast stop. Somebody had suggested they sing to pass the time. A number of the group thought it was great fun, joining in with gusto, but after only a few bottles of beer on the wall, Tricia wished she hadn't packed her iPod in her suitcase and could drown out the revelry.

Lunch at the 21 Club had been a treat for most of the group, who'd never been there before. But Chamber member Leona Ferguson, who owned Stoneham's Stoneware, looked more than a little green during the bus ride and hadn't had time to admire the restaurant's dishes or have one bite of her salad before she'd made a mad dash to the ladies' room. She'd later admitted that she'd forgotten to wear her motion-sickness patch and made the final leg of the bus journey hyperventilating into a paper bag—threatening to upchuck in her seat, which had sent her seatmate scrambling and made the bus driver in front of her break into a cold sweat. But somehow she'd made it to the pier without being sick, and everyone's spirits rose once more. Until they got inside the cavernous—and very drafty—cruise terminal where most of their group were seated. They were scheduled to board the majestic *Celtic Lady* at two o'clock, but here it was nearly two hours later and the terminal was still full.

"What's going on? What's the holdup?" grumbled a male voice behind her.

Tricia wasn't one of the lucky ones who'd managed to grab a seat, but at least she'd worn sensible shoes. Angelica had been standing in three-inch heels for over two hours. Still, the smile on her face hadn't wavered as she traveled around the group, encouraging everyone to be patient.

"I don't know how you do it," Tricia muttered as Angelica finished yet another circuit around the group.

"It's my business face. You've got one, too. The one you use with difficult customers."

"I don't usually have forty of them at once," Tricia admitted.

"That's true, but I cope the same way I've always coped. I smile and imagine myself choking the life out of each and every one of them."

"Everyone?" Tricia prompted, trying to suppress a grin.

Angelica's gaze drifted over to Antonio Barbero, who stood next to his seated wife, Ginny, and their darling angel of a daughter, Sofia, who was almost six months old. "Maybe not."

Angelica hadn't told the world at large that Antonio was her stepson. She'd wanted to keep that little piece of information a secret—and still did. As far as everyone but Tricia and Ginny knew, the four of them were just very good friends and not related by a marriage that had long ago gone south. Angelica hadn't even spoken to that particular ex-husband in almost two decades, but she'd kept in touch with the son he couldn't be bothered with, and loved Antonio as if he'd been her own child. And they worked well together on the company they'd formed a few years earlier: Nigela Ricita Associates.

A nervous Mindy Weaver bobbed and weaved around the fringe of her charges. The slight woman must have been in her early forties, and while she'd worked for Milford Travel for at least a decade, this was her first time taking charge of a tour—and it showed.

"Just a little bit longer," she called nervously over the murmur of grumbling voices.

"These things happen," Chauncey Porter called out, and shrugged.

He owned the Armchair Tourist, and Mindy had enlisted his help as her de facto mentor and helpmate on the trip.

Thanks to Angelica's business advice, Chauncey's once-failing bookshop had done a dramatic turnaround. Where he once sold used travel guides and maps, he'd branched out to stock sundries that anyone taking a trip might need: from suitcase locks to personal GPS devices, and from sunscreen to passport wallets. Chauncey got along well with everyone—with one exception: Tricia. He blamed her for the death of his fiancée some fourteen months before. She'd had no part in the woman's death, but the heart had no concept of logic. Chauncey hadn't spoken to her since that terrible night when he'd slapped her. She could have leveled assault charges, but had simply walked away. She missed his friendship.

"We've still got a bag full of peppermints if anybody needs them," Muriel Dexter called out.

"Keeps your breath fresh," her twin sister, Midge, called out.

Nobody took them up on their offer.

The elderly spinster Dexter sisters were well known in Stoneham for their rather quirky personalities and the fact that they'd chat amiably to anyone they came in contact with. Somehow the idea of individuality had never occurred to them, for despite their age they liked to dress alike and often had *fun* switching identities to fool the villagers, who found that antic anything *but* fun.

Mary Fairchild, owner of By Hook or By Book, Stoneham's craft and book shop, dodged her way across the open concourse, heading for the rest of the group. She stopped in front of Tricia. "Wow, you'd think in a building this huge they'd have better bathroom facilities. I had to wait in line for more than twenty minutes," she said. Still, Tricia could see by the sparkle in Mary's eyes that the ordeal had not deterred her.

"You've managed to stay cheerful," she commented.

"Nothing could faze me today. This is my very first cruise," Mary gushed, "and I intend to enjoy every second of it. And now that I'm single, I'm kind of hoping I meet someone."

Mary's husband, Luke, had gone to prison for murder. The divorce had come through only a month or so before. Mary was embarking on a whole new life. Tricia could sure identify with that.

"Are you looking to get married again?" Angelica said, leaning into the conversation.

"Oh, no. I want to have *fun!*"

Angelica laughed. "Well, as a four-time loser in the love department, I can't argue with that reasoning."

"I'm going to go sit back down. I'm sure glad Leona was saving my seat. I don't know how you girls have stood there for such a long time."

You could let one of us sit for a few minutes, Tricia thought, but didn't voice it. Oh, well.

At least one other person in the crowd seemed to be having a good time. A thin, gray-haired gentleman of about sixty sat on an electric scooter and zoomed between the various clusters of would-be mariners. A lot of people seemed to know him by name, and he paused to briefly speak with them before he took off for another circuit around the cavernous room. Tricia envied his seat, but not the ailment that had him saddled to the motorized chair.

A ripple of excitement seemed to go through the crowd, and Tricia and Angelica turned to see a tall, beefy woman whose hair was an alarming shade of red, stride past them in a flowing black cape, while an older, much shorter blonde-haired woman struggled to keep up with her.

"Isn't that—?" someone said.

"I'm sure it is," another agreed eagerly.

Whispers and nervous giggles broke out all around them.

Tricia immediately recognized the woman as thriller author EM Barstow. The woman's reputation for being difficult preceded her.

She'd once signed at Tricia's mystery bookstore, Haven't Got a Clue; *once* being the operative word. The woman had found nothing but fault with the store, the temperature of the coffee, the color of ink in the pens Tricia provided, with her then assistant, Ginny, and her other employee, Mr. Everett, as well. They were clumsy, they were stupid. Didn't they know how to open a book so she could quickly sign it?

Tricia looked over her shoulder to where Mr. Everett sat with his wife, Grace, and noted that he, too, was not enthused to see the author, and no doubt remembered the temper tantrum the woman had thrown when told that the cab Tricia had ordered to pick her up would be a few minutes late. Didn't they know she was *important?* Didn't they know she was used to a *limousine*, not a common cab? Didn't they know *anything?*

All eyes were upon EM as she barged ahead of a line of fifty or more passengers who'd finally been called to check in.

Her shorter companion finally managed to catch up, and EM seemed to be engaged in conversation with the woman behind the check-in desk, who shook her head and pointed to the general waiting area to the right, which was also stuffed to overflowing with weary travelers.

"Do you *know* who I am?" EM bellowed loud enough for half the terminal to hear.

All heads turned in her direction.

"Someone's not happy," Angelica muttered, raising a perfectly tweezed eyebrow.

Tricia couldn't hear the cruise terminal worker's reply, but she guessed at EM's howl of outrage that if the woman *did* know, she didn't care. Unable to suppress a smile, Tricia turned away.

Mindy finished another circuit around the Stoneham Chamber members.

"Were you able to find out what the holdup is?" Angelica asked wearily.

"When the boat docked this morning, passengers were supposed to check in with customs. It seems that four of them simply didn't. It took the crew hours to track them down. No one could reboard until they found them."

"And where was that?"

"One was in the spa. Apparently there's a deprivation tank, and she claims she couldn't hear her name repeatedly called over the public-address system."

"And the others?" Angelica prompted.

"One had her hearing aids turned off. I'm not sure about the others."

"Does this mean they're finally going to start letting people board? We're supposed to leave port in an hour," Tricia said.

Mindy looked across the way at the several thousand people all waiting their turn to check in. "Looks like we'll be a little late," she said nervously.

"Hey, look!" Chauncey called out. "They're letting the first group go through."

Sure enough, the gate had opened, and a horde of people lurched forward, dragging their luggage. EM Barstow was *not* among them. She took a recently vacated seat and, as her expression revealed, fumed.

It didn't take long before the Stoneham group was called, and everyone proceeded through the gate in an orderly fashion. As head of the Chamber, Angelica went to the back of the line, clucking reassurances to her charges like a mother hen. Tricia hung back, too. After all, they were sharing a stateroom; they might as well find it together.

Once issued their identification keycards, they passed through security, followed the stragglers, and boarded the magnificent ship. Already the sky was black, and a brisk wind whistled around the gangplank. "I hope we won't have rough seas," Angelica muttered.

"Do you get seasick?" Tricia asked.

"Heavens, no—I just don't want to fall off my heels."

"I should think you'd be ready to take them off."

"I am. But once we're settled, we're finding a nice, quiet bar. I have earned my martini—or two—for the day."

"I'll be happy to join you," Tricia agreed.

A uniformed woman stood at the bank of elevators, advising cruisers how to find their staterooms. She glanced at Angelica's paperwork. "You're on Deck 7." She signaled to a woman in a drab black uniform. "Will you please show these ladies to their stateroom?"

The young woman nodded and reached for Angelica's large case. "If you'll follow me."

"Thank you," Angelica said, and smiled.

They piled into the elevator with what seemed like far too many other people and had to jump out for the first several decks until they reached their own. A handy plaque directed them to the left. They halted in front of a door marked 7150. The uniformed woman stepped forward to open the door, but Angelica waved her away. "We can take it from here."

"I'd be very happy to help you unpack."

"No need. Thank you very much."

The young woman nodded and backed away, then turned to leave.

"Shouldn't you have tipped her?" Tricia asked.

"How long has it been since you were on a cruise?"

"Years."

"She'll be handsomely tipped—it'll be included on our final, item-ized bill. We'll also tip our own butler at the end of the trip."

"We get a butler?"

"Just one of the perks."

Angelica turned for the door and slipped her ID card into the slot, and the door opened. As it did, the lights came on inside.

"Oh, my," Tricia cried as she took in the cabin's interior.

"I was ready to jump out of my skin thinking someone would spoil my surprise," Angelica cried.

"I'm surprised, all right," Tricia said, breathless, taking in the opulent stateroom. No, not a stateroom at all; a suite of elegant rooms. "Ange, how can you afford—"

"Honey, I'm rich," she said, and somehow it didn't even seem like she was bragging. "I work hard. We both do. And who are we going to leave our money to, except each other? And Antonio, Ginny, and Sofia," she quickly amended. "I'm paying for their suite, too."

"They've got a suite?" Tricia asked.

"Not as nice as ours, but the baby will have her own room so they can have some alone time." She smirked. "We can spend time together, but have our own spaces, too, in case . . ." She waggled her eyebrows. Tricia knew what she meant, but she hadn't come on the cruise looking for love. Although her heart was broken when her ex-husband, Christopher, had died the previous summer, she wasn't interested in having a fling, either. Tricia wasn't so sure about Angelica.

"Let's get inside. My feet are killing me!" Angelica cried.

They struggled with the luggage, pulling it inside the door, tossed their coats and purses aside, and then flopped onto matching leather loveseats that faced each other. Both sisters kicked off their shoes.

"Isn't room service included in the price of the cruise?" Tricia asked. "We could order a couple of martinis."

"Yes, but I don't think it can happen until after the lifeboat drill. I'm sure we'll be hearing an announcement about it anytime now. And honestly, aren't you eager to explore the ship?"

"Yes, but you'll need more sensible shoes." She looked around the lounge and sat up straighter upon spying a magnificent cut glass vase filled with a dozen red roses, along with a sweating champagne bucket with a green bottle and gold foil-tipped top jutting out at a jaunty angle.

"Who sent the flowers and the wine?" Tricia asked.

Angelica crossed the room and checked the cards that accompanied them. "The cruise line. And why not? Ours is the most expensive suite

on the entire ship. They aim to please—and I must say, I am pleased."
She inhaled the scent of the roses. "What do you want to do first?"

"We could pop open a bottle of the bubbly while we wait," Tricia
suggested.

"Why not?" Angelica asked, and looked down at the table. "Oohhh!
Hors d'oeuvres."

Tricia joined her, her eyes widening at the sight. Eight beautiful
and delicate morsels, two each of four different kinds, graced a paper
doily on a plate, which was covered by a plastic dome. Tricia suspected
it was pink-tinged cream cheese that had been piped onto slices of
baguette. She spied what looked like smoked salmon topped with
capers, some kind of cheese sat on crackers, and the last two appetizers had pâté mounded high on yet more baguette. Tricia picked one
up and sampled it while Angelica removed the foil from the bottle. "Oh
my God, that's good."

The cork went *pop!* and Angelica poured the fizz into the flutes,
then offered one to Tricia. "This is going to be a fabulous vacation. We
are going to have a fabulous time. We are going to relax, and eat, and
not worry about gaining weight—not that you ever need to," she said
as an aside, "and have the time of our lives."

They clinked glasses and drank.

Tricia thought of this vacation as a fresh start. A way of putting
the hurt aside after the death of her ex-husband. She intended to do
just as Angelica said: to relax and read and read and read.

Nothing was going to spoil her vacation.

Nothing.

TWO

After the lifeboat drill, the ship finally left port, and Tricia and Angelica returned to their suite to meet their butler, Sebastian. The older gentleman spoke with a proper English accent and insisted on unpacking for them. But first, he poured more wine. The sisters bundled up and stood on the suite's balcony, sipping champagne and watching the lights of New Jersey slip by the starboard side of the ship as they waved and toasted the lady in the harbor. It was like being in an old Fred Astaire film—only in color! Too soon, it was time to dress for dinner, and poor Angelica never did get her cocktail. But somehow they managed to meet Antonio and Ginny at their cabin only five minutes late.

Antonio answered the door to their knock. "There you are," he said, smiling.

"Here we are," Tricia agreed, bouncing on the balls of her feet.

"Ginny is almost ready. Come in, come in," Antonio said, and ushered the sisters in.

"What a pretty suite," Tricia said. It was very like the one she and Angelica shared, but only half the size.

"You just missed Mr. Everett," Antonio said.

"Oh?" Angelica asked.

Antonio nodded. "He gave his regrets that he and his lovely wife would not be joining us for dinner tonight."

"Oh, dear. Are they okay?"

"Just tired from a long day."

"Then it's better they rest up today so they can jump into all the fun tomorrow," Angelica said.

"Are they ordering room service?" Tricia asked.

"Yes. Mr. E said they would find us tomorrow and promised to join us for dinner, as well."

"Good."

Ginny emerged from the smaller of the two bedrooms and quietly closed the door. "Sofia is asleep at last."

A knock on the door drew their attention. Antonio answered it.

"Mr. Barbero? I'm Elena Gutiérrez. One of the ship's nannies. I'll be sitting with Sofia this evening."

Antonio ushered her in. She showed him her credentials, and Ginny went over a very long list of instructions before Antonio practically had to drag her out of the stateroom.

"We will see you in an hour or so," Antonio called to Elena, firmly shutting the door behind them.

"I'm sorry I delayed us. But after all, I don't know the ship's nannies," Ginny said with concern. She walked in front of Tricia and Angelica in the narrow corridor, heading for the elevator—oops, lift, Tricia reminded herself. After all, this was an Irish ship.

"Ah, but darling girl, they do this on a regular basis. And we are only going to the restaurant. We can be paged in an instant," Antonio promised, and Tricia never tired of hearing the lilt of his slight Italian accent.

"Ginny, dear, relax. Sofia was asleep when we left. I'm sure she'll still be sound asleep when we return. That's why I booked us for the later seating," Angelica said. But that night, it seemed everyone would be eating at the same time. "Perhaps you can request Elena as your nanny for the rest of the trip, then you won't have to worry about a stranger sitting with her every time."

"Good idea. I'll look into it tomorrow."

The dress code for the first evening's meal was smart casual, and they'd chosen their attire accordingly. Angelica had sprung for a tuxedo for Antonio and was looking forward to seeing him in it. The last time he'd worn one was at his wedding to Ginny, but the handsome young man was born for formal dress. Ginny had protested when Angelica had offered to take her on a trip to Boston to buy a new wardrobe for their Irish-inspired holiday, but she'd eventually given in, and the three of them had taken time off from work to make a weekend of it. Although Ginny and Angelica had gotten off to a rough start some six years before, which was, admittedly, Tricia's fault, they'd actually bonded as in-laws.

The group paused at the hostess stand at the posh Kells Grill, several price ranges above the restaurant where the rest of the Stoneham Chamber cruisers were assigned for their meals. The dining room seated no more than twenty, but they had reserved seats and were escorted to their table beside a large window that overlooked the Promenade Deck below and the black ocean beyond.

Antonio held out chairs for all of them before taking a seat himself.

"Good evening, ladies and gentleman," said a tall, thin waiter dressed in a black tux. His accent wasn't Irish, as they might have expected, but Italian. "I am Cristophano and I will be taking care of you during our most excellent journey."

Cristophano. Christopher. The name made Tricia's heart ache, and Angelica reached for her hand under the table, squeezing it and giving her an encouraging smile, which she appreciated.

"Dove in Italia sei?" Antonio asked.

"Firenze, signore," the waiter answered.

"Anch'io," Antonio said, and laughed.

"What?" Ginny asked, puzzled.

Angelica smiled. "He asked if the waiter was from Italy. He answered Florence—the same as Antonio."

"I didn't know you spoke Italian," Tricia said.

"Well, how else was I going to communicate with Antonio when he was a boy and didn't speak English?"

"You amaze me," Tricia said, shaking her head.

Cristophano presented them with genuine (not faux) leather folders that contained the engraved menu for that night's dinner.

"How about I order a bottle of wine for the table?" Angelica suggested.

"That will not be necessary, madam. A bottle of our best champagne has been ordered for your group."

"Oh?" Angelica asked.

"Sì." Cristophano reached into his tux jacket and pulled out a card, handing it to Tricia. She read the beautiful script. *"The best for the best."*

"No signature?" Ginny asked.

Tricia shook her head.

"Ooh!" Angelica cooed. "You have a secret admirer."

Tricia looked up at the waiter. "Are you sure this was delivered to the right table?"

Cristophano nodded. "You are Ms. Tricia Miles, are you not?"

Tricia nodded. A secret admirer? Had Stoneham's chief of police ordered the champagne in an effort to woo her back? That was a stretch, since they hadn't been on a date in almost two years.

"I shall return in a moment," Cristophano said, and made a discreet exit.

The four of them smiled at one another. "I can't believe we're here—on such a beautiful ship," Ginny said, and giggled.

"How do you like your stateroom?" Angelica asked.

"Perfect. Oh, Angelica, I can't thank you enough for—"

But Angelica held up a hand to stop her gushing. "The rest of our little group doesn't have to be in on our secret, but we *are* family. A dynasty, I hope. And we will all look after each other in the years to come." Ginny blinked and Angelica laughed. "That wasn't a threat. You won't have to push me in a wheelchair when I'm old and gray. I just meant that if one of us lives well, why shouldn't we all live well?" She looked around for Cristophano. "I wish we had that champagne and we could all toast the sentiment."

Ginny frowned. "Aren't the others in our group going to be miffed when they see we have better accommodations than them?"

"I don't see why. Everyone had the option of picking their own price point for the cruise. Mindy did tell me that most of the group are in inside staterooms—no windows, no balconies—but our fellow travelers made that decision—not us—and we will *not* feel guilty." It sounded like an order.

They opened their folders to peruse the menus. Tricia studied the à la carte offerings and was considering whether she should celebrate and have the lobster Newburg with truffle-scented rice pilaf or the beef Wellington when a commotion at a table several feet away drew her attention. She looked up to see EM Barstow dressed in a riotous red and gold silk caftan that more resembled a circus tent than smart casual attire.

"This table isn't at all acceptable. It's too close to the door. There's a draft."

"Emmie," her companion pleaded, sounding embarrassed. "I'm sure it's perfectly fine."

"And I'm sure it's not!" EM declared, and didn't seem to care that her voice was carrying throughout the dining room. "This trip is costing a fortune and I want the best of the best. I demand a table with a window, and if I don't get it—"

Ginny glowered. "It's that disagreeable woman—*again!* Doesn't she ever shut up?"

"Not in my experience," Tricia said.

Cristophano arrived with another waiter, and while the newcomer set up the gleaming champagne bucket next to Antonio, Cristophano placed champagne flutes in front of each of them. "May I pour?" he asked Tricia, showing her the bottle.

"Dom Pérignon!" Ginny exclaimed. "Someone sure thinks you're hot stuff."

Tricia felt her cheeks grow warm with a blush. She spoke to the waiter. "Yes, please pour."

Nearby, EM and her companion were escorted to another table, and peace descended on the room once again.

Tricia sampled the champagne, giving it an approving nod, and Cristophano filled the rest of their glasses.

"May I take your orders now?" Cristophano asked.

"I think we'll just enjoy the champagne for a few minutes. Perhaps you could give us five or ten minutes," Angelica suggested.

"Very good, madam," he said with a curt nod.

Tricia almost expected the man to click his heels as he turned away. She turned to Ginny. "What looks good to you on the menu?"

"I was thinking about—"

"What do you mean the champagne isn't complimentary?" EM Barstow demanded of her server. "That table has free champagne."

Angelica rolled her eyes, swirled the contents of her glass, and took a healthy gulp. "Great stuff."

EM continued her loud, sour rant for another minute or two while her red-faced dining companion silently stared at the napkin draped across her lap.

"Perhaps tomorrow we'll try one of the other restaurant options," Antonio suggested hopefully.

"I'm game," Tricia agreed.

"Me, too," Ginny said.

"Why don't we talk about something else?" Angelica suggested. "Has anyone seen the list of authors who are on board and giving presentations?"

"There's a chef from the Good Food Channel. Larry what's his face," Ginny said. "I think he's going to give a couple of demonstrations, too."

"I've watched Larry Andrews on TV dozens of times; he's wonderful," Angelica agreed. "Seeing him cook in person would be heavenly."

"Nikki Brimfield-Smith's mother—that cozy mystery author—is supposed to be on board, too," Ginny said.

"Oh, yes, Fiona Sample," Tricia said. "I'd almost forgotten. It's too bad Nikki and Russ couldn't have afforded to come on the trip. It would have been lovely for Nikki and her mom to spend some quality time together."

"Nikki said her mother was going to detour to Stoneham to see her grandson after the trip," Ginny said.

"How nice," Angelica said.

"While we gush over authors, what do you intend to do, Antonio?" Tricia asked.

"I will relax with my *bambina*. I will read. And I will think about where Nigela Ricita Associates can expand its holdings in southern New Hampshire."

"You're supposed to be on vacation," Tricia chided him.

"Working with my employer is such a joy, I consider it an honor," Antonio said, giving Angelica a wink.

Tricia saw one of the leather menu folders go sailing through the air and hit the floor behind Angelica's chair.

"This menu is disgusting. How can they not offer a chicken dish for dinner?" EM demanded.

Lobster and beef Wellington weren't good enough? Tricia wondered. If EM continued her temper tantrum, they were sure to have a less-than-enjoyable meal, no matter how good the company.

Antonio reached for the champagne bottle. "May I top up your glasses?"

"Yes," the three women at the table quickly answered.

An amused Antonio quickly complied.

Although quiet music issued from the speakers, it wasn't enough to mask the harsh whispers coming from EM and her assistant. *Well, at least they aren't shouting,* Tricia thought, and sipped her wine.

Ginny, who was sitting directly behind EM, could obviously hear every word. She leaned forward. "If she doesn't shut up, someone is going to murder her. And it might just be me!"

Tricia caught sight of a woman across the aisle, who'd obviously heard Ginny. She nodded in that direction, and Ginny glanced that way. Caught, she smiled sweetly and then quickly looked away.

Cristophano returned. "Are you ready to order?" he asked.

"Extremely ready," Ginny grated.

Cristophano wrote down their dinner preferences, retrieved the menu folders, and then turned away.

"Why did you pick the diet dinner?" Angelica asked Tricia.

"Diet?"

"Yes, the spa offering is the diet meal. Didn't you see the calories and fat grams listed?"

Tricia shrugged. "Lamb just appealed to me tonight."

Angelica shook her head. "If I can reintroduce a topic," she began. "What's everybody going to do first thing in the morning?"

"I want to check out the library. I heard they've got something like six thousand books available for checkout," Tricia said. "Although I have a feeling it'll concentrate on bestsellers—and probably heavier on those from the U.K. and Europe."

"It would have been nice if we could have boarded earlier and done a walk-through of the ship," Angelica agreed. "But we've got two days at sea before we reach Bermuda."

"I was hoping to do a little poolside reading," Ginny said, "but it won't be warm enough until we get farther south. I'm going to check out the Daily Program tonight and then make my decision. Besides lectures, there are supposed to be some author signings, as well as a number of interesting panel discussions. Just being away from the pressures of the job will be nice."

"But I thought you enjoyed your work," Angelica said, sounding genuinely concerned. After all, Ginny worked for her—at least in her Nigela Ricita capacity.

"I *do* love it," she insisted. "But working with a baby—even with spectacular day care—is a lot harder than I thought it would be."

"Well, you're doing a very good job," Angelica said, which made Antonio beam as well.

Their dinners arrived and everyone dug in. The food was superb, and they were engrossed in their entrées when the dinner plates arrived at EM's table. Tricia tried not to look like she was taking an interest, but after the drama they'd already witnessed, she found it hard to take her eyes off the back of EM's head. She watched as the woman took her first bite—and then spit it out on her plate.

"You call this lobster? It tastes like sashimi—and cheap sashimi, at that!" EM declared.

"You're making yet another scene," the woman across from her grated.

"Waiter!" EM called. A chagrined female server returned to stand before the tactless author. "Take this away."

"I'm so sorry you're displeased. What may I bring you?"

"Bring me a bowl of soup—and some bread. You can't screw up bread, can you?"

"No, madam." The server quickly removed the plate and hurried away from the table.

The woman across from EM took a bite of her dinner. "I told you to get the beef. Mine is excellent."

"You have an unsophisticated palate. *I'm* the gourmand here."

As though in defiance, the woman shoveled an enormous forkful into her mouth and chewed.

A nervous Cristophano showed up at the table. "Is everything to your liking? May I get you anything?"

"I don't know about the others," Angelica said, grinning broadly, "but my lobster is superb."

"The lamb is excellent," Tricia chimed in.

"The beef is cooked to perfection," Antonio said, and Ginny nodded, as well.

"May I refill your glasses?" Cristophano asked.

"Yes, please," Angelica said, and lifted hers.

EM must have heard them, for her back had stiffened. She grabbed the napkin from her lap and threw it on the table. "I believe I'll go back to my stateroom and order room service," she said, and got up from the table. "I'll see you later, Dori."

The woman was still shoveling food into her mouth and had no opportunity to answer before EM stormed from the dining room. The rest of the Kells Grill patrons seemed to breathe a collective sigh of relief.

"Well, now," Angelica began, "let's see if we can now start to *really* enjoy our meals."

Tricia glanced at EM's dinner companion, who sported what could only be called a shit-eating grin.

THREE

Angelica wasn't about to be cheated out of the martini she'd craved for most of the day. Antonio and Ginny were reluctant to leave Sofia alone any longer that evening, so Angelica turned sad eyes on Tricia.

"Oh, all right," she acquiesced.

"We will say good night," Antonio said, stood, and pulled back Ginny's chair.

"See you in the morning," Ginny called.

The sisters watched the couple leave the restaurant.

No sooner had the heavy glass doors closed behind them when Angelica reached for her purse and retrieved the little map that had come in the tiny folder along with her keycard. She unfolded it and squinted, then grabbed her reading glasses. "Did you know there are five bars on the ship?"

"No, I didn't." And Tricia probably didn't need to, either. Still, during the past year she had patronized the Dog-Eared Page back in Stoneham. She was friendly with the pub's manager and liked the bartender, and she loved the air of conviviality the place promoted. "Where would you like to go?"

"The Commodore Club looks pretty big, but after the day I've had, I don't think I'm in the mood for crowds. And the Golden Harp is more a pub than a true bar."

"What about the Portside Bar?" Tricia said, pointing to Deck 3 midship on the map. "That looks rather intimate."

"I'm game."

They got up and left the table, heading for the lifts.

In the Portside Bar several people sat on plush, upholstered stools at the dark wood bar, but Angelica chose to settle on a loveseat in a corner. Tricia took the adjacent chair, admiring the heavy brocaded fabric. The bar was decorated in soft shades of gold and green, and several locked cabinets nearby sported memorabilia from the ocean liner's parent company's glory days the century before. She decided she'd have to return another time to take a closer look, and idly wondered if there was a book in the ship's library about a murder taking place on one of the great ocean liners from a time gone by—perhaps the *Normandie,* or the *Queen Mary.* Such a tale, steeped in the lore of the great days of ocean travel, could be a fun read.

Soon a waitress in a white uniform with green piping, and a tray in hand, approached them. "Good evening, ladies. Can I get you anything?"

"Yes, thank you," Angelica said, her smile filled with anticipation. "A dry gin martini, up, with olives."

"And the gin?"

Angelica thought about it for a moment. "Hendrick's."

The waitress turned to Tricia.

"What the heck. I'll have the same, please."

Angelica beamed at Tricia in approval as she surrendered her key-card to the waitress, who turned and headed back to the bar. "Isn't this an elegant room?"

Tricia nodded.

"I wonder if it would be feasible to put an addition onto the Brookview Inn with the same kind of ambience."

"Wouldn't that detract from people patronizing the Dog-Eared Page?"

"It would be a different clientele. I must speak to Antonio about it tomorrow."

Angelica's head rose and she seemed to be looking around Tricia, who turned to see EM Barstow enter the bar, her laptop in hand, and accompanied by someone other than her assistant.

Angelica scowled. "Oh, dear."

"I guess EM skipped dinner altogether," Tricia said.

The woman who'd joined EM was younger than the thriller author by at least three decades. Her shoulder-length brown hair needed a trim, but her black slacks and matching suit jacket were better defined *smart casual* than EM's riotous caftan. They settled at a loveseat across the way, and EM opened her laptop. Tricia turned back to Angelica. "Looks like a business meeting."

"I'm betting a lot of business will be discussed on this cruise. I intend to start networking tomorrow. How about you?"

"I'd like to line up some of the mystery authors to come sign at Haven't Got a Clue, but we're a little off the beaten track for most of them."

"That's true. But if nothing else, you could encourage them to give you their bookmarks to pass out. It's a great way to engender reader loyalty for them *and* for you."

"Good point."

The waitress returned with their drinks, setting out cocktail napkins with an image of the ship engraved upon them, returning Angelica's keycard, and giving her the charge receipt to sign. She did so, and the woman accepted the slip and turned to leave.

Angelica picked up her glass. "What shall we drink to?"

Tricia clasped her glass and thought about it for a few moments. "How about the wonderful friendships we've found in our adopted home of Stoneham?"

"Oh, that's terrific. To our friends."

They clinked glasses and took a sip. Tricia had never tasted Hendrick's Gin before. It was a revelation. "Wow, that's a damn fine martini."

"Isn't it, though?" Angelica said, smiling. And then her gaze seemed to be diverted once again to the part of the bar where EM and the other woman were sitting.

"Is something going on?" Tricia asked.

"EM and her friend seem to be having a little bit of a disagreement."

Tricia turned. Angelica might be right. EM's body language suggested she was more than a tad upset. She'd pushed up her sleeves, and Tricia could see she sported what looked like bands of a drab gray fabric that covered both wrists. It seemed an odd fashion statement.

EM's companion's expression seemed serious, but resolute.

The sisters watched for another half minute before EM rather forcefully closed the lid of her laptop, rose from her seat, and stormed out of the bar, leaving her guest still sitting there, looking like she'd just swallowed a bitter pill.

"That's not surprising, considering what a nasty piece of work EM is."

Angelica raised a hand and waved.

"What are you doing?" Tricia asked.

"Asking that woman to join us."

"Why?"

"Why not?"

Seconds later, the woman in black stood before them. "I'm sorry. Do I know you?"

"I'm Angelica Miles, and this is my sister, Tricia."

"I'm Cathy Copper."

"You're a friend of EM's?" Tricia asked.

"Actually, I'm her editor."

"Oh, how nice," Angelica said, smiling. "Won't you join us for a drink?"

"That would be lovely. Thank you."

"Tricia, can you get the waitress's attention?" Angelica asked.

Tricia looked up, raised a hand, and waved to catch the woman's eye. Cathy took the chair to Angelica's left and sat down. In no time, the waitress arrived.

"What would you like?" Angelica asked.

"Just a Diet Coke, thanks."

The waitress nodded and waited for Angelica to once again surrender her keycard before heading back to the bar.

"Have you worked with EM long?" Tricia asked, and took another sip of her drink.

"This is our second book together," Cathy said, but she didn't sound pleased.

"Oh?" Tricia prompted.

"I'm not sure we see eye to eye on where the series should go."

"Shouldn't that issue be entirely up to the author?" Tricia said, surprised by the editor's response. "I mean, she's the one with the vision for her characters."

"You'd think," Cathy said.

Tricia studied the woman's face. There was a tightness around her mouth, and for some reason Tricia wasn't sure she liked this person.

Angelica gave a forced laugh. "Has EM grown tired of writing the series?"

"Yes," Cathy said, her voice growing hard.

"Does she plan to kill off her hero?" Tricia asked.

"I'm not at liberty to say. But let's just say her previous ventures into other characters and series have not been as successful as her current work."

Tricia knew about that. EM had written another mystery series, set in nineteenth-century Philadelphia, with a scullery maid turned amateur sleuth that had not resonated with readers. It had died after only three books—which was the litmus test for the success of a mystery series.

Angelica deftly changed the subject. "Is this your first cruise?"

"Yes," Cathy admitted. "I've never done anything like this before."

"The *Celtic Lady* is a beautiful ship," Angelica said.

Cathy nodded in agreement, her expression bland. "I guess. This line is a bit stodgy for someone my age."

"Are you saying we're all old farts?" Angelica asked, straight-faced, but Tricia knew that tone of voice.

"Most of the passengers *are* of a certain age—and older," Cathy commented.

It was true that Tricia was probably twenty years her senior, so did Cathy include her in that assessment? A person like that probably couldn't begin to appreciate the experience of her elders—nor was she likely to learn from their mistakes, either.

"I'm assuming your employer sent you on this cruise," Angelica said.

"Yes," Cathy said, craning her neck—perhaps to see if her drink was on the horizon. "This isn't exactly *my* idea of a vacation."

"How sad," Tricia said.

"What do you mean?"

"That you can't find some enjoyment on this trip."

"I didn't say *that*," Cathy said defensively. "After all, this is only the first night out."

"I do hope you'll find *something* you enjoy on our voyage," Angelica said sweetly, and again Tricia knew that tone.

"If nothing else, the food seems pretty good."

"Where did you dine?"

"In the Emerald Isle Restaurant. My company stuck me in one of the cheapest rooms. I've got an inside cabin—not a window in sight."

"Oh, dear," Angelica said without sympathy.

The waitress arrived with the soft drink and the slip for Angelica to sign, then returned her keycard.

Tricia struggled to come up with another topic. "Are you scheduled for any panels?"

"Yes," Cathy said. "There are several other editors on board, and we're to speak on the first sea day on the trip back to New York."

"What will you do in the meantime?" Angelica asked.

"Try to convince my author to change her mind on the direction of her series," Cathy grated.

Had the editor said more than she ought to to people she didn't really know? Well, that was the problem with such a young person being assigned to a seasoned author. The author really *did* have a better feel for her series and characters than someone who'd only been given the assignment to shepherd a book to publication. After all, there were many, many series that Tricia had read where it was apparent that the author had lost interest in her characters long before the publisher was willing to let it go. And EM's most recent editor was far younger than herself. Had EM been insulted to be assigned such a greenhorn? Tricia would have felt that way, and was glad she was able to just read and enjoy the books in her favorite genre and not have to actually write them.

Cathy sipped her diet cola.

Angelica and Tricia sipped their martinis.

Time seemed to pass achingly slowly.

"So, why are you ladies on this little junket?" Cathy finally asked.

"We're booksellers," Tricia answered. "My sister"—she nodded toward Angelica—"owns a cookbook store. I own a mystery bookstore."

"Oh?" Cathy asked, sounding halfway interested.

"As a matter of fact, EM Barstow once came to sign at my store."

"Was she terribly rude to you and your staff?" Cathy asked, her eyebrows narrowing.

"Just a tad," Tricia lied.

"EM leads a very complicated life. She doesn't let the world in general know about her difficulties, but she has no problem taking them out on others, either."

"Oh?" Angelica asked.

"It's not my place to speak about it."

"Of course not," Angelica said, obviously disappointed.

Cathy practically gulped the last of her drink and set the glass on the cocktail table before them. "Thank you, ladies. It was very nice talking with you."

"We're glad you could join us," Angelica said, smiling.

"Yes. I hope we'll have another chance to speak before the end of our voyage," Tricia said with false sincerity.

"I'm sure we will." Cathy stood. "Until then, have a nice evening."

"You, too," the sisters chorused, and watched the editor leave the bar, her gait a bit wobbly. Had she had a drink before she'd joined them?

It was Tricia who turned to her sister and spoke first. "Well, that was certainly interesting."

"Yes. Wasn't it?" Angelica agreed. She removed the frill pick from her drink, snagged the first of two queen olives, chewed, and swallowed. "You know, I have the world's best editor. He has cut me an enormous amount of slack—especially this past year when I've had so much on my plate. I don't think I'd like to be one of Cathy Copper's authors."

"No, and I can see why. Maybe *she's* the reason EM is so grumpy."

"Perhaps," Angelica agreed, and took another sip of her drink. "She didn't seem all that grateful to her employer for sending her on this wonderful cruise. Inside cabin? Okay, not optimal. But having to sit on *one* panel as a consequence? That woman doesn't know a good thing when it's handed to her."

"Maybe *we're* just jaded," Tricia suggested.

"Nigela Ricita manages more than thirty employees, and I can't think of one of them who isn't respectful and grateful to be employed."

"Maybe that's because they know what is expected of them and are paid enough that they're happy to fulfill their obligations. I don't think editors make all that much money."

"Maybe. Perhaps it's best that I write nonfiction. I don't think I'd care to have someone trying to direct my narrative."

"And I hear the battles with copy editors can be very frustrating," Tricia said.

"Don't get me started on that topic," Angelica said with just a touch of menace.

Tricia managed a wan smile. "But you have to agree—mystery or cooking—books are our lives."

"That's true."

"I'm looking forward to finding a bookshop or two in Bermuda."

"Tomorrow we can check out the on-board shop, but as I recall from other cruises, there isn't a lot to choose from, apart from best-sellers and maritime history. Although I'm sure with so many authors on board, they'll have a ton of their books for sale."

"I'm looking forward to sitting in a comfy chair back in the stateroom, or maybe in a place like this bar, and reading for hours and hours on end with nobody bothering me. Doesn't that sound like heaven?"

"You don't intend to partake of all the wonderful panels, discussions, and demonstrations?" Angelica asked.

"Yes, but what I really want to do is just wallow in a good, long read. It's been forever since I've been able to do that."

"There'll be plenty of time for that, I'm sure. But you should schedule it for the return voyage."

Tricia polished off the last of her drink. "Do you have other plans for tonight? I understand there are a couple of nightclubs on board."

"I'm afraid my nightclub days are far behind me," Angelica said, and sighed, then took one last sip of her drink. "Maybe Cathy was right. Maybe we *are* just a couple of old farts."

"There's nothing wrong with wanting a quiet life," Tricia said. She'd experienced far *too* much excitement during the previous six years, what with the murder and mayhem that seemed to be centered in the vicinity of her shop and that had taken away Stoneham's former title of Safest Village in New Hampshire. That's why the thought of a week-long cruise had appealed to her so much.

"But, honestly, neither of us leads a quiet life," Angelica said.

"Then there's no need to worry about old fartdom," Tricia said, amused.

"I may not dance the night away, but I've got a date with my laptop. I'm going to journal about this trip and all the fabulous ideas I'm coming up with for Nigela Ricita Associates."

"You're not going to make poor Antonio work during his vacation, are you?"

"*Make* him work? Of course not. However, should he—and/or Ginny—*want* to discuss his working life with me, I'll be all ears."

They got up from their seats and headed for the main corridor and the lifts. "You can work if you want, but I've got a date with Miss Marple—and this time it isn't my cat," Tricia said.

"Looks like we'll both have a nice, quiet—and enjoyable—evening," Angelica said.

Tricia was looking forward to five more of them, too. It was just what she needed.

And yet . . . something niggled at the back of her brain telling her not to get her hopes up.

She forged ahead, determined *not* to pay attention to what, back home, she might have called her better judgment.

FOUR

After a good long read and a wonderfully refreshing night's sleep, Tricia began her first full day at sea the same way she started her days at home—with a brisk walk. After her apartment had been smoke damaged during the fire almost a year before, she'd spent a good deal of her time walking Angelica's dog, Sarge. Once winter had once again reared its ugly head, she'd had to return to her treadmill. It wasn't nearly as satisfying.

Her usual routine was to walk four miles. According to a plaque mounted midship on the Promenade Deck, three and a half circuits around the boat would equal a mile. Tricia had plenty of company, as many others on board either walked or jogged along or past her, imparting a feeling of camaraderie.

The weather was clear, but the wind was bracing as she power walked around the deck counterclockwise. She could have gone to the spa to use one of their treadmills, but as at home, she preferred the fresh air. It helped to clear her head. She dearly missed her cat, Miss Marple, but knew that she was being well taken care of by her assistant, Pixie Poe. Perhaps later she'd visit the ship's computer centre, buy some Wi-Fi time, and e-mail Pixie to see how things were going at the store and check up on Miss Marple, too. Pixie was not only cat sitting, but house sitting, as well. Tricia could picture Pixie in the evening, stretched out on the long leather couch in her living room, surrounded by books, with Miss Marple lying on her stomach. The cat and Pixie got along fine; it was Tricia who was suffering from separation anxiety. That Pixie might invite her boyfriend, Fred Pillins, to spend the night was a topic Tricia did not wish to contemplate.

Tricia returned to her shared stateroom to find Angelica clad in a plush white terry robe with *Celtic Lady* embroidered in green above the pocket, seated on one of the loveseats with a room service cart laden with pastries and other goodies beside her.

"There you are. Sebastian just brought in our breakfast tray. I figured you were out catching some fresh air. You do look rather windblown."

"You should walk with me tomorrow morning."

"I should," Angelica agreed. She changed the subject. "Sebastian also made a delivery while you were gone."

Tricia looked around the stateroom.

"Check your bedroom."

Tricia pivoted and walked the five steps to her room. The bed had been made and on it sat a wrapped gift. She picked up the rectangular box and gave it a shake. Nothing rattled. The paper was white with the words *Celtic Lady* printed on it multiple times in green ink, with a wide Kelly green ribbon and bow.

Tricia frowned. Had the person who sent the champagne to their table the night before struck once again? She wasn't sure how she felt about having an admirer from afar. She'd been stalked before, and the idea of it happening again worried her.

She returned to the lounge. "There's no card."

"Perhaps it's inside," Angelica suggested.

Tricia took a seat on the opposite loveseat and set the box on her lap, then pulled the ribbon. She carefully removed the tape from one end of the box.

"Oh, go ahead and tear the paper," Angelica admonished. "It's not like you're going to save and reuse it."

"Someone went to a lot of trouble to make the package look pretty." And the truth was she was worried about its contents. It wasn't only shirts that came in a box that size.

Removing the paper, Tricia lifted the lid and drew back the green tissue paper.

"What is it?" Angelica demanded.

Tricia withdrew a navy cardigan. Gold-toned buttons fastened the front.

"Well, that's . . ." Angelica paused. "Not especially special."

Tricia looked into the box, where she found the same kind of card that had arrived with the wine the night before. "It says, *To keep you warm during the long winter.*"

"And it's not signed?" Angelica asked.

Tricia shook her head. She set the sweater back in the box and frowned yet again.

"If nothing else, it's a thoughtful gift," Angelica said.

"Why would somebody send me a sweater?"

"Maybe you look cold."

Tricia's frown deepened.

"Would you have preferred to receive sexy underwear?"

"No!"

"Then why do you look so worried?"

"Whoever sent this and the wine is most likely a passenger on this ship."

"Why do you say that?"

"Because of the wrapping paper." She handed it across to Angelica, who glanced at it and then wadded it into a ball and set it on the breakfast cart. "Not necessarily. It's possible to order wine, flowers, or any other gift for a passenger on a cruise. I remember Mother once telling me that she received a big box of chocolates from Daddy's firm while they were on that cruise to Greece way back when."

Tricia remembered hearing that same story.

Angelica reached over, picked up a gooey pastry, and took a bite. She chewed and swallowed. "With all the good food available here, I'm going to need to go on a diet once we get home."

Tricia set the box and sweater aside, stood to shrug out of her jacket, and then set it on the back of the opposite couch before she moved to look over the breakfast items available. Among the foods on offer was yogurt, so she was good to go. She picked up one of the containers and a spoon and sat down. "Did you look over the Daily Program last night?"

Angelica licked her sticky fingers before she reached for the coffee carafe. "Yes. There's a marketing lecture at ten that could be interesting."

"What do you need to know about marketing? You're already a whiz."

"I *am*," she agreed, and poured coffee into two cups. "But I'm sure there must be *something* else I can learn. I assume you're heading straight for the library."

Tricia ate a spoonful of apricot yogurt before answering. "I don't think they open until ten. I may just go exploring in the interim. Want to come with me?"

"Maybe—maybe not." Angelica picked up a cup and handed it to Tricia. "Later, I thought I might go to EM Barstow's question-and-answer panel."

"Whatever for?" Tricia asked. "Didn't you have enough of that ill-tempered woman last night at dinner?"

"It's rather fun—in a voyeuristic way—to see someone make an ass of themselves. She's a true candidate for *Authors Behaving Badly*. I feel sorry for her traveling companion, though. Imagine having to put up with that kind of vitriol on a regular basis."

"Maybe she's paid well," Tricia suggested.

"You couldn't pay me enough to endure that." Angelica's expression turned quizzical. "Do you think they're partners?"

"I have no idea—and I really don't care to speculate."

"I wonder if EM's editor will be in the audience during her appearance."

"If she is, she may not be cheering EM on," Tricia said.

Angelica drank the last of her coffee and got up. "I'm going to get ready for the day. Are we going to meet somewhere for lunch?"

"We could. I think there's a lull in the programming between noon and three. We'll probably miss out on afternoon tea."

"We have five more days to enjoy it," Angelica pointed out.

"Where shall we meet for lunch? Or rather, how formal do you want lunch to be?" Tricia asked.

"I'm in the mood for casual."

"Then that would be the Lido Restaurant, which I've heard is more or less cafeteria style."

"That actually appeals to me," Angelica said. "Then we can have a taste of many things, in as big or small a portion as we want."

"And as many desserts as you want?" Tricia asked.

Angelica smiled. "That, too."

Sebastian appeared at the doorway to Angelica's quarters. "Ms. Miles? I've made up the bed and drawn your bath."

"Thank you, Sebastian."

The butler nodded curtly. "Please let me know if I may be of further assistance."

"We will. Thank you."

The sisters watched as their valet left the stateroom, pulling the door shut behind him.

"I could get used to this kind of treatment," Angelica said, and headed for her bedroom and bath. "À bientôt."

Tricia, too, got up from her couch, wondering what she should do with the breakfast cart. Oh, well, Angelica had ordered it—she'd let her sister worry about it.

She changed her clothes, making sure she placed the small folded map of the ship she'd received upon boarding in the pocket of her slacks, and headed for the library.

As she'd feared, it didn't open until ten. She wandered through the stately room that spanned two decks via a spiral staircase and gazed through the beveled glass on the cabinets that housed the books, sighing at the sight of all those lovely titles. She tried one of the doors. Locked. Was that to keep them safe in rough seas, or to keep them from sticky fingers that might not return them? No doubt the keycard was also used as a library card, as well as for identification and purchasing goods from the ship's stores. That was an idea. She could check out the shopping venues on board.

After consulting her map, Tricia climbed the forward stairs to Deck 3 and headed for the ship's arcade. None of the shops were open at that time of day, but she wasn't the only one who'd come to do a little window shopping. Among the gawkers was EM Barstow's dinner companion from the previous evening. She stood before the jewelry shop, staring at some of the merchandise inside a sturdy case.

Tricia moved to stand beside her. "Beautiful, aren't they?"

The woman looked up. "Out of my price range I'm afraid, but yes, they are."

"Hi. I'm Tricia Miles."

"Dori Douglas." The woman's cheeks colored. "I recognize you from dinner last night. I'm so sorry."

"For what?"

"For Ms. Barstow's behavior. She's under a lot of stress these days. I try to take up the slack, but . . ." She let the sentence hang.

"Are you her assistant?" Tricia asked.

Dori took a breath as though to answer, then held it. "Sort of. She doesn't pay me. I'm the president of her fan club."

Tricia's eyes widened. Barstow had a fan club? Why would anyone willingly want to spend a minute with that miserable woman? Tricia forced a smile, trying to reserve judgment.

"Not only is Ms. Barstow a three-time Edgar winner, she's a *New York Times* and *USA Today* bestselling author," Dori said with pride.

"I'm well acquainted with her work," Tricia said. "I'm a bookseller. I specialize in mysteries."

"Isn't it wonderful to be among so many others who are equally as passionate about the written word and are able to gush without getting strange looks and comments?"

Tricia nodded. "I've felt that way on more than one occasion." They shared a smile. "So you're acting as Ms. Barstow's traveling companion?"

Dori sighed. "I try to run interference for her. I'm afraid I haven't done a very good job on this trip. She comes across as rather abrupt"— that was an understatement—"but she's really very sweet and generous. She paid all my travel expenses. I'd never be able to afford a vacation like this on my retirement income."

"I met Ms. Barstow's editor last night," Tricia said.

Dori frowned and sighed. "She's *very* young."

"I guess everyone has to start somewhere."

"I don't see why someone fresh out of college, and with no *real* experience, should get to edit—to critique—someone as capable, and successful, as Emmie."

Did Dori really believe it, or was she just parroting what her idol had said?

"Ms. Copper said this was their second book together. Presumably she works with a number of other authors."

"Not the caliber of EM Barstow," Dori said emphatically.

Tricia was afraid Dori might be on the verge of disparaging some of the other authors on board and decided it was time to terminate the conversation. "Well, I hope you enjoy the rest of the trip."

"Thank you. You, too."

"I'm sure we'll see each other again."

"And hopefully have a more peaceful dinner," Dori added with an embarrassed laugh.

Tricia gave the woman a parting smile and headed aft. There was still so much of the ship she wanted to explore. She passed through the upper lobby area and found herself in front of a gallery of photos taken by the shipboard photographers and was startled to see a picture of herself and Angelica as they'd entered the ship. She hadn't even noticed the photographers. Though a candid, it was a nice shot. Tricia hadn't had a professional photograph taken of herself in more than a decade. Maybe she and Angelica should have a portrait taken together. Oh, and one with Ginny, Antonio, and little Sofia, too.

She was so engrossed in thought, it took her a moment to realize someone was standing at her shoulder. She looked up and recognized Fiona Sample, Nikki Brimfield-Smith's mother. "Fiona! I heard you were on board." She held her arms out to embrace the author. "It's so good to see you again."

"You're a sight for sore eyes, too."

"I'm so sorry Nikki and Russ couldn't make the trip."

"I offered to pay for them to come, but you know Russ."

"I'm afraid I do," Tricia said with a shake of her head.

"Though I hate to be away from my husband and kids for so long, I'll be heading to Stoneham to stay for a few days after the cruise. I'd love to visit your store and sign the stock."

"I always keep your books on my shelves, so there are plenty to sign."

Fiona smiled. "You're so good to me. You always have been."

Tricia had been instrumental in reuniting Nikki and her mother after years of estrangement. Too bad no one had engineered such an intervention between Tricia and *her* mother.

Fiona pushed back one of her sleeves and scratched her wrist, which also bore one of the odd little fabric bracelets like EM wore.

"What's that?" Tricia asked.

"What's what?"

"That bracelet you're wearing."

Fiona pushed back the sleeve of her cardigan. "This? It's an acupressure wristband."

"What's it for?"

"Motion sickness. On my last cruise, I wore an anti-nausea patch. It worked fine, but it left me with such terrible dry mouth that I vowed I'd never wear one again. A friend told me about these wristbands and, wearing them, I'm cured. Of course, I also brought along a little bottle of Coke syrup—just in case. Have you ever been seasick?"

"No."

"Then you're lucky." Fiona pulled the band away from her skin. "This little white button presses into your wrist. Even if it's just a placebo, it sure seems to work for me—and lots of others, too."

Tricia wondered how many other passengers would be wearing the unattractive bands on their wrists. Still, if they worked—who cared about fashion?

"When are you giving your talk?"

"I'm on a panel with several of the Lethal Ladies this afternoon at three," Fiona said.

"Oh, I love their blog," Tricia said.

"Will you be there?"

"I wouldn't miss it for the world."

"It'll be good to have a friend cheering me on in the audience. I don't do much public speaking these days. I'm afraid I'm a little rusty."

"We must have lunch or dinner before the end of the cruise—and maybe once we get back to Stoneham, too," Tricia said.

"I'd love that." Fiona looked at her watch. "Oh, my. I'm being interviewed for tomorrow's shipboard morning TV show. They're going to feature a couple of authors each day. I'll be late if I don't hustle my bustle."

"If I don't see you later today, I'll definitely see you tomorrow," Tricia promised.

"I'll hold you to it," Fiona said, gave a quick wave, and headed forward.

Tricia turned back to the display and plucked the picture of her and Angelica and took it to the desk, purchasing it. With the cardboard photo holder in hand, she retraced her steps and found the library had finally opened. All the cabinets were unlocked, and Tricia spent a happy half hour going from shelf to shelf, pulling out the books, inhaling their wonderful scent, and reading the descriptions on the back covers. Nearly all of them were hardcovers, and many were large-print editions. She thought of Cathy Copper and frowned. Did a woman that young actually read for pleasure, or did she put in her time at the publisher and go home to post selfies of herself on Instagram?

Tricia, Tricia, the inner voice inside her scolded. Maybe she was just a little burned by Cathy's attitude. Still, she'd come to find a nice book to read and was determined to find one.

As she rounded the corner, Tricia saw EM stationed at one of the library's carrels by a window. Whitecaps decorated each cresting wave outside, but in the ship's inviting library, EM's attention was intently focused on her laptop's screen. She'd come prepared to fend off distractions by erecting a small placard on the desktop that read: AUTHOR

AT WORK: DO NOT DISTURB. The sign seemed to be doing its job. Nobody seemed the least bit interested in bothering the great EM Barstow. EM wore the same acupressure bracelets as Fiona, but she'd also donned a bracelet on one hand, and a watch on the other, though neither covered the ugly fabric bands.

The man on the scooter she'd seen the previous day in the terminal rode into the library. The vehicle came to a halt, and he looked around the wood-paneled room. His expression brightened when he caught sight of EM, and then he made a beeline straight for her.

"Hi, Emmie!" he called cheerfully.

EM looked up from her laptop's computer screen, her expression hardening. "Can't you read the sign?" she asked, pointing to the placard in front of her.

"Darling, Emmie, surely that doesn't include *me*," the man said, sounding disappointed.

"I put it there especially *for* you, Arnold," EM said coldly.

Tricia looked away, perusing more titles, trying not to eavesdrop, but it seemed as though EM *wanted* those around her to listen in.

"Leave me alone, or I will have ship's security lock you away for the rest of the trip."

"It isn't a crime to visit the ship's library. And contrary to what you think, it isn't a crime for me to speak in your presence."

"It ought to be," EM grated.

"It may interest you to know that you are no longer my favorite author," Arnold said blandly.

"Which I intend to celebrate."

Tricia took a book down, glanced at the cover, and turned it over to check out the description on the back.

"I'm not even going to attend your silly panel this morning."

"Nothing I do is silly," EM grated.

"So says the massively inflated ego," the man said theatrically. "But

I'm sure we'll be seeing each other around the ship from time to time during the next few days. Perhaps if you're nice to me, we can be pals once again."

"We were *never* pals," EM asserted.

"So you say. Now. Ah, but there was a time," Arnold said wistfully.

"Go away."

"And just to remind you," Arnold continued, "we're on the open sea and U.S. laws don't apply here."

EM's gaze remained hard. "Go away!" she repeated more forcefully.

"I will, my darling, but only because I have better things to do than spar with you."

Arnold grabbed his scooter's handles and backed up. Tricia watched as he headed out the door, then turned her attention back to the book in her hand. It looked like an interesting read, and she decided to borrow it.

She glanced back at EM, who hadn't gone back to work. Instead, her gaze was fixed on the swells outside the window. Could she have actually been rattled by her brief conversation with her former fan?

Tricia moved to the next cabinet filled with tomes and studied the titles and authors, none of whom were familiar. She chose another book at random and studied the description. She opened the book and read the first few paragraphs before noticing movement to her right. EM had evidently decided the library wasn't a conducive workplace after all, and was packing up her laptop—either that, or she needed to prepare for her upcoming panel. From the look on her face, she was definitely unhappy.

Tricia replaced the book on the shelf and decided to just borrow the one book. She walked briskly to the checkout desk and surrendered her keycard. The librarian on duty swiped the card and handed it and the book back to Tricia. "Enjoy!"

"I'm sure I will," Tricia said, and headed out of the library. She wasn't sure where she'd end up on the ship to read, but she had several hours to kill before Fiona's panel and she intended to enjoy them.

A sunny day. A relatively calm sea. A book in hand.

Bliss.

And yet, part of her mind was still pondering the odd conversation she'd witnessed between EM and her former fan. What had he meant by his cryptic remark about laws not applying on the open sea?

Tricia shook her head. It wasn't any of her business. And yet, her curiosity had been piqued. The thought that someone annoyed EM as much as she annoyed others was rather amusing. Still, it was apparent that the world-famous author had been disturbed by the encounter.

What did she have to fear?

FIVE

After leaving the ship's library, Tricia settled into a sunny spot in the port side of the Garden Lounge and managed to read the first five chapters of *Why Wonder About Murder?* by an Irish author Tricia had never read before, when she looked at her watch and found it was already time to meet Angelica for lunch. She showed up on time and stood near the entrance to the Lido Restaurant, searching the faces of other passengers, looking for her sister. Instead, it was Mary Fairchild's familiar face that stood out in the crowd. She waved to Tricia and stepped out of the incoming traffic for a word.

"You look happy," Tricia said.

"I've just come from the Crystal Ballroom," Mary said, her cheeks pink, her eyes sparkling. "Did you know they give ballroom dancing lessons on board?"

"I think I heard something about it."

"The cruise line supplies gentlemen dance hosts for unaccompanied ladies. It was a lot of fun learning to do the cha-cha and mambo. My partner's name is Ed Gardener. He used to be a shoe salesman, and now that he's retired, he spends most of his time cruising and dancing. Doesn't that sound like a fun life?"

Not really, but Tricia wasn't about to burst Mary's bubble.

"Luke"—Mary's ex—"hated to dance. He even griped about being forced into it at our wedding. That was the last time he joined me on any dance floor. But learning to do those dance steps was so much fun—I felt like I could be a contestant on *Dancing with the Stars.* Tonight I'm going to the ballroom to try out these new steps, and I'm dressing to the nines. I sure hope Ed is going to be there. What a card! Maybe you should come," she suggested.

"I'm afraid I have two left feet," Tricia lied. She'd been forced to go to dancing school all those years ago. It was something her mother made her and Angelica do. Angelica took to it like a fish to water. Tricia . . . well, she could do it, but really enjoyed dancing only with Christopher. Just the thought of those happy times—and the fact that they'd never happen again—brought on another pang of sadness.

"Don't let me keep you from lunch," Tricia said.

"I'm meeting Leona. I can't wait to tell her about it, too!" Mary said, gave a wave, and entered the restaurant.

Tricia went back to scanning the faces of the other cruisers entering the restaurant. By the time Angelica showed up almost ten minutes later, she'd put the memories of herself and Christopher out of her mind. Almost.

Angelica approached, smiling and waving cheerfully.

"I was beginning to think you weren't going to show up," Tricia said.

"I'm sorry I'm late. EM's lecture—and that's just what it was—ran a little late."

"Well, you're here now. You can tell me all about it after we grab lunch. I'm starved."

The sisters entered the cafeteria-style restaurant and joined the line in front of the long stainless steel trays of food on offer. Everything looked so colorful, so vibrant—so *wonderful.*

Angelica picked up a tray, a plate, and silverware, and Tricia did likewise, following behind her.

As they inched forward, Tricia looked over the food, including more than a dozen vegetable side dishes. She sized them up while Angelica dived straight into the protein, heaping samples of shrimp, chicken, and beef onto her tray. Tricia chose a tablespoon or two of various cooked vegetables.

"Is that all you're going to have? I thought you said you were starving."

"I'm still considering my options. There's a salad bar just across the way," Tricia pointed out.

"This is a *vacation.* You're *supposed* to pig out," Angelica said, exasperated.

"That's not my style, and you know it," Tricia said.

Angelica shook her head and added some mashed potatoes to her plate, but avoided the Irish bangers.

Tricia headed for the salad bar, grabbing a bowl, setting it on her tray, and adding greens, a couple of cherry tomatoes, and a slice of cucumber. Nearby were small ramekins of pâté and what a sign promised was duck confit. Now that was a decadent treat. There could only be a couple of tablespoons in the tiny white dish, and she decided to splurge. She caught up with Angelica at the coffee station, poured herself a cup, and then followed her sister to a table by a window. The sea was a bit choppy, but the ship seemed to cut through the waves without jostling a thing.

"So, how was EM's lecture?"

"Tedious," Angelica said. "I was glad I took a notebook with me. EM must have thought I was writing down her every word, but I was actually jotting down notes for the next Chamber newsletter. I must remember to take some pictures, although I'm sure I can rely on Ginny and Antonio and the others for some candid shots. Perhaps we'll make it a double issue."

"It *is* the first trip the Chamber has endorsed," Tricia said.

"If it's successful, maybe we'll do another one next year," Angelica said, picking up her fork and diving into her mashed potatoes.

Tricia cut one of her tiny tomatoes in half. "Did EM's lecture include a question-and-answer period?"

"No, which rather surprised me. EM stood at the lectern and did a PowerPoint slideshow chronicling the life of her protagonist. Considering she writes thrillers, her talk was surprisingly dull."

"Writers are often solitary folks. They work alone for long stretches at a time. I've heard more than one author say she finds speaking to groups painful."

"Isn't it lucky I was born a social butterfly?" Angelica asked, and laughed.

"I'll say." Tricia sampled the confit. Wow! Talk about rich. She turned back to the veggies and salad before her. "Did you see anybody interesting in the audience?"

Angelica nodded. "I saw Leona Ferguson, Chauncey Porter, Grace, and Mr. Everett, and a few authors with familiar faces—but I can't remember their names—and that was about it." She attacked the beef on her plate.

"How about Cathy Copper?"

Angelica swallowed. "She was sitting in the front row. I saw her head bob a few times." She giggled. "I think she may have nodded off. She wasn't the only one."

"What do you suppose she meant last night when she said EM's life was complicated and that people didn't know she had problems?"

"EM's problem seems to be connecting with her readers on a one-to-one basis," Angelica said, and picked up her cup for a sip of coffee.

"Do you think she has health concerns?"

Angelica shrugged.

"I bumped into Fiona Sample. She told me she was being interviewed for tomorrow's on-board talk show."

"How nice. Maybe we can watch it while we eat breakfast tomorrow."

"I wonder if they'll interview EM."

"If so, I'd skip it—like I wish I'd skipped her lecture today. You were smart not to attend."

"I saw her working in the library earlier this morning. She'd even erected a little sign telling people not to disturb her. She had a bit of a run-in with one of her former readers. He seemed to take great pleasure in annoying her."

"I'm willing to bet he isn't the only one." Angelica cut off a piece of the chicken breast on her plate and sampled it. She smiled. "Not as good as mine, but not bad."

Tricia worked on her veggies for a while longer. "Will you be going to the cozy mystery panel this afternoon? Fiona will be there."

"I haven't decided. Either that, or I might visit the spa. I was considering getting a facial and perhaps a massage. We really need a spa in Stoneham. I'll have to do a feasibility study." She reached for her purse and pulled out a little notebook not much bigger than a cocktail napkin and jotted down the idea, then turned back to her lunch.

"I wouldn't mind getting a manicure and maybe a pedicure," Tricia admitted.

"We'll do it together. Maybe Ginny would like to join us. Remind me to ask her."

"Will do," Tricia said, and cut one of the baby carrots on her plate in half with her fork, her gaze landing back on the deep blue water out the window once more. "I'm so surprised how peaceful it feels being out on the ocean."

"It's not what we see out our shop windows, that's for sure," Angelica agreed.

"Do you think we'll see dolphins or whales?"

"We might. I know Ginny is hoping she will. Maybe we should have brought binoculars—just in case."

Angelica cleaned her plate and set down her knife, then noticed the ramekin in front of Tricia. "Was that duck confit?"

"Yes," Tricia said, nodding.

"Aren't you going to finish it?"

"It was very rich."

"May I taste it?"

"Be my guest."

Angelica sampled the fowl. "Oh, that's lovely. And you're not going to finish it?"

Tricia shook her head.

"I think I'd rather have this than a piece of cake."

No sooner had she scraped the last of the duck from the dish when a uniformed waiter showed up beside them. "Maybe I take your dishes?"

"Yes, thank you," Tricia said.

Seconds later, the table was cleared and the waiter departed.

"We've still got an hour before the next panel starts," Tricia said. "I thought I might read for a while longer."

"I'd like to check out the shops in the arcade."

"Been there, done that, and I ran into Dori Douglas."

"Who?"

"Sorry. EM Barstow's fan club president."

"The woman has a fan club?" Angelica asked, scowling.

"Seems so. It was Dori who sat with EM last night at dinner."

"Do we have to keep talking about that abominable woman?"

"Sorry, but she's the biggest celebrity on board."

"I beg to differ. Larry Andrews is more well known than EM Barstow."

"Who?"

"The famous TV chef. I'm dying to meet him. Maybe he'll get interviewed for the morning talk show, too."

"Food, food, food. That's all you ever think of," Tricia accused.

"It is not. I think about business first. And food is a *big* part of my business. That and shoes. I do think about shoes far more than I should. But getting back to food, I wonder if Jake at the Brookview would want to try adding duck confit to the appetizer menu." She took out her notebook once again and jotted down a few words. "We shall see."

Tricia pushed back her chair. "I'm going to find a quiet spot to read until the cozy mystery panel starts. Shall I save you a seat?"

"Sure. If I'm late, I'm late."

"Okay."

They both got up and headed toward the lifts. "I think I'll take the stairs," Tricia said, eager to walk off even just a few of her lunch calories.

"Be my guest," Angelica said, and tottered off on her two-inch heels. At lease those shoes were a tiny bit more sensible than the one's she'd had on the day before.

Tricia walked down two decks and reentered the bar she and Angelica had sat in the night before. A smattering of guests had also chosen it as a quiet place to read.

No sooner had she sat down when a waiter appeared before her. "Can I get you anything, madam?"

"Not now, thank you."

He nodded and set a napkin on the table before her. She glanced around. A napkin sat by everyone else who was reading, too. Tricia smiled. It must be a signal that meant *Don't bother this person.*

Tricia opened her purse, withdrew *Why Wonder About Murder?*, and settled in for a nice, peaceful read.

She was so caught up in the story that when she looked at her watch she noticed she had only ten minutes to make it down to the ship's theater before the program began. She got up, heading off at a brisk walk.

Tricia entered the cavernous space and walked along the broad green carpeted aisle to sit in the centre section's third row, tossing her sweater onto the seat beside her, saving it for Angelica. Up on the stage was a long table with a white tablecloth that reached the floor. Six chairs sat behind it with placards spelling out the names of the panelists. At the far right was Fiona Sample's name. Those joining her on the panel were Diana Lovell, Norma Fielding, Hannah Travis, and Victoria Burke.

So far only two of them had reached the stage. Tricia recognized them from their Facebook pages: tall and lithe Hannah Travis and the much shorter—"vertically challenged," the lady had called herself on Facebook—Victoria Burke. Tricia eyed Victoria's jacket with envy, wondering if she could track her down after the panel to ask where she'd purchased it.

Fiona arrived, greeted her fellow panelists, and then turned to the audience. She shielded her eyes from the glare of the klieg lights, spied Tricia, and waved enthusiastically. Tricia waved back.

The program was set to begin in five minutes, and the theater was filling fast. Tricia looked around, but didn't see Angelica among those filing in. Considering afternoon tea was about to begin in the Crystal Ballroom, the authors had attracted quite a crowd.

The final two panelists arrived, greeted the others, and took their seats. A woman in a Kelly green blazer—not unlike that worn by Angelica's former lover, Bob Kelly—and a long white skirt appeared—

microphone in hand—and spoke to the women before turning to the podium that divided the panelists.

"Good afternoon, ladies and gentlemen. I'm Millicent Ambrose, the *Celtic Lady*'s entertainment director." The crowd broke into an enthusiastic round of applause. Millicent held out her hands, taking in the panel. "I'm sure the ladies here need *no* introduction."

"No!" roared the crowd.

Millicent grinned and then proceeded to introduce each of the authors to thunderous applause. "This panel is entitled Cozy Free-for-all, and that means we've got an entire hour to take inquiries from the audience. Raise your hands and we'll send a runner with a microphone to take your questions."

Several hundred arms immediately shot into the air. Millicent pointed to one of the audience members not far from Tricia's seat. A tall woman with a mane of snowy hair stood, waiting for the uniformed crew member to bring the microphone to her. "Is there a lot of jealousy and competition between you ladies?"

"Only if our books come out at the same time," Hannah said with a smile, and nudged Norma.

Norma waved a hand to dispel her colleague's words. "That's not true. Hannah and I have had books come out the same time and we cross-promoted. We both sold a fabulous amount of books."

"Does cross promoting happen a lot?"

"It does with the Lethal Ladies," Victoria piped up, referring to their group blog.

"Would you help other authors promote, too?" someone else asked.

"We do it all the time, especially on social media," Diana said.

"But say your books come out the same time as a really *famous* author."

"Are you saying we're not famous?" Victoria asked, straight-faced.

"I don't know about you, but nobody offered me a limo and an all-expenses-paid trip," Hannah quipped, to a ripple of laughter.

"Define *famous*," Norma asked.

"Someone like EM Barstow."

A low murmur ran through the audience.

"Sometimes our books do come out the same time as the mega bestsellers," Diana acknowledged, "and their backlists *do* take up an inordinate amount of space on the *New York Times* list, leaving no room for anyone else. But that doesn't mean we want to *kill* them. Maybe just *maim* them."

The audience laughed, as she'd intended them to.

Millicent acknowledged another waving hand in the audience. A woman dressed in an aloha shirt stood and waited for the microphone to arrive. "My question is for Fiona Sample. Will there be any more books in the Bonnie Chesterfield mystery series?"

"I'm working on number ten right now. If you tune in to the ship's morning TV program tomorrow, you can learn about Bonnie's latest run-in with Morgan Appleton. And I might even drop a few hints about the upcoming nuptials."

Enthusiastic applause broke out. Tricia had missed reading the previous book, but she knew she had copies of it on her shelves back at Haven't Got a Clue. She'd make sure to read it when she returned home.

"We'll take another question," Millicent said, and looked over the audience as more arms were raised. She pointed to a man in a bright green sweater. He stood.

"My question is also for Ms. Sample. How's your lawsuit going against Zoë Carter's estate for stealing your work on the Jess and Addie Forever historical mystery series?"

Fiona's smile dimmed. Tricia had helped expose the fraud, and found herself leaning forward to hear Fiona's answer.

"Sorry, but I'm not allowed to speak about the ongoing litigation. But if you have a question about my other work, I'd be happy to answer."

The man shook his head and sat down, obviously disappointed by her statement.

Millicent stood a little taller. "I've got a question for all of our panelists."

Tricia looked to her left at the box seats on the upper level and caught sight of EM Barstow and her assistant, Dori. EM held one hand over her mouth and pointed at the stage toward Diana Lovell with the other. Had Diana's flip remark angered EM, whom Tricia was beginning to think of as nothing more than a common bully? And would that bully retaliate against the lovely woman Tricia had had the pleasure of hosting at her bookshop on more than one occasion, when her only encounter with EM had been so unpleasant? She hoped not.

The program had moved on and she'd missed the last question and the answers from the panelists. Millicent asked another.

"Barbara Walters is famous for asking her interviewees what kind of tree they'd like to be. Do any of you have a preference?"

The panelists giggled. Victoria Burke raised her hand. "I want to be one of those thousand-year-old oaks in England, but only as long as I can have my husband beside me, and the acorns we planted that have now sprouted to trees."

A smattering of applause followed her answer.

"Hannah?" Millicent asked.

"I'd be a willow," the author said. "Graceful and able to bend with the gentle breeze or a fierce gale."

"How about you, Norma?" Millicent asked.

"I'd be a sequoia. Tall, and straight, and resilient against the wind, weather, and fire."

"Fiona?" Millicent asked.

"In honor of Canada—my adopted country," she piped up, "I would definitely be a maple. Maple syrup is wonderful and sweet—like me!"

The audience laughed.

"And how about you, Diana?"

"I'd be an olive tree in Greece. They're beautiful; gnarled, but strong, and able to feed the world."

"Aww," a portion of the audience chorused.

Tricia smiled, pleased by each author's answer to what could have been just a frivolous question, and her admiration for each of the women rose, too.

Millicent turned back to the panel. "We've got time for one more question. Ladies, cozy mysteries always feature justice for the killer. Do you think it's possible for someone to get away with murder in real life?"

Diana laughed. "Why are you looking at me when you ask that?" The audience broke into laughter. "Turn your gaze a little farther to the right," she said, waving a hand. "There you go." Again the audience laughed. "Seriously, I would have to say yes; of course it's possible—if the killer is supremely devious. Again, why are you looking at me?"

Laughter reigned once more.

"Hannah?" Millicent asked.

"Of course I do. It's a matter of perception. If a person creates the perception that he or she is *incapable* of murder, most people will pass them over in search of another suspect. Effective deceit is based on confidence—and intelligence. Anyone with enough of those two things, as well as the ability to keep to themselves, can get away with murder."

"How about you, Victoria?" Millicent asked.

"Right in my own community there are a number of unsolved murders, many of them cold cases. That means people *are* getting away with murder. We all know this. That's what gives our books their authenticity. Well, that and all the recipes." The audience giggled. "More than that," she continued, "there are plenty of cases where people are falsely convicted of murder for a variety of reasons. Let me just say, put the cozy writers in charge of investigations and watch those rates drop. I'm willing to step up."

The audience broke into a round of enthusiastic applause, and Millicent had to wait for them to quiet down before she could ask Fiona the question. "Ms. Sample?"

"Count me in for believing that one can get away with murder. It may be harder these days, thanks to social media and the ability to make a wider swath of the public know about such cases, but as Victoria said—there are far too many cold cases for me to believe otherwise."

Millicent turned to the last of the panelists. "What do you think, Norma?"

"I plead the fifth," Norma said, giving the spectators an exaggerated wink and a smirk.

The audience laughed as one, and again rewarded the author with applause.

"Ladies and gentlemen, there you have it," Millicent said. "All five of our fabulous authors will be available to sign copies of their latest books in the second story of the *Celtic Lady*'s magnificent library. You may purchase books there or bring your personal copies with you.

"In conclusion, let's give these Lethal Ladies of mystery a hand for their wonderful repartee."

The audience broke into thunderous applause.

Tricia turned to her left once again but found that EM and Dori were no longer occupying the private box. For some reason, their absence seemed . . . well, not exactly sinister, but certainly unfriendly.

EM was a much better known author than the ladies on the stage. Not that her books were better. In many ways, they weren't. She'd just been lucky to find a wider audience. The truth was, Tricia enjoyed the books written by the authors who'd entertained that entire theater full of readers more than she had enjoyed any of EM's books. EM's style was stark; her characters devoid of any real warmth. But as the author herself seemed incapable of engendering that perception, it wasn't surprising that empathy was lacking in her work.

Lost in thought, Tricia hardly noticed that she was one of the last of the audience to leave the well-appointed theater. She sat in her comfortable seat and contemplated what she'd experienced during the last hour. There'd been an air of frivolity with an underlying current of tension.

She wished she understood what it meant.

SIX

Tricia left the ship's theater, pondering Millicent's last question and the answers the panel had given. She wasn't sure she agreed that people got away with murder on a regular basis. At least, she hoped not.

She opted out of going to the book signing and instead sought out her sister, whom she found in their stateroom, spread out on her loveseat with a pad and pen, and many pages of notes surrounding her.

"Sorry I didn't make it down to the theater. Did I miss much?"

Tricia took her usual seat on the loveseat across the way. "Everyone on the panel was charming and funny. One of the authors made a little joke about how every time EM Barstow has a new book out, her backlist takes up all the slots on the *Times* list."

"It's no joke. It happens all the time," Angelica said.

"EM was in the audience, although I can't think why. Cozies aren't her subgenre. Anyway, I saw her say something to Dori and then point at the stage. I just hope she isn't planning anything spiteful against the author."

"What could she do in retaliation?"

"I don't know. But I wouldn't turn my back on that woman in a lighted room, let alone a dark alley."

"I'm sure you're exaggerating."

"I hope so," Tricia said.

Angelica gathered up her papers, swung her legs off the loveseat, and set her notes on the coffee table. "The kitchen staff is giving a demonstration on making art from fruit. Wouldn't you love to come with me and see it?"

Angelica looked so hopeful that Tricia found she couldn't say no. That said, she decided to bring her library book and e-reader along. If things got dull, she could always escape to another world.

After a short hunt for Angelica's shoes, they headed for the Garden Lounge, where the demonstration was to take place, and found that a large group of passengers had already assembled, seated in rows of chairs pulled from the room's bistro tables and placed in front of a small raised platform that held a drum set and a bass fiddle. Tricia must have missed what the timing was for whatever combo played. A little musical interlude might be pleasant. She'd check the Daily Program after dinner to see if there was a listing. A cloth-covered table sat in front of the tiny bandstand, and on it were bowls of various fruits and vegetables, from pineapples to grapes, from peppers to heads of cauliflower.

"Drat!" Angelica cried. "We'll have to sit by the windows. We'll hardly get to see a thing."

Just then, a couple of crew members wheeled in a big mirror, not unlike the one that used to grace the demonstration area in Angelica's cookbook store—the Cookery. That is, before she had it removed so that she could expand her line of merchandise.

"Are these seats taken?"

Tricia looked up to see the Dexter twins standing beside them. "Not at all."

"Are you ladies having a nice trip so far?" Angelica asked as the sisters sat down at the little bistro table beside them.

"It's a lovely ship," Muriel said.

"And the food is divine," Midge agreed.

"But we are a little disappointed."

"In what way?" Tricia asked.

"We hoped at least one of our favorite authors would be on the voyage."

"Who did you have in mind?" Angelica asked.

"Frank Miller," Muriel said.

"And his name can't be mentioned in the same sentence without Klaus Janson," Midge chimed in.

"I'm not familiar with their work," Tricia admitted.

"They're responsible for *The Dark Knight Returns*."

Tricia blinked.

Muriel looked at her with incredulity. "They're *very* famous."

"In what genre?" Angelica asked.

"Graphic novels."

Again Tricia blinked.

"Do you even know who the Dark Knight is?" Midge asked, sounding surprised.

Tricia shook her head.

"Batman!" Muriel cried, and then giggled.

"You're into comics?" Angelica asked, surprised.

"Oh, yes. We have the most extensive collection in the entire state of New Hampshire," Midge said smugly.

"We're very proud of it," Muriel agreed. "We've even got a copy of *Action Comics* number one—the first to feature Superman!"

Midge shook her head sadly. "Alas, it's not in mint condition, so it's probably only worth a couple hundred thousand."

Tricia was back to blinking.

"You must be the best customers at All Heroes comic book store," Angelica said.

Again Midge shook her head. "Not really. Oh, Terry, the owner, has a lot of great stuff, but we head to Boston or New York for the really *interesting* stuff."

"What constitutes interesting stuff?" Tricia asked.

Muriel leaned closer and whispered, "Vintage."

Tricia nodded. "Just like I prefer vintage mysteries."

"Exactly."

"Do you ever read your older comics?" Angelica asked.

"Yes—online."

"Why online?" Tricia asked.

"We wouldn't touch our paper copies."

"Oh, no," Muriel agreed. "They're far too delicate. They must be saved for future generations."

"But if future generations can't actually touch them—read them . . . then of what use are they?"

"Historical documents," Midge declared.

Muriel giggled. "Oh, sister, now you're sounding like the Thermians from *Galaxy Quest*."

Midge tittered.

Tricia and Angelica exchanged confused looks.

"Oh my God," Muriel exclaimed, staring at the Miles sisters. "They're mundanes!"

"Mundanes?" Tricia asked. Was she being insulted?

"Yes. Obviously, you aren't into science fiction and other fandoms and can't know the joy of belonging to a group of like-minded thinkers."

Angelica frowned. "I never thought of myself as mundane. I mean, look at my shoes."

The Dexter twins leaned forward to inspect the footwear Angelica had brandished for their approval. It was a pretty shoe—red, with snappy straps and a two-inch heel. The sisters turned back to each other and hollered, "Mundane!" and then laughed hysterically.

"You have definitely been insulted," Tricia muttered to Angelica.

Before Angelica had time to reply, a man in a chef's toque stepped up to the microphone on the riser behind the table of fresh fruits and vegetables. "Ladies and gentlemen, thank you for attending the *Celtic Lady*'s fruit and vegetable carving event. You'll be amazed, you'll be thrilled, and best of all you can *eat* our sculptures!"

"Isn't this fun?" Angelica asked, beaming.

Tricia didn't answer, thankful she had her library book to entertain her during the next hour.

Angelica's attention was trained on the table before them as the first chef stepped forward, pineapple and knife in hand, to attempt the first sculpture.

Tricia opened her book and began to read, but the words weren't making much sense. It wasn't just the Dexter sisters and their comic book comic routine that had discombobulated her, but her thoughts kept circling back to the panel discussion and an unsmiling EM Barstow, who had attended to do . . . what? Ridicule the other authors? Or had she gone to deride the hundreds of readers who didn't enjoy books filled with graphic depictions of blood and gore? The truth was, Tricia skipped over those often ghastly descriptions in EM's and other thriller authors' books. The daily news was filled with far too many accounts of man's (and woman's) inhumanity to man (or woman) for her to enjoy reading the same or worse for entertainment purposes. That was why she could better enjoy vintage mysteries. The violence was off the page. Someone was usually murdered, but there was usually a reason the killer chose such an outrageous solution—at least in his or her own mind. Too many thrillers were, well, thrilling. Revoltingly thrilling. Sickeningly thrilling.

No, thanks, she thought, feeling just a tad depressed. Real life was filled with too much horror these days. She'd witnessed too much of that in her own life; the murder of her ex-husband topping the list. The fact that she would have to testify before a court of law in the not-too-distant future also filled her with dread. She would do her duty as a citizen, but she feared the experience would tear open the wound of Christopher's loss that had only just scabbed over.

"Voilà!" the chef at the front of the room cried, and Tricia looked up to see that the man triumphantly held aloft what looked like a monkey holding a lotus flower.

"Isn't it gorgeous ?" Angelica cried, applauding with enthusiasm.

Tricia frowned. "That wouldn't be my first choice of descriptor."

"Okay, then cute."

"You weren't thinking something like that would go over at Booked for Lunch, let alone the Brookview Inn, were you?"

"Probably not," Angelica admitted. "But talk about skill with a knife."

"Do you think they'll have ice sculpting, too?" Tricia asked.

"I hope so. I wonder if Jake at the Brookview would like to learn to do that."

"Shouldn't he stick to cooking and leave that to the gardener?"

Angelica glowered, obviously not amused at Tricia's attempt at humor.

While they'd spoken, three of the sous chefs had entered into a contest to carve a 3-D relief on the face of melons. In just under five minutes they'd finished. One had sculpted a sun, another the man in the moon, and the third a face that looked an awful lot like the late Lucille Ball.

"Wow—I'm impressed," Angelica murmured in awe.

Tricia shook her head and turned her attention back to her book. Yet her gaze kept wandering back to the growing number of fruit sculptures. Now, if they'd carve the Maltese Falcon, that would *really* capture her interest.

Out of the corner of her eye, Tricia caught sight of Cathy Copper standing to one side, watching the show. While the woman might have annoyed her the evening before, she looked lonely standing there. She was about to get up to signal Cathy to join her when the editor turned away for the corridor that led to the elevators, still limping a bit. Oh well. Maybe Tricia would catch up with her later. It was a big ship, but it would be easy to feel lonely with no friends or family to share the adventure with.

She turned back to look at her sister. Angelica's gaze was still fixed on the table ahead, where the fruit sculptures were piling up at an alarming rate.

Clever as the fruity carvings were, they didn't hold much allure for Tricia, who stifled a yawn. What she needed was a nice strong cup of coffee. She leaned closer to her sister. "I'm going for coffee. Want something?"

Angelica shook her head, watching the flashing knife that hacked away the excess flesh of a mango as it was transformed from a piece of fruit to a figurine.

"I'll be back in a few minutes," Tricia said.

Angelica nodded, but continued to stare enraptured at the show that continued before them.

"We'll save your seat," Midge said as Tricia sidled past the twins.

The Lido Restaurant was on the same deck as the lounge, and Tricia entered the door, stopping at the hand sanitizer. As she worked the foam between her fingers, she noticed Fiona Sample up ahead. She was alone, and Tricia hurried to join her.

"Fiona!"

The author looked up and waved. Tricia joined her.

"How do you think the panel went?" Fiona asked eagerly.

"Oh, it was great fun. You were wonderful. *Everyone* on the panel was wonderful. If you're not busy, would you join me for coffee?"

"I'd love to."

They selected mugs, filled them from the large stainless steel urn, and doctored them before turning to search for an empty table. They found one halfway down the long aisle that overlooked the ocean, and sat down.

"I'm having such a wonderful time. It's so great to connect with readers and authors I've only known via the Internet."

Tricia lifted her cup to take a sip when she saw Arnold Smith steering his scooter down the aisle. The basket in front was filled with books.

"Hi, Fiona," he called out as he passed, heading for the restaurant's exit to the stern.

"Hi, Arnold," Fiona said, sounding less than enthusiastic.

"Thanks for signing all my books."

Fiona's smile looked forced. "You're welcome."

They watched him go. When he was out of earshot, Tricia spoke. "You know that guy?"

"Everybody knows Arnold from social media. Facebook, in particular."

"How?"

"He comments on a lot of posts, but he's best known as a prize pig."

Tricia's eyebrows rose. "A what?"

"Authors have giveaways for books and other swag. Arnold enters every one of them. The idea behind the contests is for winners to give honest reviews of the books. He doesn't. In fact, he's on a number of lists from publishers who send out review copies. One of my readers discovered that when Arnold receives a shipment, he immediately lists the books on eBay. It's rumored that he makes enough money to support himself."

"That's terrible."

"And that's a lot of books," Fiona acknowledged. "During the signing after the panel, one of the authors overheard him bragging that he got a terrific discount by booking this cruise just a day ahead of sailing."

Tricia had heard about such sell-offs. The idea of just picking up and taking a trip on a whim did hold some appeal, but you had to have a carefree lifestyle to pull it off. The Authors at Sea cruise had been her first vacation in years, and if it weren't a Chamber-sponsored tour that her friends and adopted family were taking, she doubted she would have been tempted to leave her cat and her store for a week—even during the slowest time of year.

"Can't you report Arnold to the publishers?"

"It's been done—a number of times. Somehow he always knows when the publicists leave and manages to sweet-talk the new ones into adding him again. He's been doing it for years. He had us all sign those books in his basket—just our names. You can bet they'll be offered for sale before the sun sets after we dock."

Tricia shook her head. She didn't want to think about that sorry little man. "How's your family?"

Fiona's eyes lit up. There wasn't any better question to ask a mom who was proud of her kids, and Fiona launched into a joyful tale that had Tricia laughing until she had to wipe her eyes. It was no wonder the woman was a *New York Times* bestselling author. She could tell a damn fine story.

"I'm sorry to have monopolized the conversation. Tell me, what's been going on with you?" Fiona asked.

"There's not much to tell," Tricia said. "I have a new assistant since you last visited, and she's a big fan of your work."

"Oh, that's nice."

Tricia could have mentioned the fire that nearly destroyed her store, and the death of her ex-husband, but decided to keep the conversation light. "I'm going to reconfigure my storeroom into living space this spring. It'll be messy and time consuming, and no doubt cost double my contractor's estimate, but I can't wait to start."

"That sounds lovely," Fiona said.

Their coffee was long gone when Tricia checked her watch. "Good grief—the fruit sculpting must nearly be over with by now. Angelica will wonder where I've disappeared to."

"I'm sorry. I didn't mean to keep you."

"Don't worry, Angelica is a big girl. She can navigate on her own— much better than either of us, I'm sure."

"Tell her I said hi."

"I will."

They stood. "See you later," Fiona said, and headed aft.

Tricia retraced her steps to the Garden Lounge. She had a few stories to share with Angelica and again wondered about the disagreeable Mr. Arnold Smith. He'd already antagonized EM. Was he likely to do the same to others?

SEVEN

 By the time Tricia and Angelica made it to the Kells Grill, they found the rest of their party already seated, and another bottle of bubbly had been ordered. Dori Douglas gave Tricia a smile and a wave as they joined Ginny, Antonio, Grace, and Mr. Everett. EM Barstow had not yet made an appearance, and Tricia dreaded an exhibition like the one they'd witnessed the night before.

"Did you have a nice day?" Dori called to Tricia.

"Very nice, thank you. And you?"

"Wonderful."

Tricia nodded and reached for her napkin.

"Emmie isn't joining me for dinner tonight, so you should have a much more peaceful meal."

"Oh," Tricia said, and stole a glance at Angelica. Was Dori fishing for an invitation to join them?

"She's working tonight. She's eager to finish at least another chapter of her work in progress before she's called upon to do any more appearances during the voyage."

"How nice," Angelica said, and turned her attention to the champagne bottle that Antonio held to fill her glass.

"Should I invite her to join us?" Tricia muttered.

"I wish you wouldn't," Angelica said without moving her lips. Was ventriloquism another of her talents?

The waiter arrived with a plate and set it before Dori, who gave him a smile. "Thank you."

"Have a nice dinner," Angelica said, and turned her attention to the others at their table. "I'm so glad you and Grace could join us tonight, Mr. Everett. Did you have a nice day?"

"Outstanding," Mr. Everett said, sounding jovial. "Grace told me about the wonderful cruises she'd been on in the past, but I never thought I would enjoy it as much as I have so far."

They spent the next ten minutes comparing notes on the various events they'd all enjoyed, then got down to the serious business of choosing their dinner appetizers, entrées, and desserts. Meanwhile, Dori had finished her meal, and gazed out the window at the darkened sea . . . eavesdropping?

Cristophano was again their waiter and stood with his little pad ready to write down their orders.

"I'll have the caviar for my appetizer, the salmon tartare for my entrée, and the mango and passion fruit crème brûlée for dessert. And, oh, my goodness—doesn't that sound decadent?" Angelica asked, practically glowing.

"I'll skip the appetizer and have the endive salad," Tricia said.

"No appetizer?"

Tricia shook her head.

"Dessert?" Cristophano asked hopefully.

Again, Tricia shook her head.

"That's not all you're having for dinner, is it?" Ginny asked.

"Lunch was very filling. That's all I need."

"This is *supposed* to be a vacation," Angelica admonished.

Antonio held up a hand. "My dear Angelica. Tricia knows what she wants and needs."

"Thank you," Tricia said, handing the menu back to Cristophano.

"Well, I'm with Angelica. This is my vacation, and since I don't have to cook, I'm going to enjoy everything I can, because we'll be back to soup and sandwiches when we get home," Ginny said, and proceeded to order caviar, roast duck, and butter pecan ice cream.

Tricia had to admit, her mouth was watering at all the wonderful dinner selections her tablemates made, yet she felt confident in her decision. She didn't want to wage a battle of the cruise ship bulge upon returning home.

Once their orders had been taken, Antonio refilled their flutes and conversation commenced once again.

"For such a big boat, I seem to keep running into the same people all day long," Ginny observed.

"Me, too," Angelica agreed.

"What was your favorite part of the day?" Ginny asked Mr. Everett.

"The cozy authors' panel. Those ladies know how to have a good time."

"Oh, yes," Grace agreed.

"I didn't see you there," Tricia said. "We could have sat together."

"We were in one of the boxes on the starboard side," Grace said. "I must admit, it was great fun to sit there in our own little private area. I understand during the theatrical presentations that one can order champagne and hors d'oeuvres."

"What was your least favorite part of the day?" Angelica asked Mr. Everett.

He scowled. "EM Barstow's talk. It was Grace who was interested in hearing her speak. I only went along to keep her company."

"I have to admit, it wasn't my favorite part of the day," Grace said. "She is a strange duck, isn't she?"

"It wasn't the highlight of my day, either," Angelica agreed, and sipped her wine.

Tricia cringed as Dori's head now seemed cocked in their direction.

"She doesn't seem to know how to relate to people in general—and her fans in particular," Mr. Everett observed.

"Perhaps she suffers from autism spectrum disorder," Grace said.

Tricia's eyes widened. "You know, that's an astute observation." Thinking it over, Tricia reconsidered her negative feelings about the woman. Having a disorder didn't exactly excuse EM's behavior, but it certainly explained it.

A look in Dori's direction confirmed that she was definitely listening to their conversation. Would she share Grace's speculation with EM? Did it matter? Still, Tricia would feel terrible if EM sought her out and gave her a public tongue-lashing. She decided to change the subject, but was spared when the appetizers arrived at the table.

All but Tricia tucked in with evident delight.

"Would you like to try the caviar?" Ginny asked Tricia. "I've got plenty."

"That's very sweet of you, but I'm fine, thanks."

Dori pushed back her chair and rose. Tricia caught her gaze and smiled. Dori nodded and left the restaurant, allowing Tricia to breathe a sigh of relief.

Angelica tapped Tricia's arm. "I'd forgotten she was sitting right there. Do you think she heard our conversation?"

"I'm sure of it."

"Well, we didn't say anything particularly nasty."

"No, we didn't," Ginny agreed.

"I don't understand," Grace said.

"EM Barstow's assistant was sitting at the next table," Tricia explained.

"Oh, no!" Grace said, her expression troubled.

"I'm sure she's heard worse—perhaps even thought or said it herself," Angelica said defensively.

A pall seemed to settle over the table. EM Barstow had that ability—even when she wasn't physically present.

Tricia noticed Mr. Everett taking in the faces around him. "I suggest we have a toast. To happiness. Perhaps we should all try to spread a little more of it around."

"I'm all for that," Ginny said.

They raised their glasses and then drank.

Talk turned to the next day's events and the upcoming port call to Bermuda, but Tricia found she didn't have the enthusiasm to join in. Why should she feel guilty that the conversation had turned to EM with Dori listening in? She hadn't participated in it and had made only one comment.

Mr. Everett was right. They were on a wonderful vacation with great speakers and silly events—like the fruit and veggie carving—and Tricia was determined to enjoy it.

If she could allow herself to do so.

After they said good night to Ginny, Antonio, Grace, and Mr. Everett, it was Tricia who suggested she and Angelica try out another of the ship's bars that evening. "Sounds like fun," Angelica said.

This time, they went to the Yacht Club, which was sedate and as sparsely populated as the Portside Bar. They took seats facing each other, separated by a small wooden table.

"Where do you think everybody goes in the evenings?" Angelica asked.

"Probably sitting in their rooms reading," Tricia offered.

"Maybe we should check out the disco—or the Lucky Shamrock Casino."

Tricia wrinkled her nose and shook her head. "That's not my kind of scene."

"It used to be mine," Angelica admitted sadly, "but I guess you're right. The music would probably be loud enough to damage our hearing in the disco, and you may as well flush your money directly down the toilet as gamble, the way the odds are stacked for the house."

A waitress came by. "May I get you ladies anything?"

"What shall we drink tonight?" Angelica asked, her eyes widening with pleasure.

"What are you in the mood for?"

"How about a cosmopolitan. I haven't had one of those in years."

"Make that two," Tricia said, but before she could get out her key-card, Angelica had already surrendered her own."

"Very good," the waitress said, and turned away.

"I was going to get that."

"You can get the next round," Angelica said, and leaned back into her chair. "So, what's on your mind tonight?"

"I spent the last couple of days before we came on the trip thinking about the future."

"Oh?" Angelica said, leaning forward with interest.

"Now that I own the building that houses Haven't Got a Clue, I was thinking about how I could better use the space." It occurred to Tricia that she'd spilled the story to Fiona before she'd even discussed it with her own sister.

"Really? What did you have in mind?"

"Converting my storeroom into another floor of living quarters."

"What would you do with your extra stock?"

"I was thinking about converting the basement into a stock/workroom. It's just sitting there doing nothing. I spoke to Jim Stark, and he thinks he could do it in a matter of weeks."

Angelica leaned forward and rested a hand on Tricia's arm. "I'm so glad to hear you making plans for the future. After Christopher's death, I was afraid you might decide living in Stoneham was too painful."

"Sometimes it is. But the truth is, it was *my* home for much longer than it was his. My friends are in Stoneham—and so is my family. I have no intention of leaving."

Angelica's eyes glistened. "It *is* home, isn't it?"

Tricia nodded, smiling. "I thought about buying a house or a condo, but I really don't want to leave Main Street. I like the area. It's so pretty in the summer with all the flowers. And it's vibrant, too."

"In the winter," Angelica ventured, "not so much. What were you thinking of doing to the building?"

"Moving the kitchen and living room down to the second floor and building a master suite with a spa-like bathroom upstairs."

"That sounds fabulous! I hope you're going to let me help you redecorate."

"I was hoping you might volunteer."

"I may just steal the whole idea. Honestly, I've never lived in such cramped quarters as I do now. And it would give Sarge a whole new place to run around and play."

"Miss Marple pretty much has the run of the building, but I sometimes worry about her getting shut into the storeroom. This would eliminate that problem."

The waitress arrived with their drinks and returned Angelica's keycard. She signed the receipt and picked up her glass. "Here's to your beautiful new digs."

"And yours, too!" They clinked glasses and drank.

"That was a lovely toast Mr. Everett gave at dinner. He's right, of course, too. We should try to spread a little more happiness."

"Nigela Ricita seems to do that every day."

"Well, I'm sure she tries," Angelica said, and winked.

"Let's hope this new phase of our lives means a lot less trouble and strife."

"I'm for that," Angelica agreed. "And let's never hear those dreaded words *village jinx* again."

Tricia managed a wry smile. "I'm taking a vow of total disinterest in real crime and turning all my attention to that on the written page only."

"Good for you. They say curiosity killed the cat—and I don't want that happening to you, too." Angelica raised her glass and they drank on it.

Tricia sipped her cosmopolitan. *No one will ever call me the village jinx again*, she thought smugly, then frowned.

Had she just jinxed herself?

EIGHT

It was only a little after eleven when Tricia finished reading her library book and started another on her e-reader, but two hours into it she didn't feel the least bit sleepy. She kept eyeing the box on the dresser that contained the sweater. The idea that someone on board was keeping tabs on her made Tricia feel uncomfortable, as well as apprehensive. So much for her relaxing vacation. Still, she turned out the bedside lamp and settled down, but despite her best efforts, the trip to dreamland seemed to be delayed by more than just a couple of hours.

Maybe she shouldn't drink alcohol so near bedtime. More likely it was thoughts of her upcoming renovation that kept her from drifting off to sleep. She tried to banish such considerations, but the idea of making what she had often thought of as temporary digs into her real and true home was rather exciting. One entire wall of her new living room would accommodate all her favorite vintage mysteries. Perhaps she'd have someone design a special climate-controlled cabinet to hold the most fragile and valuable tomes in her collection.

The ideas kept circling and circling through her brain and wouldn't stop. Often, at times like that, she'd get up and make a cup of hot cocoa. She wasn't fussy. The instant kind from a packet was just fine.

The ship boasted twenty-four-hour room service, but Tricia didn't want to be served. The truth was, it sometimes took so long for the food or drink to make it from the kitchen that it just wasn't hot enough to satisfy.

Tricia threw back the duvet, turned on the bedside lamp, and got out of bed. Stuffing her feet into her complimentary *Celtic Lady* slippers, she donned her new sweater over her sweats, grabbed her keycard, and quietly left the stateroom.

The lights in the long corridor blazed twenty-four/seven, and if the suite hadn't included a large picture window, she was certain she might never have known if it was day or night. The doors to all the other rooms and suites were closed as she headed for the Lido Restaurant. The only sound was the ever-present thrum of the ship's powerful diesel engines belowdecks.

Tricia pressed the UP button and stood before the lift, waiting. She looked around her, feeling a little unnerved. Was it safe to roam the decks in your pj's? What if the person who'd sent the gifts was waiting somewhere to pounce?

The lift doors opened, and Tricia made sure the car was empty before she stepped inside, pressing the button for Deck 10. Would it be safer to walk back down to her stateroom, or was she just being paranoid? Then again, that kind of exercise might just get her blood churning and she'd never get to sleep.

A few other night owls sat at tables, reading or quietly conversing, and Tricia helped herself to a mug, tipping cocoa mix into it and filling it with hot water. She stirred until the powder was completely dissolved and took a tentative sip. *Ouch!* Much too hot. She poured a little out and added a little milk, then stirred again. *Ahh.* This time the temperature was perfect. She took enough sips so that she could comfortably walk the corridors without spilling her drink, and set off back to her stateroom.

Like her trip to the Lido Restaurant, Tricia met no other passengers or crew on her way back down to her cabin, but something was different as she approached her suite. The door to one of the staterooms was ajar, which was odd. The heavy cabin doors needed a wedge to stay propped open, and the door hadn't been open some ten minutes before when she'd left the deck.

"Hello?" Tricia called quietly. "Is anyone inside?"

The room was dark—which meant no keycard sat in the slot that powered the stateroom.

"Hello?" Tricia called again, wondering if anyone was inside, and if so, should she disturb them? She glanced up and down the corridor. Still nobody in sight. She sipped her cocoa, which had quickly cooled. It made no sense. Why prop open a door and then leave the stateroom vulnerable to theft or vandalism?

Curiosity got the better of her, and Tricia pushed the door fully open. "Hello."

No one answered.

She took out her keycard, slipped it into the slot just inside the door, and instantly the lights came on. The double bed looked like it had been slept in, the covers thrown back in an untidy jumble, but the room appeared to be unoccupied. Tricia used her foot to replace the wedge in the door. Had the stateroom's current resident been like Tricia and felt the need for a soothing cup of cocoa? She glanced around the lounge. The room's small desk was clear of clutter, and the loveseat was piled high with clothes that looked vaguely familiar. She tiptoed into the bedroom, where lights blazed. The complimentary slippers with the *Celtic Lady* emblem, like those she wore, sat beside the bed. On the bedside table was a pill caddy and a half-empty glass of water.

Light spilled from the opening at the bottom of the suite's bathroom's door. "Hello?" Tricia called again.

Still no answer.

She knocked on the door.

Again, no answer.

She tried the handle. It wasn't locked.

"Is anybody in there?" she called before poking her head inside.

Her breath caught in her throat at the sight of EM Barstow, dressed in a long flannel nightgown, eyes bulging, her tongue lolling, with a colorful scarf around her neck, hanging from the marble shower's rainfall fixture.

Tricia turned away from the terrible sight, squeezing her eyes shut.

Oh, crap. Now I'm the Celtic Lady's *jinx at sea!*

"Just what were you doing in Ms. Barstow's stateroom at two in the morning, Ms. Miles?" asked the *Celtic Lady*'s chief of security, Ian McDonald. He was a good-looking man, probably in his early forties. Tall, a little beefy, with a close-cropped ginger beard that Tricia might have found intriguing under other circumstances, he spoke with a slight accent, which was also rather appealing.

Tricia squirmed on the uncomfortable straight-backed chair in McDonald's tiny office. "As I've explained to you at least three times, I'd gone to the Lido Restaurant to get a cup of cocoa." She held up the empty mug she still had. "When I returned, I saw the door to Ms. Barstow's suite had been wedged open. I thought it odd and I went inside to see if everything was all right. It wasn't."

"*What* made you go inside?" he repeated gently, but firmly.

"I—" she began, about to tell him that she'd found more than her fair share of bodies since opening her mystery bookstore, but then thought better of it. "I have an insatiable curiosity about things. Maybe I'm just nosy," she offered with a shrug.

McDonald was not amused.

Tricia let out a sigh. "Did Ms. Barstow leave a note?"

"You're assuming it was suicide?" McDonald asked.

"Well, yes." Wasn't it obvious?

"And how did you come to that conclusion?"

"You mean besides the fact she was found hanging?" He nodded. Tricia shrugged. "I guess it was the pills."

"Pills?" he pressed.

"I saw a pill container on the desk, and a glass with a little water in it. I just wondered if she'd taken an overdose and then decided to make sure she carried out her attempt."

McDonald continued to stare at Tricia. He had the warmest gray eyes she'd ever seen.

"What is your occupation, Ms. Miles?"

"I'm a bookseller."

"Did you know Ms. Barstow?"

Tricia hesitated. "We'd met. She came to my store in Stoneham, New Hampshire, for a book signing several years ago."

"What was your opinion of the woman?"

Bombastic blowhard. Obnoxious. Insufferable, were the first descriptors that came to Tricia's mind, but she didn't wish to speak ill of the dead. "She wrote a good thriller."

His stare intensified. "That's it?"

Tricia nodded.

McDonald frowned. "That's not particularly helpful." He scrutinized her face. "So, you admired her?"

Again Tricia hesitated. "Not necessarily. I read her work and have customers who wouldn't want to miss her upcoming books. I'm sure they'll be disappointed to hear of her loss."

"But you won't?" McDonald guessed.

Tricia shrugged.

"Officer, my shop does sell some new releases, but I'm primarily interested in vintage mysteries."

"So you didn't like Ms. Barstow?"

"I honestly didn't know her. I dealt with her one time at my store, and I observed her here on the *Celtic Lady*, but other than that, she was a virtual stranger."

"Do you know of anyone who would want to see Ms. Barstow dead?"

Did McDonald think the thriller author had been murdered? Why? Because there was no note to support suicide? And then Tricia remembered the cozy authors' panel she'd attended in the ship's theater earlier in the day. Diana Lovell had joked that the big-name author's backlist had obliterated all chances for midlist authors to hit the bestsellers list, but it *had* been a joke. She'd hosted Ms. Lovell at signings at her own store and had found her to be not only elegant, but charming, and she loved the Perfect Posies Mysteries. Sara and Julien were two of her favorite characters. And Tricia had no doubt that while the other authors on the panel may have cursed the timing of their book releases in relation to other, bigger-name authors, they pretty much had to suck it up and accept it, hoping that when their next release debuted they might fare better. They were the victims of poor timing, like hundreds of other authors, but nothing more.

Tricia gave herself a mental shake. The woman had committed suicide. Unhappy people did it every day, leaving devastation in their wake, although she was sure that may not be the case in EM Barstow's death. Oh, sure, her publisher and a million or so readers would mourn her passing—mainly because they weren't going to get any more Tennyson Eisenberg thrillers—but those people EM had abused on a regular basis might not grieve at all.

And then there was Arnold Smith. "I did overhear a rather unpleasant conversation between Ms. Barstow and one of her readers earlier in the day in the ship's library."

"Oh?"

Tricia related what she'd heard while searching for something new to read. Should she mention what Fiona had said about the man, or was it better to let McDonald do his own sleuthing and form his own opinions on Smith?

She decided the latter.

"Anything else?" McDonald asked.

"Have you spoken with Ms. Barstow's assistant?" Tricia asked.

"I didn't know she had one."

"Her name is Dori Douglas. She's a passenger on this voyage. Perhaps she can tell you about Ms. Barstow's emotional state."

McDonald turned to the computer on his desk and began tapping on the keyboard. "Here she is. Stateroom 7045. I believe I'll have a chat with her, too."

"Will you wake her up to do so?"

He shook his head. "Until I know otherwise, Ms. Barstow's death will be treated as a suicide. Talking to her associate can wait. I'm sure she'll be extremely upset."

"Maybe not," Tricia said offhandedly.

McDonald frowned. "What do you mean?"

"It's no secret that Ms. Barstow treated her assistant abominably."

"And you have this on good authority?"

"I witnessed it more than once on this trip—and so did many of the other passengers."

McDonald frowned. "Perhaps I will go speak with her now. How do you think she'll take the news?"

Do a jig? Tricia wondered. "I really couldn't say. I've only spoken with the woman a couple of times."

McDonald nodded.

"What will happen to the body?" Tricia asked.

"We'll store it in our morgue until we get some direction from the family. It may be that it travels with us until we return to New York. That *is* where Ms. Barstow was to disembark."

Tricia nodded. Unless they kept the body well refrigerated, it could be quite ripe by the time the ship made it back to that port. That was the hazard of dying in an inconvenient place.

"May I go back to my cabin now?" Tricia asked, not that she thought she'd ever go back to sleep after finding the author dead. She had a feeling that when she closed her eyes she'd see EM Barstow's startling eyes, her mottled skin, and had there been an abrasion under her chin? She'd have to think on that. She was sure the ship's doctor and McDonald would have noticed it.

McDonald stood. "You're free to go. If I have more questions, I'm sure I'll be able to find you."

Tricia rose from her chair. "Thank you."

"Good evening," McDonald said.

Tricia glanced at her watch. Evening? Good morning, more like. It was nearly five o'clock.

NINE

 Tricia returned to her stateroom and again attempted to go to sleep, but instead of visualizing her new living quarters, her mind's eye kept revisiting the terrible image of EM hanging from her shower. Still, she must have dozed for an hour or two, she realized upon hearing noises in the lounge outside her room door. She glanced at the bedside clock and found it was after eight. Rats! She'd probably missed Fiona's interview on the ship's TV channel. Hauling herself out of bed, she put on her robe and entered the suite's common area.

Angelica stood near the stateroom's door, looking out the peephole. She turned. "I'm sorry. I didn't mean to wake you."

"I think I got about two hours of sleep all night," Tricia said, and took her accustomed seat.

"Oh, no! You must be exhausted. Is anything wrong?"

"Well, kind of . . ."

"No one is stalking you," Angelica said with authority.

Tricia shook her head.

"Perhaps you're finding it hard to sleep without Miss Marple near your feet. I know you miss her terribly. I miss Sarge, too. That's the problem with taking a trip like this. We have to leave our beloved fur-babies at home."

"They're being well taken care of, but, hang the roaming charges, I'm calling Pixie when we get into port to check up on them. I'm sure Miss Marple isn't happy sharing her home with Sarge, but I hope they have at least called a truce."

"I don't think we could have left our pets with anyone more qualified than Pixie. She loves them both."

"Yes, she does," Tricia agreed.

A knock at the door caused them to look up. "That'll be the continental breakfast I ordered last night."

Sure enough, Sebastian had arrived with a cart draped in white linen. "Good morning, ladies," he said. "May I pour you some coffee?"

"That would be lovely. Thank you," Angelica said.

Sebastian poured and handed them each a cup. "Please let me know if I can get you anything else."

"Thank you," the sisters said as he left the lounge, heading for Tricia's room to make up the bed.

Angelica sipped her coffee. "Is there anything else on your mind that's keeping you awake?"

"Besides my"—she did not say *stalker*—"admirer and upcoming renovation?" Angelica nodded. "I did have a little adventure overnight."

"Oh?"

"It started when I couldn't sleep. I kept thinking about the reno, and then I thought I'd go up to the Lido Restaurant for some cocoa. And when I came back down to our deck, I saw an open stateroom door."

"And you investigated," Angelica said with a frown. "I thought you told me you weren't going to do that anymore."

"Yes, and I meant it. But I kind of found EM Barstow hanging in her shower."

"Oh my God!" Angelica cried. "Please tell me you're fooling!"

Tricia shook her head.

"Suicide?"

"That's what the ship's security officer seems to want to believe." And if it was, then she was off the hook for being a jinx at sea. Still . . .

Angelica had noticed her hesitation. "But you don't?"

"I don't know. There was a suspicious mark under her chin."

"What do you think it was?"

"It looked like a rug burn."

"You think someone dragged her across the carpet and then strung up her body?"

"I've read a lot of mysteries over the years. Maybe I'm just the suspicious kind."

"Can you imagine the speculation that's going to go on for the rest of the trip?" Angelica asked.

"There are at least ten or fifteen mystery authors aboard. I'm sure there are going to be a lot of theories tossed around."

"What's yours?"

Tricia shrugged, got up from the couch, and examined the breakfast cart. Angelica had ordered pastries, including a couple of croissants, and two containers of strawberry yogurt. Aching to buck her usual routine, Tricia almost reached for one of the croissants. How she would have liked to set it on a plate, cut it into several sections, and then gouge some sweet butter from the small ramekin, spreading it on one of the pieces before popping it into her mouth. Instead, she grabbed one of the yogurt containers and a spoon.

"Do you think Dori Douglas could have killed EM?" Angelica asked.

Tricia shrugged, peeling off the lid. "That would be rather obvious, wouldn't it?"

"Many times it is. If EM *was* murdered, what jurisdiction would investigate, and if they discovered who did the deed, what would happen?"

"That's a good question." Tricia took a spoonful of yogurt and swallowed. "You know, sometime ago I read that Congress held hearings on just that subject. As I recall, the cruise industry didn't come out looking very good. They claim that crimes, such as theft, sexual assault, and even murder are few and far between. They claimed the odds of such things happening to a passenger were akin to getting hit by lightning."

"That's no comfort when Mother Nature has nearly electrocuted you," Angelica said. "You've found more than your fair share of dead bodies. Do you think it's a credible supposition to believe EM *was* murdered?"

Tricia thought about everything she'd seen in the author's stateroom. "Yes. And that doesn't make me feel very secure. It means there's a murderer running around the ship. There's nowhere to go to be safe, except perhaps locked here in our suite."

"Maybe we ought to employ the buddy system and stick together as much as possible."

"It couldn't hurt," Tricia agreed.

Angelica's brow furrowed. "Oh, dear. Ginny and the baby are vulnerable. I'm going to tell Antonio not to leave their sides."

"Then again, we could just be paranoid," Tricia pointed out.

"I wanted them to accompany me on this trip. I wanted the five of us to have a wonderful family vacation, and now I've put all of you in terrible danger," Angelica cried.

"No, no! Ange. I could be all wrong. I've been wrong plenty of times. There could be any number of reasons why EM wanted to kill herself. Things that wouldn't be obvious to any of us. Maybe she was unhappy with her life in general. Goodness knows she sure came across as totally miserable. She may have suffered from debilitating depression. Perhaps she had a terminal disease and didn't want to succumb from it. There could be dozens of motives for her to want to end her life."

"And what if there weren't?"

"We may never know," Tricia said. "But we shouldn't jump to any conclusions until we have more information."

"You just said the cruise industry as a whole tries to cover up crime. Do you think the Celtic line is better or worse than any other?"

"I have no idea. I guess we have to believe their PR and hope that passenger safety really is their top priority."

"And if it isn't?"

Tricia could only give an uncomfortable shrug.

TEN

 Despite Angelica's desire to stick to her sister like glue, Tricia nixed that idea—at least during daylight hours. Despite the hour, as she walked the ship's long corridors heading for the stairs and her daily exercise routine, she never came across another soul. If she had, would she have been frightened that he or she was EM Barstow's killer? Tricia wasn't sure.

Tricia pushed open one of the heavy outside doors to the Promenade Deck, noticing that though the wind was brisk, the air was considerably warmer than it had been the day before. She trailed after several others, in a counterclockwise direction, pumping her arms as she headed toward the ship's bow.

The news of EM Barstow's death had spread quickly. Tricia heard many of her fellow walkers and joggers discussing it. She, of course, offered no opinions. Nor did she want anyone—especially anyone from her group of fellow Stoneham and Milford passengers—to find out that she had discovered the body. For far too long she had been branded the Stoneham Village Jinx. She didn't want anyone spreading the word that she'd now become the *Celtic Lady*'s resident jinx, as well.

On her fifth circuit around the deck, Tricia caught sight of a troubled-looking Diana Lovell sitting on one of the teak benches nestled close to the superstructure and out of the wind, looking out at the endless vista quickly passing on the starboard side. "Excuse me, Diana?" she asked.

The author looked up. "Oh, hello."

"I don't know if you remember me. I'm Tricia Miles. Several years ago you came to sign books at my mystery bookstore in Stoneham, New Hampshire."

"Of course, I remember you. You had a darling little gray cat. Miss Marple, I think she's named."

"You have a good memory," Tricia said, smiling, but Ms. Lovell's eyes seemed troubled. "I take it you heard about EM Barstow's death."

"I don't think there are many on board who haven't."

"You're thinking about what was said on the panel yesterday," Tricia guessed.

"I'm afraid so," the author admitted.

"Ship's security seems to think her death was a suicide."

Diana shook her head sadly. "That poor woman."

Tricia decided to lighten the conversation. "Will you be at the authors' luncheon later today?"

"I wouldn't miss it," Diana said, her face brightening, but her eyes still looked troubled. Did she, too, wonder about the circumstances surrounding the author's sudden death? Mystery authors had dark imaginations—they had to in order to write about death on a regular basis. One of the most important tenets of mysteries—especially cozier mysteries—was bringing the killer to justice. If EM had been murdered, was it likely ship's security would actively look for her killer? It would be much better for the cruise line's bottom line to brush the author's death under the proverbial rug and just encourage the rest of the passengers to enjoy themselves for the remainder of the voyage.

"Are you enjoying the trip so far?" Tricia asked.

"Until I heard the news about EM, yes."

How else could Tricia steer the conversation away from that subject? "Have you met many of your readers on board?"

"Yes. It's been nice to put names to faces."

"Diana!" Tricia turned around to see Sidney Charles coming toward them. She wrote a captivating quilting mystery series. "Have you had breakfast?"

"Not yet," Diana said, standing. "I was hoping to run into you or one or more of the other Lethal Ladies."

"The weather's getting warmer. I'm going to hang out by the pool later, but first up, breakfast!"

Diana turned to Tricia. "Sidney, this is Tricia Miles. She runs a charming little mystery bookshop in New Hampshire."

"I'll have to get your address. Maybe I could come by and sign sometime."

"We'd love to have you."

"Would you like to join us for breakfast?" Diana asked.

"Thanks, but I've already eaten. I'm sharing a suite with my sister and she loves to order room service."

"Isn't it fun?" Diana said, smiling once again.

"Sure beats making the coffee myself," Tricia agreed.

"We'll catch up later," Sidney promised. "I want to get your e-mail address so we can set up a signing."

"Great. See you later."

"Hey, Diana, did you hear about EM Barstow?" Sidney asked as they entered the ship once more, while Tricia turned to resume her walk. She hadn't gone far when she saw Angelica charging toward her, with a grin as big as a child's on Christmas morning.

"You'll never guess who I just talked to!" she gushed, and dropped into step with Tricia.

"No, I won't—so tell me."

"Larry Andrews!"

"Am I supposed to know who that is?" Tricia asked.

"I mentioned him the other day. He's one of the hottest chefs on the Good Food Channel, and he's dreamy, too."

"How nice. What did he have to say?"

"I have no idea. I was starstruck. I may have actually babbled," she said, and giggled.

"Nigela Ricita babble?" Tricia asked.

"Shhh!" Angelica hissed, looking around them. "Someone might hear you."

"I'm just surprised that anyone could impress you that much."

"I think I could be a wonderful TV cooking show hostess. I've certainly got the personality."

"Your first foray into the medium came to a fiery conclusion."

"It wasn't my fault that the local TV studio burned. It was an unfortunate accident."

"I know, I know," Tricia said as they rounded the bow and started walking toward the stern of the ship.

"Anyway, Larry is doing a special demonstration in the ship's kitchen later this afternoon, and I was able to score a ticket to the event."

"Good for you."

"I may have to bow out of the authors' luncheon early."

"Oh? But I thought you were looking forward to that."

"*C'est la vie*," Angelica said. "But Ginny is going and she'll be more than happy to keep you company."

"What about Antonio?"

"He's going to babysit Sofia."

"Does he mind?"

"Not a bit. Unlike his father, he's a real hands-on dad. I couldn't be more proud of him."

"Not like our father, that's for sure," Tricia said as they avoided a couple of crewmen who were slapping some kind of clear sealer on the railing. It seemed as though maintenance took precedence over the walkers and joggers who used the deck as their outdoor exercise room.

"You're not going to disparage Daddy, are you?" Angelica asked, sounding hurt.

"No. When I was little, I thought every father only spent an hour or so a day with his children. It never occurred to me that he should play with me or read me a story. He was just not around. And from what I gathered from my friends at school, neither were their fathers."

"Well, it wasn't always that way," Angelica said.

Back then, Angelica had been the little princess. And then Tricia and her twin Patrick had been born, and Angelica had been knocked off her tiny throne. But it was only for a short while. Little Prince Patrick had taken center stage in their parents' lives . . . until he'd died of sudden infant death syndrome. Angelica remembered that life. Tricia had been an infant. She'd known only the perpetual cold shoulder from their mother, who'd wanted a son, not a second daughter. Thank goodness their paternal grandmother had been there for Tricia and Angelica, imbuing them with the love of books and reading. She'd been a sweet haven in the absence of their mother's love.

There was only one way Tricia could reconcile her mother's loveless treatment of her: mental illness. Framing her mother's behavior in that light made it understandable, though not entirely acceptable. And the fact that Tricia hadn't even known she'd had a brother until just six months before made the whole situation even more difficult to accept. But she had to. She had no other choice.

"I'm glad you have happy memories of Mother and Daddy."

"And I'm so sorry that you don't," Angelica said sincerely.

"Why don't we change the subject," Tricia suggested.

Angelica sighed. "Very well."

"Have you had a chance to sing Stoneham's praises to any of the other attendees?"

"There's a networking cocktail party this evening. A lot of authors will be there if you want to come and schmooze."

"I might do just that. What about dinner?"

"I was hoping we could have another family dinner tonight. You, me, Antonio, Ginny, and Grace and Mr. Everett."

"That sounds good to me. It would be fun for all of us to compare notes."

"I'm just worried that after EM's death Ginny won't feel good about leaving Sofia with a babysitter."

"Why not? As far as the rest of the ship is concerned, EM died by her own hand. So far only you and ship's security know. And unless someone mentions that I found EM, no one has to be the wiser."

"That's true."

"Couldn't they bring Sofia to dinner?" Tricia suggested.

"Yes, but if she cries, the other diners might not be as forgiving as our little family."

Tricia loved to think of the seven of them as family. She had depended on them during the long months after the fire at her store, and more recently when she'd grieved for her ex-husband. She thought she was long over Christopher, but his death had hit her hard. Since then, the Sunday dinners they all shared either at the Brookview Inn or in Angelica's loft kitchen were something she found she looked forward to. And now her home renovation project filled her with anticipation. Would Ginny be as interested in the project as Angelica? She could only hope.

"I'll talk to Ginny at lunch. I don't want them to hide away in their stateroom just because EM Barstow decided to take her life."

"If she did," Angelica said.

"Yeah," Tricia agreed.

They approached the bow of the ship, and Tricia slowed her pace. Something about the railing overlooking the vast nothingness of pale blue sky, the darker sea, and the ship's frothy wake bothered her. Not bothered—actually frightened her. What if some crazed individual came along and pushed you over the rail? Would the ship's big propellers chop one to pieces? The *Celtic Lady*'s speed wasn't fast, but how long could one last when flung into the cold sea, treading water with no hope of rescue and the threat of ocean predators ever at hand?

They turned the corner, heading south once again.

Tricia shook herself. Talking about EM's death had caused her paranoia to make an appearance once again. "What's next on your agenda?" she asked, hoping to distract herself.

"There's a book signing at ten o'clock. It's duty-free."

Tricia smiled. "Well, that's always good."

"Are you going?"

"I wouldn't mind. I love the fact that we don't have to check bags and can bring on and cart home as much stuff as we want."

Angelica laughed. "I just hope the bus taking us back to Stoneham will have room for all the extra baggage our tour members are likely to have after buying so many books."

"I'm sure the bus's gas—or is it diesel?—mileage is sure to plummet, because I have no problem buying my weight in books."

Angelica laughed. "Me, either!"

They power walked along the deck for another minute or so without speaking.

"How many more circuits around the deck are you going to make?" Angelica asked.

"Oh, another three or four."

"Well, then I think I'll leave it to you. I've got too much to do. See you later," she said, and headed for the door back into the ship.

Tricia continued walking toward the stern, but as she got closer, her paranoia seemed to peak and she did an abrupt about-face and started back the way she'd come. Perhaps she'd finish her walk in the ship's exercise room on one of the treadmills.

Don't be silly, Tricia told herself, and pivoted to retrace her steps. She was not going to let EM Barstow's death overshadow her vacation. If she was honest with herself, not having to run into the woman for the rest of the trip would be a tremendous relief—and she wouldn't be surprised if others felt the same way.

Tricia's power walk slowed to an amble as she came up to the rail that overlooked the back end of the ship. She stepped closer to the Emerald Isle Restaurant's big picture window and clutched the handrail, allowing other walkers and joggers to pass her.

The next morning, the ship would dock in Bermuda. Tricia suddenly found she was eager to once again step on dry land.

ELEVEN

The author signing turned out to be a lot of fun—and it seemed half of the ship's passengers showed up, making it impossible for anyone to meet all the authors. There were, however, plenty of books to be bought, and with more than thirty authors on board, Tricia and Angelica carried large book-filled shopping bags so heavy their arms were in danger of stretching to double their length.

Arnold Smith had ridden in on his motorized chair, but instead of buying books, he brought his own, and in some cases had five or six copies of a given title. Not only was the basket on his scooter filled with books, but he had two large canvas bags hanging from its handles, too. There were plenty of grumbles at his monopolizing several authors while he kept others from getting their books signed.

Tricia and Angelica had only enough time to drop off their books, meet up with Ginny, and head for the next event.

The authors' luncheon was to be held in the lower level of the ship's Emerald Isle Restaurant. Tricia, Angelica, and Ginny impatiently waited in the deck's main corridor behind scores of others.

"Isn't this exciting?" Ginny asked, her eyes wide with anticipation.

"Who do you want to meet?" Tricia asked.

"Oh, I don't care. I just like to soak up books, books, and more books. It's the one thing I miss since I stopped working at Haven't Got a Clue. And since Sofia came, I haven't had nearly as much time to read as I would like."

"She's going to be all grown up much too soon," Angelica lamented. "Enjoy every precious moment with her that you can."

"Stop it," Ginny teased. "You're making me feel guilty for leaving her with Antonio and coming to this lunch."

"I didn't mean that," Angelica said, sounding stricken.

"I know. What's so great about this trip is it's giving them some much needed daddy-daughter time together."

"Now I feel like a slave driver," Angelica declared. "Do you think I work Antonio too hard?"

"Not at all. He enjoys his job. We both do. It would just be more convenient if there were more hours in the day."

"I wonder how many of the Stoneham people will be at the luncheon," Angelica commented, changing the subject.

"I imagine just about everyone," Tricia said.

"I don't know. Some of them may be too exhausted to eat."

"Why?" Angelica asked.

"I was taking Sofia for a walk this morning and passed the Crystal Ballroom. "Mary Fairchild and the Dexter twins were having a blast doing the Texas two-step at the ballroom dance class. The Dexter twins were dancing with each other."

"Who was leading?" Angelica asked, grinning.

"Muriel . . . I think. Isn't she the older one by a few minutes?"

"They've only told us about a million times. You'd think we'd remember," Tricia quipped.

"Maybe we didn't because we're not really interested," Angelica whispered conspiratorially.

"There's going to be a dance competition on Thursday night. I think Mary wants to win."

"What's the prize?" Tricia asked.

"A trophy and one hundred dollars in ship's credit toward the winner's next cruise."

"That'll pay for a few martinis," Angelica said. "You weren't thinking of going to it, were you?"

Ginny shrugged. "Might be a little too exciting for my blood. And you'll never guess who was sitting at one of the tables they use at teatime, and only had eyes for Mary."

"Spare us the suspense," Angelica deadpanned.

"Chauncey Porter."

"You're kidding."

Ginny shook her head. "Nope. I think it's rather sweet. Maybe they'll get together, close their stores, and open a dance studio. Stranger things have happened."

Just then, the big doors to the restaurant opened and in seconds the crowd began to move forward.

"Oh, boy!" Ginny cried, sounding like a kid anticipating a double-dip ice cream cone. Her enthusiasm was infectious.

Unlike the dinner meal, where passengers had assigned seats, the restaurant had been sectioned off with tables set for ten.

"Let's get a seat near the podium," Ginny suggested. "That way we won't miss anything." She led the way, with Angelica and Tricia trying to keep up.

Tricia enjoyed dining in the select Kells Grill, but the *Celtic Lady*'s main dining hall was nicely appointed, as well. The carpets and wall coverings were done in tasteful shades of green and gold, and each linen-covered table sported a simple, but pretty arrangement from the ship's florist. On a side table sat an assortment of ornately decorated cakes that had been made to look like books. Stacked books. Books with covers from authors who'd made the trip, including EM Barstow's latest bestseller. Every one of them was a piece of art. It seemed a shame to have to cut them.

They sat down, with Ginny settling between the sisters. An engraved card with the luncheon choices sat at each place setting. Tricia scanned hers. Lobster, duck, tilapia, or a vegetarian entrée. Tricia sighed, knowing what she would order.

Ginny removed her sweater. "We should save a couple of seats for Grace and Mr. Everett."

"Good idea," Angelica said, and she, too, took off her sweater and hung hers and Ginny's on the backs of two of the table's chairs. "I think I'll order a bottle of wine for the table." She gestured for one of the tuxedo-clad waiters to join them. "I'd like a nice bottle of Chardonnay."

"Very good, madam. We have a very nice Australian."

"That'll be fine." Angelica handed the waiter her keycard, and he nodded and turned away.

"So, who do you think will sit at our table?" Ginny asked.

"I hope it's one of the cozy mystery authors," Tricia said.

"I want chef Larry Andrews," Angelica piped up. "I could talk to him for hours on only the subject of sauces."

"What I don't want is for this luncheon to turn into a makeshift memorial service for EM Barstow," Ginny said.

"Oh, dear. That would be rather dreadful," Angelica agreed.

"Someone is bound to address it," Tricia said.

"Well, they won't get a testimonial from me," Ginny said, and reached for her sweating water glass. "That woman was just plain mean to me and Mr. Everett the time she visited Haven't Got a Clue.

She was even worse than Zoë Carter's nasty assistant, and that's saying something."

"Poor Zoë and EM are both just as dead," Angelica commented, trying to see around those who hadn't yet taken their seats, no doubt looking for her favorite chef.

Zoë Carter had been strangled in Tricia's store's washroom. The expression on EM's dead face had borne an uncanny resemblance to Zoë's deathly countenance five years before.

"Is this seat taken?" asked a heavyset woman with dyed black hair. Instead of making her look younger, the color made her complexion seem washed out. She should have gone lighter by a few shades. But Tricia wasn't there to dispense fashion critiques, and simply said, "Please join us."

The woman sat down. "Hi. I'm Maria Hartley. I'm a librarian from Erie, Pennsylvania. Where are you from?"

"Stoneham, New Hampshire," Ginny answered.

"And you?" Maria asked Tricia.

"We're all from Stoneham." She indicated the three of them. "We signed up for the tour through our local Chamber of Commerce."

"That's nice. My kids paid for my trip. It's an early birthday present."

"How nice. Did one of them come with you?"

Maria shook her head. "They all have to work. But I'm having a wonderful time away from the ice and snow. I've met so many nice people. Well, except for one."

"Oh?" Tricia asked.

Maria leaned forward and lowered her voice. "That lady who killed herself. She was terribly rude to several people at her signing yesterday. I was going to buy a book, but after she chewed out one poor woman with a cane for jostling her table, I decided I'd rather have a Scotch and soda."

"Oh, you're my kind of girl," Angelica said, smiling. "I've just ordered a bottle of wine for the table. Would you like a glass when it gets here?"

"Yes. Thank you."

Two more women on the high side of fifty approached the table. They eyed the chairs with sweaters, but pointed to two that weren't reserved. "Are these seats taken?" one of them asked.

Ginny shook her head. "Feel free to join us."

The women sat down. The dress code for dinners ranged between smart casual and formal, but these ladies looked more like they were ready for a day on the beach. Each was dressed in sleeveless shirts, shorts, and sneakers. Since the air-conditioning seemed to be set at maximum, they could be in danger of catching colds.

"I'm Linda Gordon," the one on the right said, "and this is my sister Barbara."

Calls of "Nice to meet you" and "Hi" were exchanged.

Tricia looked around and saw Grace and Mr. Everett heading their way. Smiling, she waved to them.

"Hello, everyone," Grace called out. No one had a more infectious smile than Grace—unless it was Tricia's current assistant, Pixie Poe, with her flashing gold canine tooth. Grace returned the sweaters to their owners, and Mr. Everett held her chair, then pushed it in before taking his own seat. The introductions were completed just as the wine was brought to the table.

The waiter gave a sample to Angelica to approve. She did, and then she signed the credit receipt and directed him to pour for the rest of the table, as well. Mr. Everett declined, but the others seemed quite enthused.

"We've got two chairs left. I wonder who our author will be," Grace said, and sipped her wine.

Tricia looked around, but very few people were still standing.

"Angelica wants a chef. Tricia and I want a cozy mystery author. How about the rest of you?" Ginny asked.

"Definitely a mystery author," said Maria.

"We're hoping for one of the big-name romance writers," Barbara said. "I wish Nora Roberts had come on this cruise."

"She can hardly write six or seven books a year if she takes off for a cruise," Linda pointed out.

"That's true."

"Who would you like to sit with us, Mr. Everett?" Tricia asked.

"I'll be happy with anyone."

"Grace?" Ginny asked.

"A romance or mystery author would be fine with me."

They were so engaged in conversation they hardly noticed a rather short man in a baggy brown suit—sporting a bad toupee—make his way toward them. "Hello. I'm Kevin Mitchell. I've been assigned to your table."

"Welcome," Grace said politely.

Mitchell took his seat, unbuttoning his suit jacket. He reached for the crisp white napkin at the side of his place setting, shook it out, and placed it across his lap.

"I'm afraid I don't recognize your name," Angelica said. "What do you write?"

"Nonfiction," Mitchell said, and smiled.

"Oh?" Mr. Everett asked keenly.

"Yes. My specialty is deep-sea microbes."

"Really?" Ginny asked, sounding incredulous.

"Oh, yes. It's such a fascinating topic."

Tricia, Ginny, and Angelica traded skeptical glances.

"These microbes represent the very essence of life," Mitchell continued. "Did you know microbes have been found along the coast of South America that haven't changed their molecular structure in over two billion years?"

"You don't say," Angelica said, and reached for her wineglass. Tricia did likewise.

"Oh, yes. I could go on and on about it for hours."

"Please don't," Ginny mumbled into her glass. Tricia gently jabbed her with an elbow.

"I thought all the authors on board were fiction writers," Linda said, frowning.

"Oh, no. There are at least two of us nonfiction authors on the cruise."

"There're more than that. Larry Andrews is a nonfiction writer. He pens wonderful cookbooks," Angelica said.

"I hardly think a cookbook could be considered serious work," Mitchell said, his tone deadly.

"Well, it is to me," Angelica said with umbrage. "I happen to *be* a cookbook author."

"You are?" Barbara asked with interest.

"Angelica wrote a nationally bestselling cookbook called *Easy-Does-It Cooking*—and its sequel, *Easy-Does-It Holidays*. They're wonderful cookbooks," Ginny gushed. "I'm still a bit of a newlywed, and I don't know what I would have done if I hadn't had those terrific books to rely on while learning to cook."

"Oh, that's so sweet of you to say so. Thank you, Ginny," Angelica said.

"What's your last name?" Maria asked. "I may want to order them for my branch library. Or do they have them on board the ship for sale?"

"My name is Angelica Miles. I'm afraid the ship's bookstore has no copies for sale. My literary career is temporarily on hold since I was elected president of the Stoneham Chamber of Commerce. But I'll have a new one out next year. Mark my words."

"Do you have a website?" Linda asked.

"Yes, I do." Angelica reached for her purse and withdrew a couple of business cards. She handed them to Tricia, who passed them along.

"Well, that's all very nice," Mitchell said with what sounded like barely suppressed anger, "but I'm a *serious* writer. And my subject is serious, too."

"But I don't want to read serious stuff," Barbara protested. "I read for pleasure."

"My books *are* a pleasure to read," Mitchell insisted.

"What's the title of the latest one?" Grace asked, always a peace-maker.

"*Microbes: Our World in Miniature*. It's my hottest seller," he said proudly.

"What was your print run?" Ginny asked as Tricia reached for her wineglass once more.

"Nearly a thousand copies."

Tricia nearly choked on her wine.

"What was *your* print run?" Barbara asked Angelica.

"In total?" She thought about it for a moment. "I think about twenty-five thousand. Of course that was for just the first book. I'm pretty sure they doubled it for the second."

An angry blush crept up Mitchell's neck. "Of course *my* book is for people with more on their minds than baking a cake or making a pizza," he said with derision.

"Oh, I don't know," said Mr. Everett. "It seems to me that there's a lot of chemistry in good cookery."

"What was *your* occupation?" Mitchell asked, his eyes narrowing.

"I started out as a butcher."

"Like that's something to be proud of," Mitchell muttered with a martyred sigh.

"Hey," Ginny protested, ever protective of her surrogate grandfa-ther. "That was extremely rude."

"Ginny, dear," Angelica soothed, "let me handle this."

The corners of Ginny's mouth turned upward. Like Tricia, she knew that once Angelica got a bee in her bonnet, things were likely to get interesting.

Angelica sat bolt upright in her chair. "Mr. Mitchell," she began politely, "I really don't think you meant to insult my dear friend, Mr. Everett."

Mitchell's nose seemed to flair. "If he's such a good friend, shouldn't you at least be on a first-name basis?"

Tricia, Ginny, and Angelica all gasped in horror.

"Excuse me," Angelica said in a tone that Tricia considered dangerous. "But it's not your place to judge the level of my friendship for someone I dearly respect."

"Ms. Miles," Mr. Everett said, his tone placating.

Angelica raised a hand, and Mr. Everett, apparently sensing an explosion, dutifully sat back in his chair. Tricia watched as her sister took a few moments to compose herself before she spoke again.

"Mr. Mitchell," she began, "I don't mean to disparage you, but perhaps you should rethink joining this table for lunch."

"And why is that?" the author demanded.

"Because, if you make one more belittling remark, I will bite you. And I have very sharp teeth."

Mitchell looked horrified. "What?" he demanded. "What?"

Ginny burst into laughter, and less than a second later the rest of the table joined her.

"I have never been so insulted!" Mitchell cried.

"Well, maybe you'd better get out more," Barbara muttered, and giggled, already wiping her eyes.

Mitchell pushed back his chair. "I refuse to be insulted!"

"Then perhaps you should learn not to insult others," Maria exclaimed.

Tricia had to bite her lip to keep from laughing, but the pompous oaf had it coming to him.

Mitchell stood. "I don't have to stand for this."

"And evidently not sit, either," Ginny muttered into the hand she'd pressed across her lips.

"Good day!" the pompous jerk declared, and left the table.

It took only three or four seconds before all the ladies at the table broke into another round of muffled laughter.

"Oh, dear," Mr. Everett muttered in embarrassment. "Oh, dear."

"You were going to *bite* him?" Tricia asked her sister, not sure if she was appalled or terribly amused.

"Well," Angelica began defensively, "it was all I could think of at the time."

"I think it was priceless," Ginny said, and laughed, and she leaned over to give Angelica a big hug. A smiling Angelica hugged her back, and Tricia could see by her sister's expression how much the gesture meant to her.

Suddenly the waiter reappeared. "Are we ready to order?" he asked.

"Oh, yes," Tricia said, and found it difficult to keep from giggling. Somehow she managed to keep a straight face as she ordered the tilapia. Contemplating the steamed fish brought her back to solemn earth in a heartbeat. The others gave their orders, before the tuxedoed young man nodded and turned away.

"Could anyone else use some more wine?" Angelica asked, offering up the bottle.

"I could," Grace said, her smile sweet.

Angelica rose, carried the bottle around the table, and topped off Grace's glass. "Thank you, dear," Grace said, "and on more than one account."

Angelica smiled. "My pleasure," she said before returning to her seat.

"Well," Maria said, swirling the wine in her glass, "that was certainly interesting."

"Will you be buying a copy of Mr. Mitchell's book for your library?" Ginny asked, sounding oh-so-innocent.

"I think not," Maria said, and raised her glass in a pseudo toast.

Millicent Ambrose moved to stand at the podium at the head of the room. She fiddled with a microphone and tested it with the old "one, two, three" before she launched into her prepared remarks.

"Hello, everyone, and welcome to the *Celtic Lady*'s Salute to Authors luncheon. I hope everyone approves of the menu." The crowd responded with enthusiastic applause. "Before we get started on our delicious meal, I'd like to acknowledge the sad passing of author EM Barstow. Her literary accomplishments are legendary, and I'm sure we're all saddened to know there will be no more Tennyson Eisenberg books."

It was then Tricia noticed that Dori Douglas was seated at a table across the way. Considering she was the head of EM's fan club, she didn't appear to be upset in any way. EM had treated the woman poorly. Maybe the idea of never again being the object of such abuse was of comfort to her.

"We heard she committed suicide," someone in the audience called out.

Millicent looked apprehensive, and hesitated before speaking. "It does appear that Ms. Barstow took her life."

"Are they really sure?" someone else called out. "Could it have been murder?"

"Murders don't happen on the *Celtic Lady*," Millicent said firmly. "We're on a pleasant journey to celebrate books and authors. While we honor Ms. Barstow's memory, we feel sure she would want all our guests to remember her outstanding work and not the way she left this earth."

"Will there be a burial at sea?" somebody called out.

"No. Ms. Barstow's body will be returned to New York. Now, next on our agenda . . ."

"Is there going to be a memorial service?"

"There are no plans at this time."

"Why not?"

Again Millicent hesitated. "We're still gauging interest. If enough is shown, we may schedule such an event. Check your Daily Program. It will list all activities on board the *Celtic Lady*." She stood a little straighter. "I see our world-famous waitstaff is about to serve luncheon. We will continue with the program after our lovely meal. Thank you."

A smattering of unenthusiastic applause followed her remarks, and Millicent beat a hasty retreat, perhaps before she could be bombarded with any more unpleasant questions about EM Barstow's death.

Ginny leaned closer to Tricia. "She seemed pretty uncomfortable."

"Yes, she did," Tricia agreed. "When I spoke to Fiona Sample yesterday, she said she was being interviewed for the ship's morning news program. I wonder if Millicent interviewed all the authors."

"If you ask me, the ship's television stinks. We've had it on in the evenings, but mostly as background noise. I mean, who wants to watch a show about great ocean liners that have sunk when they're in the middle of a cruise?" Ginny asked.

"Not me," Angelica agreed.

"I don't mean to eavesdrop," Maria said, "but Millicent *did* interview Ms. Barstow."

"Did EM say anything interesting?" Tricia asked.

Maria shrugged. "She talked about her upcoming book and how she planned to do some research while she was in Bermuda. Isn't it odd that she had plans for the future and then suddenly decides to kill herself?"

Yes, it was.

"I wonder if they'll rerun that segment," Maria mused, then shrugged as one of the waiters presented her with a plate of lobster thermidor.

And if they didn't, was there a way Tricia could talk Millicent into letting her see a tape of the show? She'd do as the entertainment director suggested and study the Daily Program at her earliest convenience.

Tricia's lunch arrived, and as she looked around her she noticed that all but she had ordered the same thing—the lobster. Her steamed tilapia looked anemic in comparison. "Well, it looks like great minds think alike," she said, picking up her fork.

"What do you think the rest of the program will entail?" Ginny asked, reaching for a roll from the basket on the table.

"Speeches from some of the authors?" Tricia offered and tried the carrot custard that had accompanied the fish. At least it was tasty.

"Oh, I hope not Mr. Mitchell," Maria said, and scooped up a forkful of lobster.

"Perhaps it'll just be the bigger authors," Angelica said. "Could you pass the butter, please, Tricia?"

Tricia did so, looking at the basket of rolls with longing. "Who decides who's a *big* author?"

Angelica shrugged. "Perhaps whoever came up with the idea of a book-themed cruise."

That seemed plausible, but hadn't EM said that this cruise was costing her a fortune? Surely an author with her sales could well afford to pay for it—for herself *and* the president of her fan club. Had she been just a run-of-the-mill skinflint or did she have financial problems that made the trip a hardship? No, that couldn't be. EM Barstow might not be as big an author as Stephen King, but she was on a par with Patricia Cornwell, who could afford lots of neat stuff—including homes in multiple places. And yet EM had been complaining of the cost of a cruise. Her room was not as elaborate as the suite Angelica had booked, but it was still one of the top-priced cabins that allowed her and her assistant to dine in the coveted Kells Grill. If she'd been hard up for money, she could have taken a cheaper cabin option; staterooms that had a window and a small balcony. There were rooms that had just a window. And then there were rooms that were inside cabins with just a bed, a small desk, and a john, like those taken by most of the Stoneham contingent and EM's editor, Cathy Copper.

Tricia picked at her tilapia. Of course, there were degrees of hardship, and perhaps EM's complaint about the cost had been made because she had once been a starving artist, which was how most authors began their careers. Still, the fact that she'd seemed bitter about the cost was of note.

It was also odd that an author of EM's stature depended on the president of her fan club to act as an unpaid assistant. EM's sales were stellar. Tricia would have expected the woman to be swimming in moola and more than able to pay a full-time assistant to coordinate her appearances, social media, and anything else that needed to be done to keep her name out there and accessible to her reading public.

No doubt about it, the woman was an enigma, and Tricia was certainly intrigued. She glanced over her shoulder to see Dori Douglas buttering a roll, and made a mental note to seek the woman out at some point to quiz her about EM's financial state. Of course, there was a good chance EM had never confided her personal problems to someone she felt was her inferior—and the way EM treated poor Dori, it was obvious she'd felt superior to her fan club president. And how had that made Dori feel?

"You're very quiet, Trish," Angelica said, again reaching for her wineglass.

"I'm just thinking," Tricia said, stabbing a piece of steamed broccoli with her fork.

"About what?" Ginny asked, and ate another forkful of lobster.

"Nothing in particular," Tricia fibbed.

"You do look preoccupied, Ms. Miles," Mr. Everett commented.

Tricia shook her head and smiled. "I'm just enjoying this lovely lunch."

"It *is* good," Maria said, and she, too, dug into her entrée with gusto.

"And we still have dessert to look forward to. Did you see those lovely cakes they set up on the side table over there? I'll bet each of them is a different flavor. I don't know when I've eaten such marvelous cakes and desserts. It's a constant surprise. I'm sure I'll put on five or ten pounds before this cruise is over," Linda said.

She wasn't the only one who felt that way. But perhaps Angelica would let Tricia take a bite of whatever piece of cake she chose to top off her meal.

Tricia sighed. Why did she always feel guilty about indulging in any kind of treat? It's not like she did it on a regular basis.

"What kind of cake do you think lies beneath all that frosting?" Ginny asked Maria.

"Chocolate, for sure," she said with relish. "But they had an assortment of cupcakes last night at the Lido. I got one that was pistachio, and not fake—like when you get ice cream and they toss in almonds and artificial flavoring instead of the real thing."

Pistachio cake. That sounded interesting. "What else?" Tricia asked.

"I think there was strawberry and peach."

"Peach cake? I never heard of peach cake."

"If they have it at dinner tonight, I'm trying it," Maria said.

Tricia looked across the way. The ship's photographer was taking pictures of the cakes, as were a number of passengers, while a couple of waiters stood by with cake knives in hand, ready to begin to cut them. Her stomach growled.

A waitress stepped up to the table. "May I take your plate?"

Tricia nodded, and her half-eaten meal was whisked away.

"Would you like coffee?"

"Yes, please."

"I'd love a pot of tea," Ginny said.

The waitress nodded.

"Oh, look," Angelica said, "they're cutting the cakes. "I'm going to get a piece. Coming with me, Ginny?"

"Sure."

"I'll come, too," Tricia practically blurted.

Angelica started. "You will?"

"Yes. Why not?"

"It's just that you don't usually have cake."

"We've shared cake once or twice."

"*Shared* being the operative word," Angelica said. She turned to Grace and Mr. Everett. "Can we bring you back some cake?"

"I'd love a piece," Grace said. "Get anything that looks yummy."

"No, thank you, Ms. Miles," Mr. Everett said.

"Let's go!" Angelica said, and led the way.

They crossed the expanse of carpet, dodging tables and chairs, before the mass of other passengers could mob the dessert table. "I'll see if I can get a corner piece for Grace," Angelica said. "She just loves frosting."

"I hope they have chocolate," Ginny said.

"Maria assured us they would," Tricia said.

The waiters were already passing out generous slices of the cake that had looked like EM Barstow's last cover. "Not chocolate," Ginny said, frowning at the ivory cake under the gray-toned icing. It didn't look palatable.

"I think I'd rather have something different," Tricia said, wrinkling her noise.

"I'm sure it will taste fine." Angelica turned to the waiter. "What flavor is that cake?"

"It's French vanilla mousse."

"Doesn't that sound yummy."

"Yes, but the frosting," Tricia said, frowning.

"I'll have a slice of that, please," Angelica said, ignoring her protest. "In fact, two. I'm taking back a slice for my dear friend as well."

"Very good, madam."

"What else do you have?" Ginny asked as the waiter cut two slices for Angelica.

"Lemon custard, pink champagne, raspberry lemon cream, chocolate mousse, and strawberry cream."

"I'll have the pink champagne," Ginny said, and giggled.

"I'd like a small slice of the strawberry cream," Tricia said.

They collected their plates and passed Maria, Linda, and Barbara, who were just starting out for the dessert table.

"Here you go, Grace. French vanilla mousse," Angelica said, setting the cake before her.

"Oh, dear," Grace said, taking in the size of the slice. "Vanilla," she said with uncertainty as Tricia and Ginny took their seats.

"You don't like vanilla? Oh, I'm sorry. Would you rather have strawberry?"

"Oh, that sounds good."

"Tricia, you wouldn't mind giving Grace your piece of cake, would you?"

Yes, she would. Her taste buds were all set for strawberry cream. But Tricia forced a smile. "Not at all," she said, and handed Angelica her piece of cake, accepting the very large corner piece of the cake with the ugly frosting. Well, she could scrape it off if it tasted terrible.

"Thank you, dear," Grace said with sincerity. "And it's just the right size, too."

There was no way Tricia was going to eat a honking big piece of cake like the slab in front of her. Still, she'd take a few bites and try to enjoy it. She picked up her fork to plunge it into the icing but met resistance. She tried again. There was definitely something in that slice of cake that didn't belong there. She poked the icing in several places, still meeting resistance.

Angelica slid a piece of cake off her fork and into her mouth. She chewed and closed her eyes in ecstasy. "This is wonderful. I wonder if I could get the recipe. My customers at"—she paused and muttered just loud enough for Ginny and Tricia to hear—"the Brookview Inn would love this."

Tricia continued to probe the confection with her fork.

"What are you doing?" Ginny asked.

"There's something in my cake."

"Like what?" Angelica asked.

Tricia placed the edge of her fork on the top of the cake and began scraping away the offensive-looking icing. Whatever was there was still buried in the cake itself. She dug deeper. By now Maria, Barbara, and Linda were as engrossed as Ginny and Angelica.

"I think it's . . ." Tricia let the sentence trail off as she extricated a plastic card from the cake. She reached for her napkin and wiped it free of crumbs and icing, immediately recognizing what it was.

The familiar face stared up at her from the piece of plastic. EM Barstow's *Celtic Lady* identification keycard.

TWELVE

Tricia wasn't sure what she should do. If she called the waiter over to report her find, he might confiscate the keycard and then she wouldn't know if ship's security would investigate how it got into the booklike cake. One thing was for certain, it was one more piece of evidence that EM's death had not been a suicide. But would the ship's security department see it that way? Surely they must have noted it wasn't in her stateroom at the time of her death. But did that make a difference if they were going to turn a blind eye to the possibility of murder?

"What is it?" Ginny whispered, squinting to look at what Tricia held in her hand.

"Evidence," Tricia said. Cupping her hand around the card, she showed it to Ginny.

"Oh my God!" Ginny said so loudly that every head at the table swiveled in her direction.

"Ginny?" Angelica said, her tone as concerned as a new mother's, and since she was a new mother-in-law, who saw Ginny as equally important to her as her beloved stepson, there seemed to be a note of panic in her voice, as well.

Ginny stabbed her right index finger in Tricia's direction. Still shielding the card, Tricia showed it to Angelica, whose mouth had dropped open in shock. "It was in your piece of cake?" Angelica whispered.

Tricia nodded.

"What should we do?" Ginny asked.

"*We* should do nothing. But I think *you* need to talk to Officer McDonald," Angelica said.

"Yes, but how do I get his attention?" Tricia asked.

"Well," Angelica began, "maybe you just ask for him to come to you."

That seemed logical, but as Angelica had already pointed out, McDonald was probably a night-shift officer and it was after one o'clock in the afternoon. Would he appreciate being ripped from his daytime slumber to talk to her about her find?

It didn't matter. She had already spoken to him and she didn't want to try to establish a rapport with another one of the ship's crew.

"What are you going to do?" Angelica asked.

"Does anyone have a camera?" Tricia asked.

"I do," Ginny said, and reached for her purse.

"Will it give the time and date when you take the shot?" Tricia asked.

"Yes."

"Then please take a photo. Not only of me holding the keycard, but of everyone at the table. And I think I should be taken holding it with everyone at the table, just so there's no disputing the time and date of my discovery."

"You sound a little paranoid," Ginny commented.

"So be it," Tricia said.

So Ginny took eight or ten shots of Tricia holding the sticky keycard with everyone at the table.

"Now what do you intend to do?" Angelica asked once Tricia had resumed her seat.

In answer, Tricia looked around, held up her hand, caught the attention of one of the waiters, and beckoned him to come forward. "Is there any chance you could call a security officer to the dining room? Officer McDonald, if possible."

"What for, madam?"

"Because I found this"—she showed him the keycard—"in my piece of cake."

The waiter looked horrified and reached to snatch the offending piece of plastic from her, but Tricia was too quick for him. She clamped her hand around the card. "Oh, no. I'll only give this to Officer McDonald. And I'm prepared to sit here all afternoon if need be to do it, too."

The waiter nodded. "Very good, madam. I will call security. If you would be so good as to remain at your table after the luncheon concludes, I will make sure that someone from ship's security speaks with you."

"Officer McDonald," Tricia reiterated, "or I'm not giving this up."

"As you say, madam." The man bowed, pivoted, and briskly walked away.

"What if this takes a while?" Barbara asked. "Do *we* have to stay here while you wait for the security guy?"

"I shouldn't think so. But perhaps if you decide to leave, you'd give me your full names and cabin numbers, just in case Officer McDonald wants to speak with you."

"Okay. Because Larry Andrews's cooking demonstration is at two o'clock, and Linda and I don't want to miss it." Angelica came up with a notebook and pen, and the Gordon sisters entered their information before they got up, pushed in their chairs, and made a hasty exit.

"Looks like I'll be missing Larry's spectacular presentation," Angelica groused and reached for the wine bottle to top up her glass. She found it empty and frowned.

"If you don't mind, I think I'll leave, too," Maria said after writing down her information. "It was very nice to meet you all." She got up and hurried away.

"You and Ginny don't have to stay, Ange. Go ahead and do what you want to do. As long as we have the images on Ginny's phone, we don't have to worry about eyewitnesses," Tricia said.

"I'm not going to leave you," Angelica said emphatically. "But you don't have to stay, Ginny. You should go find your husband and baby and have a wonderful time."

"Are you sure?" Ginny asked, sounding decidedly unsure.

"Absolutely," Angelica said, leaned forward, and gave Ginny a hug.

Ginny pulled away. "Okay, but only because you insisted. We'll catch up with you both later this afternoon."

"It's a date," Tricia said.

Ginny got up and gave them a wave before she started for the exit.

"We'll stay with you two," Grace volunteered.

"Oh, no," Tricia said. "I really don't think it's necessary. And, in fact, I'm the only one who has to stay. I've got my e-reader in my purse. I could sit here and be entertained for hours until Officer McDonald gets here."

"Are you sure, Ms. Miles?" Mr. Everett asked.

"Yes. You two run along and have fun."

"Very well. We'll see you later this evening for dinner," he said.

"That would be splendid," Tricia said.

Grace nodded, and Mr. Everett got up and helped her from her chair before they, too, left the restaurant. It seemed as though the rest of the place had emptied, as well.

The waitstaff began clearing the tables, including the one Tricia and Angelica sat at. They left the crumb-littered tablecloth, but took off every plate, glass, salt and pepper shaker, and floral arrangement, already setting up for the early dinner crowd.

Angelica had focused her attention out the bank of windows that overlooked the boat's stern and the long river of white water churned up by the *Celtic Lady*'s huge propellers. Meanwhile, Tricia examined the keycard. How the heck had it ended up in one of the ship-made cakes? The fact that it hadn't been in EM's stateroom at the time of her death could only mean one thing: that someone had taken it after her death. And that fact certainly pointed to the probability that she hadn't died by her own hand.

Angelica turned back to face Tricia. "I wonder if the waiter could be convinced to bring us more coffee."

"You could ask," Tricia said, but since there were no members of the waitstaff within listening distance, that was going to prove difficult. "Finding this keycard in the cake might mean whoever killed EM was a member of the crew, and probably a kitchen staff member."

"Not necessarily," Angelica said. "Anybody who went on one of the kitchen tours earlier today could have dropped it into the batter."

"Kitchen tours?"

"Didn't you see the announcement in the Daily Program? There are two different types. The first is for anybody and is free. But if you're willing to pay, you can get a personal tour. Antonio and I are booked for the Friday morning extended tour."

"Really?"

Angelica nodded. "We want to see how they operate. Maybe we can learn something that we can adapt for the Brookview Inn's kitchen or another eatery we may open in the future."

"Admit it; you'd pay extra just to tour the kitchen even if you didn't run two restaurants."

Angelica offered a weak smile. "Probably."

Tricia glanced at her watch. It had been nearly twenty minutes since the party had broken up and security had been called. It was sure taking a long time for someone from ship's security to show up. Perhaps Security Officer McDonald was a heavy sleeper and hadn't heard the call. Many of the crew spoke English as a second (or perhaps third) language. Maybe they hadn't conveyed the seriousness of her find.

"Here come a couple of hunky guys in uniform," Angelica practically sang.

As Tricia had hoped, Ian McDonald was one of them.

"Ms. Miles," he said in greeting, although he didn't sound pleased. "I understand you found a piece of Ms. Barstow's property in your"— he paused—"afters."

"Yes. As a matter of fact, it was in a piece of cake baked to resemble her last book."

She held out the still-sticky keycard, but McDonald donned a pair of latex gloves before he took it from her. He pursed his lips as he studied the piece of evidence. "Where's the cake now?"

"They cleared it away. But some of my tablemates had their cameras and took pictures. I asked if they'd be willing to show them to you, and they all said yes."

McDonald passed the keycard to his associate, who had also donned gloves, and he secured the card in a plastic evidence bag.

"So, what do you think?" Tricia asked.

"I need to ponder the significance of this find."

"Ponder how?" Angelica said. "The lady didn't have it in her possession when she died. That means somebody lifted it. Could they have used it as well?"

"That's something we'll be checking."

"It sounds to me like you've got a potentially bigger crime than petty theft to investigate," Tricia said.

"And that is?"

"Murder."

McDonald looked uncomfortable. "We will consider every option."

"Just not that hard?" Angelica suggested.

"*Every* option," he repeated firmly. "Now, how can I track down the people who were sitting with you when you made this . . ." He hesitated. "Discovery?"

"We made a list," Tricia said, but since her hands were still sticky from the cake and icing, she pointed at the table, and McDonald picked up the paper.

"Thank you."

"You're welcome. Will you keep me informed on what you find out about the case?"

"We don't *have* cases on board. But we will consider what you've said."

"You better listen to her," Angelica warned. "Tricia has a knack for this kind of thing."

McDonald frowned. "Is that because you own a mystery bookstore?"

"*And* she's helped the police back home crack a few murder cases, too," Angelica said with pride. "If she wasn't more interested in reading about crime rather than solving it, Tricia would have made a marvelous detective."

"Why, thank you, Ange," Tricia said, smiling.

Angelica shrugged. "No brag; just fact."

McDonald's expression was dour, but he gave Tricia a nod. "We'll be in touch." He turned, and he and his associate headed back the way they'd come.

"What do you think?" Angelica asked.

"That unless somebody comes walking along with a sign around his or her neck that says 'I strangled EM Barstow,' they aren't going to lift a finger to try and figure out how she really died."

"One thing's for sure; it's hard to hang yourself without some kind of illumination—and without that keycard, EM's stateroom would have been as dark as a cave."

"Yes, and they know that, too." Tricia pushed back her chair. "Can you carry my purse? My hands are terribly sticky."

"Sure thing. There's a loo just around the corner from the restaurant's main entrance. You can wash them there."

They left the table and headed for the restaurant's entrance, retracing McDonald's footsteps. Tricia wasn't surprised at the ship's officers' lack of interest in upgrading EM's cause of death from suicide to murder. It was their job to protect the cruise line's reputation. But as she walked through the empty and cavernous restaurant, she found she felt more than a little worried about her own, and her friends' and family's, security.

THIRTEEN

 Since Angelica had missed the beginning of Larry Andrews's demonstration, and Tricia the next scheduled event for authors and readers, they decided to skip the presentations altogether.

"What do you want to do next?" Angelica asked wearily.

"I could use some downtime. I only got a couple of hours' sleep last night."

"That's a good idea. With everyone going to all these events, I wonder if the spa would have an opening. Wouldn't a massage be heavenly?"

"Maybe some other time."

"Manicure? Pedicure?" Angelica asked hopefully.

"Not right now. But I promise I'll go with you on the trip back to New York."

Angelica shrugged. "Okay."

"I'll walk you to the spa," Tricia offered.

"And then walk all the way back to the stateroom on your own? No way, honey."

"I don't want to spoil your fun."

"There's a soaker tub in my bathroom. There're some kind of bath salts in there, too. If I dump in a lot, it might even become a bubble bath, especially if I can figure out how to make those jets work."

"You don't mind?" Tricia asked.

"Not a bit," Angelica said, and wrapped an arm around Tricia's shoulder. "I'm really proud of you. You told ship's security what they didn't want to hear, but you said it anyway. Just don't say it too loud. I don't want to frighten Ginny."

"Will you tell Antonio?"

"Yes. But since we're now convinced EM's death was murder, I really do want us to stick together. So no going off on your own. Promise?"

Tricia nodded. "Okay."

Angelica removed her arm and they headed for the lifts. As it happened, one seemed to be waiting for them, for as soon as Tricia pressed the up button, the doors opened and they stepped inside.

Angelica pressed the button for Deck 7.

"I must say, your maternal instincts have certainly blossomed of late," Tricia observed.

"They were always there, but I wasn't able to show them back in Stoneham."

"Why?"

"Because there's this whole Nigela Ricita mystique. Honestly, I can get a lot more done with that kind of anonymity."

"The winter weather has helped keep your relationship with Antonio, Ginny, and Sofia under wraps, but what's going to happen when the baby starts calling you Nonna?"

"I've thought about that. I was hoping she'd call me Nonna Angelica, and Grace, Nonna Grace. That would be an easy way to explain it away."

"Maybe," Tricia said.

The lift doors opened and they got off and headed for their state-room. Once again the long corridors were eerily empty. They walked in silence to the stateroom, and Angelica extracted her keycard from her purse to enter their suite. Thanks to the wide expanse of windows that overlooked their balcony, sunshine poured into the lounge. Tricia was glad her bedroom was supplied with room-darkening drapes.

"I'll see you in a couple of hours," she told her sister.

"Tootles!" Angelica said, and retired to her own side of the stateroom.

Tricia was happy to see that Sebastian had returned the room to pristine condition. It seemed a shame to disturb the bed, but she really was tired. And then she saw the box on the bedside table. It was wrapped in the same paper and bow that had accompanied the sweater she'd received the day before.

"Not again," she muttered. She crossed the room in five steps and picked up the box. Heavy. And she had an inkling what she'd find when she removed the wrapping. She wasn't wrong. A sealed, one-pound box of Belgian chocolates. The card that accompanied it said, *Sweets for the sweet*.

Would Sebastian know where these mysterious gifts were coming from, or did they just arrive from the shops in the ship's arcade and he was nothing but a messenger? It was doubtful the shopkeepers would reveal who purchased the sweater and candy. If a customer in her store swore her to secrecy, she would have to respect their wishes— or forever lose a customer? Except for the champagne, the sweater and candy hadn't been expensive gifts. In fact, though they were thought-ful, they were quite pedestrian.

Tricia was too tired to even contemplate why someone had chosen her as a target of affection. She set the box back down on the night table and crossed the room to close the curtains. She pulled back the duvet, lay down, and wondered if now that she truly suspected EM's death to be murder instead of suicide, if thoughts of finding the body would ruin her slumber. She didn't have time to ponder that thought long, for in less than a minute she'd fallen asleep.

Tricia awoke to the sound of voices in the next room. She got up, checked her appearance in the mirror, and decided to drag a comb through her hair before she faced whoever was in the lounge with Angelica. No surprise. It was Ginny—albeit a very upset Ginny.

"What's wrong?" Tricia asked as she entered the lounge.

Ginny sat on the loveseat across from Angelica, her eyes welling with tears. "I can't believe I've mislaid my phone. Not only does it have the pictures we took at the luncheon today, but it's got all my pictures of Sofia on it from the past month or so. Why didn't I download them before we left home?"

"Do you think you know where you left it?" Tricia asked, feeling panicky.

Ginny looked thoughtful. "Maybe in the Garden Lounge. Antonio and I were sitting there at a table overlooking the water, looking for dolphins, turtles, and sharks. I wanted to have it handy in case we saw one so I could take a picture."

"Maybe one of the crew found it and turned it in to the lost and found," Angelica suggested.

"Where would that be?"

"I'm pretty sure at the Purser's Office. I'd be happy to go down there with you to report it."

"Thanks, Tricia." Ginny rose. "Let me tell Antonio where we're going." She hurried out the door.

"Don't let her go wandering off on her own," Angelica warned.

"I won't." Tricia glanced to her right and saw that a colorful sunset stained the few clouds in the sky. "Goodness. How long did I sleep?"

"A good three hours," Angelica said. "You'll be nice and fresh for the booksellers' meet-and-greet cocktail party later this evening. What are you going to wear?"

"I have no idea. You?"

"I haven't yet made up my mind. Something fabulous. Now, don't you and Ginny take too long reporting the missing phone. We don't want to miss anything good."

"Don't worry. I imagine we'll be back within ten or fifteen minutes."

"Good. I sure hope someone's turned in the phone. Did you notice what Ginny didn't say?" Angelica asked.

"No."

"That Officer McDonald had contacted her. Do you think he contacted *anybody* who was at our lunch table?"

"Probably not. I'll ask Ginny on the way to the Purser's Office."

"While you're gone, I'll pop over and tell Antonio our suspicions. I don't want either of them wandering around the ship on their own."

"Good idea."

A knock on the door captured their attention. Tricia answered it.

"Let's go," Ginny said.

"We'll be back soon," Tricia told Angelica, made sure her keycard was in her pocket, and closed the suite's door behind her.

They started off toward the lifts. "I take it you weren't contacted by Officer McDonald," Tricia said.

Ginny shook her head. "To be fair, until just about ten minutes ago, we hadn't returned to our stateroom since this morning."

They took the lift down to Deck 2. Luckily, there was no one in line at the Purser's Office. They approached the desk.

"Hello, may I help you?" asked a pretty, freckle-faced woman with an Irish accent and red hair almost as long as Ginny's.

"Hi. I want to report a lost cell phone."

"Can you describe it?"

"It's an iPhone. It's got a pink case," Ginny said.

"We've had several phones turned in since the voyage began, but I don't recall one that matches that description. Let me go have a look. I'll be right back."

The woman disappeared into an office.

"It doesn't look hopeful," Ginny lamented.

"Don't give up yet. Maybe the case came off," Tricia suggested.

Ginny bit her lip. "Maybe."

The woman returned in less than a minute, shaking her head. "I'm sorry. None of the phones that were turned in were iPhones. Do you remember where you last saw it?"

"In the Garden Lounge. We were there this afternoon."

"What time?"

"Maybe three o'clock."

"Did you go back there and look?"

Ginny nodded. "We even moved the chairs and tables, but had no luck."

"It may be that a staff member found it but just hasn't had an opportunity to turn it in. In case it doesn't show up by later this evening, I'll have the security guys check the video to see if someone picked it up. If so, we may yet be able to track it down."

"Video?" Tricia asked.

"Yes. All our public areas have video surveillance cameras."

"I never noticed."

"And you probably won't. They're very discreet."

"Are all the corridors covered as well?"

She nodded. "Our passengers' security is of upmost importance."

"That's good to know," Ginny said.

Certainly interesting, Tricia thought.

"Let me get your name and cabin number. Someone will contact you after the security guys have a look at the video."

"Thank you. I'd appreciate that," Ginny said. "I really need that phone. It's got priceless pictures of my baby daughter on it."

"We'll do our best," the woman promised.

"Thank you."

Tricia and Ginny turned around and headed back the way they'd come.

"Are you going to the booksellers' cocktail party tonight?"

Ginny shook her head. "I don't think so. In fact, we were thinking we might order room service and stay in tonight for a romantic evening. That is, if Sofia will cooperate."

"Sounds nice," Tricia said, and suddenly thought of her ex-husband. It was at odd times like this that she missed him the most. What hurt was knowing she'd never again hear his voice teasing her. Never see those mesmerizing green eyes.

They stopped at the bank of elevators, where Ginny pushed the button. "Penny for your thoughts," she said.

Tricia shook her head. "Just thinking that it had been a long time since I've had a romantic evening."

"You were thinking about Christopher, weren't you?"

"Just a little," Tricia admitted.

"You'll find another someone one day. Maybe he'll be Italian, like Antonio."

Tricia managed a smile. "You never know."

They rode back to Deck 7 in companionable silence. Tricia walked Ginny to her stateroom. "If I don't see you tonight, have a great evening."

"You, too. Pay attention to everything, because I want a full gossipy report about the cocktail party."

"It'll probably be a yawn."

"Like lunch?" Ginny asked, looking skeptical.

"Well, I can but hope," Tricia said. "See you tomorrow."

"Good night," Ginny said, took her keycard out of her slacks pocket, and entered the stateroom. Tricia walked two doors down and opened the door to her suite.

A barefooted Angelica had changed into a formfitting, deep blue cocktail dress that looked absolutely stunning.

"I haven't seen that one before," Tricia said.

"What? This little old rag? It's positively ancient. But I can get into it again, and it's a classic style. Did Ginny find her phone?" Angelica asked.

"No, but I learned something very interesting about the *Celtic Lady*, and I'll bet it applies to all cruise ships."

"I've got to put on my face. Come into my bathroom and tell me all about it."

Tricia followed her sister. Sure enough, foundation, blush, lipstick, and other cosmetics had been spread across the bathroom vanity. Angelica picked up one of the bottles. "So what did you find out?"

"That everywhere you go on board there are surveillance cameras."

Angelica spread some of the foundation on her fingers and began to apply it. "That's not really surprising, is it? I mean, they even have them in the Shaw's market in Milford. I happen to know that the Stoneham's Board of Selectmen have been kicking around the idea of having several of them installed along Main Street."

"Really?"

Angelica nodded. "Many of the members are still smarting that Stoneham lost its designation as the Safest Village in New Hampshire after the revitalization along Main Street. We'll probably never get it back, but they'd sure like to try. Of course," she added with a wry smile, "it's been suggested that the village just asks *you* to leave town. Some people seem to think you attract trouble."

Tricia didn't know how to refute that statement because . . . maybe it was true. Like the heroes and heroines in the mysteries she loved to read, she couldn't bear to think that anyone would ever get away with murder—or any kind of crime where someone was injured or his or her life was irreparably disrupted. It was undeniable that prosperity had brought a certain amount of crime to the village, but that was hardly her fault. "Stoneham is my home," Tricia said at last. "I'm not going anywhere."

"Good for you," Angelica said, and picked up her blush.

"But you know, learning about these cameras made me wonder if ship's security has looked to see if anyone entered EM's stateroom in the hour or so before I found her. I mean . . . if you've gone and hanged yourself, you can't leave the door open."

"Maybe she put a stop under the door because she *wanted* to be found," Angelica suggested.

"That doesn't explain the abrasion under her chin. I can't think of any other way to get an injury like that except being dragged across a short-napped rug. And I have a feeling the cruise line won't want to investigate any further. They're going to accept the suicide theory just because it's in their best interest to do so."

"Surely whoever is in charge of EM's estate will press for better answers. A woman of her financial worth is sure to be insured to the hilt. Suicide negates a death benefit payment."

"Yes, and they can have an autopsy done, and it may establish that her death was questionable, but that still doesn't mean that the cruise line will cooperate. If they follow standard procedures—the same as every other cruise line in the world—they will probably do everything they can to dispute the beneficiary's claims. As the death happened out on the open sea, there's no real jurisdiction. Nobody really cares. It's kind of like the lawless days in the Old West. Bury her on Boot Hill and who gives a crap?"

Angelica picked up the eyelash curler. "I see your point. But it can't hurt for you to ask that handsome Officer McDonald if they're considering anything other than suicide."

"No, it wouldn't. And I do feel compelled to do so. I didn't like EM

Barstow. She wasn't a nice person. She abused her assistant, she abused me and my employees when she came to Haven't Got a Clue to sign her books, but she doesn't deserve to be killed without somebody giving a damn."

"I agree," Angelica said. She picked up her mascara. "But what if the video record is inconclusive? I mean, all the killer had to do was wear a hoodie pulled down low and you'd be hard-pressed to identify him—or her."

"That's true. But if the video recording shows someone entering EM's stateroom, they have to at least consider the possibility that she was murdered."

"*Considering* is one thing. If what you've said is true—that they don't want to acknowledge the fact that crimes, including murder, can happen—will they be willing to pursue the matter?"

Tricia sighed. "Maybe not. But I feel like I have to at least try to get them to take a more in-depth look into her death. Otherwise, I don't think I could live with myself."

"I admire you for sticking to your principles. That woman was rude and obnoxious, but if nothing else, she had a talent that should be respected. Her faithful readers will be saddened that she will never entertain them again."

"Tomorrow morning I'll try to contact Officer McDonald again to see if I can convince him to look deeper into the matter."

"Aren't you forgetting something?" Angelica asked.

Tricia frowned. "What?"

"Officer McDonald works the night shift. If you try to find him during daylight hours, he's likely to be off duty."

"That's a good point. Then again, it didn't look like he'd just awakened when he came to the restaurant earlier today."

"I have a feeling that if you presented your theory to the officer on day watch that he—or she—might just blow you off. Of course, Officer McDonald might do the same thing, but if he's got an ounce of integrity, he should at least listen to you."

Tricia sure hoped that anyone working a job in security would have a modicum of integrity. The problem was that the person on the job might have all the integrity in the world, but if corporate policy took precedence, then integrity would sink like a lead weight in water. And the Atlantic Ocean was very, very deep.

"I'm ready to go, and you haven't even started getting ready," Angelica scolded.

"I wasn't going to put a lot of effort into it. What for?"

"Because—you might meet somebody. We're both terribly attractive and *awfully* available."

"This is *not* the Love Boat," Tricia countered.

"But who says it couldn't be?" Angelica said with what sounded like glee.

"There's a murderer on board—and it could be anyone. Under the circumstances, I'm definitely not looking for love."

Angelica sighed and looked at herself in the mirror and shook her head sadly. "I guess you're right. But just think, all this beauty is going to waste."

Tricia smiled. "You're full of baloney."

"No, I'm not. I'm starving. They had better have some spectacular finger foods at this cocktail party, especially since it looks like it'll just be you and me for dinner tonight. And maybe Grace and Mr. Everett."

"What has that got to do with food?"

"Nothing. I was just hoping for another family dinner."

"Ginny told me she and Antonio have planned a low-key evening."

Angelica waggled her eyebrows. "Maybe their second child will be conceived on this trip."

"Who says they want to have a second child?"

"Antonio. But Ginny is worried about the timing. She wants another baby, yet still continue to work."

"They're young," Tricia said. "What's the hurry?"

Angelica shrugged. "I thought it might be nice to have a grandson as well as a granddaughter."

"Don't push them."

"Me, push?"

Tricia gave her sister a level glare, but decided not to press the issue. "I'd better go get dressed." She left Angelica's side of the stateroom and headed to her own. She was inspecting her closet when Angelica arrived, carrying a pair of navy shoes and a clutch purse that coordinated with her dress. Of course she immediately spotted the box of chocolates.

"Where did these come from?"

"My secret admirer."

"Do you think they've been tampered with?"

Tricia turned, openmouthed—then caught herself. "Of course not. They're sealed. And they came wrapped in the gift paper from the ship's arcade."

"Okay, okay. I just wanted to make sure."

Tricia turned back to the clothes hanging in the closet.

"Tomorrow we dock in Bermuda," Angelica said as Tricia took out a blazer and inspected it. "Oh, not that, dear," Angelica advised, and Tricia hung it back up. She pawed through the hangers. "We haven't talked about going ashore."

"I wasn't sure I was going to go," Tricia said. "The area by the docks is probably just full of tourist trap shops, and none of the excursions really excited me."

"Oh, but you have to get off the ship," Angelica insisted. "I mean—wasn't that part of the idea of going on this trip? To see a beautiful island and enjoy a little sun."

"I Googled it. The average temperature in Bermuda during January is sixty-six degrees," Tricia said. "That's hardly what I'd call suntanning weather."

"It's a damn sight better than the eleven-degree weather we left back home," Angelica said.

"That's true."

"I know this fabulous restaurant. They have amazing fish dishes. I insist on taking you there."

"Insist?" Tricia asked, taking out a white blouse. She'd wear the gold brocade jacket with it and the dark silk pants. That would certainly fit the elegant casual that was the ship's dress code for the evening.

Angelica pursed her lips. "I'd *really* like to take you there. And we could do a little shopping while we're out. Wouldn't that be fun? We haven't gone shopping together in such a long time."

They'd gone to Boston with Ginny for a weekend of shopping just weeks before. Did Angelica sound just a little desperate?

Tricia shrugged. "As it's a port day, there won't be much to do on board. I guess I could go with you. But when am I ever going to have a chance to catch up on my reading?"

"Maybe we could rent a couple of chairs on the beach. It won't be too hot."

"It won't be all that warm, either," Tricia said.

"We'll just have to see what the weather's like in the morning."

"Okay, you talked me into it."

"Good." Angelica smiled. "We'll certainly have an interesting time. I'll let you get dressed." She left the room.

An interesting time? What had she meant by that?

Tricia shook her head and changed clothes. She'd combed her hair and freshened her face by the time Angelica returned, still carrying her clutch purse. "Ready?"

"As ready as I'll ever be."

They left the stateroom and headed for the lifts.

"Where is this cocktail party—and what's it for?" Tricia asked.

"It's in the Commodore Club, and it's for booksellers and authors to schmooze one-on-one. Except for bumping into them at odd moments or in the ladies' room, we really haven't had a chance to personally speak with many of the authors."

"I know. And what a dud we had for our author at the luncheon this afternoon. I hope we don't run into him at the cocktail party."

"From what I gather, all the authors were invited, but maybe he won't show. He'd probably be better off talking to librarians anyway."

They joined several others who were already waiting for the elevator. "I wish Ginny and Antonio were coming," Tricia said.

Angelica shook her head. "Neither of them are booksellers."

That was true. The Happy Domestic, that Ginny had managed for the past couple of years, did sell books, but it wasn't the store's main focus. And after the cruise she would be moving on to another position within the ever-expanding Nigela Ricita Associates organization.

By the time the lift arrived, there was quite a crowd waiting to get on. Angelica and Tricia squeezed in and rode up to Deck 10. When the car arrived, they filed out and the entire group headed for the party, but almost immediately came to a halt, as there seemed to be a line waiting to get into the club.

"I wonder what's the holdup," Angelica said.

"Maybe they're passing out name tags."

Tricia was right. When they finally got to the door, they saw the woman in charge of the ship's bookstore manning a table and handing out peel-and-stick name tags to the guests; green for the booksellers, and gold for the authors.

"Oh, dear," Angelica groused. "It clashes with my dress."

"You won't be the only one," Tricia assured her.

Once inside, Tricia took in her surroundings. Like most of the ship, the Commodore Club was a bastion of understated elegance. Dark wood clad the semicircular walls, and sumptuous upholstered chairs grouped in intimate clusters, most of which overlooked the bow of the ship, gave its patrons a wonderful view of what lay ahead of the ship. At that time of day, however, the sea was black and the sky above it was quickly turning from a dusky blue to ebony. At the back was a long bar that mimicked the shape of the room, and already had a crowd in front of it. Writers, Tricia knew, sometimes had reputations for being enthusiastic social drinkers.

"Shall we get a cocktail?" Angelica asked.

"We might want to wait until the line thins."

"Will it?" Angelica asked pointedly.

"Maybe not."

Dori Douglas stood alone by one of the windows, her gaze seemingly focused on nothing. Tricia nudged her sister. "There's Dori. I don't think she has any friends on this cruise. Maybe we should go over and see how she's doing."

"Sounds like a plan," Angelica said, and followed Tricia.

"Hello, Dori."

"Oh, hello." The poor woman sounded rattled.

"I haven't had an opportunity to offer my condolences to you on EM's loss," Tricia said, her voice soft.

"Thank you. It was a terrible shock," Dori said sadly.

"I must admit I'm surprised to see you here."

"EM's editor has authorized me to carry on and represent EM for the rest of the cruise."

"Are you sure you're up to that?" Angelica asked.

Dori nodded. "I probably knew her as well as anyone, and as president of her fan club, I can certainly talk knowledgeably about every one of her books."

That was probably true.

"We haven't had an opportunity to see or talk to Cathy since EM's death. How's she doing?" Tricia asked.

"Oh. You know her?"

"We met on our first night at sea."

Dori nodded. "I guess she's okay. She seemed more annoyed than anything else. I guess Emmie was her biggest-selling author."

Yes, Tricia could see where that might affect Cathy's corporate future.

"Not to be indelicate," Angelica said, lowering her voice, "but, what will happen to EM's body when we get back to New York?"

Dori shrugged. "I really don't know."

"Who was EM's next of kin?"

"As far as I know, she has several cousins who live in the Midwest, but from what she said, EM wasn't close to any of her family."

If she treated them like she treated her fans and admirers, that wasn't at all surprising. "Will there be an autopsy?" Tricia inquired.

Dori grimaced. "I suppose so. I mean, her death was unattended."

"Did she have any heirs?"

"I don't know. She didn't confide much in the way of personal information. Despite her paying for me to come along on this trip, we weren't exactly friends, although at one point I thought we might be."

"What changed your mind?" Angelica asked.

Dori shrugged. "A lot of little things."

"The woman was just plain *nasty.*"

Tricia, Angelica, and Dori turned at the comment made by a woman who hadn't bothered to dress for the occasion, and by the bit of a slur in her voice, Tricia suspected she may have hit the cash bar one time too many. Her name tag said Ginger French, and underneath was apparently the store she either owned or worked in, the Tattered Tome.

"Sorry to eavesdrop," Ginger said without sincerity, "but that EM was a bitch. Not many on board were sorry to hear she's dead."

"Well, I am," Dori said defiantly.

"Sure. From what I understand, she was your meal ticket."

"She was not! EM never paid me a cent."

"Then how did you afford to come on this trip?"

An angry blush colored Dori's cheeks.

"I don't believe that's any of your business," Angelica said quietly but firmly.

"Shut up!"

"Now you're just being rude," Tricia said.

Ginger went to take a swig of her drink, but found it empty. She shook the ice in her glass. "I'm going to get another."

"I think you've had enough," Tricia muttered.

Ginger glared at her, but then moved off without further insult.

"This isn't much of a party," Dori said, her voice sounding shaky. "I'm going back to my room. At least there I won't be abused by drunks. If you'll excuse me," she said, and hurried toward the exit.

"Oh, dear," Angelica said, watching her go.

Tricia had hoped to ask Dori about EM's financial state. She'd have to wait for a better opportunity.

Maria Hartley, their tablemate from the authors' luncheon, waved to them from across the room. Angelica smiled and waved back, and Maria charged toward them.

"Oh, I'm so glad to see you ladies again."

"Same here," Angelica said with sincerity. Good old Ange never met a person she didn't like—until they gave her reason not to.

"I wish we'd had more time to talk at the luncheon today before . . . well, everything happened."

"Yes, me, too," Angelica agreed.

"I'd love to hear more about your cookbooks."

"And I'm more than pleased to tell you about them," Angelica began before she launched into what turned out to be a lengthy description.

Since Tricia had proofed both of Angelica's cookbooks, she found her attention wandering during the ensuing discussion. Until she noticed Security Officer McDonald standing at the side of the room, speaking with Mindy Weaver from Milford Travel. Since Angelica was otherwise occupied, she sidled her way through the partygoers and made her way across the club.

"Oh, Tricia," Mindy called.

"Hi, Mindy. Where've you been keeping yourself?"

"I'm available for everyone on the tour, in the grand lobby, every morning from eight until nine," she said rather defensively.

"I didn't mean that," Tricia said with a bit of a laugh. "I meant I haven't seen you mingling."

"I'm mingling now." She turned to McDonald. "This is Officer—"

"McDonald. Yes," Tricia said, "we've met."

The officer nodded. "It's good to see you again, Ms. Miles."

"Are you on duty?" Tricia asked, noting that unlike just about everyone else in the room, McDonald wasn't holding an adult beverage.

"The crew are often asked to attend parties as a goodwill gesture," he said, but Tricia wasn't fooled. No doubt he was staking out the party—or, rather, its guests. Perhaps he didn't believe EM Barstow had died by her own hand, either.

"We were just talking about making port tomorrow."

"I'm looking forward to it, but not the crowds."

"The only crowds are likely to be the other passengers," McDonald said.

"What do you mean?" Tricia asked. "Aren't the winter months typically high cruise season?"

"In the Caribbean," McDonald agreed. "However, Bermuda is a good way north of that."

"I did know to expect cooler temperatures, but . . ." Tricia wasn't sure what else to say in that regard.

"The *Celtic Lady* is the only cruise ship that will dock in Hamilton."

"But that's fabulous! The shops and restaurants will be pulling out all the stops to make us all comfortable and entertained," Mindy explained.

Or were they liable to raise all the prices because they wouldn't have to compete for tourist dollars?

"Are you taking one of the excursions?" Mindy asked Tricia.

She shook her head. "Angelica wants to take me to some fabulous restaurant she knows and maybe have a little retail therapy." Tricia turned to McDonald. "Do you ever get shore leave?"

"Occasionally," he said. "But tomorrow won't be one of those days. I prefer to save my time off for when we're in home port."

"Do you have a sweetheart you visit?" Mindy asked. Like Tricia, had she noticed a lack of a wedding ring on McDonald's left hand?

"My brother, his wife, and their kids are there."

"No wife?" Mindy pressed.

"It's hard to have a family when you're at sea for months at a time."

"I'll bet," Tricia said, and sipped her drink.

"Mindy!"

Tricia and Mindy turned to find a woman beckoning to them—or rather Mindy.

"Oh, dear. It's Leona Ferguson," Mindy muttered under her breath. The queasy lady from the bus trip. "She's been a thorn in my side since she got on the bus back in Stoneham."

Leona approached. "Mindy; thank goodness I ran into you. I have a little problem with my stateroom and I can't get anyone to help me." She eyed McDonald. "Unless you could help me, sailor."

Both Tricia and Mindy started. "Leona, this is Officer McDonald of ship's security," Mindy explained.

"Maybe he can get someone to come down and unstop my sink."

Mindy's smile was forced. "I would be glad to help you in that regard." She reached for Leona's arm and began to steer her away. "If you'll excuse us."

"Oh, dear," Tricia said. "Sorry about that. Does it happen often?"

"More than you'd think," McDonald admitted.

Was this the right time to ask him about EM's death? Would she ever get another opportunity? She decided to go for it. "Have you thought any more about the circumstances of Ms. Barstow's death?"

He nodded. "Again, more than you'd think. Especially after you came up with her keycard."

"I don't suppose there were any fingerprints on it."

"Of course there were; yours."

Tricia frowned. "Just because I found her doesn't mean I killed her. And I haven't visited the ship's kitchens to drop pieces of evidence into cake batter, either."

"It may make you feel better to know that we reviewed our surveillance footage and it confirms your story."

Tricia bristled. Her *story*? Then again, it was good to know that for once she wasn't a suspect in a suspicious death.

"It's beginning to sound like EM's death fits the classic locked-room mystery scenario."

"I beg your pardon?"

"When a crime is committed under impossible circumstances. Think about it. Ms. Barstow was locked in her room. Someone came in, probably strangled her, dragged her across the rug, and then strung her up in her shower to make it look like suicide."

"How did you know she was dragged across the rug?"

"Rug burn under her chin."

McDonald's eyes narrowed.

Noting his expression, Tricia explained. "I saw it when I found her."

"You're very observant."

"That's because I read so many mysteries. I also read police procedurals and psychological suspense."

"Yes, so I heard."

"You heard?" Tricia asked, instantly wary.

"Yes. I spoke with a Chief Baker of the Stoneham Police Department."

Tricia's spine stiffened, a flash of annoyance coursing through her. "And what did *he* have to say?"

"Why are you upset?" McDonald asked.

"I don't like it when someone doubts my word."

"I didn't doubt your word, I just wanted to verify who you are and what you might have to offer in this investigation."

So, he *was* investigating.

"And what did Chief Baker"—Tricia's former lover—"have to say?"

"That I should listen to anything you have to offer. He said you have an uncanny understanding of the criminal mind."

Well, at least Grant had been kind in his recommendation.

"As I said," Tricia said, trying to keep her voice level, "I've read a lot of mysteries and true crime accounts. It's been an education."

"So I understand."

Was he making fun of her?

Tricia decided to take the high road. "I like to think that the thousands of books I've read, both fiction and nonfiction, have given me a different perspective. I've been able to help during the course of several police investigations."

"So Chief Baker said," McDonald said blandly.

And?

Tricia gazed into McDonald's hard dark eyes and had a feeling that nothing she had to add would make a difference to this by-the-book man. She felt like smacking him. Like telling him to go take a hike.

But instead she looked around the room and saw Angelica speaking with one of the mystery authors who'd joined the cruise. Those ladies—and men—were her kindred spirits. McDonald was a stick-to-the-rules security guy and probably had never had a creative idea in his life. Well, more's the pity.

Tricia forced a smile. "I'll let you go back to your work, Officer McDonald."

"My name is Ian," he said, his voice softer than he'd used during the entire conversation.

"It's a nice name," Tricia said.

McDonald shrugged, but then he gave her a sweet smile. Was he playing both roles in the good-cop/bad-cop game, or was there a chance he was attracted to her? A shipboard romance was the last thing Tricia wanted . . . but what if it was the very thing she needed to get over the loss of her ex-husband, Christopher?

Stop! her logical mind told her. McDonald had more or less called her a nosy busybody and then did an abrupt about-face. Was he messing with her mind? She decided to test it.

"Do crew members ever dine with passengers?"

He shook his head. "Just the captain."

"That's too bad. Then you've never dined in the Kells Grill?"

"No, but we have a nice dining area and eat pretty much the same food as the passengers."

"The food's been very good," Tricia admitted. And very fattening. She'd been sorely tempted to overindulge, but had always reined in that desire. She wasn't about to change a lifetime habit just because the pastries, entrées, and other desserts had such beautiful presentations.

"Will you be staying in New York after we dock?" McDonald asked.

Tricia shook her head. "We're being met at the pier by a bus and going straight home to New Hampshire."

"That's too bad."

Did he have shore leave while in New York?

"I've been to Hampshire in England, but never New Hampshire. Is it lovely?"

"Some parts are truly magnificent. They have wonderful skiing in the northern part of the state, but I live on the southern border."

"Is that where you're from?"

Was he flirting with her? What about the ship's ban on passenger-crew fraternization?

"I'm originally from Connecticut," Tricia answered. "I lived in Manhattan for more than a decade, and I loved it. But now I'm happy in a quaint little village doing what I always wanted to do."

"Selling books?"

"Yes," she said.

"Do you ever wish for a more exciting life?"

Tricia had to bite her tongue. How could she describe all the excitement she'd experienced in a tiny village and how she had come in contact with more crime than she had while living in one of the biggest cities in the world?

"The quiet appeals to me."

McDonald nodded. "I'm originally from a small village myself. When my seafaring career is over, I'll probably return there."

"I've only been to Dublin. It was wonderful."

"Maybe one day you'll venture out into the Irish countryside."

"Maybe," Tricia agreed.

"Tricia!"

Tricia looked up to see Angelica barreling toward her.

McDonald nodded. "It was very nice speaking with you, Ms. Miles."

"You, too."

McDonald moved aside to mingle with some of the other book-sellers just as Angelica arrived.

"So, what did Mr. Handsome have to say?" Angelica asked, and waggled her eyebrows provocatively.

"Not much," Tricia said, "But he's at least suspicious about EM's death." She wasn't about to mention that he *may* have—and that was a BIG leap of faith—flirted with her. If he was at sea for months at a time, perhaps he flirted with scores of women. No way was she going to get her hopes up.

"So, are you going to travel to make an appearance at Maria's library?"

Angelica sighed. "No. It's just not cost-effective. But I did agree to send her copies of my books to put on her shelves—but *only* if she promised to actually *put* them there, and not stick them in a Friends of the Library sale for a buck each—if that."

"Yes. I've heard that same lament from mystery authors way too many times," Tricia agreed.

"There are far too many people looking for freebies and not realizing that authors actually have to make a living off their writing. I'm lucky. I have other sources of income. But thousands of authors don't have that luxury," Angelica said emphatically.

"Maybe the readers on this trip will realize that by the end of the voyage."

"We can only hope," Angelica said. She looked back toward the bar. "Do you want to try to enter the line here, or go find another place to have a drink?"

"I think I'm maxed out in this locale."

"What would you want to do for dinner?"

Tricia frowned. "I'm not in the mood for fancy. I think I'd just as soon go to the Lido Restaurant and find a bunch of cooked veggies."

"Oh, that sounds so god-awful boring," Angelica said with a frown.

"Maybe for you, but I actually enjoy eating vegetables. They're full of nutrients."

"Yes, but humans need to balance veggies with protein, too."

"I try to do that," Tricia insisted.

"Not hard enough," Angelica muttered.

"Please don't press me on this," Tricia said.

"I'm sorry. I know we disagree on food. We always have. But I'm a cookbook author. I want everyone to enjoy the food they eat, and I get the feeling you don't."

"Of course I enjoy food. It's what gives us all life. And you are the best cook I've ever met. Well, you and Grandma Miles."

"She taught me everything I know," Angelica said, and gave a mirthless laugh. "If the Lido is where you'd prefer to go tonight, then that's where we'll go."

"It's not that I don't like the Kells Grill," Tricia said, "but I just don't feel like conforming to their regimented menu."

"It *is* a bit froufrou," Angelica admitted. "We're not used to that kind of dining. We're just simple folk."

"Now *you're* teasing me," Tricia said, frowning.

Angelica smiled. "Just a little. But what about Grace and Mr. Everett?"

"They know how to order from a menu," Tricia said. "If we don't show up, I'm sure they will somehow carry on."

"Yes. I'm sure you're right. And maybe tomorrow we could all assemble at the Lido Restaurant—and that way Antonio and Ginny could bring Sofia, as well. It would be nice to have the entire family together."

"I'm glad you feel that way."

Angelica looked like she might want to pontificate on some other subject but seemed to be biting her tongue. Tricia wasn't about to ask why.

"So, are you ready to leave the party?" Angelica asked.

"Yes." Tricia had an inkling of what Dori must have felt when she'd fled the affair. Suddenly her lack of sleep the night before seemed to have caught up with her. "On second thought, could we go back to our suite, order sandwiches from room service, and just stay in tonight?"

Angelica's expression wasn't enthusiastic, but she nodded. "Whatever you want, dear Tricia."

"Thank you."

"I suppose we could always eat your new box of chocolates, too."

Tricia turned a menacing glare at her sister.

"Just joking—just joking!"

The truth was, Tricia was more than ready for a drink, a light dinner, and a night of dreamless sleep—sans chocolate. She was peopled out, which didn't happen often, especially when the people were as focused on reading and books as she was. And she had much to think about.

Far too much.

FOURTEEN

At some point during the early hours, the ship had docked in Bermuda. The cessation of movement and engine noise was a welcome break, and Tricia got up from her bed and looked out the window to see the edge of the sun poking over the horizon. Sunshine and palm trees in January were sure to make this former Connecticut gal a happy camper.

Angelica hadn't made an appearance by the time Tricia left the stateroom for her brisk morning walk. She'd caught up on rest and was eager to start the day with a fresh perspective—and no morbid thoughts about EM Barstow's death—or that of a possible stalker.

The *Celtic Lady* was the only big boat in the harbor. Officer Mc-Donald's revelation that cruise ships rarely stopped in Bermuda during the winter months explained the more-than-reasonable fare they'd all paid for the trip.

The morning air wasn't what you could call balmy—probably in the midfifties—but the sun on her back was delightful, as would be the warmer temps later in the day. While she hadn't been keen to go ashore the day before, seeing the harbor and the colorful scooters zooming along the road beyond the dock made Tricia feel hopeful. Despite her vow to keep EM's death, and who might be slipping her gifts, from her thoughts, they kept resurfacing. She needed a distraction, and a trip ashore might just do the trick. She was even looking forward to shopping with Angelica. Perhaps there was a bookshop that carried British mysteries. Now that was something Tricia could get excited about.

As she power walked along the deck, Tricia wondered if Officer McDonald would think a visit to a bookshop would be exciting. She'd been about to ask him what he read when Angelica had interrupted the night before. Oh, well. There was no other opportunity to get to know the man better, and she'd never see him again after the ship docked. It was best to put him out of her thoughts and concentrate on other matters. Of course her new favorite subject was the renovation of her home. Maybe she'd find some British decorating magazines ashore. Once the ship docked in New York, she would download some decorating magazines to her e-reader. And of course, she could start checking out furniture and bed and bath ideas on Pinterest. It *could* be a lot of fun, although she wasn't looking forward to her and Miss Marple's lives being disrupted during the demolition and reconstruction phase of the project.

Tricia finished another circuit around the deck and stopped when she saw a column of passengers streaming off the ship. At the head of the line was Dori Douglas. She didn't appear to be with anyone and strode purposefully toward the road and the harbor beyond. Had she ever been to Hamilton before? Was she meeting a friend?

Tricia looked farther down and saw a smaller gangplank where members of the crew were disembarking. They looked eager for a little time off the clock. Honestly, the hours those stewards were expected to work seemed draconian.

With her exercise now finished, Tricia went back inside the ship and trundled down the stairs to her deck. When she returned to the stateroom, she found a breakfast cart once again waiting for her.

"There you are," Angelica called as she entered the lounge. "Did you enjoy your walk?"

"Yes. You can't see the harbor from this side of the ship, but you can from starboard."

"You sound pleased."

"Yes, I wasn't really looking forward to going ashore, but now I'm eager. Some passengers and crew have already left the ship. When can we go?"

"Oh," Angelica said, sounding subdued.

"Did you have something else to do this morning?"

"No." Angelica's voice was higher than normal, and though she smiled, there was a tightness around her lips.

"Is everything okay, Ange?"

"Perfect."

Tricia reached for her usual cup of fat-free yogurt and a spoon, then took her usual seat on the love seat opposite Angelica. "Have you thought about having breakfast at the Kells Grill or maybe the Lido Restaurant?"

"You don't like eating breakfast with me here in the room?" Angelica asked, sounding hurt.

"Not at all. It's just . . . I don't know. I thought it might be fun to do something different."

"Where would you like to have breakfast tomorrow?"

Tricia shook her head. "I guess it doesn't matter. I only ever eat yogurt anyway."

"Yes," Angelica said, frowning, "you do."

"You haven't answered my question. What time do you want to go ashore?"

"That depends. Do you want to go shopping first?"

"I promised Pixie I'd bring her back a souvenir of Bermuda."

"Since she only wears vintage clothes, you can't bring back a T-shirt."

"I was thinking more along the lines of jewelry."

"Have you looked over the duty-free rules for U.S. citizens? They aren't very generous. Fifty dollars if you're only here a day. After two days, it's more, but you have to fill in forms, which doesn't really matter since we leave for New York tonight anyway."

"Then I won't buy at a duty-free shop."

Angelica nodded. "Makes sense. But you'll still have to declare it."

Tricia shrugged. "I might not find anything—unless we find a shop that sells estate jewelry."

"We'll look."

"What will you bring back to Frannie?"

"Probably a bottle of rum. She'd like that." Angelica sipped her coffee. "Maybe we should go ashore early after all."

"Are Ginny and Antonio joining us?"

"Um, no," Angelica said a little too quickly, and again her voice was a little higher than normal. What was she hiding?

"Why not?"

"They want a little alone time."

"They had some last night."

"They want more, and who can blame them? They both work so hard. If it's a nice day, they'll take Sofia to the beach. She's never been before."

No, at five months old there were a lot of things Sofia hadn't done.

Tricia scraped the last of her yogurt out of the container, ate it, then returned the container and spoon to the cart. She stood. "I'm going to shower and change so I can be ready whenever you are."

"I'd better get ready, too. We're going to have fun—just the two of us."

Tricia studied her sister's face. Fun? Not if the worried look in Angelica's eyes meant anything.

Just what did she have planned?

The day was bright, but the breeze was cool, and Tricia was glad she'd donned one of her sweater sets—this one pale blue. It went so well with the color of the sky. Their keycards were scanned as they left the ship amid another small group of passengers at a little after eleven. They had no idea where they were going, but just followed the others along the concrete pier.

"We have to take a ferry to Hamilton," Angelica said.

"Oh? I thought we were just going to walk around the wharf. There's supposed to be a nice mall. And there's the National Museum of Bermuda."

"Oh, you don't want to go to any stuffy old museum," Angelica chided.

"Yes, I do."

"No, no. I've got a surprise for you," Angelica said.

"Oh?" Tricia asked. Here it came. Surprises weren't always welcome, and the timbre of Angelica's voice let Tricia know that whatever was about to happen wasn't necessarily going to be good.

"I've made arrangements for us to have lunch at the famous Hamilton Contessa Hotel."

"What for? Except for breakfast, all our meals on the boat are at one restaurant or another. Or will we be able to sample some of the local cuisine there?" Tricia asked hopefully.

"Um . . . maybe—maybe not," Angelica said, giving Tricia no other explanation. "Oh, look, there's the ferry boat. Let's hurry. We don't want to miss it and have to wait for the next one."

Tricia didn't want to take *any* ferry, but she dutifully followed Angelica.

They did just make it aboard, for no sooner had they got on when the crew cast off and the boat started chugging toward Hamilton.

It was a pleasant twenty-minute ride, especially since Angelica struck up a conversation with one of the locals, who gave them some good tips for places to shop. And they found that the hotel where Angelica had made reservations for lunch was within walking distance of the pier—if you didn't mind a bit of a hike.

"I don't mind. In fact, I miss walking Sarge. Oh, hell, I miss *Sarge!*" Tricia said. "Did you bring your iPad? Maybe they'll have WiFi at the hotel and we can FaceTime Pixie and Frannie to see how Sarge and Miss Marple are doing."

"I didn't think to bring it," Angelica admitted. "And anyway, I think we have some free computer time on the ship. We can do that later today."

"Whatever," Tricia said, and then winced. She hated that expression.

They bid their new friend good-bye as the ferry landed, and they, and everyone else, disembarked.

It was such a pleasant day that Tricia didn't at all mind the walk to the big pink hotel and resort, which seemed to loom up at them as they approached, and for once Angelica had worn sensible walking shoes, so they made it in good time.

They approached the main building, and a doorman welcomed them with a toothy smile. "Welcome to the Contessa, ladies. Can I help direct you somewhere?"

"We're here for lunch."

"Ah, through the lobby and to your left." He opened the door for them.

"Thank you."

Angelica darted inside, and Tricia followed. The bright, elegant lobby was filled with columns, richly upholstered furniture, crystal chandeliers, and a sumptuous carpet. The reception desk anchored the right edge of the room, and large glass doors on the opposite side were opened, leading to the hotel's restaurant. A podium stood outside, with a maître d' in a white tux, holding an armful of large menus.

"This is nice," Tricia said.

"May I seat you ladies for lunch?"

"We're meeting someone," Angelica said.

"We are?" Tricia asked, confused.

Angelica craned her neck to look into the restaurant. "Oh, I see them. We'll just go ahead and join them," she said.

"As you wish," the maître d' said with a nod.

"Who do you know in Bermuda?" Tricia asked.

"Just a couple who happen to be visiting the same time we are."

Tricia assumed it was one of Nigela Ricita's business contacts and followed Angelica. However, her stomach lurched when she recognized the man and woman seated at the table for four that overlooked the beautiful harbor. Her parents: John and Sheila Miles.

"Mother, Daddy!" Angelica cried, and hurried toward them. They turned at the sound of her voice. Tricia felt heat rise up her neck, and her cheeks began to burn. She couldn't seem to make her feet move and stood there, staring.

It had been nearly five years since Tricia had seen her parents. Her father looked tanned and relaxed. Their retirement years in Rio had apparently been good for him. He mother looked well, but her skin was pale. She avoided the sun at all costs. Being in the sun caused wrinkles, and she had very few, but then she'd had more than one face-lift and some other work done over the years and looked more than a decade younger than her true age. She had not risen from her seat, though Tricia's father had stood to give Angelica a hug.

"It's so good to see you both," Angelica said, and turned, bending down to give their mother a kiss on her offered cheek.

Dumbstruck, Tricia still just stood there. It seemed like her feet had taken root.

"Tricia," Angelica called. "Come and say hello to Mother and Daddy."

Tricia shook herself and moved forward on unsteady feet. John strode forward to meet her halfway. "There you are, princess," he said, and gave her a hug. Tricia returned the embrace, albeit without much enthusiasm. The shock of seeing her parents had rattled her so much that she found it hard to speak. "Hello, Daddy."

John stood back. "Come and say hello to your mother." He took her by the arm and led her to the table.

Tricia stood there for a long moment, just staring at her mother, who just stared right back. "You're looking well," Tricia managed.

"I *am* well," Sheila answered, her chin jutting forward in what Tricia could only think of as a defiant manner.

Did Sheila know that Angelica had finally confided the Miles family secret that had kept Tricia and her mother from having a loving relationship? Tricia didn't know, and now was not the time to ask. Angelica had said her mother would never speak about it, and Tricia believed her.

"Angelica, darling. Come sit by me," Sheila said, indicating the chair next to her.

Angelica braved a smile for Tricia and sat down. She patted the back of the empty chair next to her. "Come sit."

Tricia did so, and her father pushed in her chair before he sat back down. It took all Tricia's willpower not to kick Angelica under the table.

A glass of Scotch, neat, sat in front of John's place, but it looked like their mother was drinking only water. Suddenly Tricia craved a double martini and hoped Angelica would order for them. She needed a good belt of something to help her get over the shock of seeing her parents.

"Isn't it a small world?" Angelica asked, her voice still higher than normal.

"It certainly is," Tricia agreed grimly.

"I'm so happy you girls could join us for lunch, but unhappy your ship takes off this evening. It hardly gives us time to do more than chat," John said. He turned to Tricia, his expression darkening. "We were very sorry to hear about Christopher."

So sorry they couldn't call, e-mail, or send a card during the past six months?

"It was a terrible shock," Tricia agreed.

"We've never had a murder in the family before this," Sheila said coolly. "It's all so . . ." She wrinkled her nose. "Tawdry. But then you *were* divorced, so . . ." She let the sentence hang.

Again Tricia's cheeks burned. Thankfully, a waiter showed up. "May I get you ladies something other than water to drink?"

"I'll have a dry Beefeater martini, up, with olives," Angelica said hurriedly.

"The same please," Tricia said, somehow managing a smile.

"I'll have another," their father said, indicating his Scotch.

"Ma'am?" the waiter asked Sheila politely.

Sheila smiled sweetly. "I don't feel the need to drown *my* sorrows." The waiter nodded and turned away.

"Martinis? My, you girls have certainly grown up," John said.

"We're both fabulously successful businesswomen," Angelica said.

"Do tell," their mother said with a hint of sarcasm.

"I have my darling little cookbook store, a funky retro café, and part interest in a bed-and-breakfast." Tricia waited for her to expand the list, including her Nigela Ricita holdings, but Angelica refrained from mentioning anything else. "Since being elected president of our local Chamber of Commerce, I've had to put my writing career on hold, but it's giving me lots of time to think about what direction I want my literary career to take."

"Hopefully away from cookery," Sheila muttered.

"Everybody's got to eat," Angelica said, her tone light.

"I'm very proud of you," John said, then picked up his glass and sipped his Scotch.

"Tricia's fabulously successful with her wonderful mystery bookstore, too."

Sheila sighed loudly. "Mysteries are just so . . . common. Besides, I thought you said the place burned to the ground."

"Oh, I'm sure I told you that the store had reopened just in time for the Christmas rush," Angelica said, and Tricia didn't doubt her. "It's even prettier than it was before. And Tricia has two of the sweetest employees, whom we count among our dearest friends."

"Oh, no! I hope you don't socialize with the help," Sheila said, frowning.

"As a matter of fact, one of them joined us on the voyage," Tricia said.

Sheila's frown deepened.

"Didn't you say that stepson of yours joined you on the trip?" John asked Angelica. "We haven't seen him since he was just a boy. Did he ever learn to speak English?"

Angelica's smile was tight. "Of course he did; and he speaks fluent French, as well. Antonio works for a big developer and manages the beautiful old inn in Stoneham, among other projects. I'm sorry he couldn't be here today, but his darling wife was feeling a little queasy. I'm sure after a day in port she'll find her sea legs and be just fine."

Tricia studied her sister's face. Oh, Angelica lied beautifully. No doubt she had no intention of offering Antonio, Ginny, and baby Sofia up as objects of their mother's disdain or ridicule. Too bad she hadn't thought to include Tricia in that plan.

Luckily, the waiter arrived with the drinks, setting them on white cocktail napkins. "Are you ready to order?"

"Thank you, but we could use a few minutes. We have oodles to talk about," Angelica said, her voice tight.

The waiter nodded and turned away.

Oodles to talk about? Maybe *she* did. . . .

"Well, what shall we drink to?" John asked, picking up his glass.

"How about family?" Angelica suggested.

"Excellent," John agreed, and the three of them clicked glasses. Sheila sat back in her chair.

Tricia noticed that Angelica took as big a hit of that fine drink as she did.

The four of them looked at each other. Angelica smiled. John smiled. Tricia smiled. Sheila didn't. The quiet dragged on. Tricia found her gaze traveling out to one of the ferries chugging its way across the harbor.

The quiet dragged on.

"So, what made you decide to visit Bermuda? It's got to be cooler than Rio this time of year," Tricia said. Innocuous conversation seemed the best approach.

"When Angelica said you'd be coming down to our part of the world, we decided it would be a wonderful opportunity to see our girls," John said.

We? Tricia wondered.

"Well, *you* did, dear," Sheila said. "I find it quite cold here."

Angelica's laugh seemed forced. "Nothing like the temps back home in Stoneham."

"If you're both so wildly successful, why can't you leave your businesses in the hands of your lackeys and winter in warmer climes?" Sheila asked.

"My employees are *not* lackeys," Tricia said firmly.

"Nor are mine," Angelica said, sounding more than a little hurt.

"Then if they're so capable, you should be able to trust them to run your businesses while you enjoy the fruits of your labors."

"I enjoy working," Tricia said. "I always have."

"Is that true for you, too, Angelica?" Sheila asked, an edge of disappointment creeping into her voice.

Tricia turned to look at her sister. For years she'd believed that Angelica's only business experience had been as a sales clerk in a failed boutique. Obviously their mother had no idea of what Angelica could do or had accomplished.

"Yes," Angelica said. "And I'm happy. In fact, I'm happier than I've ever been."

"And what about your social life? Or does being so wrapped up in your work mean you have no time—and maybe won't be attractive—to men who could make your life so much easier?"

Tricia's mouth dropped. What century was her mother living in?

Angelica managed a lopsided smile. "Gosh, I'm hungry." She picked up her menu. Tricia did likewise. "What looks good to you, Mother?" she asked.

Sheila tossed her head. "I'm having the fresh greens with balsamic vinaigrette."

"Tricia's keen to try some of the local cuisine, as am I," Angelica said, perusing the menu. Unfortunately, there didn't seem to be anything with a local flair available to them.

"I want a steak," John said. "How about you, Angelica?"

"Well, the mixed grill sounds good."

"Tricia?" John asked.

Tricia's gaze slipped down to the entrées. Nothing really appealed to her but she had to eat something. "The duck with citrus sauce over rice sounds good."

"Duck is extremely fatty, and rice is incredibly carb heavy. Are you sure you want to order that?" Sheila asked, eyeing Tricia critically. "It looks as though you've packed on a few pounds since we last saw you,"

That wasn't exactly true. Tricia had gained a total of five pounds in the last year, which she attributed to the stress of her store burning and Christopher's death. And, as her doctor had also affirmed—she was at a time in life when it wasn't as easy to shed pounds as it might have been a decade earlier. She still wore the same-sized clothes and they weren't exactly tight, either.

Tricia glanced in her sister's direction. Angelica was an inch or two shorter than Tricia and weighed a good twenty pounds more, and yet their mother deigned to criticize *her* for her menu choice?

"Oh, Mother, don't be silly. A good stiff wind would blow Tricia away," Angelica admonished, and then her eyes darted to Tricia, her forehead furrowing in distress.

"Would you prefer I have nothing?" Tricia asked her mother. It was an effort to keep her voice level.

"Do what you want, dear," Sheila said, her tone simpering, and then she shrugged.

Tricia closed her menu. "I believe I'll pass on lunch," she said, taking another sip of her martini. Her gaze drifted to Angelica, who'd abandoned distress and had apparently moved on to anger.

"Me, too," Angelica said. She closed her menu as well, setting it back on the table.

"Girls, girls," their father chided, "don't be like that."

"Like what?" Angelica asked, her voice hardening.

"Ange, please don't," Tricia muttered.

"Trish," Angelica warned.

Tricia knew that tone. "Please don't," she tried again. "It's not worth it."

"Dear, dear sister. You couldn't be more wrong."

Tricia watched as Angelica seemed to inflate before her, her expression growing hard. "Mother, I have cut you a lot of slack over the years, but no more."

"Why, Angelica, whatever do you mean?" Sheila asked, her tone innocent.

"I've stood by for far too long allowing you to disparage my sister, and I won't stand for it any longer."

"Angelica?" their father asked, sounding confused.

"Patrick died of SIDS," Angelica stated.

The mention of their long-ago deceased brother caused Sheila's eyes to widen in sudden fury and her cheeks to redden.

"You've always blamed Tricia for Patrick's death, but the truth is he probably died because he was sleeping on his tummy. Most moms put their babies to sleep on their tummies back then and you probably did, too."

"That's what I was *told* to do. Are you saying *I* caused his death?" Sheila asked sharply.

"No. And neither did Tricia. But because she lived and Patrick didn't, you've punished her for decades. It's got to stop."

"Ange!" Tricia protested.

Sheila's expression hardened.

"Tricia would never tell you how much your poor treatment of her has hurt, but I'm telling you now."

"Ange, please!" Tricia pleaded.

"Yes. Please spare us," Sheila said diffidently.

Angelica turned to their father. "Daddy, how could you have let this go on for so long?"

The poor man shrugged. "I have to live with her," he said apologetically.

Angelica pushed back her chair and stood. "Trish, let's go. Maybe it's not too late for us to have lunch with our *real* family back on the ship."

Never had Tricia felt such affection for her sister. She stood. "It was lovely to see you again, Daddy." Tricia bent down to brush a kiss against his cheek.

"Don't go," he implored. He looked up at Tricia. "I'm sorry, princess. Your mother's tart words seem to bother you. I thought . . ." But whatever he thought, he said no more.

Tricia smiled. "Good-bye, Daddy. I love you." She turned to her mother. "I love you, too." But then she turned and headed for the lobby, wondering if she would ever see her parents again.

Tricia didn't wait for Angelica to follow and left the opulent lobby for the sunny expanse of sidewalk outside the hotel. She headed back toward Front Street with her head held high, but at an easy pace, not sure what to think of the altercation at the restaurant. She hadn't wanted Angelica to say anything about her relationship with their mother, though perhaps in the long run clearing the air was the best thing that could have happened. That her mother wouldn't apologize hadn't been a surprise, but for some reason Tricia felt a sense of relief—of closure.

She walked half a mile or so until she saw a bench in a small patch of green by the side of the road. She sat down and looked at her surroundings, so different than Main Street back in Stoneham. It was then that a wave of homesickness hit. Tricia dug into her purse and plucked out her phone, punching in the number she knew by rote. It rang twice.

"Haven't Got a Clue. This is Pixie. How can I help you?"

"I wanna come home," Tricia practically wailed.

"Tricia, is that you?"

"It's me. I miss you and Miss Marple something terrible," she admitted, afraid she might begin to cry.

"Oh, and we miss you, too. But you've got nothing to worry about—except maybe for paying the rent next month. Business has been practically nonexistent. Did you know we got nearly a foot of snow overnight?"

"No, I didn't."

"And another six inches yesterday. Gosh, I envy you. You sure are lucky to be someplace warm and sunny."

Again Tricia took in her surroundings. Palm fronds swayed, while all around beautiful flowers bloomed, and the breeze—while not sultry—was pleasant.

"How is Miss Marple?"

"She's right behind me on her perch. Do you want to say hello?"

"Yes, please."

"Go ahead," came Pixie's muffled voice.

"Miss Marple. It's me, your mom. I love you."

Tricia felt her eyes fill with tears as she heard "*Yow!*" issue from the tiny speaker in her phone.

"Good girl," Pixie told the cat, then came back on the phone. "Are you having a good time on the cruise?"

"Well, not really."

"Uh-oh. You didn't find anyone dead, did you?"

"Well, kind of."

"Oh, no!"

"Yeah. EM Barstow."

"That was *your* ship?" Pixie asked, sounding incredulous.

"I'm afraid so."

"Aw, gee. You have the rottenest luck."

"Don't I just?" Tricia agreed.

"Everybody else is safe, though, huh? Angelica, Mr. E and Grace, and Ginny and Antonio and Sofia, right?"

"Yes, they're all safe."

"I'm glad of that."

"How are Miss Marple and Sarge making out sharing the apartment at night?"

"Well, let's just say your cat's glad Sarge doesn't jump on shelves or the furniture. But, he's really been no trouble. Although I think he likes going back to the Cookery for the day. Frannie says he watches the door, just hoping Angelica will walk through it."

"Well, luckily we'll be home in another three days."

"I'll bet that's an eternity in dog time."

It felt like an eternity in people time, too.

"Your phone company is going to slam you with charges for this call," Pixie warned.

"I don't care. I just wanted to connect with you and Miss Marple and make sure everything at the store is fine."

"We've got grub in the kitchen and piles and piles of books to be read. What else could we want?"

Yes, what else?

"Even if we get snowed in, Miss M and I will be fine, so don't you worry."

Tricia heard the tinkle of a bell in the background.

"Oh my God—it's actually a customer!" Pixie practically squealed. "Gotta go. See you on Saturday."

"Okay, bye." Tricia hit the off icon and replaced the phone in her purse. Well, that was nice. Sort of. Now what could she do?

The sun really was much stronger in Bermuda than it was back in Stoneham, and Tricia pulled a pair of sunglasses from the case in her purse. She still had a long walk to return to the road that led back to the ferry landing, so she got up and headed back the way she and Angelica had come just an hour before. But instead of taking the turn, she kept walking until she came upon a more commercial area. She paused in front of a jewelry shop and stared at the contents on offer.

An assortment of pretty rings in a variety of stones sparkled under the carefully placed spotlights. It was then she became aware that her thumb was absently twisting the diamond engagement ring on her left hand. Christopher's dying wish was that she wear it once again, and she had honored it. But he was gone forever, and as she had never anticipated a reconciliation between them, it was time again to take the ring off. She admired an opal setting and, on impulse, decided to see if they had something similar in her size.

Ducking into the shop, Tricia tried a duplicate of the ring in the front window, as well as several others, and then made her purchase. She also bought a sturdy chain, hung the diamond ring from it, and donned it, tucking it inside her blouse. She also saw a lovely jeweled starfish pin that she thought Pixie might like to wear, and bought it, too.

As she exited the store, she saw a dispirited Angelica walking toward her, and she paused. "That took a while," she said in passing.

Angelica sighed. "Too long. I had a feeling you wouldn't go straight back to the ship. I'm so glad I caught up with you."

"Are the three of you still speaking?" Tricia asked.

"Barely. I don't want to share with you what else Mother had to say." Angelica's lips trembled, and she looked like she was about to succumb to tears. "I'm sorry I didn't tell you about Mother and Daddy being here. As you can tell, Mother didn't want to come. Daddy insisted, although they're staying here for a week. Daddy has professional contacts here, and he thought it might be nice to combine business with pleasure."

Tricia certainly hadn't been pleased by the unexpected meeting.

"Are you awfully, terribly angry with me?"

Tricia sighed. "I should be, but I'm not. Truly. I can't blame you for wanting to promote a little family harmony. Unfortunately, it just wasn't going to happen. And it sounds to me as though you may have burned some bridges."

"You mean compromised our potential inheritances?"

"Yes."

Angelica shook her head and smiled. "Darling, Tricia, you and I don't need our parents' money. It would be wonderful if they left it to a truly needy charity."

"Such as?"

"I would wish for it to go to local pet charities, or for the care of sick people with no resources. Or food pantries. Or literacy."

"But you don't think they will?"

Angelica shook her head. "No. It's possible they'll cut us out completely and leave all their assets to the colleges they went to so that the sports programs can thrive and the schools and coaches can get even richer. I feel so sorry for those young athletes who play their hearts out, receive nothing, and aren't good enough to go on to the NFL or NBA."

Tricia shook her head. "I've always felt the same way."

"*We* will leave a better legacy. We'll leave our assets to places that truly need them. And a little to Antonio, Ginny, and Sofia, too," she added. Angelica glanced down at the new ring on Tricia's finger. "Looks like you were indulging in a little retail therapy."

"It's cheaper than consulting a shrink."

"That all depends on how much you bought. Opals are supposed to be unlucky, you know."

"What does it matter? I've already been branded a jinx. I don't think the ring can bring me any more bad luck than I've already had."

"Where's Christopher's ring?"

Tricia fingered the chain around her neck.

"That's a good idea," Angelica said. She wound her arm around Tricia's and they began to walk toward the road that would take them back to the ferry landing once again.

"Antonio, Ginny, and Grace and Mr. E have probably already eaten lunch. I don't know if any of the restaurants on the boat will even still be serving by the time we get back."

"Afternoon tea is right around the corner," Tricia suggested.

"Ooh! You're right. We haven't had an opportunity to indulge. And I think today is the champagne tea. That could be fun."

"I could use a little fun," Tricia admitted.

Angelica's smile was full of sisterly affection. "Then champagne tea, here we come."

FIFTEEN

During the ferry ride back to the wharf, Tricia told Angelica about her call to Pixie.

"I'm glad Sarge and Miss Marple aren't battling it out, but I will be glad to see my little man in three days. After this afternoon, I must admit I'm feeling a little combat weary."

Tricia didn't comment.

The gangplank was filled with other passengers returning from shore, and Tricia wondered if they'd make it through the gauntlet in time for afternoon tea. Still, they headed back to their suite to change into more formal attire.

Sebastian had once again done his magic, transforming the suite to its glory, and once again there was another gift waiting for Tricia. This time, it was flowers; her favorite calla lilies. The card said, *For someone special*.

"Well, somebody sure knows what you like," Angelica said. "This has to mean that whoever is sending you gifts knows you pretty intimately."

Tricia wasn't sure she liked that descriptor. She'd had intimate relations with two men during her time in Stoneham: Russ Smith, who was now happily married to someone else, and Chief Grant Baker, who had been out of her dating picture for quite some time. Still, how many of the villagers had seen the scores of lilies delivered to her shop on her birthday three years before? While she dressed for tea, Tricia did a mental head count of the local men who had signed up for the Authors at Sea cruise. The most eligible was Chauncey Porter, who couldn't stand the sight of her. He wasn't exactly her type, though, either.

For someone special. Tricia had felt anything but special during the visit with her parents, but that hadn't been her fault, and she swallowed down a pang of regret that her mother would never forgive her for something she had no part in causing.

For someone special.

Was it possible her father had had the flowers delivered in the hours since they'd parted at the hotel? Maybe, but it didn't seem likely. Did he even know calla lilies were her favorite blooms?

Tricia tried to put such thoughts out of her mind and looked at herself in the full-length mirror on the outside of her closet, admiring the crisp white blouse and long black skirt. She grabbed a black clutch, placed her keycard in it, and met Angelica in the lounge. She looked stunning in a floral suit with heels that had hoisted her to an inch taller than Tricia.

"I must confess, I'm really looking forward to this," Angelica said as they left the stateroom and headed for the lift.

A cellist sat on a small stage, playing what sounded like a piece of classical music, when Tricia and Angelica entered the Crystal Ballroom. All the little round tables were covered with lovely white linen, while the enormous crystal chandelier glowed overhead and the luxurious carpet surrounding the wooden dance floor softened their steps.

They sat at one of the empty tables and turned their attention to the cellist.

"Isn't this lovely?" Angelica asked, looking around the elegantly appointed room.

"I wish we'd done this before today," Tricia said in agreement.

They hadn't done much talking on the ferry ride back to the wharf where the *Celtic Lady* had been berthed, but Tricia had never felt closer to her sister than she had during that brief journey. Happily, that feeling had stayed with her upon their return to the ship.

They watched in silence for several minutes as the white tux–clad waiters methodically set the tables with gold-rimmed china and beautiful cutlery, and the rest of the room filled with their fellow travelers.

"I meant to mention before now that when I was walking down Front Street, I saw Dori Douglas coming out of an office supply store," Angelica said.

"Really?" Tricia asked. "I wonder what she needed there? Surely not a ream of paper. Did she have a bag?"

"She seemed to be carrying several, but I don't know what she might have purchased there. Perhaps she was just stopping at any shop she came to."

"I suppose she could have been souvenir shopping; but wouldn't she have found more items like that on the wharf near the ship?"

"You'd think," Angelica said.

One of the waiters paused at their table, setting out linen napkins and silverware. Another stood behind him with plates, cups, saucers, and champagne flutes. "Thank you," Angelica said, giving them both a smile.

Another waiter appeared with a sugar bowl, creamer, ramekins filled with sweet butter and clotted cream, and two small jars of jam.

"Everything is just so lovely," Angelica gushed.

"Very nice," Tricia agreed.

Another waiter appeared with a tray heaped with an assortment of finger sandwiches and petite scones.

"Madam?" he asked Angelica.

"Oh, they all look so lovely. I'll have one of each," she said, and watched as the waiter plucked the sandwiches and a scone with a set of silver tongs.

"And you?" he asked Tricia.

"I'll have one of the cucumber sandwiches and one of the salmon."

"That's all?" Angelica asked, taking her napkin, shaking out the folds, and placing it on her lap.

Tricia looked up at the waiter. "That's all, thank you."

The waiter nodded and turned away, only to be followed by another with a large white teapot rimmed with green and gold. "Tea?"

"Yes, thank you," Tricia said, letting him pour.

"I'll have a cup, too," Angelica said.

The waiter poured another cup before turning away.

"Why did you only get two tiny sandwiches?" Angelica asked.

"I'm pretty sure they're going to have little cakes. I wanted to save room for one."

"*Little* is the word. I've seen them up at the Lido Restaurant."

"When did you go to the Lido for tea?" Tricia asked.

"On more than one occasion to get a coffee fix, and simply had to check out what else they had on offer. After all, I *am* a restaurateur."

Tricia picked up the delicate triangular salmon sandwich and took a bite. It was wonderful, but was already half gone.

"Do you mind if I bring up a potentially painful subject?" Angelica asked at last.

Tricia turned to face her. "I thought we agreed not to talk about Mother."

"Well, this concerns her peripherally. I'm talking about your eating habits."

"My what?" Tricia asked, confused.

"Until today, I'd never noticed the way Mother constantly criticized every morsel you ever put in your mouth."

"You're exaggerating," Tricia said with a shake of her head.

"No, I'm not. Have you ever enjoyed a meal in your entire life?"

Tricia scowled. "Of course I have."

"You eat yogurt for breakfast; back home you eat a tuna plate almost every day for lunch; and when you come to my house for dinner, your portions are minuscule."

"You know how hard I try to maintain my weight."

"A little *too* hard. Why?"

"Because I don't need to eat any more."

"Don't *need*—or since childhood have been bullied not to *have* more? And not to *enjoy* what you have?"

Tricia thought about her sister's questions. There had always been a little voice in the back of her head telling her what she should and shouldn't eat. Until that moment, she hadn't recognized that voice as being her mother's. And suddenly she thought of her fifth birthday party.

Angelica had been ten and had been enlisted to help—something she'd been mortified to do. The little girl guests—dressed in their party best—had all sat around the big dining room table, laughing and then singing "Happy Birthday." Tricia made a wish (for the kitty that she had never received), blown out the candles, and then Angelica had cut the big sheet cake into slabs three or four inches in size, plopping them onto plates for the ten or so of Tricia's schoolmates—none of whom she remembered some forty years later.

Tricia had held her fork and was about to dive into the white cake with pink frosting roses when she'd heard a voice behind her say, "Uh-uh-uh!" She'd turned around to see her mother towering over her, frowning. "Do you want to grow up to be a fat, ugly, repulsive person who nobody will ever love? Someone to be made fun of?"

Tricia remembered being puzzled by the question, and she'd shaken her head, frightened by the images her mother's words had evoked. Still, she'd whimpered, "But it's my birthday."

Her mother had looked at her and had shaken her head. Tricia well remembered the terrible weight on her soul as she'd carefully considered her mother's words. Not wanting to disappoint the person she needed the most, Tricia had set down her fork and pushed the cake aside.

"Aren't you going to eat that?" Angelica had asked, horrified.

Tricia remembered again shaking her head.

"Good. Then I will."

Angelica had grabbed the plate, sat down at the table, and had plunged her fork into the sea of white and pink icing. Tricia had had to swallow hard as she watched Angelica practically inhale the lovely confection. And when she'd looked back at her mother, she'd found her gaze planted squarely on Angelica, smiling broadly.

Tricia looked down at her plate and frowned. She remembered so many Christmas dinners when she'd had a teaspoon of each item served—but no more, and then going to bed hungry.

On their first trip away as a couple, she and Christopher had gone to Portland, Maine, for a long weekend. He'd ordered lobster for both of them, but she'd picked at hers, taking a bite of the corn and maybe one or two of the boiled potatoes, totally bypassing the drawn butter. He'd been disappointed she didn't want to finish her meal, and had appropriated what was left of her entrée.

Several times she'd shared pieces of Angelica's decadent carrot cake with Ginny, always taking the smaller half—and never the one with the most icing—and then feeling guilty for having eaten it at all.

And yet, despite the memories that had assaulted her, instead of wanting more, Tricia suddenly found she'd lost her appetite.

"It never occurred to me before this afternoon, but Tricia, darling, you've been a victim of parental abuse your entire life."

Victim? That wasn't a word Tricia wanted to be associated with. Indoctrinated? Yes, perhaps that was a better explanation, but it wasn't any more palatable—and wasn't that ironic?

Their mother had punished Tricia for the death of the brother she had never known—a death she hadn't caused. Angelica was right. That was child abuse. And yet . . . why did she still cling to the hope that one day her mother would suddenly forget her errors of the past and love her unconditionally?

It was a pipe dream. And when Tricia thought of her mother, she didn't have kind words to apply to her vision of the woman. And what about her father? He had known how Sheila treated his younger daughter and hadn't interceded. Yet when she thought of her father, Tricia associated him with the word *downtrodden.* Beaten. Dominated. Weak willed. And yet, she loved him. He'd always called her his princess. He had never called Angelica by that pet name.

Yes. When she'd looked into her father's eyes, she'd *felt* like a princess. Had he accorded her that moniker because he knew how her mother had repeatedly browbeaten her? Yes, he must have, because he'd told Angelica he'd been spineless to counter his wife's abuse because *he had to live with her.*

There was only one person in Tricia's—and in Angelica's—life who had given unconditional love: their Grandma Miles. At that moment, Tricia felt an overwhelming gush of love for that selfless woman who had taught Tricia the love of books filled with mystery, and Angelica, books filled with the love of cookery. She'd picked up on what each girl was most interested in and had encouraged that pursuit.

"Trish," Angelica said, bringing Tricia back to the here and now. "What are you thinking about?"

Tricia sighed. "That you may just be right." Again she looked down at her plate and yet did not want to take a bite of the cucumber sandwich or what was left of the tiny salmon sandwich.

At that moment, a waiter with a bottle of champagne showed up at the table. "Shall I pour?"

"Please do," Angelica said with a nod.

He did so, and the bubbles frothed up before settling down in the glasses—and then he topped them up again.

"Thank you," Tricia said, giving the bored waiter a wan smile. He nodded and turned away.

Angelica's expression was somber. "How does one undo a life of coercion?"

"Are you suggesting I should consult a shrink?"

Angelica looked thoughtful. "Maybe you should."

Tricia again looked down at the tiny rectangle of bread, butter, and cucumber, which looked so delicate and inviting, yet there was nothing she could think of that would activate her appetite.

"Perhaps it's time for a toast," Angelica said, picking up her champagne flute.

With reluctance, Tricia picked up her glass, but there was nothing on earth she wanted to celebrate. The day had been full of too many painful memories and surprises.

"This sister," Angelica said, indicating herself, "has the best sister in the world."

"Now you're joking," Tricia said.

"No, truly. I couldn't have asked for a kinder, smarter, more generous sister than you. I'm so sorry we weren't closer when we were growing up, but I now realize exactly why that was."

"You promised we weren't going to talk about her." No need to clarify who *her* was.

"That's all behind us now. You're my sister, and you're my best friend." Angelica moved her glass to clink Tricia's.

"You're my best friend, too."

Angelica smiled, her eyes growing moist.

They drank, and the bubbles tickled Tricia's nose. "Good stuff."

"It sure is." Angelica set her glass back on the tablecloth and picked up the cucumber sandwich on her plate, taking a bite. "I wish I'd brought my phone so I could have taken a picture of the table setting and these darling little sandwiches. We'll have to do this again before we return to New York. We're going to begin afternoon tea at the Brookside Inn the first weekend in April. I thought it might be fun to have a trial run for the Chamber members. What do you think?"

"I think they'd love it. I know I would."

"Good. The Brookview Inn's sous chef's specialty is pastries. I want to give her an opportunity to shine."

"If you do that, you might not have her much longer," Tricia pointed out.

"Ah, but when she goes on to work at bigger and better places, she'll tell everyone where she got her break, and that will be fabulous PR for the inn."

"Everybody wins?" Tricia asked, amused.

"Why not?"

Tricia found herself smiling. For many years she'd been too blinded by her animosity toward her sister to notice the depth of Angelica's generous nature.

"The next time we have tea, we should try to get Grace, Mr. Everett, and Antonio and Ginny to join us. Wouldn't that be fun?"

"Our real family," Angelica had said of them back at the Hamilton Contessa Hotel. Yes. That's just how Tricia thought of them.

She let out a breath and reached for the cucumber sandwich on her plate, taking a nibble. The combination of bread, sweet butter, and cucumber was delightful. She ate the rest of it and enjoyed every last morsel.

SIXTEEN

 Angelica decided that after such a stressful day she needed a deep tissue massage and a nap, and went off to book the former or attempt the latter. Tricia went back to the stateroom and changed clothes, filled her tote bag with several books and her e-reader, and went off in search of somewhere to rest, relax, and possibly reflect, although the latter wasn't going to be high on her list of things to do.

The temperature never did go up to where she thought it would be warm enough to sit by the pool (unlike some sun-starved passengers), and she decided to find a cozy niche in the ship's Garden Lounge.

The ship seemed quiet with so many of its temporary denizens off to take in the sights in Bermuda, and she found a seat in the sun with no trouble.

Tricia read for nearly an hour before she looked up from the page and out the window to the pier below, where she saw Cathy Copper approach a man holding a duffel bag. He wasn't a lover, or even a friend, for Cathy offered her hand and the man shook it. They stood looking at the big ship for a couple of minutes, conversing, and then Cathy led him to the gangplank. Was he going to board the ship?

Tricia sat back in her comfortable chair, placing a bookmark between the pages of her book and setting it aside. Who could the mysterious man be? Was he from EM's publishing company? Could he be a member of EM's family here to claim the body, or at least accompany it back to New York? Tricia's curiosity was certainly piqued, and she wondered if she might accidentally run into Cathy again at another of the cruise's book-related functions—or maybe later that night at one of the bars.

"Tricia?"

Tricia looked up to see Ginny heading in her direction without Antonio or Sofia.

"There you are. Angelica thought you might be here."

"Did she get her massage?"

"I don't think she ever made it down to the spa. She's holding court at the Portside Bar, talking with a bunch of authors. She seemed to be doing Chamber networking."

Tricia sighed. "I don't think Angelica knows how to relax."

"I think she's having the time of her life," Ginny said, smiling.

Tricia nodded. "You may be right."

"We did have a moment to speak, though." Ginny's voice softened. "I'm sorry things didn't work out with your visit with your parents."

"So, Angelica let you and Antonio in on the secret of the big reunion, but she kept it from me?"

"Don't be angry with her, but, yes, she did discuss it with us. She strongly discouraged us from meeting your mother."

"As I thought," Tricia muttered.

"It was your father who wanted the meeting."

"Really?"

Ginny nodded. "When he found out the two of you were making the trip, he engineered the meeting, but I guess Angelica was worried that if you knew you wouldn't want to come on the cruise. I guess your mother didn't know until this morning that the two of you would meet them for lunch."

They'd both been duped.

Tricia shook her head. "When you think about it, the situation is really quite pathetic."

"I understand your mother's loss, but I would have thought she'd have poured all her love into you, instead of blaming you for that loss."

"There's no explaining the ways of the heart," Tricia said sadly. "But oddly enough, I feel a sense of closure. I love my mother; I always will. But I don't know as I need to have her in my life."

"As a new mom, I can't imagine what it would take for Sofia to feel that way."

"That's because you love her unconditionally."

Ginny's smile held a touch of sadness. "That's true. And I feel terribly sorry for your mother. She has no idea what she's missed." Ginny lunged forward and gave Tricia a hug. She pulled back. "I know that nobody can ever compensate for the loss of a mother's love, but since I found out that Angelica was Antonio's stepmother, I've felt that we were all family. I feel proud to think of you as the big sister I never had."

"Oh, Ginny," Tricia said, her lower lip trembling, her eyes filling with tears. "Thank you," she somehow managed to say.

"And I have good news. I found my phone!"

Tricia raised a hand to wipe her eyes. "Where was it?"

"Antonio found it tucked down the side of Sofia's stroller."

"That's one mystery solved."

"Yes. We took it to the ship's security officer and they downloaded the pictures from yesterday's lunch. Apparently, they've now spoken to everyone who was at our table."

"And?"

"If they've come to any conclusions, they weren't sharing it with any of us."

That wasn't surprising.

"I guess we've done all we could to redirect their thoughts away from the idea that EM committed suicide and to look at the possibility she was murdered."

"Why would you say that?" Tricia asked.

"Oh, come on. You had to think it was murder right from the get-go. If her keycard wasn't in her cabin's power slot, how could she have seen what she was doing to hang herself?"

So Ginny, too, had noticed the significance of that little piece of the puzzle.

"Angelica didn't want you to worry and was concerned you'd be upset about Sofia's safety."

Ginny sighed. "I admit it: I'm not comfortable knowing there's a killer on board, but then how much safer are we back home where a murder seems to happen a couple of times a year? But I don't think I want to leave Sofia with a sitter anymore, especially since she may have picked up the sniffles."

"Angelica and I were talking about perhaps taking the rest of our meals at the Lido Restaurant. That way we wouldn't have to wait for the late seating and could all have dinner together without worry about the baby making noise."

"She's liable to make noise, but at least we wouldn't have to get all dressed up. It was fun the first time, but it's getting old fast. I think if we stick together—especially during the evenings—we'll be fine. Can you believe our vacation is already half over?"

"Time has gone by fast," Tricia admitted. "But I must admit I'm psyched to get home and start renovating my apartment and the new storeroom."

"I've learned a lot during my time at the Happy Domestic. I'd love to help you pick out colors and accessories."

"I think Angelica's got her heart set on doing that—but I'm sure she'd be thrilled to share that duty with you. I like the exposed brick, and I want to make sure there's an entire wall of floor-to-ceiling book-shelves in the new living room."

"Oh, that's a given," Ginny said, and laughed, then sobered. "Are you okay?"

"You mean am I okay to be left alone?"

Ginny nodded.

"I'm perfectly safe in any of the common areas. Remember, we're all on Candid Camera," she said, nodding in the direction of one of the dark globes that was mounted on a wall in the corner of the room.

Again, Ginny laughed. "You're right about that. Okay, I'm going to catch up with Antonio. We're heading for dinner at the Lido around six thirty if you want to join us."

"We had a very late lunch. I'm not sure we'll be hungry by then."

"That's okay. If you make it—you make it. If not, we'll catch up in the morning, okay?"

"Right. See you later, then."

"Bye."

Tricia watched as Ginny retraced her steps, heading for the lifts.

The late-afternoon sunshine felt wonderful, and Tricia turned her gaze back to the pier. A number of couples were ambling along the dock, hand in hand, making their way back from their time on shore. Among them were a few stragglers, including Dori Douglas. She carried several plastic bags, and Tricia wondered if she'd been buying souvenirs. She frowned. Dori had been gone an awfully long time. Tricia glanced at her watch—almost eight hours. Dori must have done a *lot* of shopping.

Tricia picked up her book once more, but found she could no longer concentrate on it. What she needed was a pick-me-up. After all, she hadn't had an opportunity to finish her lunchtime martini. Okay, she had had a glass of champagne during afternoon tea, but that hadn't hit the spot. Champagne was for celebrating, and while she felt good about her relationship with Angelica, the events at the Contessa had left her feeling relieved, but mildly depressed. Alcohol was a depressant, but at that moment Tricia really didn't care.

She collected her book and bag and started off for what was becoming her favorite of the ship's bars.

It was early, and the drinking crowd was sparse, but Tricia smiled as she saw a familiar face sitting by the window gazing out over the harbor. She approached.

"Penny for your thoughts."

Angelica looked up and smiled. "There you are."

"I see you started without me," Tricia said, eyeing the untouched martini that sat on one of the ship's embossed cocktail napkins. "I was waiting for you."

"Lies. Otherwise you would have ordered one for me, too."

Tricia sat down and looked up to see a waitress coming toward her, carrying a tray with yet another martini.

"Just in time," Angelica told the waitress, and surrendered her keycard. They watched as the waitress retraced her steps to the bar to make the charge.

"Have you become psychic?" Tricia asked in awe, and reached for her glass.

Angelica smiled and did likewise. "Maybe. What shall we drink to?"

"Home," Tricia said, and they clinked glasses. "As lovely as the ship is, and as terrific as the food is, the truth is . . . I miss my cat. I miss my bed. I miss my store. I just want to go home."

"We'll be on our way tomorrow," Angelica said.

"I may bow out of the rest of the activities and just be lazy and read."

"Sounds like a plan," Angelica agreed.

Tricia took a sip of her martini. She was really beginning to like them. "I caught up with Ginny, and we're on for dinner at six thirty."

"I hope I can work up an appetite by then," Angelica said.

"There's always soup."

"That's true. And rolls—with butter. Lots and lots with butter!"

That actually sounded pretty good to Tricia.

"Anything new happen?" Angelica asked.

"It's only been a couple of hours since we talked."

"A lot can happen in a couple of hours," Angelica said.

"Well, I did see Cathy Copper meet someone out on the pier. A man," Tricia said coyly.

"Really," Angelica asked, her eyes widening. "A lover?"

"I don't think so. They shook hands."

Angelica scowled. "Well, that's no fun." She looked up and over Tricia's head and blinked in surprise. "Speak of the devil."

Tricia looked around, and then turned back to her sister. "That's him," she whispered.

Cathy and the stranger stood talking by the open entrance to the bar. The man had lost his duffel. He'd probably stowed it in his cabin.

"I didn't know we were picking up any passengers," Angelica said.

"Neither did I."

Angelica's smile widened and she waved, and then gestured for the couple outside the bar to join them. Tricia turned to see a thin-lipped Cathy and the newcomer approach. "Looks like you found a new friend," Angelica said, grinning.

"Harold Pilger," Cathy began, "this is Angelica and Tricia Miles. They're booksellers." She didn't sound thrilled.

Harold reached down to shake their hands. "Nice to meet you. Were you friends of EM's?"

"Uh, no," Tricia answered honestly.

Harold shot a puzzled look at Cathy.

"Harold is a lawyer who works for my publishing company."

"Ah," Angelica said, nodding.

"So you're on board representing the publisher's interests?" Tricia asked.

"You could say that," Harold said, his gaze wandering over to the bar.

"Did you fly into Hamilton?" Angelica asked.

"Yes. I got in last night. I stayed in a lovely pink hotel that over-looked the harbor."

"The Hamilton Contessa?" Tricia guessed.

"Why yes. Have you ever stayed there?"

"No," Angelica answered emphatically.

Harold blinked, apparently startled by her blunt tone.

"Are you investigating EM's death?" Tricia asked.

Again Harold blinked. "Investigating?"

"Perhaps I should have said *looking into*," she amended.

"I guess you could say that," Harold said, but he didn't sound all that sure.

"Harold and I have a lot to talk about," Cathy said, sounding more than a little uncomfortable.

"Don't let us keep you," Angelica said.

"I hope you enjoy your few days at sea," Tricia said.

Harold nodded. "It was nice meeting you." He turned to Cathy. "Shall we snag a table?"

"Yes. We'll see you ladies around," Cathy said.

"I'm sure you will," Angelica said, plastering on a smile.

The couple gave them a parting nod and headed for the other side of the bar.

Tricia sat back in her seat. "Interesting."

Lorna Barrett

"Very interesting," Angelica agreed.

"Why would a lawyer come on board?" Tricia mused.

"Perhaps Cathy didn't believe EM's death was suicide any more than you do. Perhaps she called her boss and they sent someone to make inquiries on the publisher's behalf. EM was no doubt worth a *lot* of money to them."

"There could be a provision in her will allowing the estate to authorize someone to continue writing with her name. There are plenty of authors who've died, yet still crank out bestselling books—either written by ghostwriters or with a lesser-known author's name in a much smaller font on the cover. Tom Clancy is a prime example. Other times, a family member has taken up the reins of a series. Felix Francis immediately comes to mind."

"I never read any of their books."

"You've missed out," Tricia said with pity.

"The original books or the *after-death* books?"

"Both."

The sisters thoughtfully sipped their martinis. "You know," Tricia said at last. "I've been thinking about the night I found EM."

"Oh! Why would you want to revisit that terrible event?" Angelica asked, chagrined.

"Not so much *what* I saw—but what I *didn't* see."

"And what was that?"

"Her computer."

"Perhaps she'd packed it away for the night."

"I don't think so. I mean, I never saw her without it. I'll bet she had it plugged in every night so that it would be fully charged so she could take it to various places on the ship and write."

"You did say you saw her writing in the library on our first day at sea."

"And she brought it to the bar that first night to show Cathy her ideas about where she wanted her series to go."

188

"Do you think the killer stole it?"

"Could be. I wonder if Cathy was allowed into EM's stateroom, didn't see the computer, and either immediately called her bosses—"

"Very expensive at sea," Angelica said.

"—or fired off an e-mail to let them know the computer was missing. It may have held the only copy of her latest work in progress."

"Surely she had a flash drive or uploaded it to the cloud," Angelica suggested.

"Internet connections can be spotty at sea."

"As I have found out," Angelica agreed. "But I still think any writer would be a fool not to have backup. I mean—accidents happen. I once spilled a cup of coffee on my laptop. Good-bye, laptop!" She looked around Tricia to take in Harold and Cathy across the way. "I still don't understand why they'd send a lawyer. Wouldn't a private detective be a better choice?"

Tricia took another sip of her martini. "Maybe. Perhaps they're looking for a legal loophole to do a little snooping for the publisher. A private eye wouldn't have that kind of pull."

"That makes sense," Angelica agreed. "But suppose they *do* find out something that proves EM's death was a crime and not suicide?"

"In some places, suicide *is* still considered a crime."

"And how are you going to arrest a corpse?" Angelica asked wryly.

"Make the heirs pay for any costs associated with investigating the death. And, of course, most religions consider suicide to be a sin."

"That's an angle they may not have thought about. Did EM have strong religious convictions?"

"Maybe. I suppose they'd have to ask her family and friends."

"Do you think Dori would know?"

Tricia shrugged. "Maybe. Speaking of Dori—it seems she had quite the shopping excursion. She came back to the ship loaded down with plastic bags."

"I thought she was broke."

"That's what that rude bookseller thought, but who knows? I don't go around broadcasting my financial status—and neither does anyone I know."

Angelica sipped her drink thoughtfully. "Do you think Mr. Pilger will want to question Dori?"

"Undoubtedly. She makes a good suspect, if only because of the way EM treated her in public."

"The woman had no manners—and probably no friends, either," Angelica commented.

"And yet both Dori and Cathy defended her, saying she had problems not apparent to people outside her inner circle. Then, of course, there was Grace's assessment of her personality."

"Yes," Angelica agreed. "I do try to see the good in people, but I must admit it has been a challenge when thinking of EM Barstow—and I never even had to deal with her directly."

"Let's change the subject. What do you think you'd like to do tonight?" Tricia asked.

"I believe there's a darts tournament in the Golden Harp pub. Since the Dog-Eared Page opened, you've gotten very good at it. Perhaps you should enter."

"I've been lucky," Tricia agreed, "but I have a feeling that the competition on board could be too fierce. I prefer to play for fun."

"We could go watch and maybe have another martini."

Tricia smiled. "Maybe." She looked up and saw the ship's entertainment director standing in the aisle outside the bar, speaking with another crew member. "Oh, look. There's Millicent Ambrose. I've been trying to catch up with her." Tricia set her glass down on the table and rose from her seat. She walked purposefully toward the entertainment director, who noticed her approach and quickly dismissed her colleague.

"Hello, Millicent. I'm sorry to interrupt," Tricia began.

"Not at all. How can I help you?"

"I don't know if you remember me. Tricia Miles." Tricia extended her hand.

"Very nice to bump into you again," Millicent said, but it was obvious she had no recollection.

"I understand you interviewed EM Barstow before her death."

"Yes, we ran it yesterday."

"There was so much going on that day. I'm sorry I missed it. Is there a chance it'll be shown again before the ship returns to New York?"

"Yes, but not until Friday, I'm currently working on a new introduction and then a tribute. Being at sea, it's been difficult getting biographical information and testimonials."

"Oh? But her editor and assistant are both on board."

"Really? I'd love to speak with them; perhaps film additional interviews."

Tricia gave Millicent Dori's and Cathy's names, but didn't think it was wise to mention that Cathy was sitting mere feet from them.

"Thank you. This is brilliant. My conversation with EM was the last official interview she gave. We'll be offering it to the networks. It should be great PR for the cruise line."

Yes. And it was too bad Tricia would have to wait days to see it. Still, what were the chances EM said something cryptic that might point to her killer?

Tricia forced a smile. "I'll look forward to seeing the program, as I'm sure a large portion of the passengers will, too."

"It'll be spectacular," Millicent promised. "Perhaps we'll even rerun it in prime time. Excuse me, dear. I really must run."

Tricia watched as the entertainment director charged off down the corridor, only to be intercepted by yet another passenger. *C'est la vie.*

Returning to her former seat, Tricia picked up her glass once more.

"Learn anything new?" Angelica asked.

"Only that Millicent's interview with EM will rerun on Friday morning."

"Her show airs at the crack of dawn. You'll have to set an alarm or ask for a wake-up call," Angelica advised.

"I'll do what I have to. I'm not about to miss it."

Angelica shook her head in what looked like consternation. "You're getting too involved. And what for? You have no stake in this."

"You forget; I *found* the poor woman. I intend to observe only, and if I learn anything of note, I'll report it to the person or persons most likely to follow up on it. In this case, that would probably be Harold Pilger. He wasn't on board when EM died. He has no personal stake in any of this, but the people—or rather corporation—he represents certainly do."

"Whatever you do, keep it impersonal. I don't even want you talking to Dori or Cathy again. I want you safe. You have a business to run and a home to renovate. You have goals, and friends and family who love you."

Including a possible stalker, Tricia reminded herself.

She didn't want to think about it.

Tricia glanced at her watch. "Rats. We've already missed dinner with Ginny and Antonio."

"Oh, dear. What should we do about dinner?"

"Nothing much. What did you have in mind?"

"You know, fish and chips might be just the thing at the ship's pub."

Angelica frowned. "After that tea, I'm not sure I'm all that hungry."

"But I didn't fill up. I may be ready for dinner in another hour or so. You don't have to come with me if you don't want to."

"What? And sit alone in our room?"

"The Daily Program said the ship's TV channel was repeating the documentary on ocean liners that sank," Tricia said with amusement.

"Which is not what *I* want to see," Angelica exclaimed.

Tricia smiled. "If you only want an appetizer, that's all you have to order. But I've never experienced mushy peas and I think I might like to try them at least once."

Angelica glowered. "Better you than me. Do we need to change?"

Trisha shrugged. "I'll bet if we arrived buck naked nobody would care."

"Well, I would," Angelica declared.

Again Tricia smiled, feeling content—something she hadn't experienced in quite a while. "Why don't we have another round—and on me, this time—and then make our way to the Golden Harp?"

"I'm for that," Angelica said, and drained her glass. She looked around, caught the waitress's attention, and motioned her to attend to them.

Once the drink order was taken, Angelica turned back to Tricia. "Now, let's have no more talk about EM, her death, or anything else sordid. We're on holiday," she said, using the European expression for *vacation*. "Deal?"

"Deal," Tricia readily agreed. Except . . . What if something interesting came up?

Just for a moment, she wished she'd crossed her fingers before answering.

SEVENTEEN

The Golden Harp wasn't rocking, because they were playing traditional Irish music when Tricia and Angelica arrived at a little after nine, but the atmosphere was certainly cheerful.

"Oh, dear. There isn't a free table in the whole place," Angelica said with chagrin.

Tricia looked around the low-ceilinged room and saw Fiona Sample sitting with a number of other authors at a large table in the back of the pub. Tricia caught her eye and waved. As she hoped, Fiona gestured for her to join them. "I think we just got lucky," Tricia said, and motioned for Angelica to follow.

"Hi," Tricia called, and stopped in front of the table.

"Hey, Tricia. Are you going to compete in the darts tournament? Nikki tells me you're one of Stoneham's best players."

"Oh, she exaggerates." But Tricia enjoyed hearing the compliment nonetheless. "You remember my sister, Angelica."

"Hi, Fiona. It's good to see you again."

"And you, too!"

"We came for fish and chips, but it looks like we should have arrived a lot earlier."

"We've only got room for one more, I'm afraid," she apologized.

"Oh, we can squeeze in another chair for your friends," Lethal Lady Helen Evans said. Tricia had briefly met her at the author signing the previous day.

"Sure we can," Carmen Hammond agreed. "Ladies?"

Suddenly the women and lone male at the table started scooching their chairs aside to make room. Angelica snagged another chair from a table for four with only three occupants, and the sisters edged in between Norma and Sidney, facing Fiona across the table. Fiona made the introductions.

"So, what's the consensus of opinion on EM Barstow's death?" Angelica asked, and Tricia felt like kicking her under the table. So much for her request not to broach the subject.

"Oh, she was murdered," Hannah Travis said confidently.

"Absolutely," Victoria Burke agreed, and sipped the last of her drink.

"But that's not what we've been led to believe," Tricia said innocently.

"Of course not. They don't want to panic the passengers," Helen said.

"What makes you think it was murder?" Tricia pressed.

"They're pulling your leg," Norma Fielding said reasonably. "Will somebody see if they can snag the waitress? I need another Guinness."

"I could use another martini," Angelica muttered.

"As far as we know, there's no evidence to point to anything other than suicide," Diana Lovell agreed.

Tricia glanced askance at Angelica, who'd pursed her lips, no doubt in an effort not to giggle guiltily.

"Of course, there were plenty of people who probably could have cheerfully strangled the woman," said the lone male at the table. It was thriller writer Steven Richardson. Tricia had read and enjoyed most of his books.

"Why do you say that?" she asked.

"Her split personality."

"Oh?" Angelica asked. "I thought nasty was her only way of life."

"She could also be passive-aggressive. I said right—she said left, just to be contrary."

"Oh, yeah," Fiona agreed. "We were once on a panel together and were asked some innocuous question that required only a yes or no answer, but EM went on some kind of tangent that infuriated not only her fellow panelists but the audience members as well. She pretended to be totally clueless about it, too."

Tricia saw movement in her peripheral vision and then suddenly Arnold Smith's motorized chair came to a halt practically in Carmen Hammond's lap. "Hello, ladies and gentleman. Any chance I could join you?" From the looks on the authors' faces, the answer was a definite "No!"

"We're stretched pretty thin here, Arnold. How about a rain check?" Lorelei Garner asked. She was the only Lethal Lady to whom Tricia hadn't been personally introduced at one point or another during the trip.

"Yes," Carmen quickly agreed. "We've still got two days aboard this lovely ship. How about meeting for lunch at the Lido Restaurant?"

From the expressions on the faces of the rest of her tablemates, Tricia was sure poor Carmen would have to suffer lunch alone with the bore.

"Sure thing, Carmen. I think I'll cruise around the deck and come back a little later. Maybe one of you guys will leave and make room for me," he said pointedly.

No one commented.

Arnold gave a wave and started for the door. Tricia waited until he was out of earshot before speaking. "EM hinted that Arnold had stalked her."

"She wasn't the only one," Sidney Charles commented.

"Oh?" Tricia asked.

"Several women in our circle of author friends have received threats that were traced back to Arnold."

"What kind of threats?" Angelica asked, sounding concerned.

"Being smeared on social media," Fiona said. "Arnold's an Internet troll. Cross him and he posts negative reviews about your books, or he'll make nasty blog comments. And he has a legion of fellow creeps who will do likewise."

"What kind of person would do that?" Tricia asked.

"A bully," Norma said. "I saw that all too often during my years as a school nurse. "You're a psychologist, Helen; what do you think?"

"Bullying is much more about the bully than the person who's on the receiving end. These types are angry, entitled, and at their core, extremely insecure. So, they adopt the 'I'll get you before you get me' way of life."

"Do you think Arnold ever threatened EM with physical harm?" Angelica asked, probably worrying about Sofia, Ginny, and Antonio.

"Just because he rides around in a motorized chair doesn't mean he's without physical strength," Hannah said.

A waitress arrived and took drink orders for those who wanted a refill and dinner orders for Tricia and Angelica. Everyone surrendered their keycards and Tricia felt sorry for the poor waitress who had to figure out everyone's drink orders and charges. Still, it gave her time to absorb what she'd just learned. Arnold Smith a stalker? Had he begun his mini reign of terror with EM with seemingly innocuous gifts like wine, a sweater, chocolate, and flowers? Tricia glanced at Helen Evans, who was not only a talented fiction writer in a number of genres, but as Norma had pointed out, a clinical psychologist, too. Would she have time to speak to Tricia further on the subject or was it unfair to ask for a professional opinion when the poor woman was on vacation?

The answer was a resounding yes.

Besides, if Tricia had ever wanted to seek professional help, she'd have done it in regard to her relationship with her mother, and that was now a moot point as far as she was concerned. No, she was more interested in what motivated people like Arnold to menace others. She'd certainly read enough fiction on the subject, but it might be interesting to read some true crime accounts. Perhaps the ship's library would have a book on that topic. She'd have to check.

The drinks arrived, along with the dinners Tricia and Angelica had ordered.

"What's that you're drinking?" Angelica asked Diana.

"Malbec. It's a wine from Argentina. Lovely. A little fruity with a smoky finish." She looked around the table at her fellow authors. "Anyone want some of these gorgonzola chips?"

Steven reached for one. "Thanks."

Angelica shook her head, picking up her martini and taking a sip.

Hannah sipped her margarita. "Here's a question I've always wanted to ask a group of authors. Have any of you ever known a murder victim?"

"Tricia has," Angelica piped up. "Let's see. . . ." She counted on her fingers, quickly running out of them. "At least ten . . . including her ex-husband."

All eyes turned to look at Tricia, who was about to take her first bite of mushy peas. "I didn't kill any of them," she said, sounding defensive.

"Of course not," Angelica said quickly, reaching for her martini glass and taking a very large sip.

"How were they killed?" Victoria asked aghast, then took a slug of her Jameson on the rocks.

"Let me think. The first one was stabbed. One had the brakes on her car tampered with. Um, a couple of them were strangled. One was bludgeoned to death. Oh, and I can't forget poor Deborah, who died when a plane crashed into the village gazebo—now that was a bizarre one. Then there was—"

"I think they've heard enough," Tricia said with consternation.

"That's a lot of bad luck," Diana commented.

"Yes," Angelica agreed. "That's why she has the reputation as the village jinx."

Tricia winced, grinding her teeth at that hated nickname.

"She also helped the police solve many of those murders. Of course, she didn't have to solve poor Christopher's murder."

"Christopher?" Victoria asked.

"Her ex-husband. He was killed right in front of us—in front of a bunch of witnesses. It was horrific."

Hot tears stung Tricia's eyes at the memory. Why did Angelica have to mention it—just when she thought she was getting over his death?

"He saved my life," Angelica went on, sounding just as teary, and took another gulp of her martini. When she put the glass down, Tricia appropriated it.

"Ange, I think you've had enough," she said quietly.

"You poor thing," Helen said, looking at Tricia. "Actually both of you. It must have been terrible."

"Oh, it wash," Angelica whimpered, slurring her words. Now she was getting maudlin.

"Eat your dinner," Tricia urged gently. Angelica should have eaten something before imbibing all those martinis. Tricia took the long-delayed bite of mushy peas and scowled, unable to see the appeal. Instead, she set down her fork and tore open the packet of malt vinegar, sprinkling it across her chips. *Ah, much better.*

Angelica picked up her fork and poked at the piece of fish on her plate, pouting. Tricia dug in. The fish—and the chips—was excellent. She took another bite. She really had needed sustenance.

"Tricia!"

Tricia turned around to see Ginny pushing Sofia's stroller and accompanied by Antonio. They halted in front of the table. "We missed you guys at dinner."

"We're having it now," Tricia said, cutting the end of her fish with the fork.

"I don't think I want mine," Angelica whimpered, pushing her plate aside.

"I'm afraid Angelica has had a little too much to drink," Tricia said, and chomped on another chip. Never had a French fry tasted so good.

Antonio frowned, "Angelica, my dearest. Would you like us to take you back to your suite?"

Angelica nodded and sniffed.

Antonio pulled the chair back and helped Angelica to her feet. She sniffed again. "It was very nice meeting you all."

A chorus of "same here" followed.

"Thanks for taking care of her. I'll be back to the cabin after I finish my dinner," Tricia said.

"I'll sit with her to make sure she's all right."

"Thank you, dear," Angelica said, and patted Antonio's cheek.

"We'd better go," Ginny warned, turning the stroller around. "See you later, Tricia."

Everyone watched Angelica go.

"Is that her son?" Diana asked.

"Uh . . . no." Tricia wasn't about to reveal Angelica's secret that Antonio was her stepson—not in front of Fiona, whose daughter was a fellow Chamber of Commerce member. "He's . . . he's a friend. A good friend."

"I'll say," Hannah said, and sipped her margarita.

"You've had a lot of shattering experiences," Helen commented. "If you ever need to talk, I'd be glad to listen."

At that moment, Tricia didn't want to think about anything unhappy. Enjoying her dinner was her top priority, and she was clearing her plate in record speed. She swallowed. "Thank you, Helen. Maybe we could talk sometime tomorrow about stalkers. I may have one of my own."

"Oh?"

Tricia nodded and reached for her own martini, taking a sip. "Since we boarded the ship, I've been receiving little gifts." Little? A bottle of Dom Pérignon could not be called a trinket, but the other gifts were all well under one hundred dollars each. Still, the price tags had probably accumulated to the tune of five hundred dollars or more, which wasn't inconsequential, either.

"Have you received any threats?"

Tricia shook her head. "No. In fact, Angelica insists I've got a secret admirer."

"Let's hope it's just that," Norma agreed, but looked worried just the same.

Victoria drained her glass. "It's time for me to turn in. Big day tomorrow."

"Oh?" Tricia asked.

"It's our next-to-last day on the trip, and I intend to enjoy every minute of it. What are the rest of you doing?"

"There's that editors' panel tomorrow. That could be quite interesting, especially since EM's editor is going to be on it," Sidney said.

"Oh, yeah?" Carmen asked. "I wasn't going to go to it, but maybe now I will."

"What's she likely to reveal? Why print runs are such a secret?" Hannah asked with a laugh.

"Or why authors aren't consulted when it comes to book covers?" Steven asked.

"I have a wonderful editor," Norma said. "I wouldn't trade her for a bag of gold."

"How about two bags?" Hannah asked.

A smile crept onto Norma's lips. "Well, maybe."

Victoria stood. "I'll see you all tomorrow. Good night."

Most of the rest of the women at the table drained their drinks and joined her, voicing their good-byes, but Steven still had half a pint left in his glass and moved down the table, taking the chair across from Tricia, who still had most of her martini—as well as Angelica's—before her. He watched as she polished off the last of her fish, and smiled. "I love to see a woman who enjoys a good meal."

Tricia wiped her mouth with her napkin. "Oh?"

"My ex-wife was a slave to counting calories and excessive exercise. I'm happy to see you aren't stuck in that mentality."

Oh, if he only knew.

"I love your Toby Amsterdam series," Tricia began, making small talk, "but I do wish you'd write another Oscar Moore story."

Steven shrugged. "Yeah, well, they didn't sell quite as well. I have to write what pays the bills—and my alimony."

Tricia nodded in understanding. She could have gone after Christopher for alimony, but he'd been more than generous with their divorce settlement, no doubt because of guilt for leaving her. And when he'd died, he'd left all his assets to her, but financial security was no substitute for his friendship. At least when he'd left this earth, they'd still been friends, which apparently was more than Steven could claim.

"Maybe I'll write another book for Oscar one day," Steven continued, "but my fans demand that I write what they like best—not what I'd prefer to work on."

"You don't like the Amsterdam books?"

"Not at all. But there's only so much time in the day, week, month, and year."

"I get that," Tricia said, and picked up her glass to take yet another small sip. "I understand you live in Massachusetts. I just so happen to own a mystery bookstore in southern New Hampshire. Would you consider coming by to do a book signing sometime?"

"Only if I could have dinner with you, too."

"Well, that's a given," Tricia said glibly. Maybe she'd had too much to drink, too. She cleared her throat. "But you wouldn't want to come until at least April—maybe even June or July—when the tourists return. That's when I could best expect to round up an enthusiastic audience for your talk or reading."

"Why don't we e-mail—or better yet talk about it sometime in the future?"

Tricia squinted at the handsome man who sat across the table from her. "Do you flirt with every woman you meet?"

"Not every woman. But I've known most of the other authors who sat at this table for quite a while. The fact that they welcomed you as a friend must mean they respect, or at least like you."

Tricia really knew only Fiona, but she had met and hosted several of the other authors at her store during the past five years, too. "Thank you," she said, gracefully accepting the compliment.

"And I'm assuming that since you own a mystery bookstore—and have the good taste to read my work—that you're someone I could talk to on practically any subject."

"I like to think I'm well informed on most subjects."

Good grief, Tricia realized, she was flirting right back. She picked up her glass once more, sipping the last of her drink, then set it down again. "I've enjoyed our conversation, but I really should go check on my sister. We're traveling together."

"Do you two make a habit of it?"

"This is actually the first vacation we've been on together since we were children. My sister not only owns a cookbook store, but she's a cookbook author as well."

"And do you have any literary aspirations?"

Tricia shook her head. Her specialty working at the nonprofit organization had been writing grant applications—and she'd been good at it, too. Should she consider attempting to write a mystery? With all she had on her plate? The answer was: not anytime soon.

Tricia folded her napkin and stood. "I really must go check on my sister."

Richardson rose, too. "May I walk you to your stateroom?"

Hadn't he heard her mention she might have a stalker? Could Steven Richardson be that stalker? But he'd only met her half an hour before. The corridors were likely to be empty. Then again, video surveillance would follow them every step of the way. Still, ship's security wasn't keen on looking for EM's killer—would they do any more to protect or prosecute an attacker or rapist? And Richardson wrote about serial killers. Surely he knew just about every way to kill a victim.

Tricia swallowed and forced a smile. "That's very nice of you, but you haven't finished your drink. I'm sure I'll make it just fine to my stateroom."

"As you wish. But let me give you my business card so that at some point we can set up that book signing." He reached into his back pants pocket and pulled out his wallet, extracting a card and handing it to her.

"Thank you."

"Maybe we could have a drink tomorrow sometime."

"That would be very nice. It's not a big ship. I'm sure we'll bump into each other at least once before we dock."

Richardson smiled. "Then, until we meet again."

"Good night."

Tricia turned to leave, but before she had walked too far down the corridor, she looked back to see if Richardson was following her. He hadn't. Instead, he'd wandered over to watch the darts tournament.

She continued to the stairs. Steven Richardson seemed like a nice enough guy. Knowing he hadn't followed her made her actually look forward to that promised drink.

Tricia pulled out the keycard from her slacks pocket and inserted it into the suite's lock, then opened the door. She immediately heard a low groan and found Antonio seated on what she thought of as her couch, while Angelica had her feet propped up, leaning back against her own loveseat, pressing an ice bag to her forehead.

"I think I'm dying," Angelica wailed, her lower lip quivering. "I haven't been drunk for at least ten—maybe fifteen—years and I *do not like it!*"

Tricia turned her gaze to Antonio. "Poor Angelica has been sick, but perhaps now she will feel better," he said hopefully.

"I puked my guts up. I will *never* recover!" Angelica wailed.

"Oh, yes, you will," Tricia said kindly, and moved to stand beside her sister, clasping her hand. "I can take over from here," she told Antonio. "Go be with your family."

"Ah, but Angelica is also my family," he asserted.

"No, no," Angelica insisted. "I'm fine now."

"But you just said you were dying," Antonio reminded her.

"It only feels that way. I'm sure by tomorrow I'll be much better. Please, go back to Ginny and Sofia."

Antonio sighed and stood, then crossed the three feet between the love seats. "Okay. But only because you insist, and dear Tricia is now here."

"I promise, this will never happen again," Angelica vowed.

Antonio bent down to kiss his stepmother on the forehead. "See that it doesn't," he said, but without rancor. He turned to Tricia. "Feel free to call if you need my help."

"I'm sure I can handle the situation."

Antonio nodded, then stepped forward to give Tricia a peck on the cheek. A rush of affection for him filled her, something she hadn't felt during her visit with her parents earlier in the day. Antonio would never know how lucky he was. Then again, maybe he did.

Tricia followed him to the door. "We'll see you tomorrow."

"Good night," Antonio said, and Tricia closed the door behind him. She turned to her sister. "Will you be okay?"

"Eventually," Angelica said, and sank farther into the loveseat. "Thank goodness for Sebastian, who supplied the ice pack, otherwise I'm sure I would have died." She rested the back of her right hand dramatically against her furrowed brow.

Talk about a diva!

"Is there anything I can do to make you feel better?" Tricia asked.

"No," Angelica said piteously. "Just stay here and keep me company for a little while, will you?"

Tricia sat down on her love seat, which was still warm from Antonio's body heat. "I will."

"I'm so embarrassed," Angelica whimpered. "What will all those mystery authors think of me?"

"It doesn't matter. I know what *I* think of you. That you're a very strong woman who had a terrible day."

"Oh, no! It was *you* who had the terrible day, and it's all my fault."

"Not really," Tricia said. "You've spent far too many years running interference between Mother and me. You don't have to do that anymore. I'm fine, and that's also because of you."

"Things will work out," Angelica said.

Yes. They usually did.

"Did I miss anything by leaving the party early?"

"Well, that hunky author Steven Richardson hit on me."

Angelica opened one eye. "He did?"

Tricia nodded.

"And?"

"He wants to have a drink with me before the end of the cruise."

"You said yes, I hope."

Tricia shrugged. "I left it open. If we run into each other—I'll go."

"Good."

"Why good?"

"Because you need a man in your life."

"Oh, don't start that."

"You took off Christopher's ring, so you're obviously ready."

"To have a long-distance relationship with an author I just met not an hour ago? I don't think so."

"If nothing else, having a drink and a nice conversation with an attractive man will help you break back into the relationship game."

"You make it sound like a date on training wheels."

"Exactly," Angelica said with a little too much enthusiasm, and winced at the timbre of her voice.

"I don't know why you're so worried about my social life, when you've had none for almost two years."

"I'm extremely socially active," Angelica countered.

"Maybe in your capacity as head of the Chamber of Commerce. You, personally? Not so much."

"Our Sunday dinners with family are social."

"But you're not likely to meet anybody new that way."

"Stoneham isn't exactly a hotbed of eligible men," Angelica conceded, and readjusted the ice bag on her brow.

"Frannie suggested I try online dating."

"Yes, she mentions it to me on a daily basis, too."

"She seems happy," Tricia commented. "But I've got too much on my plate right now."

Angelica sighed. "Me, too. I just hope that when we find the time to date, we won't be too over the hill to enjoy it." She looked at Tricia. "I think I owe you an apology."

"What for?"

"I asked you not to talk about EM's murder anymore, and then I went and opened my big mouth in front of all those authors."

"That was the martini talking," Tricia said kindly.

"One martini too many, I think."

"I wouldn't worry about it. I think they enjoyed discussing it."

"I'm glad I didn't mention your part in trying to solve it. What would they think about that?"

Tricia grimaced. "That I'm a pathetic wannabe sleuth trying to live the life of one of their characters. Wouldn't that get a few laughs?"

"What you've done in the past is dangerous, and I'd be happy if you'd just find a nice, safe hobby."

"Like what?"

"Like . . . renovating your home."

"I could drop a hammer on my toe and break it," Tricia said.

"Now you're just being silly."

"And I think *you* need to go to bed and sleep off your liquid dinner."

"You're right about that." Angelica carefully sat up, swinging her legs off the loveseat. "The thing is, I'm not sure I can walk all that way under my own power."

"Then I will help you," Tricia said, and got up from her seat. She crossed the space between them and grasped her sister's arm, helping her to stand. Angelica swayed for a moment or two before she found her sea legs. "Please never let me drink so much ever again."

"I'll put that on my perpetual list of things to do," Tricia promised with a wry grin. She helped Angelica to the bedroom, got her ready for bed, and pulled the covers up to her neck and kissed her on the forehead. "Now, go to sleep and have sweet dreams."

"Thank you, Trish. You, too," Angelica said with heavy eyelids, and immediately fell asleep.

Tricia switched off the bedside lamp and pulled the door until it was ajar, then retreated to the lounge. Should she watch TV? No, that didn't appeal to her. She left a lamp alight in the lounge in case Angelica needed to get up in the night, and retreated to her own room. It wasn't all that late, and she had a novel to finish, but before she settled down in the comfortable upholstered chair with a good book, she sampled a couple of the chocolates in the box sent by her secret admirer/stalker and found them to be superb.

Oh, what had she missed during the past forty years?

And then she plucked yet another chocolate delight from the box and thoroughly enjoyed it.

EIGHTEEN

Considering everything that had happened the day before—with all its unpleasant implications—Tricia had no trouble falling asleep, and slept like the proverbial log. In fact, she overslept, since she'd forgotten to set her alarm.

The ship seemed to be fighting a heavy sea—not enough to make her feel queasy, just enough to make her aware that they were traveling the Atlantic Ocean in January. She was sure Fiona would be wearing the compression bands on her wrists today. Raindrops beaded the windows and Tricia decided she would skip her power walk around the deck that day. In fact, she decided to skip exercise altogether, and showered and changed before she entered the suite's lounge, where she found Angelica sitting in front of the television. She turned down the sound.

"There you are, sleepyhead. I was beginning to think I should put my compact's mirror under your nose to check to see if you were still breathing."

"I did sleep like the dead," Tricia admitted, and stopped before that morning's breakfast cart. She found a carton of vanilla yogurt and nothing else but crumb-littered plates. Frowning, she poured herself a cup of coffee and sat down on what she thought of as her loveseat.

"How are you feeling this morning?"

"I have just a wee bit of a headache. I was wondering if I ought to indulge in the hair of the dog."

"You asked me not to let you drink too much ever again," Tricia reminded her.

"Yes, I guess I did. Coffee will have to do." Angelica turned off the set. "You missed Millicent's interview."

"Not the one she did with EM."

"No, but boy did she hype the fact they're going to show it again on Friday. You'd think she'd snagged an audience with the Queen or something."

Tricia sipped her coffee and changed the subject. "The weather looks dreadful."

"We've had the best of it," Angelica agreed. "According to Millicent's weather report, we'll be stuck inside for the rest of the voyage."

"There's plenty to do—or nothing, if we're so inclined. Maybe I should do just that: rest up. Once we get back home, I've got a ton of work to do and lots of plans to make."

A smile tugged at Angelica's lips. "You almost sound happy. I haven't heard that tone in your voice for a long time."

"This trip has had more downs than ups," Tricia admitted, "but I also feel like a great weight has been lifted off my shoulders."

Angelica frowned. "Mother?"

Tricia sipped her coffee thoughtfully. "Yes, but I've also been thinking a lot about Christopher. Getting away from the daily grind—if only for a few days—was good for me. I think I'll try to make that a priority in the future—at least for a couple of days every month—even if I just sit in my apartment and decompress with a good book."

"You deserve it. We both do."

Tricia gave her sister a skeptical glance. "So says the workaholic."

"We've both got good people working for us—people we trust. It would be fun for the two of us to get away now and then."

Tricia hadn't meant to include Angelica in her downtime plans, but now wasn't the time to mention it. She drained her cup and stood. "I think I'll go in search of sustenance."

"There's yogurt on the cart," Angelica said.

Tricia wrinkled her nose. "I was thinking of something a little more substantial. Maybe I'll mosey up to the Kells Grill. I've only had dinner there. I wonder what they serve for breakfast."

"Want me to come with you?" Angelica offered. "After all, there *is* a murderer running around the ship." She was still dressed in a nightgown, robe, and slippers. By the time she showered and changed, they'd be serving lunch.

"Hopefully whoever killed EM is preoccupied with the most important meal of the day and won't be planning any mayhem until later in the day. But let's meet for lunch. How about the Lido Restaurant at one?"

"Good. I'll track down Antonio and Ginny and see if they want to join us. Mr. Everett and Grace, too."

"Great. I'm just going to grab my book and e-reader and then I'll be off."

By the time Tricia returned to the lounge, Angelica had retreated into her own half of the suite. Tricia made sure her keycard was in her pocket before she closed the door behind her. She decided to walk up the three flights to the Kells Grill, and when she got there found only a couple of stragglers seated at the tables. She glanced at her watch. She'd made it only ten minutes before they stopped serving.

"Ah, Ms. Miles. It's been days since we saw you," Cristophano greeted her, and smiled.

"Do you work all three meal shifts?"

"Sì. Can I get you some coffee?" he asked as he handed her one of the leather-clad menus.

"I think I'll have a nice cup of tea."

"Irish breakfast tea?"

"Sì."

Cristophano nodded and headed for the beverage station across the room. Tricia only had time to turn on her e-reader before he returned with a pot of hot water and a tea bag. "Would you like a few moments to study the menu?"

"Yes, thank you."

Cristophano nodded and respectfully retreated.

Tricia glanced at the menu. The full Irish breakfast looked inviting, with its fried eggs, rashers of bacon, grilled tomatoes, mushrooms, sausage, baked beans, and sautéed potatoes. Tricia smiled and closed the folder. She set it on the table beside her and noticed Dori Douglas sitting at a table in the corner of the exclusive restaurant, the remnants of her breakfast before her, gazing out at the roiling gray seas, looking distinctly unhappy.

Cristophano returned. "Are you ready to order, madam?"

"Yes." Tricia handed him the menu. "I'd like the full Irish breakfast."

"Feeling particularly hungry today?" he inquired.

"I feel as if I've been starving for decades," Tricia admitted truthfully.

"Very good." He turned and headed for the kitchen.

Tricia wondered if she should speak to Dori but decided against it. She wanted a quiet breakfast with delicious food and intended to enjoy every moment of it. She turned her attention to her e-reader, studied the titles on the main page, and decided to choose something a little darker to go along with the day's weather, but before she could open the file, Dori stood, noticed her, and headed in her direction.

"Hello, Tricia. Would you mind if I joined you?"

Yes, I would. Still, she forced a smile. "I'd be delighted."

Dori took the seat opposite Tricia.

Tricia waited and waited, but Dori didn't initiate conversation.

"Is everything all right, Dori?"

"I had a very unpleasant experience last evening that still has me upset."

"Oh?"

Dori nodded. "I decided to treat myself and have a drink in the Chart Room. but when I got there I found a rowdy group of EM's fans discussing the possibility that she was murdered instead of committing suicide."

Was the whole ship buzzing about that possibility?

"One of them knew I was the president of EM's fan club and told them so," Dori continued. "Then they started debating whether *I* had the motive and opportunity to kill EM. Me, the woman who took care of her. I hid from the world the fact that EM was a sour, disagreeable woman. I answered her fan mail. I wrote and posted the updates to her blog and website. No one else in the world knew that I was the public face of the late, great, miserable EM Barstow," she said bitterly.

"Perhaps they just imbibed too much," Tricia suggested.

"They were drunk, all right. But I was scared they might come after me. I practically ran back to my cabin. I'm not sure I want to go back to any of the ship's common areas, in case someone comes after me."

"I'm so sorry," Tricia said, feeling bad for the poor woman.

"I thought this trip would be the chance of a lifetime. Instead, it's been a nightmare."

There weren't a lot of high spots for Tricia, either, but her problems were insignificant compared to Dori's. "Is there anything I can do to help?"

Dori sighed. "No. I just needed someone to talk to. Thank you for being a sounding board."

"I'm sorry I couldn't be of more help."

"Maybe I could hang around with you today and tomorrow."

Oh, God, no!

"Although I own a mystery bookstore, I seldom get the chance to lose myself in a book. I'm afraid my plans for the day are to find a quiet place to read. I don't think I'd be good company," Tricia explained.

Dori's expression hardened. "I understand." But it was apparent she didn't. She stood. "Well, I guess I'll be on my way. I wouldn't want to keep you from anything *really* important." She pivoted and stormed off toward the door.

"Dori!" Tricia called after her, but the woman yanked open the etched-glass door and passed through it without a backward glance.

Tricia sighed. She'd been polite. That Dori had taken offense wasn't her fault. She'd let far too many people make her feel guilty if she dared contradict their vision of how she should react. Those days were over. Her mother's latest rejection had convinced her that if she wanted to plow forward in life—finally be her own person—she was going to have to cease to allow other people, including Angelica, to dictate who she was and what she'd do.

Sorry, Dori, but the rest of this trip is mine, Tricia thought defiantly.

Cristophano appeared with a plate in hand. "Your breakfast, madam."

"Thank you."

"May I get you another pot of hot water?"

"No, thank you. I'm fine."

"Very well, madam."

Again, Tricia was surprised that Cristophano didn't click his heels as he bowed. "Do let me know if I can get you anything else."

"I will, thank you."

Cristophano nodded and retreated.

Tricia looked at the virtual banquet on her plate and picked up her fork and knife before diving into the best breakfast of her life.

The Garden Lounge was the perfect place to spend the day reading. Unfortunately, it wasn't a unique idea, as the cheerful, expansive room was jammed with other passengers who'd come to the same conclusion. The lights had been turned up to compensate for the gloomy skies and dark sea surrounding the ship, and with so many lively conversations going on Tricia knew there'd be no quiet to be found. She turned and headed for the stairwell. She'd look for a more tranquil spot to read, starting at the ship's lowest deck.

She'd nearly made it down to Deck 2 when she saw Mary Fairchild round the landing on her way up.

"Hey, Tricia!"

"Hi, Mary. What's up?"

"Busy day. Have you made plans for tonight?"

"No. Why?"

"Tonight's the big dance competition and I'm a little nervous. I've been having trouble with the paso doble."

"I beg your pardon?"

"A quick Spanish two-step."

"I'm sure you'll do fine."

"I'm hoping they stick to the more basic stuff. Still, after studying the competition, and unless a ringer shows up, I'm pretty confident," Mary admitted. "But part of the scoring relates to audience approval. I'm trying to track down everyone from our group and ask them to please come and cheer me on."

"What time does the contest start?"

"Nine in the Crystal Ballroom. Please say you'll be there."

Tricia considered ballroom dancing as exciting as watching paint dry, but Mary was a friend, and there wasn't anything she'd do to hurt the woman's feelings. "Sounds like fun. Unless something comes up, I'll do my best to be there."

"Thanks. Did you know Diana Lovell, the mystery author, was going to be one of the judges?"

"No, I hadn't heard that. I didn't know she was a dancer."

"She's not. But she's been a devoted fan of every season of *Dancing with the Stars*, and she knows her stuff."

If you say so, Tricia thought, amused.

"Now, I'm off to the shopping arcade to buy a new dress. It'll cost the moon, but I want to make a spectacular impression on the judges."

"I'm sure you'll look beautiful."

"And then I'm going back to my cabin to practice some more dance steps. No one will say I'm not prepared for this."

Tricia's smile broadened. "Well, as they say in show business, break a leg."

Mary laughed. "I hope not!" She gave a quick wave and continued on her way upstairs once again. Tricia trundled down the last of the stairs to Deck 1 and considered entering the theater's ground floor, but when she looked inside the cavernous and empty auditorium, she reconsidered. There was a murderer running loose. Did she want to be alone in such an isolated area of the ship? No.

The Grand Lobby was elegant, with polished chocolate marble floors and a magnificent mahogany staircase that soared three levels high, with a sparkling chandelier twinkling above. Scattered around the area were a number of tables, chairs, and plush loveseats—and like in the Garden Lounge, all of them were occupied. Tricia mounted the stairs and ascended to Deck 2 only to find that the Portside Bar and the lower level of the ship's library were also overflowing with passengers who'd been driven inside by the weather. Turning right, she headed down the corridor, stopping to admire some of the paintings on display, before she headed on toward the Crystal Ballroom. Many of its tables and chairs were occupied by people like her who'd sought a quiet sanctuary. This would do. The only conversations she heard were whispered as she crossed the expansive ballroom, settling on the port side next to a large expanse of window that was no more than ten or twelve feet above the roiling sea. She sat there for a good five or ten minutes, just watching the ocean's fury. Oddly enough, she felt at peace. Still, after a time, she turned her chair inward toward the tranquil room and consulted her book. She had plenty of time before the editors' panel would take place in the ship's theater. That was something she didn't want to miss.

She'd read for fifteen or twenty minutes before she looked up to see Harold Pilger sitting alone at one of the ballroom's tables on the other side of the deck. Closing her book, Tricia gathered her things, rose, and crossed the ballroom and the aisle beyond.

Pilger's gaze was fixed on the ocean rushing by outside the large droplet-spattered window. A yellow legal pad sat before him on the table, along with a pen. Several pages had been folded under the pad, but it looked like he'd paused to compose his thoughts.

"Penny for your thoughts," Tricia said.

He looked up. "Oh, hello."

"How are you enjoying your trip, Mr. Pilger?"

"Call me Harold. I'm sorry, but I've forgotten your name."

"Tricia Miles. Were you waiting for someone?"

"No. Just sitting here jotting down some thoughts."

"May I join you?"

He stood. "I'm sorry. Where are my manners? Please sit."

Tricia took the chair across from him at the small table, and Pilger turned the pad over. Rats! She couldn't get a peek.

"To answer your question, yes. I'm enjoying the trip so far, although it's a bit of a working vacation."

"Oh?" Tricia asked, glad she hadn't had to push to get him to open up. That is, *if* he was about to open up. He might be willing to do so, if she first made a confession.

"Mr. Pilger—"

"Harold," he insisted.

Tricia smiled. "Harold. I think you should know that it was me who found EM hanging in her stateroom bathroom."

Pilger's eyes widened, his mouth dropping open. "I take it ship's security didn't mention my name."

"No. Thank you for coming forward to speak with me."

"As Cathy told you, I'm a bookseller. I specialize in vintage mysteries—but I'm also well acquainted with the work of most contemporary mystery authors as well. And, I've read a lot of true crime accounts." He nodded. "So, I thought you might be interested in what I saw the night of EM's death."

"Very much," he admitted. "I take it you don't believe her death was suicide."

"No. Did they let you see the body?"

He shook his head. "No."

"I noticed there was an abrasion on the underside of her chin. As though she'd been dragged across the carpet in her stateroom. Also, her keycard was missing. I had to put mine into the slot in order for the lights to come on. I doubt she could have hanged herself in pitch blackness."

He nodded, listening intently. "Anything else?"

"I saw no sign of her laptop computer. I never saw her without it."

"Yes. It's missing," he confirmed.

"I thought perhaps you came on board to try to ascertain whether her death was suicide or murder."

"She *was* heavily insured," Pilger admitted. "Fidelity Mutual of Connecticut will not pay out for a suicide. Therefore, anything I can do to prove EM was murdered will benefit my employer."

Tricia nodded. "EM's stateroom keycard was recovered the morning after her death," Tricia began, but didn't go into details about where and when. "I don't know if someone on board had used it to buy goods or drinks. If so, I'm sure ship's security could check video to find out who did."

"I'll be speaking to Officer McDonald again later this afternoon. I'll be sure to ask."

"Have you spoken with Dori Douglas, EM's fan club president?"

"Yes. She very graciously offered to help us in any way she could."

"It was EM who introduced me to her editor, Cathy Copper. Was she the last one to speak to EM before her death?"

"I don't believe so. Ms. Douglas told me she'd spoken to EM before retiring on Monday evening. We believe she was the last to see Ms. Barstow alive."

"Has Officer McDonald corroborated that?"

Pilger frowned. "He hasn't been forthcoming with much that can help me determine what actually happened. I suppose I'll be trading letters with the cruise line's lawyers to get what little information they'd be willing to share."

"It's too bad. Their first priority should be finding out the truth—even if it would be inconvenient for them to admit a crime was committed."

Pilger nodded.

"Harold, did you know the ship has hundreds of cameras monitoring the public areas twenty-four/seven?"

"So I noticed," Pilger said, and nodded toward one of the Plexiglas domes that hid a camera on the ceiling not far from them.

"I wonder if we could persuade Officer McDonald to let us review the video from those cameras."

"Do you think they'd still retain those images after so many days?"

"It couldn't hurt to ask."

Pilger eyed Tricia suspiciously. "And what do you get out of it if we uncover the truth about EM's death?"

"Nothing more than personal satisfaction. I have no literary aspirations. I wouldn't write a tell-all exposé for the tabloids. But I'd feel I was doing a service to EM's legions of fans who will want to know the truth about her death. You might be surprised, but fans of her writing will not only grieve for the loss of their favorite author, but for the loss of her characters, as well."

"Do you feel that way about Agatha Christie?"

"I was just a little girl when she died, but I often wonder what else she might have written had she lived another one, five, or even ten years more."

Pilger nodded. "I understand."

"Are you a mystery reader, Harold?"

The lawyer shook his head. "I deal in facts. I read true crime because I prefer operating in the real world. I have no affection for fiction."

"That's too bad," Tricia said. The man had no clue. According to George R. R. Martin, "A reader lives a thousand lives before he dies, the man who never reads lives only one." Tricia believed it heart and soul. She was way beyond that thousand-life threshold. Still, the two of them did have a common goal: to find out the truth behind EM Barstow's death.

"Are you willing to approach Officer McDonald about reviewing those ship's video logs?"

"Yes. And the sooner, the better."

Tricia nodded. "He seems to work erratic hours, but we could at least approach the ship's security team."

Pilger picked up his legal pad and pocketed his pen. "I should go now. There are probably hundreds of hours of video to review. The sooner I start, the sooner I'm done."

Tricia pushed back her chair and rose.

Pilger stood, too. "Ms. Miles—Tricia," he amended. "I don't think it's a good idea for you to accompany me."

"Why not?"

"I'm on board in an official capacity, and you're—"

"Just a wannabe sleuth?" she offered. He hadn't minded her telling him things about EM's death that he hadn't known. Was he afraid that she—a lowly retailer—might come across yet more pieces of information that could be used to prove his theory and look more knowledgeable—and capable—than someone who'd passed the New York bar?

"Well," he began, but didn't seem to have a placating comeback.

"I completely understand," Tricia said. And how. She forced a smile. "I'm sure we'll run into each other before we dock in New York. Good luck with your investigation."

"Thank you. And thank you for understanding."

Again Tricia forced a smile. "Have a nice day."

"You, too."

Tricia strode off, unwilling to resume her seat across the way. She'd find somewhere else to pass the time until the editors' panel, which was still a good two hours off. And maybe she'd count the minutes until this far-from-pleasurable cruise was to end.

NINETEEN

Tricia found a quiet niche in the Wee Dram bar and read for more than an hour before she thought to look up and note the time. *Good grief!* It was already five after one. She'd told Angelica she'd meet her at the Lido Restaurant at one o'clock.

Once again Tricia gathered up her things and this time hurried to the nearest bank of lifts. Two minutes later, she entered the busy restaurant, walking its length until she spotted a table for six with a high chair squeezed in.

"There you are," Angelica scolded, but she sounded more relieved than annoyed.

Tricia took the only empty seat, next to Grace. "Sorry I'm late. I've been reading."

"So we figured," Ginny said, handing Sofia an arrowroot biscuit to gum.

"Did you check out the food on your way to the table?" Grace asked.

223

She held her fork, ready to spear a piece of lettuce from the salad in front of her.

"No. I'm not really hungry. I had an enormous breakfast."

"And what was that? Half a bagel?" Ginny guessed, and laughed.

"No. The Kells Grill's full Irish breakfast."

"How much were you able to eat—a quarter of it?" Antonio asked. His plate contained grilled salmon in a wine sauce with some angel-hair pasta on the side.

"No. All of it."

The heads of the other five adults at the table all snapped to look in Tricia's direction.

"All of it?" Angelica asked. "But that's a massive amount of food."

"I know," Tricia said. "But the fresh sea air made me hungry."

"Don't tell me you did your usual four-mile power walk on the deck in this weather," Ginny said.

"Oh, no. I was afraid I'd be swept overboard. I just took a quick sniff outside." Okay, that was a lie, but it could have happened that way. "Anybody do anything interesting this morning?"

"I had a massage. It was heavenly," Angelica said, attacking one of the rolls on her plate, and then smearing it with a thick pat of butter.

"And while she did that, I had a pedicure," Ginny said. "Wanna see my blue toenails?"

"I'll pass on that," Tricia said, and smiled.

"And while they did that—I wrote a presentation to make to my employer, Nigela Ricita, about changing the menu at the Brookview Inn."

"Surely Ms. Ricita doesn't expect you to work on your vacation?" Grace chided him.

"Oh, no. But it is my pleasure to take this experience and apply it to my vocation in any way I can."

"I don't know," Grace said, cutting a cherry tomato in half. "Seems like you should be having more fun."

"But my work *is* fun," Antonio said, glancing in Angelica's direction and winking.

"I hope you'll suggest these wonderful pork chops," Mr. Everett said.

"What kind of sauce is that?" Tricia inquired.

"Honey hoisin. Absolutely marvelous. All the meat has been superb." As a former butcher, Mr. Everett knew a good cut when he ate it.

"Are you sure you don't want anything?" Angelica asked her sister.

"I may swipe a couple of cookies for later this afternoon. After the editors' panel."

"You won't have long to wait," Ginny said. "The panel ends at two."

"Oh, no. I'm sure it starts at two," Tricia said.

"'Fraid not," Angelica agreed. "I looked at the Daily Program before Ginny and I went to the spa. It definitely started at one."

Tricia glanced at her watch. She'd already missed half of it. This day was *not* getting any better.

"Was there something you wanted to hear at the talk?" Grace asked.

"Just what EM Barstow's editor had to say about the future of her Tennyson Eisenberg series."

"Surely there's no future if the author has died," Antonio said, and twirled pasta around his fork.

"Oh, no," Tricia, Angelica, Ginny, and Grace said in unison, and with conviction.

Antonio shook his head. "I fear I will never understand the publishing business."

"You aren't alone, my boy," Mr. Everett said, reaching for his cup of coffee.

Tricia pushed back her chair. "I'm going to see if I can catch the last half of the panel."

"Where will we meet later?" Angelica asked.

"I'll probably park myself in one of the bars. They seem to be a quieter destination than the bigger common areas on the ship."

"If we don't track each other down, let's meet at the Portside Bar for cocktails at five," Angelica suggested.

"Only if you promise not to start without me. Remember what happened last night."

"How could I forget," Angelica said with a little shudder. Antonio couldn't seem to hide a grin.

"See you later," Tricia said to a chorus of good-byes. She had no patience to wait for the lift, and strode straight to the forward staircase, which was virtually empty. She made it down the stairs to Deck 1 in less than two minutes, and hurried to the theater. It was standing room only on that level, and Tricia wished she'd thought to stop at Decks 2 and 3 first, since several of the box seats seemed to be vacant.

The audience was intently listening to one of the panelists: a woman whose placard said Claire Lawford. "We've seen a lot of changes in the industry over the past decade, especially with the consolidation of so many publishing houses." The rest of the panelists—including Cathy Copper—nodded sagely, and the moderator encouraged each of them to give their take on what the next trends in genre fiction might be.

Tricia had a feeling she had probably missed the most juicy information, which had no doubt been dished at the beginning of the discussion. And she was right. Under other circumstances, she probably would have hung on to every word the editors said, but she had wanted to hear one piece of news, and it was not brought up. She looked around the auditorium, but didn't see anyone she knew among those seated. Perhaps her best bet was just to wait—and confront—Cathy Copper.

Confront sounded a little antagonistic. She'd invite Cathy for a drink and if she accepted, she'd find a way to introduce the subject.

It took another ten minutes for the discourse to wind down before the moderator thanked the panelists, and the audience reacted with an enthusiastic round of applause. Soon the murmur of voices grew in pitch as the spectators rose from their seats to file out of the auditorium. Tricia stepped out of the way as the large room emptied, her gaze fixed on the panelists, who stood on stage, speaking with each other.

Only a few stragglers remained when the panelists headed for the stairs that led down to the rows upon rows of now-empty seats. Tricia started down the main aisle. "Cathy!"

Cathy looked up. "Oh, hi, Tricia. Thanks for attending the panel. I'm shocked that so many people thought we had anything of interest to say."

"I wish I could say I was here for the entire program, but I'm afraid I got my times mixed up and only got to hear the last half of the discussion. I thought maybe we could go to one of the bars and get a drink and you might fill me in on what I missed."

Cathy looked about ready to refuse, but then seemed to think it over. "That sounds nice." She held out a hand. "Lead the way."

Since the Golden Harp pub was on the next level up, they headed up the forward staircase and easily found a place to sit near one of the portholes that overlooked the still-choppy sea. The ocean was a darker shade of gray than the gloomy skies above, and Cathy's expression seemed just as dour as they ordered a round of drinks. A glass of Chardonnay for Tricia, and another diet cola for Cathy.

Tricia surrendered her keycard while Cathy looked out the window and sighed. "I had no idea the weather would be this appalling," she said, sounding subdued.

Tricia had to admit, when she thought of a cruise, she pictured sunny skies and a warmer climate. "Bermuda was nice."

"While it lasted," Cathy grumbled.

"Were you able to take in any of the sights?"

"Just the wharf. Half the shops were closed because the tourist season won't officially start for another couple of months."

What a bundle of negativity. Cathy's expression was so dour, Tricia half expected her to burst into tears at any moment.

"I take it you didn't find the panel to be very interesting."

She shrugged. "I've heard it all before."

"Based on the audience's reaction, I don't think they did."

Again Cathy shrugged.

Tricia wondered if she should ask about EM's characters' futures, but then the waiter arrived with their drinks, setting them down on cocktail napkins embossed with a golden harp. Tricia signed the receipt and the waiter moved off. She picked up her glass. "Cheers."

Cathy picked up her own glass, but didn't join the toast.

"Did Mr. Pilger bring news from your supervisor about the fate of the Tennyson Eisenberg series?"

"It will go on. I'd like to take a shot at writing them."

"Really?"

"I think I know them well enough to pull it off. It could even be an improvement. I think you're aware of my feelings concerning the direction EM wanted to take the series. No one could reason with that woman."

Was Cathy referring to EM's passive-aggressive nature?

"Oh?"

"She wasn't entirely stable—mentally, that is," she added dryly.

"Did you see signs of mental illness in her before the trip?" Tricia asked, feigning innocence.

Cathy nodded. "Sadly, yes. She'd been practically paranoid about protecting her vision of her series and its characters. She didn't take into account what her publisher—and more importantly—her readers wanted. She was determined to kill off Tennyson Eisenberg." Good grief, the woman sounded positively offended by the thought.

"Conan Doyle did the same thing with Sherlock Holmes, but eventually relented and his grateful readers benefited with many more stories to enjoy."

"These days, readers are a *lot* more discerning," Cathy commented.

For one so young, Cathy certainly was cynical.

"What plans does the publisher have in mind for the series now that EM is gone?" Tricia asked.

"I'm sure they've had top-level meetings on just that subject. I probably won't be told until I go back to the office on Monday."

"I suppose it will be business as usual for you."

Cathy nodded. "EM and I weren't in contact on a daily basis. In fact, we rarely spoke. We conducted most of our business by e-mail. And, in fact, a lot of times I would be e-mailing Dori Douglas, the president of her fan club, who was acting as her virtual assistant. She handled a lot for EM, who didn't pay her a nickel," she said as an aside. "I don't know how EM convinced the poor woman to take on that kind of responsibility. I know I wouldn't have done it."

Of course not. It seemed as though Cathy could barely stand the woman, which must have made working together nearly unbearable—for both of them.

"I suppose now that your panel is over you're free to do as you please for the rest of the cruise."

"One whole day," Cathy agreed. "It's too bad Internet access is so expensive on board. I'm going to have a lot of e-mails to go through when I get home."

Did she mean personally or for her job?

"I did load several manuscripts on my tablet, and I'm going to make an effort to read them before I get back to work. A couple of them look really interesting."

"Mysteries?" Tricia asked hopefully.

"Literary fiction. That's what I prefer to read. I have an English degree from Dartmouth."

"So do I," Tricia said.

Cathy immediately brightened, as though she'd found a kindred spirit in a sea of genre readers. "I'm working toward my master's. My thesis is on eighteenth-century women poets."

Oh, dear. That subject had been done to death by nearly half of Tricia's classmates. She'd chosen pulp fiction, which hadn't been a favorite subject of her professor, but she'd still received an A.

"Were you in a sorority?" Cathy asked.

"Kappa Delta." For about a month. Tricia just hadn't fit in and preferred to spend most of her time away from class reading. She'd left the sorority house and had ended up with Pammy Fredricks as a roommate.

"I was in Sigma Delta," Cathy said, sounding disappointed. If they'd been sorority sisters, would Cathy have wanted to hang out with Tricia? "Being a Sigma Delta sister was one of the highlights of my life," she said wistfully.

And what were the lowlights?

"Do you get to New York often?" Cathy asked. "Maybe we could have lunch together sometime."

My, what a change of attitude—and all because they'd gone to the same college.

"This is actually the first time I've gotten away since I opened my store almost six years ago."

"Retail is difficult," Cathy agreed. "Didn't you aspire to more?"

Was she actually interested in the answer?

"I worked at a nonprofit for almost a decade. It was challenging work, but I always had my heart set on opening a mystery bookstore."

Cathy sighed, probably biting her tongue so as not to make a nasty remark about that particular brand of fiction. "I often think of what I might do when I retire."

"I didn't retire," Tricia asserted. She was, after all, only twelve or thirteen years older than Cathy. "I got divorced. I received a nice settlement and decided to make a change."

"Didn't you say you were located in New Hampshire?"

Tricia nodded.

"Don't you miss the excitement of the city?"

"Not really. Life has not been at all dull since I moved to Stoneham." Not when some of the villagers now referred to it as the death capital of New England.

"I may have to drive up there to have a look," Cathy said. She certainly seemed a lot more affable than she'd been ten or so minutes before—kind of like a fair-weather friend. Tricia had had enough of those friendships, and now she wished she hadn't blown off Angelica and her Stoneham family at lunch to mark time with Cathy. Oh well, there was always dinner, where she could reconnect.

Tricia drained her glass. "It's been a busy day."

"For me, too," Cathy admitted.

"I'll be staying up late tonight—at least late for me—to go to the big ballroom dance competition. Are you going?"

Cathy shook her head. "I find competitive *anything* to be a total bore."

"One of my friends thinks she has a shot at winning."

"I walked past the Crystal Ballroom when some of the classes were going on. Lot of old farts were doing the mambo. It was hysterical."

Tricia didn't appreciate her friend being called an old fart. "I'm sure they're all young at heart."

"And they ought to be careful they don't *strain* their hearts," Cathy said, and laughed.

"Aerobic exercise is good for everyone."

Cathy's gaze dipped. "Sometimes a little *too* good."

Talk about a non sequitur.

Tricia rose. "I'm sure we'll be bumping into each other before the end of the cruise."

"As it's a small ship—it seems inevitable."

"Have a great evening," Tricia said, grabbing her tote, and headed for the aisle. She hoped that would be the last time she spent time with Cathy Copper.

TWENTY

It was nearly five, and Tricia was already sitting in the Portside Bar when Angelica practically came bouncing into the room. Tricia had parked there after her encounter with Cathy Copper, content to sit in the corner and read while other passengers came for a drink or two and then wandered off again.

She sat up straighter and put her book on the cocktail table in front of her. "You're in a good mood."

"And why shouldn't I be?" Angelica asked, sitting down in the adjacent brocaded chair. "It turns out there are three other Chamber of Commerce presidents on the cruise. We met for drinks and had a fascinating chat about intrastate marketing."

"Drinks?" Tricia asked, unable to keep the disapproval out of her voice.

"Pardon me, I should have said 'coffee.' I promise you, so far nothing stronger has passed my lips today." She signaled the waitress. "But that's about to change."

"Where did this happen?"

"In the card room. Lovely little niche. Too bad we don't play cards. It seems to be where the eligible men gravitate—except they all appear to be over seventy. What have you been up to? Did you ever track down Cathy Copper?"

"Oh, yes."

"Did she say anything interesting?"

"She went to Dartmouth."

"She's an alumnus?" Angelica asked, sounding disconcerted.

"Sigma Delta."

Angelica rolled her eyes. "Well, that explains everything about her."

"Now, now," Tricia chided. "Those kinds of rivalries are far in our past."

"You're right," Angelica said, sounding contrite. "And after the wonderful afternoon I've had, I'm not going to think about past jealousies. After all, there's virtually no one I'm envious of."

"Then you're a very lucky person."

"You're jealous of someone?" Angelica asked, surprised.

"Not at all."

Luckily the uniformed waitress arrived to put an end to that subject.

"I'll have a gin and tonic," Angelica said.

"Oh?" Tricia asked.

"Sure. After yesterday, I'm going to pace myself. And G and Ts are kind of like martinis on training wheels, right?"

Tricia shook her head before turning to the waitress. "I'll have one, too, please. And could we have a bowl of crisps with that?"

"Certainly," the woman said as Angelica handed over her keycard. "I'll be back in a few moments with your drinks." She nodded and headed back toward the bar.

"Crisps?" Angelica sked.

"I skipped lunch, remember?" Tricia said.

"Oh, yes. So you did." She settled back in her chair. "I take it you haven't been back to the suite since this morning."

"No, why?"

"Because, your secret admirer has struck again."

"Oh, no."

"Oh, yes," Angelica said, grinning.

"What is it this time?"

"Looks like jewelry."

"You didn't open it?"

"My name is *not* on the card," Angelica pointed out. "The wrapping paper is from one of the arcade's shops. I'm going to guess it's a necklace. Or perhaps a pin."

"I wish you'd brought it with you—then there'd be no suspense."

"As a matter of fact," Angelica began, and then opened her purse. She withdrew the little package.

"I should have known," Tricia said, and sighed.

"Open it, open it!" Angelica encouraged.

"This time there's a card," Tricia said, and worked at the envelope's seal. The card within was printed, as though by a computer. *"To remember your Irish cruise."*

"Get to the good stuff," Angelica pressed.

Tricia worked her thumbnail under the tape on the end of the square box and unwrapped it. Removing the lid, she couldn't help but smile.

"What is it?" Angelica demanded.

Tricia turned the box so that Angelica could see the silver Celtic knot pendant on a chain.

"Oh. That's nice," Angelica said, obviously disappointed.

"It *is* nice."

"I saw the same one—and maybe that's it, for all I know—for about thirty dollars. I guess your secret admirer doesn't have a lot of cash lying around."

"I think it's pretty."

"You're not creeped out about getting it?"

"Well, a little," Tricia admitted. "I wonder if I should wear it. If I do, maybe whoever sent it will see it and finally come talk to me. I'd much rather know who's behind all these little gifts than to have it hanging over me. I mean, what if it doesn't stop when we go home?"

"Do you want me to fasten it for you?"

"I can do it," Tricia said, removing the necklace from the box and putting it around her neck. It looked pretty and stood out well against her black sweater set.

The waitress arrived with the drinks and a silver bowl filled with potato chips, giving Angelica back her keycard and the receipt, which she signed. "Pretty necklace."

"Thank you. Would you mind disposing of the box and wrapping, please?"

"Not at all," she said, scooping it up and setting it on her tray. "Let me know if you need anything else."

"Thank you," Angelica said. She picked up her drink, removing the sliced lemon from the rim and squeezing it into the tonic. She took a sip. "Different than with a lime, but I could get used to it."

Tricia sipped her own drink. *Not bad.* "Has the gang made dinner plans?"

"Because of the dance competition, we thought it best not to have dinner at the Kells Grill. We'd probably miss the first hour. But it *is* formal dress tonight. We'll just have to have an early dinner at one of the other on-board restaurants and then get ready for the floor show."

"I rather like the Lido Restaurant," Tricia said. "I like the whole smorgasbord presentation. It reminds me of being back in college." Although that thought brought Cathy Copper back to mind, and Tricia really didn't want to go there yet again.

"We should have tried one of the other on-board restaurants."

"You mean where you pay extra for some exotic cuisine?"

"We can afford it."

"I know; but it's just such a bother."

"Tonight is our last chance to dress to the nines. It'll be casual the night before we dock," Angelica lamented.

"I brought way too many formal outfits. I'll probably never have an opportunity to wear them again, either. At least, not in Stoneham."

"We could go on another cruise," Angelica suggested, sounding hopeful.

"Maybe."

Tricia sipped her drink.

Out in the corridor, Arnold Smith rode past the bar on his motorized scooter. *What an odd duck*, Tricia thought. Despite the fact that so many of the authors—and his fellow readers—seemed to know him, he appeared to be without comrades. Still, from what she'd seen of the man, Tricia didn't feel inclined to offer him the hand of friendship and ask him to join her and Angelica. From what she'd observed, he wasn't at all a nice man and seemed intent on pushing boundaries— and making a pest of himself at the same time.

Was he just a loser, or should she pity such a man who obviously lacked polish? Perhaps that's why he'd stalked EM Barstow. Could he have recognized her as a kindred spirit and her rejection of him forced him into rescuing his bruised ego by asserting his own warped sense of authority? He certainly seemed to enjoy bullying the authors, who were polite, and probably afraid to court his wrath and to challenge even more abhorrent behavior.

After all, he might just be a murderer.

Tricia frowned, reaching for a handful of crisps. But that didn't make sense. The man had health issues; perhaps a bad back or a weak heart that had forced him to use a scooter rather than walk. There was no way he could have pulled EM across her cabin's carpet and then strung her up in the shower. No way. But somehow Tricia wasn't sure about the guy. If he was adept at stalking, who knew what else he was capable of?

"You're awfully quiet," Angelica said.

"Just thinking," Tricia said, and munched another chip.

"Of what?"

"Of who could have killed EM."

Angelica pouted. "You're not going to start that again, are you?"

"It was just a passing thought." Or two. Or four. Oh, hell—many thoughts. She reached for another handful of crisps but found the bowl conspicuously empty. Did the ship's stores include flavored crisps? Barbecue? Sour cream and chives? Salt and vinegar? Pickle?

"That's a quizzical expression you're sporting," Angelica commented. "Now what are you thinking of?"

"Nothing important."

The already dark sky outside the rain-splattered windows seemed to be growing a deeper shade of gray by the moment. "It'll still be winter when we get home the day after tomorrow," Tricia said.

"I don't know about you, but I feel revitalized by this trip; eager to take on new, challenging projects. Don't you feel that way, too?"

There were many projects to tackle, but Tricia wasn't sure she felt invigorated by travel. More weary, actually. But that wasn't what Angelica wanted to hear. Christopher would still be gone, there was a lot of work ahead with the reconfiguration of her home—while trying to keep her business open. Oh, what a mess. And yet Angelica was right. The year ahead would be challenging—perhaps even life changing—but she decided right there and then that she would look at it as a positive. There'd been too much negativity in her life.

She looked down at the pendant that rested on her chest. It was pretty. Someone had put some thought into the gifts she'd received while on this trip. She decided that unless someone showed up demanding her attention, she would look at the presents for what they were: an appreciation. Because if she thought about each and every one of them, they were tailored to her likes. Then again, there'd been that box of candy. She hadn't been known for having a sweet tooth. Otherwise, the gifts had been trinkets from someone who knew her well.

Tricia looked over the rim of her glass, her gaze falling on Angelica's face. *Good grief!* Could Angelica be her secret admirer? She'd known Tricia suffered from depression since Christopher's death. She'd really pushed to get Tricia to sign up for the cruise. Had she sent the gifts before their stop in Bermuda as a setup to misdirect Tricia from considering the fact that she'd be confronting their mother? Angelica had certainly been nervous about the reunion.

Yes! The gifts could be viewed as a diversion. And today's pendant was yet another feel-good Band-Aid to help heal her wounded heart.

It certainly couldn't hurt to ask.

"My liquor level has plunged," Angelica remarked, eyeing the ice and nothing more in her glass. "Shall we go for another round?"

"Yes. Why not? But this time it's on me."

"That sounds fine." Angelica raised her right hand into the air, waving to get the waitress's attention.

They reordered and the waitress retreated before Tricia decided to test her theory. "I've been thinking . . ."

"Well, that was obvious."

"About these gifts," Tricia continued, and fingered the chain that hung from her neck.

"And?" Angelica asked.

"It's obvious whoever sent them knows me well."

"I'd say so."

"And is probably on this trip."

"Possibly." Was Angelica hedging?

"I think if there was malice attached to them—that the giver wanted something in return—he or *she* would have tried to corner me by now."

"Again, a possibility," Angelica acknowledged. "It sounds like you're about to make a pronouncement. Who? Who do you think it is?"

"Well, how about you?"

"Me?" Angelica asked, surprised.

"Yes, you."

"But why would I do that?"

"To cheer me up."

Angelica seemed to think about it for a moment. "You're right. It *would* be in character for me to perform such a generous act. I'm only sorry that I didn't think of it first."

"So, it's not you?" Tricia asked, disappointed.

Angelica shook her head. "Sorry. But think about it. I would have never sent you that box of chocolates."

"You're right. That was the only miss among the hits. Oh, well. I guess I'm back to square one, then."

"Sorry," Angelica apologized.

Tricia sipped her drink. "Did we decide about dinner?"

"No, but we're going to rendezvous at the Crystal Ballroom with the others for the dance contest, so I guess we're on our own."

"The Lido?" Tricia suggested.

"The Lido it is. Drink up. After we eat, we're going to have to change. I'm sure everyone will be dressed to kill, if you'll pardon the expression."

The whole idea of a dance-off seemed a bit silly to Tricia, but she had promised Mary she'd try to attend, and really, she didn't have anything better to do but read . . . and, oh, how she wanted to do just that.

She picked up her glass and drank the remnants. She eyed Angelica over the rim. "I'm ready. Let's go."

TWENTY-ONE

Tricia looked at herself in the mirror and wasn't displeased with what she saw. She'd bought the new cocktail dress during the shopping trip to Boston she, Ginny, and Angelica had made before the cruise, although she hadn't been entirely sure she'd get the chance to wear it. The bodice of the little black dress bore sequins, and the jacket was tailored, giving the illusion that she was taller than her five-foot-seven-inch frame. She'd condescended to buy a pair of low heels instead of her usual flats, but she knew Angelica, in stilettos, would still tower over her. How she could wear those shoes that not only threatened her Achilles tendons, but conspired to topple her, remained a mystery to Tricia.

She left her bedroom and switched off the lights. The door to Angelica's side of the suite was open, and Tricia found her sister in the bathroom touching up her makeup. "Almost ready?"

Angelica whisked the blush brush across her cheeks one more time, then inspected her lipstick, which was perfect. "I am now. Isn't this going to be fun?"

"I don't know about fun, but I hope Mary at least places."

"She doesn't honestly think she can win, does she?" Angelica said, shooing Tricia into the lounge and turning off the light behind her.

"She said she felt confident."

"Well, then let's hope she does. It sure can't hurt to have the entire Stoneham contingent rooting from the sidelines."

The sisters gathered up their purses, making sure their keycards were inside, and left the suite. As usual, the corridors seemed curiously empty until they came closer to the lifts, where a small crowd was waiting. In no time, the doors opened and they all crowded inside. The button was already pressed for Deck 2. It looked like the dance competition was the big draw that evening.

Tricia and Angelica followed the crowd to the Crystal Ballroom and were surprised to find a packed house. "Oh, dear. Where will we sit?" Angelica asked, looking around, but then Tricia saw Mr. Everett standing at a ringside table for six on the far side of the room, waving.

"It's good to have friends in high places," Tricia said, and nudged Angelica to follow.

Mr. Everett was decked out in a dark suit with a sedate maroon tie, while Grace was dressed to the max in a navy sequined full-length gown. "Oh, Grace, you look gorgeous," Angelica said.

"I haven't been this dressed up in ages," she said, and actually giggled.

"You look very handsome, too, Mr. Everett," Tricia said as she sat, and Mr. Everett pushed in her chair, then did the same for Angelica.

"Thank you."

Just then, a waiter in a white tuxedo arrived with a champagne bucket and bottle of bubbly. "Oh, this is a nice surprise," Angelica said.

"I thought it might be nice to toast to Mary's success," Grace said.

The waiter poured a smidgeon for Grace to taste; she approved the selection, and the waiter poured for the four of them. "To Mary." They raised their flutes.

"To Mary," Tricia and Angelica said.

"To Ms. Fairchild," Mr. Everett chimed in.

They drank. Angelica was the first to speak again. "I'm surprised to see such a big turnout. I mean, I knew ballroom dancing TV shows were big, but didn't realize they had such broad appeal."

"The Brits have had ballroom dance shows for ages. It never went out of fashion there," Grace pointed out. "And the Irish are spectacular dancers, too."

"I take it Antonio and Ginny will be arriving soon?" Angelica asked.

"There was some talk about them not getting a babysitter," Grace said. "Perhaps one of them will come."

"Ginny didn't sound too enthused when she mentioned it yesterday," Tricia said.

"Oh, dear," Angelica said, sounding disappointed.

And then, as if she'd wished on a star, Antonio appeared, resplendent in his black tuxedo. For a moment, Tricia wasn't sure if her sister might combust from the fierce look of maternal pride that seemed to radiate from her. "Sit by me, sit by me," Angelica encouraged Antonio.

"Why of course, dear lady," Antonio said as Tricia moved to the next seat to accommodate them.

"No babysitter?" Tricia asked.

"Ginny is content to spend the evening with a good book—one she bought at the author signing the other day. What have I missed?"

"Nothing so far," Tricia assured him as Mr. Everett leaned over to pour him a glass of champagne.

"I was concerned I'd miss the beginning of the competition," Antonio said, consulting his watch. "They must be running late."

From across the room, Tricia saw that EM's publisher's lawyer,

Harold Pilger, stood in the aisle at the far end of the ballroom. He seemed to be scanning the plethora of tables that ringed the dance floor in horseshoe fashion, finding no openings. He caught her eye and waved. *Oh no*, she thought as Pilger wasted no time and charged forward, dodging around the tables until he made his way to where Tricia sat.

"Is this seat taken?"

"Well—"

"No," Angelica said affably. "Please join us."

Pilger sat next to Tricia, giving her a thankful smile. She made the introductions as a string of well-dressed men and women emerged from the side of the stage. Each of the men had a cardboard placard hanging on his back with large black numbers against a stark white background. Mary and her partner, Ed, the retired shoe salesman, were number fifty-seven, although there couldn't have been more than twenty couples on the dance floor and lined up at the side of the room.

Millicent Ambrose stepped onto the small dais, moving to stand next to a microphone stand. She looked elegant in a white sheath with a bolero jacket piped in navy blue, giving her a nautical flair. Trailing behind her were three other people, one of whom was author Diana Lovell, who waved to her blog sisters who occupied another of the ringside seats. One of the other judges was Cathy Copper, followed by a man Tricia didn't know. Why would Cathy be judging a dance contest, especially after making such rude comments about those who took lessons? Although Tricia had to admit she didn't exactly seem thrilled to be there. Had Millicent cornered her and gotten her to agree during a moment of weakness?

Tricia watched as the judges sat on chairs behind a draped table with placards giving their names. Meanwhile, a combo began assembling on the other side of the stage, consisting of a sax player, a guy with an electric guitar, a fellow with a stand-up base, and a drummer. All were dressed in black tuxes, looking dapper. On the sidelines were several still and video photographers. No doubt a professional DVD of the event would be available for purchase come morning.

Millicent tested the microphone, then addressed the crowd.

"Good evening, everyone, and welcome to the *Celtic Lady*'s Dance Challenges. Our judges this evening are author Diana Lovell, celebrity chef Larry Andrews, and editor Cathy Copper. Let's give them a warm round of applause."

The audience did just that.

"And let's not forget the wonderful Jerry Hammond Combo."

More applause followed as the band members took a bow.

"We'll start out with the first heat, progressing until all contestants have had a chance to strut their stuff"—the audience roared—"and then the eliminations will begin. And now, let's dance!"

The lights above the audience dimmed, and the band launched into a jaunty tune with a Latin beat as the competitors began to mambo.

"Isn't this fun!" Angelica practically squealed.

Tricia had to admit the twirling disco ball, the sparkling dresses, and the men all dressed in tuxes—some of them in tails—were rather exhilarating. Best of all, Mary and her gentleman dance partner seemed to be the best of the passenger contestants. Tricia watched them moving back and forth in perfect synchronization and wondered how Mary had hidden such dancing talent from the entire village for so long. Had she taken classes as a child? There was a story there; Tricia hoped she'd get to hear about it before their bus rolled to a halt back on the streets of Stoneham.

The judges seemed to be carefully watching each of the contestants, jotting down notes, pointing at various dance teams, and consulting with one another. Meanwhile, Angelica topped up the champagne glasses. The music was so loud, and there were cheers and catcalls, with the audience calling out the numbers of their favorite contestants, that conversation was impossible. Tricia had had no idea that audience participation would be so exuberant. Everyone seemed enthused. Everyone but Harold Pilger, whose gaze seemed to be fixed on the judges more than the contestants.

After the music died, the next group of dancers took to the floor. This time, the band played a tango. Tricia noticed Mary, now on the sidelines, carefully checking out her competition. All the couples were good, but Tricia couldn't seem to sit still as she waited for the tune to finish and the last group of contestants came onto the floor to dance a waltz.

When the tune ended, the contestants went back to stand with their peers, looking nervous as the judges conferred for several tense minutes.

"Do you think Mary will be called back?" Grace asked anxiously.

"She has to," Angelica said with authority. "She and her partner were the best in her group."

Finally, the judges handed Millicent a card, and she approached the microphone once more. "From the first group, the judges have called back contestants forty-four, thirty-two, and fifty-seven!"

The ballroom broke out in raucous applause, whistles, and cheers.

"Thank goodness Mary made the first cut," Tricia said with relief.

"I can't believe how much I'm enjoying this," Angelica said, grinning. "Now I want to learn ballroom dancing."

"I do not think Ginny would be interested, but I might like to try it. Perhaps we should take lessons together, dear lady," Antonio said.

Angelica's mouth dropped in shocked surprise. "Do you mean it?"

"I would not say so if I didn't mean it."

Angelica grinned. "Wouldn't I look stunning on the dance floor in a flowing gown adorned with feathers and sequins?"

"You look lovely every day, Ms. Miles," Mr. Everett said with sincerity.

"Oh, you're just saying that because it's true," Angelica replied, and the rest of the table dutifully laughed. Expect for Pilger, that is. He was still watching the judges.

The competitors had assembled on the dance floor once again.

Millicent announced they'd be doing a foxtrot, and the band began to play. Once again, Mary and her partner were obviously the best dancers. Their posture and timing were impeccable. They looked as though they'd been dancing together for a lifetime, not mere days, and Tricia marveled at their skill. It was no surprise, therefore, when they passed every round of eliminations.

There were only three couples left on the dance floor after the judges gave their scorecards to Millicent. "And for our last round, our dancers will be performing the cha-cha!"

Hoots and cheers of approval rang out through the ballroom as the dancers assembled on the floor once more.

"This is the final dance. I know Mary's going to win. I just know it!" Grace cried with glee, and raised her hands in the air, clapping with wild abandon. Tricia stifled a giggle as she noticed a blush rise up Mr. Everett's neck, stalling at his cheeks as he took in his usually poised wife, who'd given in to her unbridled enthusiasm.

The music started, and all eyes turned to the dance floor once again. It was obvious to all assembled who were the best dancers: Mary and her partner. Tricia found herself watching their fleet feet and inwardly counted, *One, two, cha-cha-cha—one, two, cha-cha-cha!* There was no way those two weren't going to win the competition.

Tricia's gaze was so fiercely focused on the couple, that it took a moment or two before she noticed movement in the aisle across the ballroom. Arnold Smith rode his scooter up and down, his gaze fixed not on the dancers, but on the crowd at ringside. It looked as though he was trying to figure out the timing to cross the dance floor. But surely he wouldn't be thoughtless enough to try such an irresponsible move.

Suddenly Arnold hunched forward, taking aim, and seemed to gun the scooter's speed control before he barreled right into the middle of the floor, just missing the stunned woman contestant in the flowing green dress and her equally flabbergasted partner.

"Oh, no!" Tricia cried, jumping to her feet as Mary cha-cha-cha'd with her back to the jerk on the scooter. The crowd cried out with a warning that came too late as Arnold plowed right into Mary, who flew into the air, nearly somersaulting over the scooter's handlebars and falling into an inelegant heap on the floor. Her scream of pain cut through the din, and the drummer kept the beat while the sax player blew a sour note and the guitarist stopped in mid-chord.

Chaos seemed to reign as several men and women in formal wear rushed onto the stage to see if they could help—Tricia among them.

"Don't touch her, don't touch her!" Norma Fielding cried as she, too, rushed onto the dance floor. "I'm a nurse."

"She got in my way!" Arnold protested angrily from the sidelines, where he sat parked on his scooter.

"What were you thinking?" a woman cried.

"Mary, Mary!" called a familiar voice. Chauncey Porter wormed his way through the crowd.

Poor Mary sat on her backside, her beautiful ball gown ripped in several places, tears streaming down her face, giving her raccoon eyes, as she wailed in pain. Her left foot was positioned at an impossible angle. Tricia's stomach did a flip-flop. Had it snapped right off?

"Please, please!" Millicent called from the dais. "Could everyone *please* leave the dance floor!" But no one appeared to be listening.

Chauncey crouched down beside Mary, who grabbed onto him like a lifeline, sinking her fingers into and wrinkling his dark suitcoat as she buried her tear-steaked face into his chest, while her dance partner stood to one side, wringing his hands in obvious anguish. "Dear lady, dear lady," he lamented in a thick Irish brogue.

"Mary, is there anything I can do to help?" Tricia asked.

Mary turned a murderous eye toward Tricia. "*You* told me to break a leg. Well, it looks like I did. Are you happy?"

Tricia's breath caught in her throat. *Break a leg* was an expression used to wish good luck to entertainers at large. How could she have known—or wished—such a fate on her friend?

Suddenly a hand clamped around Tricia's shoulder, pulling her away from the woman in such terrible pain. It was Angelica, of course. "Come back to the table," she said, her voice low and kind.

Tricia fought tears, but she knew that since Mary was in agony, she was probably incapable of listening to Tricia's explanation of what she'd meant when she'd uttered the now-prophetic phrase.

Angelica led Tricia back to the ringside table, and they resumed their seats. Mary let out yet another anguished wail of pain, which made everyone wince.

"Mary didn't know what she was saying," Angelica told her sister, patting her hand. "You did not cause her to break her leg. It was that horrible, thoughtless Arnold Smith."

Tricia hadn't even been aware that Angelica was aware of the inconsiderate oaf who'd caused far too much strife for the authors and other passengers. "But—" she begun.

"Hush!" Angelica ordered in the same tone she used to keep her dog, Sarge, from barking.

The ship's medical team arrived and rushed onto the dance floor, dragging a gurney piled with tackle boxes full of equipment behind them.

"Poor, poor Mary," Grace said, her voice shaking.

"What about the contest?" Pilger asked. "Do you think they'll continue with just the other two couples?"

Everyone at the table turned to glare at him.

"What? It's an honest question," he said, oblivious to his lack of tact and compassion.

"As soon as the medical personnel leave, I think we ought to go back to our cabin, dear," Mr. Everett told Grace.

"Yes, my pet. I think you're right. I've had far too much excitement this evening."

"I think I shall do the same," Antonio said.

"I don't know about you, Trish, but I'd like to hit one of the bars. I'm going to need a shot or two to help me forget the sight of Mary's foot going the wrong way."

As if to emphasize that observation, Mary let out a bloodcurdling scream as the medical personnel moved her onto the gurney.

Tricia buried her face in her hands, fighting tears. She heard a sloshing noise, and then Angelica pressed her champagne glass into her hands. "Drink this." The glass was full, but all the others were now empty. Angelica must have poured the contents of each into Tricia's empty flute. She drank it down in one gulp.

As soon as the medical personnel had removed a still-wailing Mary from the dance floor, the rubberneckers began to disperse. Tricia looked around the room to find that most of the rest of the contest's spectators, as well as the contest's judges, had already discreetly departed.

"Would you like me to walk you to your cabin?" Antonio asked Grace and Mr. Everett.

"Since we're going the same way, it would be very nice," Grace said, sounding grateful.

"Will you be all right?" Antonio asked Tricia.

She braved a smile. "As long as I have my big sister along—I think so." She gave Angelica a wan smile. Angelica leaned close and gave her a hug.

"Not to worry. We'll be fine," Angelica said.

Antonio stood, moved behind Grace, and helped her up from the table. "Good night, ladies."

"Yes, good night," Grace said, and Mr. Everett nodded.

"Good night," Tricia and Angelica chorused. They watched the three depart before speaking.

"Well, what bar would you like to patronize tonight?" Angelica asked.

"The Wee Dram bar always seems to be the most quiet. I think I could use that right now."

They stood and headed for the aisle. They were among the last of the audience to leave the ballroom.

The deck's main thoroughfare seemed oddly empty, and they walked in silence to the bar. They sat down in chairs at the far end of the small room, but it took only a few moments before one of the waitstaff noticed them.

"What can I get you ladies?" the waiter asked.

"Two Beefeater martinis, up with olives," Angelica ordered, and surrendered her keycard.

"And some crisps, too, please," Tricia added.

The waiter nodded, turned, and headed for the bar.

"I didn't think you actually liked potato chips."

"Of course I do. Doesn't everybody?"

Angelica shrugged. She sat back in the brocaded chair and gave a heavy sigh. "I just can't believe anyone would be so—so callous, so rude. Did you notice that Arnold Smith didn't even apologize to Mary? I'd say there was cause for a lawsuit. I hope the videographer captured the whole thing, although with hundreds of witnesses, that may not even be necessary."

"If he could do that, I could well believe he would stalk authors like EM Barstow."

A man walked up to the bar. Tricia craned her neck and recognized Steven Richardson, whom she'd met the night before at the Golden Harp. She watched as he ordered a drink. He turned, saw her, and waved. She smiled and waved back.

Angelica's head swiveled back and forth, observing them. "Why don't you ask him to join us?"

"We did say we'd have a drink together," Tricia said, then waved a finger, indicating Richardson should join them. He nodded and indicated that he'd wait for his drink first.

The waiter collected the martinis and brought them over, setting them and the snack bowl on the table, then waited for Angelica to sign for the drinks before he departed. Richardson was only a few moments behind.

"Hello, Tricia. I'm sorry, I didn't catch your name."

"Angelica. Very nice to meet you, Mr. Richardson. I've read and enjoyed your books."

He sat. "Thank you."

"Angelica's an author, too. She writes cookbooks. I get to taste her test recipes."

"You're a lucky woman," Richardson said, and raised his glass. They toasted.

"Were you at the dance competition?" Angelica asked.

Richardson frowned and shook his head. "A terrible end to what had been a fun evening."

"You and the other authors said Arnold Smith could be a menace. He sure proved himself to be just that tonight," Tricia said.

"Do you think a man that heartless could have killed EM?" Angelica asked Richardson.

"I wouldn't want to point any fingers, but he's certainly guilty of depraved indifference when it came to plowing into that poor woman on the dance floor."

"She's a friend of ours," Angelica said, casting a worried look at her sister.

Tricia *hoped* Mary would still consider her a friend.

"What did you think about the panel of judges?" Richardson asked.

"I heard that Diana Lovell is a big ballroom dance aficionado, which is why she was asked to judge," Tricia said.

"They probably asked Larry Andrews because he's well known, thanks to his cooking shows," Angelica added.

"But doesn't it seem strange they would ask a book editor to judge a dance contest?" Richardson asked.

"That's what I thought, too," Tricia agreed, frowning. "Surely there were others with more celebrity they could have tapped for the job."

"One would think," Richardson said, and sipped what looked like Scotch on the rocks.

Angelica glanced at her watch. "Oh, my! Look at the time. It's been a big day for me. I think I'll just toddle off to bed."

"Do you want me to walk you to the cabin?" Tricia asked.

Angelica snagged her glass and stood. "Oh, no. I'm sure I'll be fine. As long as I don't run into Arnold, that is."

"I won't be long," Tricia said.

"Stay out as long as you like," Angelica said, and waggled her eyebrows suggestively.

Tricia let out a sigh. "Good night."

"Good night. Nice talking to you, Steven."

"And you."

Angelica waved and headed out of the bar.

Tricia reached for a couple of potato chips and then pushed the bowl toward Richardson. "I don't know what brand these are, but they're marvelous."

Richardson tried one and swallowed. "Taste pretty normal to me."

Tricia smiled. "I don't eat them very often; maybe that's why they taste so darn good." She picked up another and popped it into her mouth just as Arnold Smith pulled up outside the bar on that blasted scooter of his. Thank goodness he'd come from a different direction than Angelica had gone.

Irked, Tricia watched as he climbed off it without any hint of disability and sauntered over to the bar, where he sat down. Of course, not everyone who rode a scooter or used a wheelchair had an affliction that affected their legs. She supposed he could have a heart condition or some other invisible malady that kept him from being totally mobile.

"What else do you know about Arnold?" Tricia asked Richardson. "For instance?"

"What's his disability?"

Richardson frowned. "I've heard rumors that he has none."

"What?"

"Well, maybe an ingrown toenail. He uses that scooter to cut through lines and get special treatment."

"Is that what you've witnessed, or did someone share that with you?"

"The latter. A bookseller in Pittsburgh complained about him. Arnold crashed an after-hours event she held for a dozen authors to sign stock. They were serving beer and wine and Arnold had a little too much to drink. He confided to her that buying a used scooter was the best investment he ever made. It garners a lot of sympathy—at least until people find out what he's really like."

"How come you didn't mention this at the Golden Harp last night?"

"Some of the other authors already have legitimate beefs against Arnold; I didn't want to incite them to riot."

"Someone ought to call him out on it," Tricia said testily.

"The man apparently has no conscience," Richardson said, resigned.

Maybe it was the mixture of champagne and martinis, but Tricia's patience with the oaf evaporated like spilled water in the desert. She stood. "I'm going to give him a piece of my mind," she said, and, without waiting for a word from Richardson, she stomped her way across the bar.

"You should be ashamed of yourself!"

Arnold looked up from his glass of cola. "What?"

"For what you did in the ballroom to poor Mary Fairchild not an hour ago."

"Who's that?" he asked, without sounding terribly interested.

"The woman you ran down with your scooter."

"I didn't run her down."

Tricia's mouth dropped open in shock. "Well, what do you call what you did?"

"She was in my way. These things happen," he said with a shrug.

For a moment Tricia just stood there, dumbfounded. "There were hundreds of witnesses who saw you blatantly charge into the Crystal Ballroom and knock poor Mary down."

"What are you so angry about? It wasn't you who got hurt."

"She's my neighbor, and we have a mutual friend: Roger Livingston, *Esquire.*"

Arnold frowned. "Esquire?"

"That means he's a lawyer, and if you're smart, you'd better find one for yourself, *fast!*"

"Are you threatening me?" Arnold asked, anger tingeing his voice.

"No. Just warning you." And with that, Tricia turned on her heel and made her way back to where Richardson still sat. She plunked down in her chair, grabbed her martini, slopping a little on the polished surface of the cocktail table, and took a mighty gulp.

Richardson watched her, his mouth twitching until it finally ended up in a lopsided grin. "Bravo, Tricia."

She shrugged, just a teensy bit embarrassed and still very angry.

His smile was short-lived, however. "You might feel better confronting Arnold, but I'm afraid you may have just made a target of yourself, too."

"I can take care of myself," she said, and this time her hand was steady as she took a much smaller sip of her drink.

Richardson's gaze wandered back to the bar, and so did Tricia's. Arnold was swallowing his cola with remarkable speed, then slammed the empty glass onto the bar, shattering it, startling the bartender, who'd been polishing the beer taps. Arnold didn't bat an eye at this further violent outburst and marched back to his scooter, climbed aboard, and gunned it. He looked absolutely ludicrous, leaning forward as if to push the little electric motor for more speed.

"Go, Arnold, go!" Richardson called, causing Arnold to look up. Thank goodness no one was in his path, for he lost control of the scooter and crashed into the nearest wall, scraping the beautiful woodwork.

"Sir! Sir!" the bartender called, and hurried from behind the bar.

Arnold didn't appear to be hurt—just angry. The scooter seemed to have stalled, and he got off and kicked one of the small rubber tires.

Tricia clamped a hand over her mouth to keep from laughing aloud.

Frustrated, Arnold stalked off down the corridor with the bartender and waiter struggling to catch up with him—whether to inquire about his health or the damages to the wall, Tricia wasn't sure.

Richardson's smile was wry. "Well, that was certainly an interesting end to the evening."

Tricia's smile waned. "You're calling it quits for the night?"

"Oh. No," he backpedaled. "I wouldn't mind having another drink and talking so we can get to know each other better."

"You're just saying that because I put you on the spot."

"No, honestly. I wouldn't have sought you out if I wasn't interested."

Interested? Yes, but . . . Oh, what the heck. He was a nice man and the fact that she might never see him again after tomorrow shouldn't enter into it.

"I'd like to get to know you better, too," she said, and leaned back farther in her chair, noticing her glass was nearly empty. The bartender returned solo from his confrontation with Arnold, and Tricia wondered if the waiter and Arnold were on their way to the ship's security department for a little chat with Officer McDonald. She sure hoped so.

"Why don't I get us another round?" Richardson suggested.

"That would be very nice. And don't forget to ask for another bowl of crisps," she added, noticing the bowl on the table was now empty.

"Righty-o!" Richardson said, and got up from his chair, heading toward the bar.

Tricia watched him, glad she'd taken off Christopher's engagement ring and that the opal she now wore was on the ring finger of her right hand. She was being silly. But right then she felt like indulging in a little silliness. Her life had been far too serious for too long.

Here's to your future, girl, and a brand-new start.

And Tricia downed the rest of her drink.

TWENTY-TWO

"Tricia! Wake up," someone said in a harsh whisper, so close Tricia could feel the heat of hot breath in her ear. She opened one eye to see Angelica, dressed in her *Celtic Lady* bathrobe, hovering over her.

"You *did* still want to see Millicent Ambrose's interview with EM Barstow, right? It'll be on in a few minutes."

After all she'd had to drink the night before, Tricia had been sure she'd awaken with a hangover, and was happy it hadn't come to pass. But she had enjoyed her lengthy conversation with Richardson. She'd even let him walk her back to the suite, and they'd shared a pleasant kiss. Perhaps it would have been more intense if she hadn't been aware of being a star attraction on one of the ship's video display screens.

Tricia threw back the covers as Angelica scurried out of her room and back to the lounge. She had no time to dress, and grabbed the robe from her own closet, hurrying after her sister.

As usual, Sebastian had already arrived with a cart filled with breakfast goodies. Angelica poured a cup of steaming coffee into a mug, doctored it the way Tricia liked it, and handed it to her. The breakfast cart had more food on it than it had had during the rest of the trip, and there was a noticeable absence of yogurt. Tricia smiled and used tongs to set two croissants and pats of butter on her plate before gouging some raspberry jam from one of the small jars. She sat down on her loveseat, setting her breakfast on the cocktail table before her.

Angelica picked up the remote and switched on the TV. "I hope this show is worthy of us getting up so early on our last real day of vacation."

"Me, too."

Except for the *Celtic Lady* logo against a Kelly green background, the screen was blank. Tricia concerned herself with buttering her croissant while Angelica plopped a couple of Danish on a plate, but left the plate on the cart. "Before I forget . . ." Angelica moved to the table by the entry. "Sebastian left this."

"Not another gift from my secret admirer!"

"Looks like it." Angelica retrieved a flat box. This one was wrapped in plain white tissue.

Tricia didn't even try to save the paper and tore it off. She lifted the lid and gasped.

"What is it?" Angelica demanded.

"It's . . . it's . . ."

Tricia handed the box over to her sister. Angelica looked at the aged paper cover and frowned. "It's an old magazine."

"Oh, Ange, it's the holy grail of mysteries: Poe's short story 'The Murders in the Rue Morgue,' the first modern detective story!"

Angelica sniffed. "Oh." She handed the box back, returned to her seat, and picked up a Danish.

Tricia dared not touch the antique magazine. She'd read the story numerous times. She'd even bid on an original copy of the magazine some ten years before only to lose it to someone with deeper pockets.

Only four people on Earth had known about her obsession to actually own an original copy. Two could never have afforded it, and another was dead.

Tricia now knew who her anonymous benefactor was and smiled.

The TV screen suddenly came to life. A jaunty Irish jig played in the background and the words AT SEA WITH THE *Celtic Lady* in a distinctive Irish script were superimposed over a shot of Millicent Ambrose. Tricia set the box aside as the words faded. A smiling Millicent sat in a forest green chair that looked like it might have once lived in one of the ship's fancier bars, her legs crossed at the ankles, her skirt covering her knees. The camera moved in for a closer shot. She looked rather pleased with herself, no doubt because she hoped to flog the show to the networks upon their arrival in New York—if she hadn't already done so.

"Good morning, cruisers, and welcome to *At Sea with the* Celtic Lady. I'm Millicent Ambrose, your ship's entertainment director. Today we'll be revisiting an interview I did with author EM Barstow before her unfortunate and untimely passing just days ago." She bowed her head, her expression growing somber.

"This woman missed her calling. She should have been an actress," Angelica said sourly.

"It's all showbiz," Tricia agreed, and took a bite of her croissant.

Millicent prattled on. "After the taped interview, one of Ms. Barstow's colleagues will join us to tell us about the *real* EM Barstow. So, without further ado, let's get on with the show."

"I told you," Tricia said with a wry smile.

The screen went to black for a second or two before it came to life once more. Millicent sat in the same forest green chair, wearing the same uniform, her smile just as plastic as ever. The camera moved in for a closer shot.

"Good morning, cruisers! Millicent Ambrose here, your *Celtic Lady* entertainment director. Welcome to our program. We've got loads of wonderful information to share about our upcoming landfall, as well as tidbits on some of our celebrity cruisers, but first the weather. The forecast calls for clear skies and bright sunshine, with winds gusting to five knots."

Tricia tuned out while Millicent dutifully reported the air and water temps, gave an update on the miles traveled so far, and the miles left until they docked in New York. Why hadn't the woman edited that part out of her show? Perhaps they didn't have the facilities. Or was it because she was in love with the sound of her own voice? Tricia wished she had a fast-forward button on the TV's remote, but she didn't dare hit the mute button for fear she'd miss something.

Finally Millicent got to the point.

"Today my guest on *At Sea with the* Celtic Lady is *New York Times* and *USA Today* bestselling thriller author EM Barstow." The camera pulled back. "Good morning, EM. May I called you Emmie?"

"Good morning, Millicent," EM said, all business, "and no, you may not."

Millicent seemed taken aback by the reply. Obviously she'd known that EM's close associates called her that, but EM made it clear Millicent wasn't one of them.

"Er, I understand you've won just about every mystery-writing award given on the planet," Millicent said, just a little disconcerted.

"Yes."

Again, Millicent looked startled by the blunt answer. "Have you had to build new bookshelves to hold them all?"

"Yes," EM answered once again, with no hint of amusement in her voice.

Millicent pasted on a smile, and Tricia could see this was going to be a difficult interview to watch. Poor Millicent. Still, as the ship's entertainment director, she'd probably suffered through hundreds of such dialogues with the famous and near-famous over the years.

"Because of the popularity of the Tennyson Eisenberg series, you must have had a lot of wonderful experiences to celebrate over the years."

"Yes. But the truth is I've lost my anonymity. I can't walk the streets of New York or Boston without being constantly recognized."

Talk about delusions of grandeur. Tricia had read that many public figures actually *liked* living in big cities because the denizens weren't impressed by celebrity. It was the blasé factor. It took a lot more than a bestselling book to enamor the New York crowd.

"My life has been threatened on a number of occasions," EM continued.

And maybe that was because the woman had been skipped when the chip for civility had been given out.

"Have you been stalked?" Millicent asked, aghast.

EM nodded. "Several times."

"What other kinds of threats have you encountered?" Millicent asked.

"My e-mail and bank accounts have been hacked—"

Was that the source of her money problems?

"And my home has been broken into and valuable items stolen."

"Surely not by any of your fans."

"Fanatics," EM clarified.

"It must have been terrible for you."

"Yes. But, I've stepped up my security measures, and I'm happy to say all that seems to be behind me." *Oh, yeah?* Then why did her mouth look so tight? Was it just because Arnold was also on the cruise? During their encounter in the ship's library, it had seemed as though EM was more annoyed with the jerk than afraid of him.

"What kind of hobbies does a bestselling thriller author enjoy?"

Millicent asked, changing the subject. "I know Patricia Cornwell pilots a helicopter. Do you have a dangerous hobby?" she asked eagerly.

"I live vicariously through my characters; that's all the excitement I require."

Millicent plowed on, changing the subject. "What do you do in your free time?"

"My work takes up a great deal of my time," EM said firmly. "This voyage is the first downtime I've had in several years. Even so, it's definitely a working vacation. I'm writing my next, what may be my *last*," she said firmly, "Tennyson Eisenberg book, as well as juggling other projects."

"Your fans will be sorry to hear that," Millicent said with just the hint of a scold in her voice.

Some journalist! Why hadn't she pursued that answer?

"Would you care to tell us a little about your other writing projects?"

"No," EM replied, staring straight into the camera. It was positively unnerving!

Millicent's smile wavered, but by then she seemed resigned to receiving tactless, blunt answers to her questions. "I understand you contribute to a number of charitable organizations."

EM nodded. "My favorite is for therapeutic horse riding."

Millicent blinked—and Tricia did likewise. "I wouldn't have thought of you as an equestrian. Your characters don't ride, do they?"

"No. When I was a young girl, I dreamed of owning a horse. I would like to have a stable of them. They're beautiful creatures. But I simply don't have the time to devote to a horse, or any other animal, although I also support a number of horse rescue organizations. In fact, I once owned such a stable."

"Once?" Millicent inquired.

"Yes, for children and teens with learning disabilities, autism, and those who'd been injured."

"Did you sell it?"

EM shook her head. "The manager robbed me blind."

Whoa! Those were lawsuit words.

"I nearly went bankrupt," EM continued. "I've found it hard to trust anyone since."

Well, that explained a lot.

"Do you ride English or Western?" Millicent asked.

"Western. But I haven't ridden in over forty years. Still, there's a barn not far from my home. I often go there to feed the horses carrots. Sometimes I pick up a curry brush, as well. It's very relaxing to take care of such placid creatures."

Obviously no stallions in those stalls, Tricia thought.

"Do you have a favorite breed?"

"No. They're all beautiful to me."

Horses? Oh well, Tricia liked to repair the injured spines of books as a hobby—that is, when *she* could find the time.

"Would you like to tell us a little about your next book?"

"No."

Millicent's lips pursed. "How about the book that's currently available for sale? The one you'll be signing later today for your fans on board."

"Readers are free to check my website for details."

It was a shortsighted answer, since not everybody was willing to pay for WiFi access at sea.

Millicent's bright smile didn't extend to her eyes. "Thank you so much, Ms. Barstow, for being my guest today on *At Sea with the* Celtic Lady."

"It was my pleasure," EM said, her mouth a straight line. Didn't the woman ever smile? How sad that the only joy she seemed to have had during her life was brushing or feeding a horse. But then, she probably related better to them than people.

The screen went black before Millicent returned, this time with a nervous-looking Dori Douglas sitting in the guest chair beside her.

"Joining us today is Ms. Barstow's personal assistant, Dori Douglas. Hello, Dori."

"Hello, Ms. Ambrose. And I was Emmie's *virtual* not personal assistant. We communicated almost exclusively over the Internet."

"And why was that?"

"Probably because Emmie didn't like to talk face-to-face with people."

"Why would she admit that?" Angelica asked before taking another bite of Danish.

"Shhh!" Tricia warned.

"She enjoyed being eccentric," Dori continued. "It added to her mystique."

"But you knew the *real* EM Barstow. Care to share with us an example of this mystique?"

Dori bit her lip. "Well . . . she had a vast collection of model horses."

"She did mention her love of those magnificent creatures."

"I think she liked to play with them," Dori admitted.

"Oh?"

"Sometimes she'd Skype me and I could see her collection in the background. The next day, they'd be in a different order."

"Perhaps she dusted them on a regular basis," Millicent suggested.

"Every day?" Dori asked.

Millicent's smile widened and she went on. "What are your plans now that Ms. Barstow has passed on?"

"Pretty much the same as they were before she died. I'll continue to spread the word about Emmie's books so that people don't forget those wonderful characters or their creator."

"Aw, that's very sweet," Millicent cooed. The camera pulled in for a tighter shot of Millicent. "I'm afraid that's all the questions we have time for right now. I had hoped to interview Ms. Barstow's editor, but she wasn't available before airtime."

Had the program been prerecorded, or had Cathy Copper simply refused to be a part of the broadcast?

"Well, cruisers, as it's your last day on board the beautiful *Celtic Lady*, I want to remind you that you'll be disembarking after everyone has spoken with customs officials, so have your passports ready and wear a smile, and you'll be through it in a heartbeat.

"And now, let me wish you a happy day and hope that you'll soon join the *Celtic Lady* on one of our transatlantic crossings, or one of our exciting journeys to foreign lands. Until then, happy cruising!"

The camera pulled back. The Celtic script appeared once more, this time giving credit to Millicent and her camera crew before the screen went to black, and then green with the *Celtic Lady* logo emblazoned on it.

Angelica picked up the remote and switched off the set. "Well, that was certainly boring."

"Yes, it was."

"What were you hoping to pick up from watching EM's interview?"

"I don't know. But my bet is something she said has something to do with her death."

"And how will you figure that out?"

"I may not be able to," Tricia said truthfully. "I wonder if Harold Pilger watched the show."

"Did he even know the interview would be rerun?"

"Maybe. It was mentioned in the Daily Program, and I'll bet the ship's channel advertised it as well."

Angelica stood. "Despite the weather"—she looked toward the gray sky and the choppy sea outside the lounge's window—"I intend to do as Millicent said and enjoy my last day aboard the *Celtic Lady*."

"Doing what?"

"First up, Antonio and I have that in-depth kitchen tour. It may be the highlight of the entire cruise. After that, I might do some last-minute networking, then maybe a little shopping, and another visit to the spa. I won't have time for that once we return to Stoneham. I've got too many plans and ideas to implement. What are you going to do today?"

"Read."

"Are you planning on seeing Steven Richardson again?" Angelica asked, raising an eyebrow.

"It would be nice if I bumped into him, but if I don't, I'm okay with that, too."

"Oh." Angelica sounded so disappointed.

"This isn't the Love Boat," Tricia reminded her.

"Yes, but . . . you came back to the suite so late last night. . . ."

"I'm sorry if I woke you."

"No, you didn't. I was just lying there . . . wondering if you'd been murdered."

"Don't you guilt-trip me. Admit it; you left the bar last night hoping I'd indulge in a little hanky-panky."

"I did nothing of the sort," Angelia claimed, but Tricia knew a lie when she heard one.

"You're a busybody, Ange," Tricia accused.

"And so what if I am. Nothing would get done if I didn't give certain situations a helping hand."

That was true, but when it came to her love life, Tricia didn't need an assist. Well, that wasn't exactly true. She didn't *want* an assist.

She stood. "I'm going to shower and change and see if I can't stake out a claim to a nice, quiet reading nook."

"Will we regroup for lunch?" Angelica asked.

"We can. How about the Kells Grill at one?"

"Okay."

"Good," Tricia said, and picked up what she knew would be the final gift from her admirer. "See you later."

Tricia went back to her bedroom, set the box on the night table, and then chose her outfit for the day before heading for the shower. While washing her hair, she decided to try to find Mary Fairchild to see how she was doing, and hoped Mary would let her at least apologize—not that she'd had a hand in the accident.

That decided, Tricia finished her ablutions. Despite her plans for a quiet day of reading, she had a feeling it could be a very busy day.

TWENTY-THREE

As it turned out, it wasn't hard to find Mary; she was holding court in the Garden Lounge. Gathered around her were a number of other members of the Stoneham contingent, including the Dexter sisters, Grace Harris, Mr. Everett, Leona Ferguson, and Chauncey Porter.

The Dexter sisters seemed to be hovering, dressed alike, their hands clasped, and looking only to please, they resembled a couple of mirror-image bookends. "Can I get you a fresh cup of tea?" Muriel asked.

"Or coffee," Midge suggested.

"Cookies? Pastry? Pie?" Muriel recommended.

"Can I get you another pillow to put under your leg?" Midge proposed.

"Thank you, ladies, but no," Mary said. Her cheeks were pale, but her smile seemed genuine.

"What's the prognosis?" Grace asked.

"The ship's medical team was able to stabilize the break, but I'm afraid I'm going to have to see an orthopedic surgeon when I return home."

"Oh, dear. How will you manage the shop?" Mr. Everett asked.

"I have no idea. I can't go back to work with my leg like this."

"If I may," Tricia interrupted.

Mary's gaze traveled to meet Tricia's, then dipped to the cast that began at her toes and traveled up past her knee. It was obvious she *did* hold a grudge.

"If my employees are willing, I'd like to volunteer their time to help you in your shop until you're back on your feet. Or I'd be happy to pay for someone to come in temporarily."

Mary's lips pursed, and the blush that rose up her neck brought some much-needed color to her cheeks. "I couldn't accept that."

"I'd be more than happy to volunteer a few hours of my time every week until you can manage," Mr. Everett said.

Mary managed to raise her head. "That's incredibly generous of you. Thank you."

"I'm sure we can rally a number of other shop owners to help in one way or another," Leona said.

"Perhaps the Chamber of Commerce would be willing to ask all members, as well," Grace said.

"You're all too kind," Mary said sincerely, and chanced a glance at Tricia, who nodded. "Thank you."

Grace rose from her chair. "Now, dear, if there's anything you need, you just let us know."

"Yes, please do," Mr. Everett echoed.

"Don't worry, Midge and I will wait on poor Mary hand, foot, and finger, until we get home."

"Yes," Muriel agreed.

"That really won't be necessary," Mary insisted.

"Oh, but we wouldn't have it any other way," Midge persisted.

Mary braved a smile, although it seemed as though she'd already grown weary of the twins' attention. Chauncey, too, seemed disconcerted. He'd been the one to comfort her directly after the accident. Could he be sweet on dear Mary?

"We'll talk later," Tricia said, and was surprised when Mary reached for her hand.

"I'm sorry, Tricia. It was thoughtless of me last night to say—"

"You take it easy," Tricia interrupted her.

"I will," Mary promised as Chauncey slipped into the seat Grace had so recently vacated.

"I'll take care of her," he said with authority, and Tricia had no doubt he would. Perhaps the *Celtic Lady* was a Love Boat, after all.

Tricia gave them both a wave and crossed the Garden Lounge, finding a seat at one of the bistro tables on the other side of the expansive room. She removed her e-reader from her tote bag, switched it on, and stared at the lines of text but didn't start to read; too many troubling thoughts occupied her mind. She turned her gaze toward the angry sea and stared at the waves and the dark, puffy clouds that seemed to hover over the ship.

"Tricia?"

Tricia turned to see Fiona Sample walking toward her. "Would you mind a little company?" she asked as she approached the table.

"Not at all."

Fiona settled on the opposite chair. "Wasn't it awful what happened last night at the dance contest?"

"Yes. The woman who got hurt is from Stoneham—one of the booksellers on Main Street."

"That's terrible. I wonder how she's doing."

"I spoke with her a few minutes ago. She's hurting, and has to have surgery when she returns home, but I think she'll be fine."

"I hope she has a good attorney."

"That, too," Tricia agreed.

"Almost all the cozy authors got together at the Golden Harp after the contest. The consensus is that Arnold killed EM Barstow."

"Do you really think so?" Tricia asked.

"After that move he pulled last night, I wouldn't be at all surprised. Rumor has it that the NYPD will be waiting at the dock to arrest him for assault."

"If that's the case, why hasn't ship's security taken him into custody?"

"He can't really go anywhere."

"No, but he could be a menace to other passengers."

"Perhaps he got a stern warning. I can't say I've seen him today. Maybe he's under house arrest. All I know is, I feel a lot better knowing security is at least watching him. And I must say I'm looking forward to leaving the ship tomorrow. I'll have a few peaceful days visiting Nikki and my new grandson, and then it's off to home for me."

"I agree. If nothing else, it's been an interesting trip. But enjoyable?" Tricia shrugged.

"I feel the same way." Fiona glanced at her watch. "I'd better get going. I want to get my packing done this morning so that I won't have to rush to do it tonight to get the bags out in the corridor by the eight o'clock curfew."

"I'd forgotten all about that," Tricia admitted. "Maybe I'll hike back to the cabin and do the same."

Fiona rose. "See you later—and if not, when we get to Stoneham."

"Okay. See you."

Tricia placed her e-reader back in her tote, got up, and pushed her chair in, then headed for the forward stairway. It was usually quicker to walk than wait for one of the lifts.

She started down the carpeted stairs at a brisk pace. As she rounded the landing that opened to her deck, she saw a uniformed officer standing in front of the lifts.

"Officer McDonald!" she called.

He turned at the sound of her voice. The lift doors opened, but instead of stepping in, he moved to meet her at the bottom step. "Ms. Miles?"

"Good morning."

"Not the best weather I've seen, but not the worst, either," McDonald admitted.

"I'm grateful for that."

"Is there something I can help you with?"

"I wondered about Arnold Smith. The rumors are flying."

McDonald frowned. "Yes. I've heard them."

"Are they true?"

"Which one are you referring to?"

"That Mr. Smith has been put under house arrest."

McDonald nodded. "After studying the video, our security department decided it would be safer for everyone—Mr. Smith included—if he didn't interact with the rest of the passengers."

"Will he be arrested upon our arrival?"

"The New York police do not have jurisdiction over acts that occur at sea."

"I was afraid of that."

"However, Ms. Fairchild is free to file a civil suit against the gentleman."

"After what he did last night, Mr. Smith proved he's no gentleman."

Again McDonald nodded.

"Some of the authors think Mr. Smith was capable of killing."

"Our security team watched hundreds of hours of video to ascertain his whereabouts on the evening of Ms. Barstow's death. He went to his cabin about ten o'clock and didn't leave until nearly eight the next morning."

"You're sure?"

"I reviewed the video myself."

Tricia nodded.

"Ms. Miles. I don't care what the rumors are; the truth is Ms. Barstow took her own life."

"How can you say that without an autopsy?"

"That would be up to a medical examiner to determine, but we have no evidence to turn over to any U.S. law enforcement agency."

"Can't or won't?"

McDonald glowered.

"Okay, okay," Tricia said in what she hoped was a placating tone. "I appreciate you speaking with me once again."

McDonald seemed to hesitate, as though he wanted to say something, but then thought better of it. "It has been my pleasure," he said at last, with none of the impatience she'd expected. "Perhaps you'll sail with us on another *Celtic* cruise sometime in the near future."

"Perhaps," she said, and gave him a small smile.

McDonald tipped his head and touched the brim of his hat with the first two fingers of his left hand. "Happy sailing."

"You, too."

Instead of waiting for the lift, McDonald started down the forward staircase, and Tricia headed down the starboard corridor toward her suite. Fiona wanted to believe that Arnold Smith was a killer and that keeping him locked up in his cabin kept the rest of the passengers and crew safe, but Tricia wasn't sure. She also didn't believe McDonald's assertion that EM killed herself.

That meant there could still be a murderer wandering the *Celtic Lady*'s corridors.

TWENTY-FOUR

Angelica was already seated at their usual table in the Kells Grill, perusing the leather-clad menu, when Tricia arrived. There was no sign of the rest of their regular family group.

Tricia sat down. "Good afternoon."

Angelica looked up, but she wasn't smiling. "Maybe not."

"What do you mean? Didn't you have a good time on your tour of the ship's kitchen?"

"Oh, that was fabulous."

"Then what's wrong?"

Angelica sighed, setting her menu aside. "Nothing, really. Sofia kept Ginny and Antonio up all night, so not only was he distracted during the tour, the poor man was exhausted. I finally told him to go back to his cabin and catch a nap."

"What's wrong with the baby?"

"Ginny thinks she's cutting a new tooth, poor little thing."

Cristophano approached the table. "Good afternoon, ladies. Would you like to start with a glass of wine?"

"Just coffee," Angelica said without adding a thank-you, which was unlike her. She really must have been bummed. "We'll need a few minutes."

"Very good," Cristophano said with a curt nod, and departed.

Tricia picked up her menu and skimmed it. Everything sounded so delicious—so decadent. "Do you think I could learn to cook?" she blurted.

Angelica looked up, startled. "You, cook? I've only been encouraging you to try for nearly six years. Of course you could learn to cook. For me, it's as natural as breathing. What makes you ask?"

"All the wonderful food on this trip. The dishes are probably way beyond my abilities, but I think I'd like to give it a try. I've always admired the way you chop vegetables—just like a chef—and you never cut yourself."

"Once you learn the trick, you could be slicing and dicing like a pro."

"Maybe we could do it together. I think I'd like to make lasagna."

"Lasagna?" Angelica repeated as though astounded.

"Or maybe make homemade bread. Pixie was telling me how her boyfriend, Fred, has a bread machine and how good their apartment smells when they use it."

"Oh, no—bread needs to be kneaded by hand. It gives you such a sense of peace—and accomplishment—when you first cut the loaf and spread a layer of sweet butter on it."

Peace and accomplishment? Tricia smiled. That sounded so *right*.

Cristophano appeared with a pot and poured the coffee, then took their orders. Afterward, the sisters chatted amiably about their beloved grandmother Miles and how she'd taught Angelica to cook. Cristophano delivered their meals, and then after cleared the table.

"What are you going to do for the rest of the afternoon?" Angelica asked.

"Read."

"Oh, come with me to the spa."

Tricia wrinkled her nose. "I don't think so."

"Please? It'll be fun." Angelica insisted.

Tricia let out a heavy sigh. Sometimes giving in to Angelica's whims was the only way to get her sister off her back, although this time she knew she'd actually enjoy more of her sister's company "Well, okay."

Of course they had to walk down several decks and almost the entire length of the ship to get to the spa, not that it would have counted as brisk exercise, for Angelica couldn't walk all that fast in heels. "Since we don't have appointments, we may not be able to get facials or a massage," she warned.

"I was thinking more along the lines of a manicure," Tricia said.

"Or a pedicure," Angelica agreed. "It's been ages since I've had one. We really do need a day spa in Stoneham. As Chamber of Commerce president, I'm going to see if I can find a suitable building and then recruit someone from Nashua."

"Sounds like a sensible plan," Tricia agreed.

The comforting tones of pastel greens and blues of the gurgling floor-to-ceiling water feature outside the entrance to the Sea Nymph Spa promoted an air of tranquillity. A young, red-haired lass stood behind a white podium. "How may we help you ladies?" she asked with just the hint of an Irish accent.

"We're such bad girls. We don't have an appointment, but we were hoping to get manicures and possibly pedicures," Angelica said.

"I'm sure we can accommodate you. Come this way."

Since this was Angelica's party, Tricia followed her to a reception area where they again surrendered their keycards in order to pay for the services available. It rather irked Tricia that the ship's services always scanned their cards *before* they could order a drink or do anything else, when in the real world you paid for meals, goods, and services *after* they were delivered or performed. She frowned at such thoughts. She really did need a few hours in a spa to chill out.

Another young woman approached the desk; her uniform, a plain white, knee-length dress with green piping on the bodice, matched that of the hostess and receptionist. "Good afternoon, ladies. My name is Siobhan, and I'll be your spa guide today. Have you visited the Sea Nymph Spa before?"

"Yes," Angelica answered.

"No," Tricia piped up.

"Then let me give you a quick tour before your treatments. This way, please."

They followed after her, taking in the sights as they walked.

"Here is our fitness centre," Siobhan said, waving a hand in that direction.

Tricia and Angelica leaned into the doorway of the large, glass-encased workout area, which gave a panoramic view of the angry steel gray waves being cut by the ship's bow, as well as the murky sky above.

To Tricia, the ship's fitness centre could have doubled as a modern-day torture centre. Every station—from the elliptical and spin bikes, to the treadmills, to the weights area—was occupied by sweating passengers dressed in workout clothing, much of it emblazoned with the *Celtic Lady* emblem. Tricia recognized a number of authors using the equipment. Harold Pilger sat on a spinning bike and gave a wave, while in the corner Cathy Copper received guidance from a spa trainer as she did bench presses. Chauncey Porter walked briskly on one of the treadmills. He'd lost at least fifty pounds a little over a year before and had kept the weight off through diligent exercise. Tricia often saw him power walking through the streets of Stoneham in the early morning and late at night, even though he'd lost his most-recent exercise buddy.

"Our salon is this way," Siobhan said, and led them past a well-equipped beauty parlor. Among the clients was Mary Fairchild, seated in her wheelchair, her dripping hair being snipped by a young man dressed in white. She looked happy—perhaps because the Dexter twins had not accompanied her.

"Tricia! Angelica!" she called, waving a hand in the air.

"May we take a moment?" Angelica asked.

"Of course," Siobhan cheerfully agreed.

The sisters made their way across the room. Every station was occupied by women having their roots touched up, getting their hair trimmed, and one woman on the high side of sixty was admiring the green streak that had been added to her bleached-blonde mane.

"I'm so excited," Mary said, staring at herself in the mirror before her. "Right after I spoke to you this morning, Tricia, I was approached by one of the ship's officers. Aren't they the nicest people in the world? They offered me a total makeover."

Probably in hopes of avoiding a lawsuit, Tricia thought grimly.

"I've already had a manicure." Mary offered up her bloodred nails in evidence. "I'm scheduled for a massage, a body scrub, and a session with a makeup artist. I can't remember when I've had so much fun!"

"They're certainly doing a good job of pampering you," Tricia agreed. "What are you ladies here for?"

"Oh, just a manicure and pedicure," Angelica said.

"You're going to love it," Mary practically squealed.

"Madam, would you like me to trim your bangs?" asked the young man, in a French accent.

"Oui," Mary said, and giggled.

"We'll let you get on with it," Angelica said, "and hope to see you later to take in the final results."

"Despite my infirmity, I intend to enjoy every minute left on this cruise—especially now that I know that idiot with the scooter won't run into me again."

"What are your plans?" Tricia asked.

"Chauncey and I are going to have dinner together tonight in one of the exotic restaurants. He's been so sweet to me since last night. I couldn't have managed without him holding my hand throughout the whole rigmarole of X-rays and everything else."

"He's a nice man," Tricia agreed. *Except that he held an unreasonable grudge.*

"Ladies," Siobhan said, reminding the sisters that they had somewhere else to go.

"We'll see you later," Angelica said, giving Mary's arm a pat and turning to follow their spa guide.

"You'll be in treatment room four," Siobhan said once they were back out in the corridor.

Once inside the treatment room, they were handed *Celtic Lady* terry cloth robes that weren't as sumptuous as those in their cabins, but were more than adequate as cover-ups. The room was painted a soothing shade of blue and contained two big, soft-padded leatherlike chairs with footbaths before them, and movable tables that housed clippers, emery boards, orange sticks, and neatly folded white towels.

"If you'll please be seated," Siobhan said, waving a hand in the direction of the comfy chairs. "Can I get you ladies anything to drink? Green tea? Perhaps a refreshing glass of cucumber and lime–infused water?"

"We're fine, thank you," Angelica said. She turned to Tricia and mumbled, "I'd rather have a gin and tonic."

"Shhh!" Tricia admonished.

"Your nail technicians will be with you shortly," Siobhan said. "Please let any of our staff know if you need anything."

"We will. Thank you," Tricia said.

Angelica picked up a brochure that showcased the rainbow of nail varnishes available, running her index finger down the columns.

"Did I mention that I ran into Officer McDonald again this morning?" Tricia asked.

"No. What did he have to say?"

"Not much. I get weird vibes from him. He gets annoyed with me when I mention my theories about EM's death, but then he hints that he'd like to get to know me better."

"He's probably like that with a lot of women passengers. I mean, he's not allowed to fraternize, and yet he's stuck at sea for months at a time. He's probably lonely and, like me, you've held up well despite the years."

Tricia frowned, unsure if she'd just been insulted. She shook herself. "Did you hear that Arnold Smith has been confined to his cabin?"

"Oh, is that what Mary meant? It seems a prudent measure. The man is a menace."

"I wonder if he'll sue the cruise line. There certainly seem to be enough unfortunate events to warrant a plethora of suits."

"You may be right."

Two young Asian women entered the treatment room, and in no time the sisters were soaking their hands and feet in warm water.

"I think I could get used to this," Angelica said, sighed, and sank deeper into her comfy chair. But Tricia couldn't seem to relax. Something niggled in the back of her brain. Something she'd seen since they'd entered the spa—something that should be important, but she couldn't for the life of her think what it could be—and she knew it would bug her in the hours to come.

TWENTY-FIVE

Angelica had insisted that the sisters go for the works at the Sea Nymph Spa—and it was much later than either realized by the time they left and returned to their suite to get ready for dinner. The dress code may have been deemed casual for that night, but Angelica donned a tailored black silk pantsuit with a crisp pink blouse, while Tricia opted for one of her usual sweater sets—this one in apricot. The porter had already picked up her luggage and that was about all she had left to wear.

The Kells Grill was practically empty when the sisters met up with Grace, Mr. Everett, and Ginny and Antonio. The new parents seemed antsy about leaving Sofia with the sitter, and settled for appetizers, hurrying to eat so they could get back to their cabin to check on the baby, who'd been fretful all day.

"Those poor dears," Grace lamented as she tucked into the last of her sautéed trout. "I don't think they got to enjoy much of the day."

"Did you?" Tricia asked.

"Oh, yes. And we'll have to hurry, dear," she told Mr. Everett, "if we're going to make curtain time for tonight's play."

"I had no idea it was so late," Mr. Everett said, setting his knife and fork aside. "Dearest, we really should leave now."

Grace's smile widened and she turned her gaze to Tricia. "Would you please tell Cristophano not to bother with our desserts? I hate to think of them being wasted."

"We will," Tricia promised, and waved as two of her favorite people got up from their chairs and left the restaurant.

"Looks like we're shutting down the place," Angelica said, swirling the last of her wine in her glass. "Why don't we go back to that lovely little bar, the Wee Dram, and have a nightcap?" she asked Tricia.

"Why not?" Tricia agreed.

As promised, she flagged down Cristophano and canceled all their dessert orders before the sisters departed the restaurant and retraced their steps from the night before and found the bar, which had only a few scattered patrons. They sat down in the chairs they'd previously occupied and waited for one of the staff to come take their order.

"What will you have tonight?" Tricia asked. "Another martini?"

"I'm in the mood for something that must be sipped in minute quantities to be truly enjoyed. Perhaps a brandy or a glass of Grand Marnier."

"Oh, that sounds good. Maybe I'll have the same."

Soft music issued from hidden speakers. It seemed to be all around them—not coming from any specific direction.

"It was so good to see you actually enjoying your food for once."

"Dinner was excellent," Tricia agreed. "But don't get used to it. Starting tomorrow, I'll be back to my usual regime."

"That's too bad," Angelica said. "I was hoping you'd made a change for the better."

"Eating healthy is a good thing."

"Yes, but too much of a good thing isn't healthy for your spirit," Angelica suggested.

Maybe. Maybe Tricia would allow herself more treats. Maybe she'd stick to her usual habits during the week and allow herself a few indulgences on weekends. Yes, that seemed like a reasonable compromise. She decided not to share her new resolve. "Why don't I just go to the bar and order the drinks?" she asked.

"Would you be a dear and do so?"

"I'd be happy to." Especially since Angelica had charged so much to her personal account, Tricia felt like she ought to flex her financial muscles. After all, she wasn't exactly destitute thanks to Christopher's generosity.

"I'll be back in a flash," Tricia said, and got up from her seat, heading for the bar.

The bartender was washing glasses as she approached. She read his name tag. Georges. As expected, the man had a French accent. "May I help you, madam?"

"Yes. Two glasses of Grand Marnier, *s'il vous plaît*?"

"Ah, *oui*, madam."

Tricia watched as the Frenchman poured the liqueur, then held out his hand for her keycard.

Drinks in hand, Tricia approached Angelica but saw another couple had also taken up residence.

"Mary, you look gorgeous," Tricia said in greeting.

"I feel gorgeous," Mary gushed. It looked like she was wearing a new dress as well.

"Hello, Chauncey," Tricia said as she handed Angelica her glass.

"Tricia," he said, his voice subdued. He didn't look at all happy to see her. If he'd known she was in the vicinity, would he have wheeled Mary over to converse with Angelica?

"Can we offer you a drink?" Tricia asked.

"No, thank you," Chauncey said, and shifted in his chair so that he wouldn't have to look at her.

Tricia took her seat, suddenly feeling self-conscious. Well, this certainly wasn't going to be a pleasant conversation—at least for her.

"We haven't had much of a chance to talk, Chauncey. How are you enjoying the trip so far?" Angelica asked.

"Wonderful. It's been years since I've been able to afford a vacation—but thanks to your business advice, my shop is back in the black."

And Tricia had loaned him the money to buy the stock that had afforded him the opportunity to do so, but she wasn't going to mention it and apparently neither was Chauncey.

"How do you think Mindy's doing her first time leading a tour?" Angelica asked.

"Excellent. She quizzed me for tips before we left, but she really hasn't needed my help at all—which is all right by me. It gives me more time to enjoy the programs and the joys of cruising." He looked over at his companion. "And Mary's company."

Mary blushed, a shy smile tugging at her lips.

"Have you met any celebrities?" Angelica asked.

"Quite a few of the authors. I had hoped a travel writer, like Rick Steves, could have made the trip, but I've enjoyed talking with every-one I meet."

"I'd hoped for another opportunity to speak with Chef Larry Andrews. I wonder what kind of suggestions he'd have for the Booked for Lunch menu," Angelica pondered.

Chauncey laughed. "Probably to offer fewer burgers and sand-wiches."

"Don't you listen to him," Mary chided. "Your menu is perfect as it is."

"Have you met any other celebrities?" Angelica asked.

"Just Cathy Copper."

"Cathy Copper?" Tricia repeated, surprised, but Chauncey didn't look in her direction.

"We met her, too," Angelica said. "She's an editor with one of the big publishing houses in New York."

"She is now," Chauncey said, "but that's not her biggest claim to fame, and I'm amazed you don't recognize her name."

Angelica looked over at Tricia, who shrugged.

"Don't keep us in suspense," Angelica said. "Who is she—or *was* she?"

"Cathy Copper was on the fast track to become an Olympic champion in gymnastics until her accident."

"Accident?" Tricia asked.

Again, Chauncey ignored her, but spoke directly to Angelica. "A terrible fall during the nationals. The subsequent surgeries weren't entirely successful, and she never competed again."

That explained Cathy's limp, and also the crack she'd made about those in competition.

"That's terrible," Angelica agreed. "How old was she at the time?"

"I believe fourteen."

"How sad. Was she glad to be remembered?"

"Not really," Chauncey admitted. "I think she was actually embarrassed. It's hard to be washed up at fourteen, but she seems to have adjusted better than a lot of former athletes."

Maybe not, Tricia thought.

"Have you been networking with other booksellers?" Angelica asked, abandoning that thread of conversation.

Chauncey launched into a soliloquy of each and every bookseller he'd spoken with since boarding the ship almost a week before. Angelica usually enjoyed the topic, but when he didn't give her an opportunity to participate in the conversation, Tricia could see her sister's patience begin to wane. And though they'd both been slowly sipping their drinks, the glasses were long since empty when Chauncey finally seemed to wind down. Would his windbag tendencies be detrimental to what seemed to be a budding relationship between him and Mary?

"It's been such a lovely evening—after such a lovely day," Mary said wistfully, "but I must admit I'm running out of steam. It's going to be a hectic day tomorrow. I think it's time I turned in. Chauncey, would you be so kind as to wheel me back to my cabin?"

"I'd be delighted." He rose from his seat. "See you tomorrow, Angelica."

"Good night, Tricia—Angelica," Mary said as Chauncey pushed the chair out into the corridor.

The sisters watched them leave.

"That was rather rude of Chauncey not to even acknowledge you," Angelica commented.

"It's okay," Tricia assured her. "I'm used to it."

"If he and Mary do end up together, perhaps he'll thaw a little toward you."

"Perhaps," Tricia admitted, distracted.

"What're you thinking?" Angelica asked with a note of disapproval evident in her voice.

"After hearing what Chauncey had to say, I think I know how Cathy could have killed EM."

"And?"

"Well, it would be extremely dangerous, but I'm betting a trained gymnast could have scaled the side of the ship along the balconies until she came to a certain cabin, then open the door from the balcony to the stateroom."

"Are you crazy? One false move and she'd fall overboard. And besides, she's got a bum leg."

"She'd need upper-body strength, that's for sure. But we saw her working out with weights at the exercise area of the spa."

"That's true," Angelica admitted, "but why would she kill EM? She was Cathy's meal ticket, or at least a part of it."

"We'd have to talk to her to get some more infor—"

"No!" Angelica declared. "If she *did* kill EM—and I think your theory is totally ridiculous—what makes you think she wouldn't come after you?"

"Because you'd be with me—my hedge against attack."

"No. No. No!"

"But we only have a few hours before we dock in New York. Once Cathy is off the ship, she's pretty much assured of getting away with murder, because you know the cruise line won't pursue justice."

"And it's not your responsibility to do it, either."

"But—"

"May I remind you that you didn't even *like* EM Barstow?" Angelica said, her voice growing strident.

"She may not have been a very nice person, but that makes it even more essential that someone cares enough to see her killer apprehended."

"You're a dreamer."

"But I'm not the only one."

Angelica frowned, then her gaze rose.

Tricia looked up to see Antonio rushing toward them. *"Mamma mia!"* he cried as he approached.

"What's wrong, darling boy?" Angelica asked, rising to her feet.

"It's Sofia. She's very sick. Ginny has rushed her to the ship's medical centre. I knew you would want to be there with us."

"Of course I do," Angelica said, sounding frantic.

"I'll come, too," Tricia said.

"I'm sorry, but there is limited room for visitors," Antonio apologized.

"That's okay—go!"

Angelica turned back to Tricia. "Promise me you won't do anything stupid—like confronting Cathy."

"Who, me?" Tricia asked, feeling panicky.

"Yes, you!"

There was no time to argue. "You have my word."

Angelica turned to Antonio. "Let's go."

Antonio grabbed his stepmother's hand and practically pulled her out of the bar.

Tricia resumed her seat, not knowing what to do next. She'd promised Angelica she wouldn't do anything stupid, but that didn't mean she couldn't do *something*—even if that meant simply wandering the ship's corridors to walk off her worry about Sofia. And perhaps she should wait outside the ship's theatre to intercept Grace and Mr. Everett to let them know about the baby. But then what could Tricia tell them? Antonio had said Sofia was sick, but *sick* covered a lot of territory. A fever? An infection? Convulsions? The more she speculated, the higher Tricia's anxiety level grew.

Tricia left the bar with no clear destination in mind—she just felt the need to *move*!

The corridors were virtually empty on the final night of the cruise. Perhaps most of the passengers had left their packing until the last minute. Tricia passed the photo gallery and briefly paused to look for pictures of her little Stoneham family. The ship's photographers had taken appointments for portraits. Why hadn't she or Angelica insisted on having one or more of them made? What if something dreadful happened and Sofia—?

She wouldn't even let herself finish that terrible thought.

Tricia continued on, charging up the forward stairs until she got to the Lido Deck, thinking she might get a cup of coffee. She'd always found comfort in a steaming cup of joe. She wanted to be clearheaded when she learned Sofia's fate. But before she got to the restaurant, the door to the deck opened and Dori Douglas burst inside, wearing a knitted cap and a winter coat—nearly barreling into Tricia.

"What's wrong?" Tricia said, noting Dori's red cheeks, which she wasn't sure were a result of just the cold outside.

"Nothing—nothing!" Dori shouted shrilly. "Get out of my way!"

"What were you doing out on deck in this weather?" Tricia demanded, stepping in front of the woman so that she couldn't escape.

"None of your business."

"Were you talking to Cathy Copper?"

Dori's head snapped up, her eyes widening, but she didn't reply.

"Did you confront her—or did she confront you?"

Dori's eyes blazed. "That's none of your business!"

"You've got to tell the authorities what you know about EM's death. You owe it to her!" Tricia blurted.

"And tell them what?"

"That she didn't die by her own hand. That she was murdered."

"And how do I do that? I have no proof—and I suspect you don't, either. If you're smart," Dori continued, "you'll go lock yourself in your cabin and stay there until you're allowed to leave the ship in the morning. That's what I intend to do."

"Make sure your balcony door is locked tight, too," Tricia warned.

Dori's eyes grew even wider, but not in umbrage—in pure terror. "Let me go!" she shouted, and pushed past Tricia, practically running in her haste to get away.

If Tricia thought she'd felt panicked before, she felt totally freaked now. It seemed no one on the entire ship cared enough to see justice done. And suddenly Tricia felt like a relic. Integrity was all-important to her, even if it wasn't to the population at large.

She charged for the door Dori had come through and burst onto the deck. Snow fell, giving the overhead floodlights a soft glow and covering parts of the wet deck. She looked left and right but saw no one. Cathy had not come inside through the door Dori had used. Did that mean she was still on deck? If so . . .

Tricia darted back inside, grateful for the warmth that enveloped her, but then she charged aft, almost running through the nearly empty restaurant, wondering if she might see Cathy out by the outdoor pool—and if she did, what would she do?

Tricia exited the restaurant and entered the short corridor, which led to the glass-topped door that overlooked the deck outside. As she studied the empty expanse of teak, what she'd seen and heard for the past few days began to fall together like the pieces of a puzzle. On impulse, she pushed through the door. Again, the air was biting, the sky above a murky gray obscured by the lights that illuminated the deck.

Tricia walked far onto the deck, hugging herself to retain her body heat. There was no sign of Cathy. She approached the rail that overlooked the black ocean behind the ship, the churned-up water leaving a frothy gray wake behind.

"What are you doing here?" a shrill voice demanded.

Tricia whirled and nearly slipped on the icy deck. Cathy Copper stood before her, wearing a bulky parka over dark slacks, her feet shod in black flats.

"I came out to get a breath of fresh air," Tricia lied. "I need to go back to my cabin now. It's time to put out my luggage for the porters."

"Bullshit," Cathy spat. "You came out here looking for me, didn't you?"

"Why would I do that?"

"Because you're a busybody."

Hadn't Tricia accused Angelica of the same thing?"

"I've spoken to a number of people in your tour group and they all said the same thing: you can't keep your nose out of other people's business," Cathy said.

Did the rest of the Stoneham passengers honestly think Tricia was a meddlesome troublemaker?

"I don't listen to gossip," Tricia said loudly to be heard above the sound of the wind and the ocean waves, and started to edge away from the rail.

"Don't move!" Cathy ordered.

"I'm cold! Unlike you, I don't have a coat."

"I want to know what you *think* you know about EM Barstow's death, Little Ms. Snoop."

"She's dead and nobody cares."

"Nobody but *you*," Cathy mocked.

"You sure don't."

"That woman wasn't fit to breathe the same air as the rest of us."

"And why was that?"

"You tell me."

"I'm betting it all stems back to the failed horse therapy academy."

Cathy's eyes widened. *Ha!* Tricia had scored with that salvo.

"You were an injured athlete who was crushed by the reality that you'd never make the Olympic team. Riding those gentle therapy horses restored your confidence—until the farm folded in bankruptcy. EM took care of the horses—but not the children who depended on them."

"She abandoned forty-seven of us," Cathy said bitterly. "She never gave a damn about people. She could fake it with her writing—she was smart enough to figure that out—but she never had a genuine loving feeling for another human being."

"And you did?" Tricia accused.

"What do you mean?"

"You killed EM without a qualm, and you hoped to pin her death on poor Dori Douglas."

"She's not as innocent as you might think," Cathy grumbled.

"Why? Because she objected to being treated like a servant while volunteering her services?"

"Dori's a chump."

"And you're a murderer," Tricia accused, feeling thoroughly chilled.

Cathy's expression hardened. "EM was working behind the scenes to get me fired from my job."

"And you were trying to take over her characters."

Cathy grimaced. "You're like the rest of her sheeplike followers, thinking of those imaginary people as though they were real. EM did, too, because she didn't have any friends—she didn't know how to *be* one."

"But there was more to the story, wasn't there? The horse farm went bankrupt—and you know why. I'm guessing you wouldn't have snapped if EM hadn't talked about it during her interview the other day."

Cathy's lips pursed, and for a moment Tricia thought she might cry, but then her anger resurfaced. "EM was a vindictive woman. She took legal action, filing suits right, left, and center. She ruined my mother. EM hounded her until—"

"Until she hung herself?"

Cathy said nothing.

"And that's what you did to EM."

Still, Cathy said nothing. Did she know Millicent intended to flog the show to the networks? Was that why she'd decided against being interviewed?

"How did you finagle becoming EM's editor?"

"It wasn't coincidence," Cathy bragged. "I worked harder than any of the assistants. I stood out from the rest because of that."

"And how did EM feel when you got the job?"

Cathy's face twisted into a scowl. "She didn't even recognize my name. It wasn't until I confronted her in her stateroom that she made the connection. Even then, she didn't believe me."

The biting wind seemed to pick up. Tricia had never been so cold in all her life, and she knew that she had to get back inside before hypothermia set in. Still, she needed to know more.

"Why did you leave the door to EM's stateroom ajar?"

"So some sap would find her, keeping ship's security from looking for me."

"That sap was *me*," Tricia said bitterly.

"Ha-ha!" Then Cathy sobered. "Unfortunately, security didn't seem to give a damn who killed EM."

"What happens now?" Tricia asked.

"You're going to have an accident—a fatal accident."

Tricia shook her head. "I don't think so," she said with as much calm as she could muster. "And you won't get away with EM's death, because I've shared my theory with Officer McDonald, Harold Pilger, and more." Well, she would have, if she'd had the chance. If nothing else, Angelica knew, and hell had no fury like Angelica scorned.

Cathy's sneer deepened.

"Take a look behind you; there are cameras all over the deck," Tricia said.

"Liar."

"There are cameras all over the ship!"

"Nobody saw me enter EM's stateroom."

"Are you sure? Maybe they're waiting until we get to New York to bag you."

For the first time, Cathy seemed to hesitate, and Tricia eased a step away from the rail. But then Cathy's expression hardened once again. "You're full of shit—and I *told* you not to move."

"I don't have to listen to you."

"No, you don't!"

Cathy lunged forward, but instead of trying to run, Tricia dropped to the icy deck. Cathy skidded, screamed, and by the time Tricia turned, there was no sign of her.

"Cathy!" Tricia hollered into the wind, scrambling to her feet.

She heard no reply.

Tricia grabbed the frozen rail, but all she could see was the gray wake at the back of the ship as it chugged farther north.

TWENTY-SIX

The bus ride from New York back to Stoneham was a lot quieter than it had been on the reverse course a week before. Everyone seemed subdued. The driver had reserved the seat behind him for Mary, who'd been carefully brought on board by the *Celtic Lady*'s medical personnel, and arrangements had been made for the Stoneham Fire Department's EMTs to help her off when the bus arrived back home. Meanwhile, Chauncey hadn't left Mary's side. When the two of them looked at each other, it seemed as if they shared a special connection. Oh, how Tricia missed that kind of relationship.

Angelica hung back with Mindy, the tour guide, to wait for the stragglers, and Tricia boarded the bus. She saw Antonio and Ginny had settled several seats from the back while a smiling Sofia sat on her mother's lap, showing no ill effects from her troubles the night before. On the other side of the aisle, Grace sat by the window with Mr. Everett next to her. Tricia bent down to have a word with him.

"I want to thank you for all the lovely gifts."

"Oh, dear," Mr. Everett lamented. "What gave me away?"

"'The Murders in the Rue Morgue.' Only you, Ginny, and Pixie knew how much I coveted an original copy." Well, Christopher, too. "They were lovely gifts, but I don't understand why you gave them to me."

Mr. Everett's head seemed to droop. "You've had a terrible time these past few months. I hoped my little gifts might bring you a smile or two."

"That they did." Tricia leaned closer and brushed a kiss on his wrinkled cheek. "Thank you again, Mr. Everett. You're the kindest man I've ever known."

Mr. Everett blushed.

Tricia patted his shoulder, then stood and shrugged out of her coat, placing it on the rack above, and took the seat behind Grace. A minute later, the last of the Stoneham group boarded and Angelica made her way up the aisle. She shucked her coat, placing it on one of the empty seats behind them, and sat beside Tricia as the driver pulled the door shut and they moved away from the curb. Angelica said nothing, but opened her briefcase, took out a notebook, and completely ignored her sister.

Tricia spent most of the ride staring out the window, not taking in the scenery that zoomed by and not communicating with Angelica, who was still furious to find out she'd been on deck with Cathy Copper just before she'd fallen overboard.

Angelica had returned to their suite from the ship's medical centre after midnight, when Ginny and Antonio returned with baby Sofia to their cabin. She'd been unhappy to find Tricia was not tucked in for the night. When Tricia had finally left the ship's security department, it was well after two in the morning, and she'd been surprised to find her sister had waited up for her, angrily pacing the floor.

"Of all the stupid, unreasonable, and thoughtless things to do! What if it had been *you* who'd gone overboard?"

Tricia had had no answer, and had been very happy to change the subject and inquire about baby Sofia. The ship's doctor diagnosed an ear infection, but was reluctant to give the baby antibiotics. She did, however, prescribe anesthetic ear drops and ibuprofen, which had reduced the fever and given Sofia, her parents, and Angelica, some much-needed relief. Upon waking, Ginny had called her pediatrician back home and had an appointment for late in the day.

That was one happy ending.

Of course, Tricia wasn't sure what to make of the conversation she'd had with Dori Douglas that morning as she and the rest of the Stoneham contingent waited in the Shamrock Casino for their group to be called to disembark.

Dressed in a red and white ski jacket and pulling a little black suitcase behind her, Dori ignored Tricia, who hurried over to intercept the woman. "Dori."

Dori pretended not to hear her.

"Dori!" she called again.

Finally Dori deigned to acknowledge Tricia's presence. "What do you want *now*?"

"Did you hear?"

"About Cathy? The whole ship has."

"Have you spoken with ship's security?"

"They hauled me out of bed last night and interrogated me for over an hour before they finally told me I was free to go. Don't hold me up," she warned.

"The line is stalled," Tricia observed, which was true. "I figured it out, you know."

"Figured *what* out?" Dori grated.

Tricia lowered her voice. "When you went ashore in Bermuda, you were seen coming out of an office supply store."

"So what?"

"You made a purchase—and no doubt in cash—of a flash drive."

"Now, why would I want to do that?" Dori asked.

"To store the contents of EM's hard drive."

"No one ever found her missing laptop."

"No, because you tossed it overboard after Cathy left it on your balcony."

"You have no proof of that, and neither does ship's security."

"What do you hope to gain?" Tricia pushed. "Are you going to hold EM's last manuscript for ransom? Try to blackmail the publisher?"

"That wouldn't be very smart—and it's also illegal."

"So, theoretically, what would someone have to gain from stealing something they didn't intend to exploit?"

"Perhaps nothing more than knowledge. It's a pretty powerful feeling to hold a secret."

"And what secret would that be?"

"Knowing how it all ends. Not just the book she was working on, but all the rest of the books she intended to write."

"Why would someone want to deprive her readers of that information?" Tricia asked, puzzled.

"Because nobody else knows. Nobody else will *ever* know."

"What about the flash drive?"

"It's taken care of," Dori said smugly.

"They could search your luggage."

"They won't find anything."

Could she have asked someone to take it and mail it to her? As head of EM's fan club, Dori probably knew scores of her fans. Was one or more of them on board? Could she have asked one of them to take possession of the drive and send it to her at a later date?

"If you'll excuse me. The line is moving again. When I get home, I have a lot of work to do for the fan club."

"Why bother? It's not like you'll make any money on it."

"Of course I will. I take care of the website—for a nominal fee—which the estate will continue to pay. I have all EM's books linked with affiliate codes from all the major online retailers. I get a kickback for every single book that sells off the site."

"Did EM know that?"

"Of course not. She was too arrogant to listen to me when I tried to explain it. She signed a waiver and . . . now I just sit back and collect the money every month."

"But if more of her books went into production, you'd make even more."

"You don't think EM's death is going to be the end of the Tennyson Eisenberg books, do you?"

No, she didn't.

"Someone else will write them. They won't be as good, but they'll sell and sell and sell. And thanks to Mr. Pilger, I negotiated a deal with the publisher. I get to represent their interests at various reader conferences and collect speaker's fees. With EM gone, she can't offend people right, left, and center anymore. In fact, in a year or two, I'll have people thinking of her in glowing terms. I intend to canonize her," she said blithely.

Good luck with that, Tricia thought.

"Now, if you'll excuse me."

Tricia watched her leave the ship, then had to scramble to grab her things when the Stoneham group was called.

She'd been surprised that Officer McDonald was waiting for her at the security checkpoint. He motioned for her to step out of line and speak to him out of earshot of the others.

"Have you heard anything?" Tricia asked.

"The Coast Guard hasn't found a trace of Ms. Copper," McDonald said gravely.

Tricia shook her head. Cathy had been wearing that down parka, which would have weighed a ton when soaked with frigid water. There was no way she could have survived in the sea for more than a minute or more even if she'd been able to shuck the heavy coat. The thought that she may have been chewed up by the ship's propellers made Tricia shudder.

"Will there be any investigation into EM Barstow's death?"

"I'll be speaking with NYPD within the hour."

"I don't suppose you could keep me apprised of the investigation."

"Perhaps," he said.

Tricia dug into her purse and came up with one of her business cards. "I'd appreciate it."

McDonald placed the card in his left pants pocket, but Tricia could see the hint of a smile at the corners of his mouth. Maybe he *would* actually call her.

"Have a safe ride home, Ms. Miles."

"I hope your next cruise is without incident," Tricia replied. McDonald nodded, turned, and headed back down the corridor.

Tricia had to hurry to catch up with the rest of the Stoneham group. Just as she was about to board the bus, she'd seen Harold Pilger hailing a cab. She wished she'd had another opportunity to speak with the attorney, and wondered if she might look him up when she got back home. Then again, was he liable to tell her anything she didn't already know—if he wasn't sworn to secrecy? She wasn't sure.

"We're almost home," Angelica said curtly. They were the first words she'd spoken in more than an hour.

Tricia tuned in to her surroundings as the bus turned off Route 101 and onto the road that would take them into Stoneham.

The bus began to buzz with the sounds of people gathering their belongings. Everyone seemed more than ready to go home. Since they were seated near the back of the bus, Tricia didn't bother to collect her things.

As they pulled into the municipal parking lot, Tricia noticed a figure dressed in a black topcoat and fedora approach the lot. "Ange," she called sharply.

Angelica stood in the aisle, trying to help Ginny stuff Sofia back into her snowsuit. "What?"

"Look out the window."

Angelica bent down and her jaw went slack. "Good heavens! It's Daddy!"

"Daddy?" Ginny asked.

"Our father," Tricia affirmed.

"Oh, my."

Most of the others were already off the bus, but Angelica lowered her voice to a whisper. "He doesn't know about—you know," she said, referring to her Nigela Ricita identity and empire, "and I don't want him to know. I'm so proud of the three of you, and I want him to meet you, just not right now."

"Do not worry," Antonio said, patting her back. "We will get off the bus and will talk later, no?"

"Yes. And thank you." Somehow Angelica managed to give all three of them a kiss.

"What are we going to say to him?" Tricia asked.

"I'm more interested in what he's got to say to us," Angelica answered.

They donned their winter coats, hats, and scarfs, and headed down the aisle, with Angelica leading the way. By the time they got outside, most of the others had collected their luggage and were trudging toward their vehicles.

John hurried to meet them. "Surprise!" he called, but sounded unsure of what kind of welcome he would receive.

Angelica hurried over to him, throwing her arms around him. "Daddy, what are you doing here?"

"I came to see my girls."

Tricia stood waiting. Angelica pulled away, and John held out his arms to her. "Princess?" he asked quietly.

Tricia stepped forward, giving him a gentle hug; her welcome not nearly as enthusiastic as her sister's had been. "Where's Mother?"

"Home. In Rio."

"What made you decide to come all the way to snowy New Hampshire?" Angelica asked.

"I wanted to see where you live." John shivered in his long, heavy coat. "Funny, I don't remember winter ever being this cold." He looked at Tricia. "I came here to apologize to you both, but mostly to Tricia."

"Oh, Daddy, you don't have—"

"Yes, I do. I just wanted you to know that I'm proud of both my girls, and I hope you can find it in your hearts to forgive me."

Tricia almost gave an automatic *"But there's nothing to forgive"* before she realized it would take her a long, long time to forgive, and she would certainly never forget, either. "Why don't we go inside somewhere and talk."

"My apartment is just down the block," Angelica suggested.

"I know. I've been to your store and met your dog. I've eaten lunch in your café. I'm staying in the B and B you've got an interest in, too. They're all very nice."

Angelica smiled shyly. Even at fifty years old, a compliment from her father still meant the world to her.

"You've got a nice store, too, princess."

"Thank you, Daddy."

John reached for the handle of Angelica's big case. "Now, let's get all your things and go home."

Home? Did that mean he intended to stay in Stoneham for an extended length of time?

The sisters looked at each other, as though reading each other's minds. *Uh-oh!*

CELTIC LADY RECIPES

Angelica returned from the Authors at Sea cruise determined to replicate the food they served at the Kells Grill and Lido Restaurant.

BEEF WELLINGTON

1 beef tenderloin (2 to 2½ pounds)
ground black pepper (optional)
1 egg
1 tablespoon water
1 tablespoon butter

2 cups finely chopped mushrooms
½ cup medium onion, finely chopped
1 sheet puff pastry, thawed

Heat the oven to 425°F. Place the beef into a lightly greased roasting pan. Season with the black pepper, if desired. Roast for 30 minutes or until a meat thermometer reads 130°F. Cover the pan and refrigerate for 1 hour.

Reheat the oven to 425°F. Whisk the egg and water in a small bowl. Heat the butter in a 10-inch skillet over medium-high heat. Add the mushrooms and onion. Stir often and cook until the mushrooms are tender and the liquid is evaporated. Unfold the pastry sheet on a lightly floured surface. Roll the pastry sheet into a rectangle 4 inches longer and 6 inches wider than the beef. Brush the pastry sheet with the egg mixture. Spoon the mushroom mixture onto the pastry sheet to within 1 inch of the edges. Place the beef in the center of the mushroom mixture. Fold the pastry over the beef and press to seal. Place the seam side onto a baking sheet. Tuck the ends under to seal. Brush the pastry with the remaining egg mixture. Bake for 25 minutes or until the pastry is golden brown and a meat thermometer reads 140°F.

Yield: 6–8 servings

LOBSTER NEWBURG

2 egg yolks, beaten
½ cup heavy cream
¼ cup butter
2 tablespoons dry sherry

½ teaspoon salt
1 pinch cayenne pepper
1 pinch ground nutmeg
¾ pound cooked lobster meat, broken into chunks

In a small bowl, whisk together the egg yolks and heavy cream until well blended. Set aside. Melt the butter in a saucepan over low heat. Stir in the egg yolk mixture and sherry. Cook, stirring constantly, until the mixture thickens. Do not boil. Remove from the heat and season with salt, cayenne, and nutmeg. Add the lobster. Return to the pan on low heat and cook gently until heated through. Serve hot over slices of buttered toast.

Yield: 4 servings

CARROT CUSTARD

14 ounces carrots, peeled and cut into 1-inch pieces
2 tablespoons (¼ stick) unsalted butter, at room temperature
2 eggs
½ cup milk
3 tablespoons evaporated skim milk
½ teaspoon freshly grated nutmeg
½ teaspoon salt
Dash of black pepper

Preheat the oven to 375°F and put the rack in the middle position. Butter a 9-inch-round cake pan and set aside. Put a kettle of water on to boil. Boil the carrots until very tender (about 30 minutes) and drain. In a food processor, with a metal blade, process the carrots with the butter for 10 seconds. Add the remaining ingredients and process for 30 seconds more, until it's well pureed. Adjust the seasoning if necessary. Pour the mixture into the cake pan and put the pan in a large ovenproof pan. Pour enough boiling water around it to come halfway up the side of the cake pan. Place in the oven and bake for 30 to 35 minutes. The mixture will be firm and set. If using immediately, allow enough time to let it rest for 10 minutes after it has been taken out of the water. If you intend to reheat it later, leave it in the pan. When ready to serve, loosen the edges gently with a knife and invert it onto a serving plate.

Yield: 6 servings

STRAWBERRY CAKE

1 cup butter, softened

2 cups granulated sugar

1 3-ounce package strawberry-flavored gelatin

4 eggs (room temperature)

2¾ cups sifted cake flour

2½ teaspoons baking powder

1 cup milk, room temperature

1 tablespoon vanilla extract

½ cup strawberry puree made from frozen sweetened strawberries

Preheat the oven to 350°F. Grease and flour 2 9-inch-round cake pans. In a large bowl, cream together the butter, sugar, and dry strawberry gelatin until light and fluffy. Beat in the eggs one at a time, mixing well after each addition. Combine the flour and baking powder; stir into the batter alternately with the milk. Blend in the vanilla and the strawberry puree. Divide the batter evenly between the prepared pans. Bake for 25 to 30 minutes or until a toothpick inserted into the center of the cake comes out clean. Allow the cakes to cool in their pans over a wire rack for at least 10 minutes. Frost with sour cream icing or your favorite flavor icing.

Yield: 6–10 servings

SOUR CREAM FROSTING

1 cup butter, softened
½ cup sour cream
4 cups confectioners' sugar
½ tablespoon vanilla extract

Combine the butter and sour cream and beat with an electric mixer until well blended. Gradually add the confectioners' sugar. Add the remaining confectioners' sugar and blend thoroughly. Add the vanilla extract and continue blending until the frosting is smooth and creamy. If you like a thinner frosting, add more milk until you get the consistency you desire.